LIVING WILDER

WILDER SISTERS SERIES, BOOK ONE

LĒIGH TUDOR

TUDOR

Copyright © 2021 Leigh Tudor
www.leightudor.com
Living Wilder
Wilder Sisters Series, #1
Cover design by Damonza
Copy editor: Theodora Bryant
ISBN: 978-1-7367915-0-9 (ebook)
ISBN: 978-1-7367915-1-6 (paperback)

All rights reserved.
No part of this book may be reproduced in any form or by any electronic or mechanical means, including information storage and retrieval systems, without written permission from the author, except for the use of brief quotations in a book review.

This book is a work of fiction. Names, characters, establishments, organizations, and incidents are either products of the author's imagination or are used fictitiously to give a sense of authenticity. Any resemblance to actual persons, living or dead, events, or locales is entirely coincidental.

*This book is dedicated to my girlfriends, aka,
Dirty Girls Reading Books
(you know who you are).
I made sure my heroines capture those
things I love the most about all of you;
they're fun, flirty and fierce.
But more importantly, they love one another unconditionally*

PROLOGUE

"Math is sometimes called the science of patterns."

—Ronald Graham
Credited as one of the principal architects of the rapid worldwide development of discrete mathematics

Findling, Utah
Division of Child and Family Services [DCFS]

"When did the drawings begin?" Dr Halstead asked. Hands behind his back and eyes narrowed, he regarded the agitated fourteen-year-old girl through the observation window.

The teenager slumped in her chair with her skinny arms crossed, a perpetual grimace on her face. Her knee bounced up and down with the uncontrolled energy of a drug addict.

"We're not sure. She's been less than cooperative," Dr. Bancroft said. "We ran the tests you ordered. Which by the way, thank you for the funding. Never would've been approved by the state."

Dr. Halstead ignored the platitude. "Head trauma from the accident?"

"Confirmed."

"Damage to the left hemisphere?"

"Affirmative."

"Latest brain scans?"

They appeared before him. He turned to shove the scans into the lit monitor next to the window. He viewed the mid-sectional MRI images of the teenager's brain in the sagittal, coronal, and axial planes. He had reviewed previous scans, but these were the last to come through. All looked highly promising.

Conclusive.

"Drawings?"

Bancroft handed those over, too.

After a quick perusal, Halstead turned slightly toward the third man in the room, standing quietly by the door. Without a word, the man moved to his side.

Halstead didn't bother to make polite introductions or explain the man's role to Dr. Bancroft. Information was to be shared on a need-to-know basis. As it stood, he was the only one who needed to know that this man was a Mensa elite with a documented IQ of over one hundred and sixty.

A renowned mathematical prodigy.

The man viewed the drawings one-by-one, which to Dr. Halstead resembled nothing more than a Spirograph drawing, a game he used to play as a child.

"Assessment?"

"Fractals," the man said without taking his eyes off the page in front of him. "Meticulously drafted." He pointed at one of the patterns. "Here she's illustrated mathematical roulette curves. And here she's drawn hypotrochoids, and epitrochoids, among other highly complex geometric patterns."

Halstead's focus turned to Bancroft. "Math scores, prior to the accident?"

Bancroft opened a folder and referred to the contents. "Algebra one. She barely skated by with a D," the psychiatrist said, and then hesitated before adding, "then failed geometry."

The Mensa member holding the drawings looked up at Dr. Bancroft with wide eyes. "Extraordinary."

Halstead continued. "The sisters? Still not exhibiting similar results from the accident?"

Dr. Bancroft shook his head. "No signs of brain trauma."

Halstead contemplated that fact. No problem. He would create the trauma, which would make for a far more interesting study.

He held out his hand toward the drawings, which were reluctantly returned by the mathematical genius who cost a fortune to fly from his remote home in Copenhagen to the equally remote town of Findling, Utah. A costly endeavor for only a few moments of his expertise.

Nonetheless, worth every penny.

It was time to initiate a human connection.

Without a word, he walked through the door and into the room on the other side of the observation window.

The agitated teenager sat up, and as expected, she did her best to exhibit bravado as opposed to fear.

He approached the table slowly. "Good morning. I'm Dr. Halstead." He reached out his hand.

She glared, unmoved, at his outstretched hand.

"Come now, what is it you young people say these days?" He softened his tone alongside a warm smile. "You're not going to leave me hanging?"

After some hesitation, she reached out. "Ava," she whispered. After a quick shake, her arms re-crossed but with less overt agitation. "And nobody says that anymore, unless they're old or lame."

He nodded with a smile at her slight, and pulled out the chair across from her to sit down. "Can I ask you a couple questions about these drawings, Ava?"

"I've already answered a billion stupid questions. Ask Mr. Bancroft."

"Dr. Bancroft is a psychiatrist. I'm a neuroscientist."

She shrugged as if unimpressed. "What do they do?"

"That's a great question, Miss Ava. Neuroscientists study the development and function of the nervous system, which includes the brain—the area in which I specialize."

He fanned her drawings on the table facing her, pointing at the one in the middle. "Would you mind telling me what this is?"

She looked over her crossed arms, exerting as little effort as possible. "That's a fern."

"This is what you see when you see a fern?"

She nodded.

"Can you explain what you see? Like this table. What do you see when you look at this table?"

She shrugged one shoulder, glancing down. "It's hard to explain."

"Can you try? With more information, I can better understand and then I can help you to understand."

Eyebrows drew together as she chewed on her bottom lip.

He tilted his head. "Do you want to understand, Ava?"

Once again, she shrugged, looking away from the drawings and fixating on the window, which was too high to view anything of consequence.

Halstead stroked his chin, deciding to redirect his questioning strategy. "I hear you've caused quite a stir at your foster home."

Her crossed arms visibly tightened. "They won't let me see my sisters."

He pulled another folder out on the table and opened it, repositioning his bifocals. "Your foster parents claim they separated you from your sisters because you disobeyed one of the house rules. No food after hours." He looked at her, over his bifocals. "You were caught stealing food out of the refrigerator around midnight."

Her eyes turned to the color of a dark storm. "The food was for Mara and Charlotte."

He looked back down at the contents of the folder. "They also claim to be feeding you and your sisters three adequate meals a day."

She snorted. "That's a lie. They don't cook enough food for everyone. The other cretins grab it right off your plate before you even have a chance to sit down."

"I take it the 'cretins' are the other foster children?"

She nodded, her knee back to bouncing.

Very good. It was easier to work through irritation than distrust. "So, they separated you as punishment?"

She nodded again, her eyes filling. "Charlotte's only five. They just sit her in a chair and expect her to fend for herself. I have to help her, and by the time I'm done all the food's gone. Mara's so scared, she just hands her food over to the older kids." She swiped at her eyes with a quick hand.

Despite her level of agitation, he found it promising that she was confiding in him. He needed to position himself as an ally as opposed to another obstacle in her life.

"Deplorable," he said. Shaking his head, he pulled off his bifocals, and rubbed his eyes. "I'm so sorry, Ava."

She shrugged, looking to the side. "I've told our social worker. She's useless."

He remained quiet, his elbows on the table and his hands clasped at his mouth. He allowed some time to transpire as if contemplating the circumstances. "I'd like to propose something."

She fidgeted in her chair, and then looked up, but only as far as his chin.

"I'd like you and your sisters to live with me."

Her eyes moved to his. "You mean, like, adopt us?"

He nodded his head once. "That's right."

Her eyes narrowed. "You're not some creepy old perv that likes little girls, are you?"

He chuckled. "No, Miss Ava. I'm just a lonely old man who doesn't have any children, or a family for that matter, and would very much like to have one with you and your sisters."

She continued to stare, expressionless.

Processing, undoubtedly.

"I'd also like to help you to better understand your visions. The way you see things. I can help you understand what's happening up here." He patted his forefinger to his own temple.

"No funny stuff?"

"Well, I hope you and your sisters will be happy and have fun living with me, but only the appropriate kind between a father and his daughters."

He watched her mind at work, hope clashing with distrust. He understood the source. Dr. Bancroft had told him that the girls' foster parents were rather suspect, at best; the wife, an unscrupulous woman whose primary source of income was from a disability claim and a husband who had been questioned in the past for inappropriate touching of some of the older girls under his care.

And then, as if hope won out, she whispered. "I see shapes and angles in everything."

He tapped the middle drawing with his finger. "Even with a fern?"

"Yes. It's like I see everything different from before."

"Before?"

Her lips rubbed together and her eyes squeezed shut and reopened. "Before the accident."

"I see." He allowed that significant piece of information to sink in.

Picking at a loose string on the cuff of her sweatshirt, she asked, "Can I think about it?"

He raised one eyebrow.

"The whole living with you thing."

"Of course. Take all the time you need. I won't do anything until I hear from you." He stood. "This is your decision, Ava. Your protective instincts are strong. But you don't have to do this alone. I know you'll do what's best for you and your sisters."

He stood and walked around the table, pausing at her side. "You let your case-worker know, and I will move heaven and earth to get you and your sisters under my care. Your sisters will never have to worry about having enough food. And I'll help you to better understand this." His hand touched the drawings.

She looked up and nodded, her expression now a mixture of skepticism and hope.

"Goodbye, Ava." He turned and walked out of the room.

Bancroft instantly sidled up next to him as he stepped into the observation room. "Would you like me to start the adoption paperwork for Ava?"

"Yes," he replied, walking past him, ready to make his way back to the research facility. "But I'll be taking all three. Make sure everything's in place as quickly as possible."

The psychiatrist nodded, taking notes.

"There's no distant relatives who might disrupt our plans?"

"None," Bancroft assured him. "The parents died on impact and were both only children; their own parents were deceased. Despite a lengthy search, no relatives were found to assume custody of the girls."

Halstead then addressed the Mensa member in the room, who was no longer of need to him. "Dr. Bancroft, please see that our guest gets a ride back to the airport." He stopped before exiting. "One last thing. You've been submitting your résumé for a number of positions at the research facility."

Dr. Bancroft's eyes widened. "Yes, sir, and if I may say—"

"No," the doctor interrupted, "you may not. Once the children are legally under my care, you may join my staff. Do we understand each other?"

He nodded, standing tall. "Absolutely. Consider it done."

CHAPTER ONE

"If people do not believe that mathematics is simple, it is only because they do not realize how complicated life is."

—John von Neumann
Theory of *Games and Economic Behavior,* 1944

Findling, Utah
Halstead Research Center
Eight Years Later

Ava lay on her bed, her arms behind her head, waiting for the sealed door to her suite to open. She and her sisters were usually given free access to certain rooms within the Center, but today they were in lockdown.

She didn't mind.

Totally worth it.

First thing that morning, she'd been informed by her digital calendar that the day's agenda had changed. Rather than a full day of tutors, sparring, and assignment debriefing, she'd be meeting up with her sisters to view their so-called father's funeral.

Remotely, of course.

She smiled.

And then fear crept in like an uppercut to her good mood.

Don't think about what you've done. Think about what you need to do next.

Rubbing her eyes with the pad of her palms, she told herself that everything was going according to plan. She just needed a distraction. Something to pass the time and to dampen the anxiety that bubbled inside her head.

She glanced at the folder on the side table and considered running through the pre-approved brain teasers. She sat up and looked inside the manila folder. Today's theme covered topological vector spaces.

Rolling her eyes, she pushed the pages away. She could do those with her eyes closed. Literally.

As she paced back and forth in her closet-sized room, her eyes crept toward the door, wondering what she would find on the other side when it finally opened.

Heavily armed security guards, ready to escort her outside the Center and into a waiting police car?

Stop it. No one was taking her anywhere.

Not without a fight anyway.

She considered watching one of the DVDs she'd picked up in a back alley in Hong Kong while on a job last spring, but without the time to get through an entire movie, she deferred to a more physical distraction.

Dropping to the floor, she did twenty sets of push-ups. Some one-handed, others with intermittent claps as she pushed off the floor with her hands.

Afterward, she leaned against the bed to allow her heart rate to settle and noticed the stack of books on the side table next to the folder. She had been reading them to Charlotte a few nights ago.

Flipping open one of the contraband Little House books by Laura Ingalls Wilder, she sifted through the pages. She loved the story of an American Midwest family undergoing hardships, with a Ma and Pa who loved them unconditionally.

As if that were a real thing.

They were silly, romantic books, and at twenty-two, she was way too old and entirely too jaded to be reading them. But she read them anyway. These days, for Charlotte.

The books had been given to her years ago by a sympathetic attendant who was fired the next day for providing non-approved reading material to a patient at the Center, a serious infraction.

Ava had managed to hide the books before they could be confiscated, claiming that someone had already disposed of them.

Noting the time, she quickly gathered the books and knelt in front of the cabinet beneath the sink. She pulled at the square of sheetrock at the back wall, placing the books between two studs. After replacing the piece of plaster and moving bottles of toiletries to help camouflage the frayed edges, she wiped her hands on her shorts and sat impatiently on her small bed. Tapping one foot uncontrollably.

The digital clock on her screen moved to 10:00 AM. Her throat clogged with what felt like shards of glass as the door to the suite whispered open.

She stood and instantly moved into a fighting stance, her heart palpitating.

But no one was on the other side.

No guards, no handcuffs, and no indication that her soul-damning deed had been exposed.

Following the calendar's instructions to go to the viewing room overlooking the lecture hall, she made her way through the familiar labyrinth of corridors, well aware of the restricted access to certain rooms. Rooms that had been securely and remotely locked, supported by biometric devices requiring fingerprints for the final entry.

She'd learned from eavesdropping on conversations between the staff, that others were housed in separate annexes of the campus; she could only guess for how long and for what purpose. But what she did know was that a large part of the Center's security measures hinged on isolation. The less interaction with others, the higher the level of control.

And the doctor was all about control.

But not anymore.

Ava placed her finger on the biometric reader to the observation room, hoping for the same outcome.

The pneumatic door whisked open.

And again, nothing to trigger a combat position.

Mara, two years younger than Ava, lay on her back on one of the conference room tables, repeatedly throwing a stress ball against the ceiling, while fourteen-year-old Charlotte subconsciously hummed a complex tune, her arms propped on the audio console, observing the funeral beyond the wide expanse of windows overlooking the lecture hall.

The doctor lay in repose inside a gold-leaf lacquered coffin. The insides tufted in a garish green-satin lining, with bright orange carnations cascading over the sides. He lay so quietly and at peace, it was hard to believe he was in the same lecture hall where he had once pontificated before his staff.

Ava raised an eyebrow and grinned. "They sure did a shoddy job on his makeup."

Hearing her sister's voice, Mara kicked off the table with unrestrained enthusiasm. "Omigod Ava, can you believe it? How much you wanna bet the old geezer is knee-deep in the fiery pits of hell?"

"We can only hope," Ava said.

Mara grabbed Ava's arm and moved her closer to watch the proceedings. "It's like watching a train wreck. I mean, look at his face. Whoever applied his makeup must have suffered a seizure mid-application and failed to blend. Check out those rosy cheeks and his snow-white pompadour. And I'm not sure, but I think he's wearing lip gloss. Who do you think authorized that?"

"Good question," Ava said, a tilt to her head and wearing an unrepentant grin.

Mara nudged her shoulder. "So, what's the probability of one delinquent genius hacking into the doctor's funeral plans and making a few alterations?"

"I'd say statistically low, Mara," Ava replied, shaking her head. "That person would have to disable the biometric devices going into the doctor's personal quarters, lift his laptop and hack into his encrypted files with the intent to change his instructions for an austere and tasteful service."

Mara shook her head. "What I would give for him to see this. He looks like Liberace having a bad hair day. This is so fucking great."

"Language," Charlotte sing-songed, still watching the service below.

Mara leaned closer to the window, turning her head to the side and squinting her eyes. "Is he wearing a gold satin smoking jacket?"

Ava nodded, biting her thumb between her teeth. "With a ruffly pirate shirt."

Charlotte paused her humming to look at Ava with wide eyes. She pointed below. "You did that? Jeez, Ava, what if you had been caught?"

Her younger sister was a rule-follower, always fretting that their visitation hours would be reduced because of her sister's blatant irreverence for the doctor and his research.

Ava waved her hand. "Please. I've been hacking into systems on behalf of the doctor for years. He just made the mistake of thinking he'd taken the necessary measures that would keep me from hacking into his."

Those moving through the processional made their way one-by-one to the casket, some stricken with grief and others weeping into their handkerchiefs. A few of the younger staff members appeared bored, going through the motions and waiting their turn to pay their respects with their eyes glued to their mobile devices.

Ava chuckled darkly. Nothing like viewing your adopted father's funeral to help you forget you were a virtual prisoner in a highly secure, state-of-the-art research facility.

Charlotte yawned, also losing interest. "They say he died in his sleep."

The Center-wide memo, alerting the staff of the details surrounding his funeral noted the cause of death as "natural causes."

Ava pulled at her lower lip, contemplating why the Center would lie about how he died. She knew for a fact that he went down eating a pastrami on rye covered in questionable condiments. Because after she got through with them, there was nothing natural about them.

But her sisters didn't need to know the gruesome details. Plausible deniability and all that.

She did wonder, with admittedly sick fascination, what had run through his mind as he choked on his fat-laden sandwich with extra mayo and Dijon mustard.

Such a plebeian way to go for one of the world's most venerated scientists. Ava had spent the past few hours visualizing his death.

He glibly begins to eat his sandwich and then becomes inexplicably dizzy. He grabs the sides of his desk as nausea sets in, followed by foam dripping from his mouth.

Realizing, with his last dying breath, that he'd been poisoned.

Oh, how she hoped during that moment in time, he thought of her as the culprit. What she would give to watch him take his last breath, knowing that she was the one responsible for extinguishing it.

Patricide: the Latin word for the killing of one's father. Just another karmic checkmark to add to her long list of transgressions with zero regret.

She leaned on the console, overlooking the ostentatious memorial service with intense satisfaction and maybe a little self-doubt.

Did her stark lack of remorse substantiate his claims against her? Claims that she was insane and a harm to herself and others. Was it wrong that after years of lies, experiments, and blackmail, all she felt was relief?

She was so close to finally being able to relax and exhale now that the man who stood between her and her sisters' freedom had finally met his just reward.

Pulling in another deep breath, her solar plexus expanded, and she attempted to release some of her pent-up anxiety.

So close. But there was still so much to do.

Mara began bouncing the stress ball against the wall and catching it. "I have this intense desire to dance around his casket singing ding-dong the mad fucking scientist is dead."

Charlotte turned, giving Mara the stink eye for her cursing.

"An event which would, ironically, fail to raise an eyebrow. We *are* crazy, after all." Ava said, pushing herself onto the console, sitting with her back to the window.

Charlotte paused her humming as she leaned over the console with her chin in her hands. "That must be why we weren't permitted to attend the funeral. Not that I mind, he didn't seem to like us very much. But still, we were his legal daughters, right?"

"They would never allow Mara and me to mingle among the staff without sufficient security. No telling how we might react, being so mentally imbalanced."

Mara snorted. "Couldn't risk the chance of us cackling like hyenas and wearing prom dresses covered in pig's blood."

"Pig's blood is so nineteen-seventies," Ava said. "I'd like to think we could be more creative than that."

Charlotte shook her head. "Please, if you two were so dangerous, why would they allow me to be alone with you? Not to mention, send you all over the world to math conferences and art shows."

With Charlotte's back to them, Ava and Mara glanced knowingly at one another.

Through the window, one of the staff members broke down in tears, clutching a photo of her mentor to her chest. Not only had they passed out 8x10-inch glossies of the doctor, but they also hung a

10x12-foot portrait from the wall of curtains overlooking the bereaved. Photoshopped, of course, giving him extended jowls and bushy eyebrows.

Charlotte asked, "If you didn't know him, wouldn't you think he looked like your everyday grandpa?"

"If your grandpa was the spawn of Satan," Mara said, popping her gum and catching the ball.

"He was always nicer to the people who worked for him than his own family," Charlotte commented.

"We weren't family," Mara refuted. "We were lab experiments turned cash cows."

The crying woman was led out of the room ahead of the casket by one of her sympathetic peers.

How ironic to watch two opposing reactions to the doctor's passing: those following his casket who'd willingly helped him to realize his scientific vision, and those of his three adopted daughters, who were the unwilling recipients.

Ava closed her eyes, pushing back on the pixelated geometric lines surrounding the casket. Lines that typically made sense out of chaos and allowed her to see the beautiful symmetry in the mundane.

Not today.

Today, they were harsh reminders of why she and her sisters were in this jacked-up familial mess.

She inhaled and compartmentalized the guilt. There wasn't time for ruminating about the past. Her plan was in place. She had gotten them into this, so she was going to get them out.

Clearing her throat, she said, "Okay, here's the deal." She caught the ball on the return to grab Mara's attention. "We've talked about getting out of this place. Now's the time but we have to move quickly. We have to leave tomorrow."

Charlotte turned toward Ava, staring at her with furrowed eyebrows. "What? How?"

"She's right," Mara agreed. "They're distracted. "Everyone's attention is on Halstead's death and the funeral."

"That's right," Ava said. "And honestly it couldn't have come at a better time. It's rare when we're all three at the Center at the same time." She nodded toward the slow procession. "Look at them. They're grief-stricken. We can use it to our advantage. This is it. This is our time, our time is now, right here."

Mara nudged Ava's shoulder. "Way to misquote *The Goonies*."

Charlotte sucked in and looked up. "Ooh, such a good movie."

To their surprise, the door to the viewing area whisked opened, catching them off guard.

Mara grabbed a nearby microphone sitting atop an audio-control panel, and pulled it behind her back as a makeshift weapon. Her reflexes were getting sharper, but sometimes, she was a bit of a hair-trigger.

Case in point, they were in the Center, not on assignment, and standing inside the door was Dr. Jasper Bancroft, Halstead's personal lackey. He wore a lab coat buttoned to his throat, carrying his ever-trusty iPad.

CHAPTER TWO

"A man is like a fraction whose numerator is what he is and whose denominator is what he thinks of himself. The larger the denominator, the larger the fraction."

—Leo Tolstoy
Russian author, *War and Peace*

Although a cog in the intricate system that kept them under the doctor's control, Jasper was certainly no physical threat. Rather, he instructed others to perform his muscle work for him.

But after years of sparring and combat training, the security guards and orderlies the size of double-wide trailers were of little consequence. These days, very few even bothered to get close enough to exact any power over them.

Just wasn't worth the pain from an unexpected knee to their junk or a side kick to the head.

And as a result of the girls becoming stronger and more lethal, Dr. Halstead's power and control came in the form of extortion as opposed to physical force, with Jasper being his go-between when it came to dealing with his troublesome adopted daughters.

God, how many times had Ava fantasized about shoving that iPad up his unspectacular backside?

His eyes were murky and his hair was thinning, teetering on a comb-over. Not a good look for a man in his thirties. On top of that, he smelled like a combination of antiseptic and ass.

He stood straight with his back stiff and one hand folded over the other, holding his precious iPad. "Good to see you girls paying your respects."

Mara loosened her grip on the microphone as she nodded her head toward the funeral in process. "We heard *Kill Bill* was playing in the lecture hall." She tilted her head with a saucy smile. "And you know how we love us some Uma."

He looked her up and down with disdain. "That would explain your poor choice of attire for the funeral of the man who took you in and gave you a home."

Mara clucked while batting her eyes, sporting a black corset, cutoff shorts that would only pass a brothel's dress code, and black combat boots. "The only thing the doctor gave us was a whale of a funeral to watch." She sighed, nodding her head toward the now slow-moving casket. "Good times."

Ava played along. "Who was the decorator for this little shindig? I'm loving the green, orange, and gold combo. It's so . . . neuroscientist meets white-trash-lottery-winner."

Ignoring her, Bancroft said, "You being the oldest of this delinquent threesome, I thought you might try to set an example."

Ava glanced down at her red booty shorts, white tank top foregoing a bra, and red patent leather stilettos. "What? I find this ensemble to be the perfect attire given the circumstances."

After completing an assignment, Ava and Mara used what little time they had to purchase the most risqué clothing possible to piss off Jasper and embarrass the doctor. Initially, their questionable clothing choices ended up in the incinerator, until the doctor and his minion realized their attire meshed well with the fabricated stories of psychotic deviant behavior.

Ava turned one stiletto inward. "Dang it, I knew I should have gone with the dominatrix boots."

Mara's eyes widened. "Yaasss, I love those!"

Nothing short of intense satisfaction surged through Ava. Messing with Jasper was certainly small compensation for their shitty life, but at least it provided a modicum of relief.

But as of today, the doctor was dead, and there was light at the end of the tunnel.

Ava turned to share her mirth with Charlotte, and noticed she had discreetly moved farther to the corner of the room. Oddly, her younger sister's eyes were downcast, her thin braids hanging in front of her, and she looked scared.

Like, swallowing-rocks scared.

She stood hunched over as if to divert attention from herself, wearing her usual plaid skirt that reached her knees, and a white polo shirt. Smaller than most fourteen-year-olds, the doctor had purposely isolated her from the real world, and as a result, she was terribly shy. And now, she appeared to be doing her best to make herself as small as possible.

Ava squinted her eyes at Jasper. What the hell? Was Charlotte afraid of Jasper?

Why had she not noticed this before?

Jasper tapped the iPad on the metal desk. "I have more important things to do than discuss your blatant levels of impropriety. Charlotte has a concert in Prague tomorrow evening and needs to prepare. Madame Garmond is looking for her as we speak."

Ava's eyes widened. "Are you serious?"

Regarding his iPad, he said in a flat tone, "I'm always serious."

Tomorrow was go time. By the time all three of them were back at the Center, things would have settled, and protocols meticulously followed.

Ava positioned both arms on the table and leaned toward him. "That's not happening, Jasper."

"I'm beyond thrilled to inform you that it's not up to you, Ava."

Her eyes narrowed. "Charlotte's father keels over and you expect her in Prague the next day to play the piano? What will people think? That you're the boss man now that the doctor's taken a six-foot nosedive?"

The iPad slammed onto the table.

All three women jumped at this uncharacteristic behavior. Ava noted Mara's grip tightening once again on the microphone.

Jasper leaned over the table, chuckling eerily, shaking his head. Pushing from the table, he turned toward them. "Spare me," he hissed. "Like any of you care that he's gone." His voice shook like gravel.

He sauntered toward Ava and she bristled, but it was more with shock than fear. Jasper never got this close to her. He knew what she'd been trained for and what she was capable of, and that she was in an excellent position for a Japanese chokehold.

She refused to break eye contact.

"You think you're so special, Ava?" The muscle in Jasper's jaw ticked, and she realized it was his breath that smelled like ass. "You think anyone here gives a damn about your opinion? You're nobody. *Person* non-grata. You'd do well to remember that you're *anything* but special."

Her eyes turned to slits, willing to play the baiting game to see what he had up his sleeve. "I guess you could say I have a healthy self-image. How about you?" She moved around him slowly, purposely antagonizing him. She stopped inches from his ear. "Still telling yourself you're a big man despite a less than average-sized ball sack?" She purposely glanced at his crotch and then backed up to watch the vein in his neck pulsate. "Not to worry. I'm sure even your lackluster sperm count could muster up a sea monkey or two."

He chuckled, atypical bravado considering he didn't bring any orderlies with him for protection.

"Oh, Ava, you needn't worry your little head about my ability to procreate. Time will tell. But right now, there's so much yet to be done." And then his thin lips turned up. "With Charlotte."

Ava's heart missed a beat as he turned toward her cowering sister. "Come here, Charlotte," he said, with an overly large grin, waving her over theatrically. "Come on now, don't be shy."

Charlotte made her way toward Jasper like she was working her way through sludge, or a Cambodian mine field.

"That's it," he said, putting his arm around her shoulders and pulling her into his side.

Charlotte swallowed as if she might purge, standing stock-still and hunched over.

"I have some good news," Jasper said, running his spiny fingers down Charlotte's braid. "You're looking at the only son, and sole heir of Dr. Halstead's assets, as well as the new director of this fine research facility."

Ava tried to absorb his words as she contemplated how many bones she could break in the hand fondling her sister's hair.

"On top of that, and this is the really good part, ladies, so pay close attention," he paused for dramatic effect, "I have been named as Charlotte's guardian."

Charlotte sucked in what sounded like a sob.

And that's when Ava knew.

That sick fuck.

Mara shook her head, not quite catching on. "You're *his* son?" she asked, pointing toward the windows overlooking the hall, and then as if to clarify, "*Halstead's* son?"

His eyes turned from his perusal of Charlotte to Mara. "And they call you a genius. Wow. Yes, I'm the doctor's son. *Blood*-related."

He pulled Charlotte closer to his side in a jovial manner,

speaking to Ava and Mara as if they were challenged. "So, when I say Charlotte is going to perform at a piano concert in Prague—Charlotte is getting on a plane to perform at a concert in Prague. In the meantime, you two have an assignment on the books. You depart in the morning as well."

"We could refuse," Mara argued, but Ava already knew Jasper's answer. She'd heard it too many times from the doctor.

She felt her pulse race as their options diminished.

"Please do," he said, as if an open invitation. "And I will tell every criminal you and Mara have ever crossed paths with, who you are. Heck, I'll even lead them to you." He lowered his voice. "Exonerating the Center of any wrong-doing, of course. I mean, you *are* evil geniuses. There was only so much we could do to contain you." He repositioned his grip, clasping Charlotte by her upper arm. "I think we all know the great lengths some of them would go to track you two down. And there's no telling the extent of their revenge.

"And what about the artwork you pilfered?" he said to Mara. "I'm sure there's a number of investigators who would love nothing more than inside information on the individual who painted all those replicas." His beady eyes moved to Ava. "And the woman who masterminded the swaps."

Ava waited for it. The prick wasn't done yet.

"At the very least," he said with a shrug, "I'll make sure you never see Charlotte again."

And there it was.

A sick feeling lodged in Ava's chest. It was like he'd memorized the doctor's personal handbook, *Mind Manipulation for Assholes*.

Grinning, he moved toward the door, oblivious or uncaring that he pulled a resistant Charlotte with him.

Ava's heart pounded in her chest as intricately laid plans began to fall to pieces. It was happening all over again. They were being blackmailed, but this time by someone who had more to gain than just funding the Center and furthering his research.

And Charlotte was going to pay the price.

Charlotte openly cried, making Ava wonder how long and to what extent this had been going on.

Today, it was going to stop.

Jasper turned toward the exit, and with nothing more than a nod to Mara, the microphone was moving across the room with the speed and precision of a Chinese flying guillotine, landing a clean strike to the back of his head. The force was insufficient to take him out, but enough to give them time and the upper hand.

Releasing Charlotte's arm, he fell to one knee, his shaking hand moving to the back of his head where blood dripped on his white coat. Ava, in position, knuckle-punched him in the temple with enough force to cause death, or at the very least, hemorrhaging. Jasper fell face forward onto the floor.

"Mara, tie him up," Ava instructed, searching his pockets for his key badge.

Charlotte backed into a table and fell into a chair with her hand to her mouth. "Oh, my God."

Ava felt for his carotid artery and found his pulse. She glanced at Mara. "Alive."

Mara's head ducked underneath the audio console and lifted a set of bundled cables. She pulled a small Bushcraft knife from her combat boot, found the locking mechanism on two cable ties. Moving beside Ava, she took the ties and methodically slipped them over his wrists and loafers.

"How do you know how to do that?" Charlotte asked, watching Mara. "What was he talking about? He mentioned criminals and . . . and replicas?"

Ava ignored her questions, working in lockstep with Mara, as if it were a pre-orchestrated event.

Charlotte didn't know quite everything about their circumstances. In this case, certain assignments and a variety of crimes they were blackmailed into committing. But now wasn't the time to explain.

Ava reared back on her haunches, talking to herself. "The badge will only get us so far. We'll need his fingerprint to get out of the Center." She looked up at Mara as she pulled the last cable tie taught.

Mara nodded, pulling the Bushcraft back out of her boot. "Fingerprint."

Ava lifted and extended his arm as Mara firmly gripped his index finger, lowering it to the floor and lifting her knife.

"Oh my God, no!" Charlotte shouted, holding out her palms to stop them.

Ava looked over her shoulder, and her heart wrenched at her sister's stricken face. "Char, we don't have time for this."

Charlotte shook her head frantically. "Please, don't do it. We just ... can't."

Ava looked toward the ceiling and sighed; mercy was not an emotion she embraced much. But Charlotte was innocent, and blissfully unaware of what she and Mara had become.

Giving Jasper's repulsive, prone body a quick glance, she made her decision and gave Mara a look that said today was a day of firsts.

Mara nodded and lifted Jasper's arms as Ava helped heave his inert body over Mara's shoulder.

"Lead the way," Mara said, as she repositioned him for better balance.

CHAPTER THREE

"The highest form of pure thought is in mathematics."

—Plato
Athenian philosopher during
the Classical Period in Ancient Greece

Ava skirted through hallways, scoping out the corridors, which were uncharacteristically empty. Apparently, the longstanding employees of the research facility were busy standing graveside.

She navigated each hall with a growing sense of relief. The empty corridors allowed them to move swiftly and avoid unnecessary force.

In truth, the entire staff wasn't a horde of evil scientists. The real shit heels were the ones who knew the truth behind how the sisters came to the facility, the doctor's personal sycophants: Jasper; Ms.

Garmond, also known as Charlotte's "handler"; and the facility's neurosurgeon, Dr. Vielle, dubbed "Dr. Vile" by Ava and Mara.

The others? They bought into the doctor's mocked-up psychological profiles labeling Ava and Mara as borderline psychotics, struggling with reality and spewing conspiracy theory nonsense.

Why all the cutting-edge security? Just as the doctor explained to his existing staff and new hires, the means necessary to ensure the older sisters didn't escape the grounds and wreak their psychotic havoc on the unsuspecting locals.

And what a pitiful picture he painted for himself. The benevolent doctor taking in three orphaned sisters, only to discover the older ones harbored severe mental disorders, including, but not limited to paranoid schizophrenia and antisocial personality disorder, not that dissimilar to the diagnoses of several notorious serial killers.

Lucky for the sisters, and the community at large, the doctor was the best guardian possible in terms of studying their psychotic tendencies, potentially discovering new treatments and at the very least, controlling and subduing their erratic behavior.

And let's not forget the sisters were certified geniuses, making it all the more critical that the staff avoids buying into any elaborate stories or emotional pleas for help.

Which meant Ava and Mara had no one to talk to or confide in, other than each other. With few exceptions, the staff worked around them, dodging them at all costs and treating them as if they were virtually invisible.

Ava's greatest fear was that after years of endless tutoring, questionable experimental treatments, and constant threats of separation from her sisters due to non-compliance, that she might, in fact, be just a little bit crazy.

At the very least, a tad unstable.

Ava had reached another badge-reader, and they were fast working their way through an area of the facility they'd only used when departing on assignment.

Thankfully, with Mara's ninja level of fitness, her pace never slowed, nor did her breathing become labored.

Ava turned a corner, waved them through, and stopped in front of a security door with a biometric reader. Mara turned, and Ava lifted Jasper's finger. The door opened, and they stepped into a small, enclosed room with another door at the end, a mantrap.

Unsure as to why alarms weren't sounding off from the security cameras lining each of the corridors, Ava kept moving forward until they reached the door at the end of the mantrap, lifted Jasper's finger, and placed it on the last reader.

The door began to open, and they held their breath as to what they might find on the other side. Ava half expected a team of combat-trained security guards at the ready to bring them down. After inflicting some gratuitous pain, of course.

"Don't let them touch Charlotte," Ava instructed as they leaned against the wall.

They held their breath and then—nothing.

To the left was an office behind glass. A single security guard sat with his back to the window as he watched the graveside ceremony from one of twelve surveillance monitors.

Ava sighed with relief at their luck. The doctor's funeral was a gift that just kept giving.

Ava turned to Mara and Charlotte, forefinger to her mouth, indicating to be quiet and quick. They each moved past the window to the front vestibule, stopping short at an outdoor exit. Ava waved Mara and Charlotte back as she peeked outside at the parking lot. Her heart began to beat wildly. Jasper's Mercedes was parked in the space next to the doorway.

She turned to Mara, her two fingers turning in a circle. Mara nodded and moved accordingly, allowing Ava access to Jasper's pockets. She shoved her hand into his lab coat and then a pants pocket and grinned as her fingers touched metal, pulling out a ring of keys.

Ava whispered, "I'll open the trunk. The lid will help shield us as we dump him inside."

"Just let me throw him in a closet and be done with it," Mara argued.

Ava shook her head. "It'll buy us more time if we leave him in the woods outside of town." It would be hours before Jasper woke up, found the trunk release, and managed his way out of the woods. Without allowing further argument, she slipped out the front door.

No one in sight.

Her fingers brushed the trunk icon on the key fob and it popped up soundlessly.

Gotta love German technology.

She motioned Mara over, and they moved quickly through the door toward the car, dumping the man into the cavernous trunk. Charlotte bounced on her toes behind them, scanning the parking lot for witnesses.

Ava pushed the trunk icon on the key fob, and the trunk lid lowered soundlessly.

"Hand over the keys," Mara said, holding her hand out toward Ava.

Ava shook her head. "I'm driving."

"We both know I'm the better driver. Give me the keys."

Ava balked. "We're not doing this 'fast and furious' style where you crash through the security gates, alerting everyone within a fifty-mile radius."

"Fuck that shit. We need to burn tires if we expect to make it out of here."

Ava spoke slowly. "I've got the keys and I'm calling the shots." She hesitated, telling herself to address the topic later but just couldn't hold back. "And don't think for one minute that I didn't notice the knife in your boot," she hissed. "That knife is mine and you know it."

Mara's eyes narrowed, waiting too long to respond. "It's my knife. I picked it up last month during the job in Vienna."

"That's a flat-out lie. It was hidden in the hole I made in the sheetrock behind my bathroom mirror. *And* it has my initials engraved on it."

"Who the fuck does that?" Mara asked, throwing her arms up and leaning toward Ava. "Who puts their initials on a weapon they're going to use to *off* somebody?"

Charlotte gasped, the older sisters forgetting she was there.

Crap. So much for protecting Charlotte's innocence. Cooling her temper, Ava bent at the waist, holding her little sister by her forearms. "We don't 'off' anyone unless we have to, Char."

Mara snorted and rolled her eyes. "Oh, *that* helped."

Charlotte looked at them as if they were strangers. "Who-who are you?" She looked at Mara. "You told me you were traveling to art exhibits"—and then to Ava—"and you were attending math conventions."

"Those weren't total lies," Mara said with weak conviction. "We hit one or two . . . a few years ago."

Again, they were wasting time.

"We'll address this later," Ava asserted. "But now we have to focus on getting past gate security." She opened the driver's-side door and slipped behind the wheel, and Mara entered through the passenger door, as Charlotte scooted into the back seat. Once everyone was settled, Ava pressed the start button. The engine turned over softly, almost purring.

So close. Just one more hoop to jump through. Security going out of the facility was just as stringent as going in. It was in their best interest to get through without causing any alarm or suspicion. But if that wasn't possible, Ava would have to channel her sister's driving skills and burn some tires.

Her heart pounded in her chest as she pulled up to the security gate and lowered the car window.

She didn't recognize the guard. That was good. Freakishly good. Annnddd—he was young, early to mid-twenties. She twisted her body with one arm over the door, her cleavage in perfect view.

"Please, be straight; please, be straight. . . ." she repeated as he opened the sliding glass partition.

She glanced down to see if her heart might literally explode from her chest, noticing that due to the amount of adrenaline coursing through her body, her nipples could literally cut glass. Huh, perfect timing for some sexual manipulation.

That said, despite seducing a number of marks over the years, this one was by far the most important. Failure was not an option.

She smiled brightly at the young guard who was gaunt, compared to the gorillas that usually manned the main entrance of the facility.

"Hi, we're Jasper's nieces. He told us to go on back to the hotel." She lowered her voice to a sultry setting as if letting him in on a secret. "Uncle Jasper said we weren't properly dressed for a funeral."

His eyes were pasted to her chest. He folded one arm over the other and leaned down. "Yeah, uncles are funny that way."

Bingo. Hetero at 11:00.

"Tell me about it." She rolled her eyes. "We came for a visit and out of nowhere, some guy he works for ups and croaks. We show up for the funeral, like he asked, and well—" She leaned back so he could see the rest of her inappropriate ensemble. "He just about split a gut when he saw what we were wearing."

He leaned farther out the window as his eyes took in her bootie shorts and candy-red stilettos.

He took a long swallow. "For the record, I think you look just fine."

Ah, how cute, he was flirting with her. But this was no time for drawing out her sexy skills. "Really? Why, aren't you the sweetest?"

Mara mumbled in the background. "Who are you channeling? Ellie May Clampett?"

Ava discreetly waved her back with her right arm. "If you could just let us through, we'll be out of your hair."

"No problem," he said, and Ava's heart palpitated with success. "Hand me your security pass. I can let you through."

Hmm, a security pass.

Shit.

During assignments, when driving Ava and Mara to the private airport, Jasper always gave the guard a pass to get both in and out of the facility.

Think. Think. Think.

"Shoot," Ava said with her bottom lip pulled out, "Uncle Jasper has the darned pass." She put the car in reverse. "Just let me go back to the gravesite and tell him the sexy security guard needs it. He won't like it, but rules are rules."

The hapless guard, encouraged by the compliment and perpetually smitten with the points protruding from her shirt, appeared conflicted. Recognizing opportunity, Ava put the gear back into drive. "When do you get off work, Mr. . . .?"

"Walker," he replied. "Jake Walker. I'm off at nine."

"Well, Mr. Jake Walker, I plan on having a late-night swim." She leaned closer to him with her chin on her arm, batting her eyelashes. "Why don't you meet me at the hotel pool when you get off work?"

Ava could barely hear Mara's low, biting voice. "Jesus H. Christ. You've got the acting skills of a D-minus celebrity. This shit's never going to fly. Fucking go!"

"I tell you what," Jake Walker said with promise in his eyes, "it'd be improper to interrupt Dr. Bancroft during such a solemn time. Why don't you ladies go on to the hotel."

Ava exhaled. Ahh, Jakey-boy was so losing his job.

He scratched the back of his head. "By the way, which hotel are you ladies staying at?"

Fuck.

. . . the name of a local hotel.

"Umm, the one up Highway 47," Ava said, impressed she remembered the highway but legitimately struggled with a hotel name. She and Mara were never allowed outside of the facility unless escorted, all while getting briefed on their upcoming job as their driver drove them to the airport. She and Mara had traveled the world but knew nothing of the local town. "What's the name . . .?"

"The Hotel Pompano?" Jake offered. "That's where some of the other mourners are staying."

Ava smiled wide and snapped her fingers. "That's it, the Hotel Pompano. I guess I'll see you at the pool a little after nine, Mr. Jake Walker. Oh, and if I don't show up right away, it's because I'm waiting for Uncle Jasper to fall asleep."

He winked. "I'm sure it'll be worth the wait."

The security arm began to rise. Ava couldn't believe their good luck. And then Lady Luck just as quickly kicked them in the balls.

"Wait a second."

Jake Walker reappeared at the window as Ava's heart all but beat out of her chest. She pressed the brake to the floor, her other foot ready to mash down on the gas pedal.

"I fuckin' told you," Mara griped.

The young guard leaned back down on his arms in the window. "What's your name?"

Ava exhaled again, and slowly eased her left foot off the brake.

"Ellie," Ava said with a wink. And just to irritate Mara a tad bit more, she added, "But my friends call me Ellie May."

―――

Mara suggested a zigzagging, backtracking, and then moving forward approach to their route as well as changing out vehicles along the way. All in the hopes of confusing anyone who might be tracking them.

After a couple days of driving, they finally reached Albuquerque and decided it was safe to find a room and get some real sleep. And with the cash Ava lifted from the wallet of the still unconscious Jasper before closing the trunk on him one last time, they were able to snag a used laptop at a nearby pawn shop, and to pay for the night at a rundown roadside motel.

Ava sat at a small table while Charlotte and Mara slept on the one double bed. She stared at her computer screen, making some last-minute inputs until the screen began to blur.

She was too tired to continue her work and too weak to keep the memories of that fateful day at bay, when she'd followed the doctor out of the padded room, and he'd led her to Charlotte, who was recovering from surgery. Ava didn't want to believe it—it was her worst-case scenario realized. A high-risk brain surgery where the soulless bastard, Dr. Vile, had created lesions in sections of her sister's young brain that Halstead had hoped would trigger certain skill sets, or levels of genius.

Similar to the surgery he'd performed on Mara just a year prior. Surgery he'd promised Ava he would never perform on Charlotte as long as Ava and Mara remained "cooperative."

As a result of her surgery, Mara had begun to show an aptitude for art. It began as a mild interest and then expanded into a full-blown obsession. The doctor was beyond ecstatic at the outcome, proving out his hypothesis and earning him international attention. And then the doctor brought in an art mentor for Mara, and that's when her work morphed into something truly special.

Ava would check on Mara throughout the day, between studies with her own mentor, and noticed her sister looking pale and drained of energy.

After long artistic frenzies which could last days, Mara would spend the same amount of time, if not more, sleeping. When Ava approached the doctor about her concerns, he'd wave it off as just "catching up on her sleep."

Leaning on the flimsy tabletop, she covered her face with her hands. She could recall standing over Charlotte in the recovery room, grasping her hair and shaking her head in disbelief. History had repeated itself. Despite everything she and Mara did to comply with his demands, he'd cut into their little sister's brain.

The twelve-hour days of study and endless testing of their progress, a never-ending series of events that left them stumbling to their beds at night was all for nothing. Yet, at the time, completely worth every minute to protect their younger sister from a surgery fraught with risk.

When Ava confronted Halstead regarding his broken promise, she realized the true level of duplicity and betrayal from the man who'd promised her otherwise.

He told her she was a selfish and immature child, incapable of appreciating the sacrifice Charlotte had made for the greater good of science. That *her* selfless act would allow for scientists all over the world to help others like her, below average in intelligence and without any worthwhile defining characteristics, to reach their true potential.

As if Charlotte had had a say in the matter.

As if Charlotte were somehow lacking before the surgery.

If she were honest with herself, deep down, Ava knew it was imminent. With Mara's continued success, more questions and theories were hypothesized that could only be verified by conducting yet another experiment that required another surgery. And again, one of Ava's sisters became a human guinea pig at the express pleasure of one fucking mad scientist. Three, if you count Bancroft and Vielle.

Ava later discovered that Mara had been isolated in another room and under sedation during Charlotte's surgery on standby in the event they needed her for a blood transfusion, as she and Charlotte shared the same blood type. Post-surgery, Halstead gave orders to keep her sedated in light of the issues they were having with Ava.

Ava closed her laptop, extinguishing the only light in the room with the exception of the streetlights that peeked through the metal blinds. Charlotte's small frame was plastered against Mara, which gave Ava a sliver of the bed to settle into.

Tomorrow was a big day, quite literally the culmination of years of planning. Planning her sisters were virtually unaware of. And although unexpected, Jasper's interference had worked out to their benefit.

She smiled, wondering if he'd managed to find the trunk release on the S550. Mara had wanted to disable the glowing green button, but Charlotte wouldn't allow for it, saying that he might not survive otherwise. And despite him being a lowlife scumbag, she would not be a party to murder.

Pulling more covers over herself, she snuggled down, knowing she'd done everything she could to protect herself and her sisters. First thing in the morning, they'd work on disguising themselves in the likely event that authorities were looking for them. And then she would take her sisters home.

She only hoped that Wilder, Texas was the right choice.

She'd made that last-minute decision while sleep-deprived and time-restricted, the name of the town eliciting a warm feeling in her solar plexus. Wilder, Texas reminded her of those series of books she'd loved as a child. Ava used to read them to Mara and Charlotte, assuring them that one day they would leave the Center and have a father like Mr. Ingalls to care for them.

She was years older now and knew there was no one to look out for them except her. As she told herself a million times, she'd got them into this mess and she'd get them out.

Ava fell asleep to dreams of an idyllic home. A home where new memories would be made and where they were safe. She prayed that would be the case.

CHAPTER FOUR

"It is impossible to be a mathematician without being a poet in soul."

—Sofia Kovalevskaya
First woman to obtain a doctorate in mathematics, to be appointed a full professorship in Northern Europe, and to work for a scientific journal as an editor

"Oh, hell no," Mara said, white-knuckling the dashboard of the Ford Escort Sedan, her eyes wide. "Tell me this isn't it, Ava."

Ava curled one finger around her newly minted, shoulder-length platinum-blond hair. The wood-shingled house looked straight out of a scene from *The Walking Dead*.

"What? It's perfect." She swallowed. The only perfect thing

about the house was the fractal patterns and elegant geometric lines she alone could see.

"The house is secluded, so you can paint, and Charlotte can play the piano without anyone the wiser." A crow lit on the splintered rail of the front porch. An omen. Her smile faltered. "And it's the best I could find in forty-eight hours."

"I love it!" Charlotte said, bouncing in the back seat, the fourteen-year-old sprite of a sister forever the optimist. "It's home. I can feel it in my bones. We can start over and build a real family."

"It's an abomination," Mara grumbled, turning to her sister in accusation. "Tell me this is temporary. As in one night, two tops."

"Six months."

Charlotte clapped her hands. "What's the name of the town? Where do we live?"

Ava clenched her eyes shut. "Wilder." She turned her head toward the driver's window, ignoring Mara's head jerk and open-mouthed expression.

"Seriously? *Wilder*? Texas?" As expected, Mara dropped her head to the dashboard, repeatedly, as Charlotte bounced out the car door, humming with delirious joy, skipping up the porch steps.

Ava began to second-guess herself. Maybe Wilder, Texas wasn't such a good idea? There were those still at the Center who remembered her obsession with the series, for one. And just lately, she'd been reading them to Charlotte.

Ava quickly followed Charlotte, partly to distance herself from Mara. "Be careful. The realtor said the place has been empty for eighteen months. The key should be under the concrete troll next to the front door."

Charlotte held up the key as if she'd found a hidden treasure, and Mara sided stealthily up next to her older sister. Just as Charlotte skipped through the front door, Mara had Ava in a headlock.

"What the fuck, Mara," Ava gasped, her fingers wrapped around her sister's solid forearm.

"Wilder-*fucking*-Texas? Are you serious?" The pressure increased.

"It's not what you think."

"Oh, pray tell, what could I be thinking? That you picked our new home, aka hideout, based on your obsession with a TV show set in the godforsaken prairie in the eighteen-hundreds?"

"Of course not," Ava said weakly, her face reddening with the increasing pressure, "that would be . . . crazy." She weakened alongside the lie, Mara's hold relaxing slightly. Recognizing a window of opportunity, she grabbed her sister's thigh, bringing them both to land in a pile of dust.

"Jesus, Mara, shave much?"

Mara gasped, finding her head in her sister's armpit. "Please, your deodorant quit back in fucking Abilene, you delusional shrew." She flipped Ava over, gaining the advantage. "This has got to stop, Ava. Get your head out of Michael Landon's ass, and get a grip on reality. We're running from some really sick criminal shitholes and your head is in the clouds, searching for fucking Pine Nut Grove."

"It's Walnut Grove, you illiterate. And all I'm trying to do is bring some normalcy to Charlotte's life."

Mara pushed Ava's cheek into the dirt, making her spit and cough. "Normal is not a fucking TV show," she panted. "A TV show that people at the Center know you're obsessed with."

"A TV show based *on a series of books*." Not sure of the significance of that, but by God Ava wasn't going to be labeled crazy.

When they'd first arrived at the Center, those contraband books were the only link she had to an idyllic childhood. After spending tireless days working on mathematical formulas, graphing tangents, and reading through hundreds of financials searching for anomalies on behalf of Doctor Halstead, she'd pull the books from under her plastic-sheathed mattress and dream about a life she desperately craved for herself and, more importantly, her sisters. It wasn't crazy. It was . . . a coping mechanism.

Because in truth, their jacked-up life was her fault and her responsibility to make it right. She had to fix it. Fix them.

What better place to do that than a small prairie town in Texas?

Ava gained a foothold, twisting her torso, pinning her knee on Mara's chest. "I had forty-eight hours to find a town with a secluded house for rent. I created new identities for us . . . and hacked half a dozen government agencies to embed them online." She moved her knees over Mara's biceps, putting as much pressure on them as possible. "I did this, by the way, at night after driving all the way from the Center while you snored and drooled on my pillow. Here's a tip: You may want to wash off your dime store mascara before sleeping on other people's pillows. Jesus, where were you raised, a fucking barn?"

Mara lifted her head. "No, a medical facility, where our laptops were blocked from online stores like Sephora."

"How many times have I told you that for every night you sleep with your makeup on, you age seven years?" All of Ava's body weight was digging into her sister's arms, and one of Mara's legs was attempting to wrap itself around her neck for leverage. "How many times, Mar?"

"That's enough."

The entangled sisters froze instantly. Ava looked up sheepishly at their little sister, standing on the front porch, her hands where her hips might be in a couple of years. Ava pulled away, slowly dusting herself off as Mara did the same.

"You both promised."

She was right. They did promise. While driving along winding rural roads, and then backtracking those same routes to confuse any potential trackers, there was plenty of time to talk. Ava and Mara answered as many of Charlotte's questions as honestly as they could without providing too many graphic details. This included a high-level explanation of the contracted jobs the doctor had coerced them into executing.

Quick wit and their so-called individual gifts were oftentimes the edges they needed to crack a safe, replace a priceless painting with one of Mara's replicas or scale the side of a twenty-story building only to be greeted by an enemy with a Glock 26 or a SOG Bowie knife.

Some were military-type assignments that involved intel gathering or hacking into high-security databases. After some time, the sisters questioned whether they were the good guys or the bad guys. The longer they were in the field, the blurrier the lines of morality became and the more they began to rebel.

When they forced the doctor's hand, he threatened them with Charlotte's future, stating that if they found their assignments questionable from a moral perspective, then it was time to indoctrinate Charlotte into the fold: discontinue her concert performances and begin combat training.

And then he dangled the idea of submitting Charlotte to more brain lesions to uncover levels of genius that were more lucrative than being a piano prodigy. That freaked them out and shut them up quick.

There was nothing more frightening than the experimental shit that went on behind closed doors at the Center. And she vowed to do whatever it took to protect Charlotte from another of the doctor's "trans-cranial" procedures.

"What?" Ava shrugged her shoulders. "We're just joking around. You know how sisters are."

"No." Charlotte shook her head. "That's not how sisters are. Wrestling and throwing each other in the dirt is what brothers do. Sisters support and love one another, share their clothes, and paint each other's toenails."

Ava doubted the truth in that statement but she'd be damned if she was going to be the one to break her sister's idyllic bubble.

Charlotte remained undeterred. "You both promised. You promised we could start over and have a normal family."

"It's okay, Char, really," Ava said, jogging up the steps. "We're just letting off steam. But we're going to stop. Right, Mar?" She turned to her sister, widening her eyes, compelling her to chime in.

Thankfully, Mara complied. "All good, li'l bit." Mara shook the dust from her newly cropped pixie cut. "But you may want to cut us some slack as we figure out what normal is. We've been living in a rather sterile, nonstandard living environment for the last eight years."

"You were cursing," Charlotte added, refusing to cut them any sisterly slack.

Mara coughed, both her and Ava looking everywhere but at their sister. Freak of nature that she was, it was as if she'd been born from an entirely different gene pool.

Ava confessed, "You're right. Mara and I were cursing. Which is a bad habit and one we promise to break. Right, Mara?"

"Fuck, no."

Ava turned her head slightly and Mara rolled her eyes and recanted. "I meant, heck, yeah."

Ava continued, "So your call. You want to start a 'swear jar' where we have to put money in it every time we cuss?"

"Or you could make us do hours of calisthenics as punishment," Mara offered enthusiastically, which to her would have been anything but.

Ava watched as Charlotte beamed, an idea blooming.

And then she blurted out, "Church."

Silence. Except for maybe mosquitos buzzing, and the aforementioned crow cawing in the woods behind the house.

"Come again?" Mara all but choked.

"Church!" Charlotte reiterated with exuberance. "I've seen on TV sitcoms where families go to church to ask for forgiveness, pray to a guy wearing a floral headdress, and drink wine." She looked at Ava beseechingly. "You love drinking wine."

Ava swallowed. "I do . . . like wine, that is." She glanced at Mara, who stared back at her with a "the-last-place-in-hell-I-wanna-go-is-church" look.

"That's it, then," Charlotte said smugly, as if she'd just determined how to dispose of toxic waste. "Each time one of us swears, we all three have to go to church that Sunday." Charlotte looked at each of her sisters with a deliberate expression. "That's what normal families do."

Ruminating over the concept of attending church, Ava and Mara pulled several 7-Eleven bags out of the vehicle they'd commandeered from last night's hotel parking lot. The fifth car they'd absconded with, and for now, the last.

Which reminded Ava that she had to anonymously send money to the owners, their addresses found and noted by Charlotte inside each of the glove compartments.

Walking inside, Ava took mental notes.

The house was furnished. That was a plus. There was a washer and dryer in what appeared to be a mudroom.

All good if you didn't mind the contents being circa 1962. Which also appeared to be the last time the place was cleaned.

Despite this, Charlotte squealed through the house like it was The Bvlgari Resort in Dubai.

Ava and Mara walked around, slowly perusing the place, exhibiting far less enthusiasm than their little sister. Ava scrunched her nose as Mara held up a crocheted afghan, which looked to have been a home to field mice.

Ava kept glancing at her from the corner of her eye, waiting for her to lose her shit.

Finally, she spoke. "How are we paying for this lovely hovel?"

"I made a few bank transfers."

"You didn't have much time. Are you sure you didn't leave a trail?"

"No trail."

"How can you be sure?"

"I'm sure."

"How? I've watched you hack for days and weeks, covering your tracks. You didn't have days, let alone weeks to prepare for this."

Moving into the kitchen, Ava opened the pink refrigerator with flare fins that extended out on the front edges like a Cadillac. A far cry from the ultra-modern aesthetic of the Center. "I've been making small transfers over the past four years."

Ava glanced up at Mara, and her heart warmed as she watched one side of Mara's lip turn up. "You've been planning for this?"

"I knew the time would come. I wanted to be prepared."

"How much?"

Ava looked inside the oven. Relatively clean.

"We're flush." She didn't want to sound too full of herself. "Enough to send Charlotte to college . . . and then some."

Give or take a cool half mil.

"Ava." At the sound of Mara's voice, she suddenly felt awkward. It was atypically soft, making Ava's heart feel too large for her chest. She knew that voice. She had heard it before. It was a voice from her childhood. So soft and kind. Their mom's voice.

Mara pulled her arm, gently forcing her to look at her. Their eyes caught, and Ava thought her throat would burst from the gratitude in her sister's amber eyes.

"Thank you."

And it felt so good. So good to have something of consequence to celebrate. Not the thrill of the hunt or the success of a heist, but something that mattered far and above the circumstances that were forced upon them.

"Okay," Mara's brash voice was making a comeback. "Let's talk names."

Ava gave a short nod. "Let me get the laptop."

Within minutes, details outlining their new identities were displayed on the laptop. As Mara turned the first few pages, Ava held her breath.

"Mercy?" Mara asked, looking up at Ava with high eyebrows.

Ava nodded.

"Mercy, *fucking*, Ingalls?"

Well, that lovely sister-moment was short-lived.

"And you're . . . ?" She scrolled down. "Oh my God, you're Loren Ingalls."

"Who am I?" Charlotte asked, bounding in the room. "What's my new name?"

Mara once again stared at Ava as if she'd lost her mind. "Why, you're Carrie Ingalls. I don't even have to look at your folder."

Ava cleared her throat. "Cara. Her name is Cara Ingalls."

"Oooohh, I lovvve it! Thank you, Ava! It's just like those books!" She hugged her as if the name was lyrical.

Mara snorted as she reared back in her chair. "Even Charlotte remembers the books."

"It's fine," Ava reassured her, not entirely sure that was the case. "It doesn't really matter what our names are since we have all new accounts with complete histories. And a set of government documents with our new names that appear to have been initiated years ago." Ava turned to Charlotte, who didn't pick up on Mara's fuming. "Here's the thing, Char, we can no longer go by our old names. Charlotte, Mara, and Ava no longer exist. Moving forward, we're Cara, Mercy, and Loren. Got it?"

"Got it . . . Loren." She grabbed her hand, pulling her toward the staircase. "Let's pick out our rooms!"

Mara, now Mercy, followed them up the staircase. Ava, now Loren, could barely hear her mumble, "Great. We're the fucking Ingalls living in a little house on the prairie."

CHAPTER FIVE

> "Mathematics has beauty and romance. It's not a boring place to be, the mathematical world. It's an extraordinary place; it's worth spending time there."
>
> —Marcus de Sautoy,
> British mathematician, *The Creativity Code: Art and Innovation in the Age of AI*, 2019

Two days and thirty-one swear words later, Sunday arrived. On Saturday, Cara insisted they go shopping for "church clothes." According to their chaste sister, leather *bustiers* and bootie shorts were indecent and unseemly.

After a trip to the nearby Wal-Mart, which was forty-nine miles away no less, they went in search of what Cara deemed "appropriate church clothing."

It didn't take long before Loren and Mercy realized their angelic little sister possessed the fashion sense of a repressed eighty-year-old nun and the tenacity of a third-world dictator. Twenty minutes into their first attempt at a sisterly right-of-passage, it turned into the razor's edge of sisterly bloodshed.

The shorts Mercy held up were too short. The skirt Loren cooed over, indecent. Loren merely touched a gray tee printed with the words, *Size Matters, Just Ask Pluto,* and Cara's eyes narrowed to threatening slits as she hissed, "No. Just, no!"

When did their timid baby sister become so crazy-assed, holier-than-thou?

"Madame Garmond," Cara preached while sifting through a bin of granny panties, "says that a young lady is defined by her choices."

"Garmond?" Mercy grumbled, pulling the panties Cara put into their cart back into the bin. "The old lady who traveled with you during concerts?"

"Madame Garmond took care of me while traveling, and at the Center," Cara explained, making Loren cringe as she tossed a pair of beige panties into the cart. "She was my teacher, my caregiver, and my protector."

Loren watched Cara carefully. "She protected you from Dr. Bancroft?"

Cara paused and shrugged her shoulders. "Sometimes." She continued her search, then added, "Sometimes they would argue."

Loren kept quiet, allowing her sister to determine how much she wanted to share.

"Madame Garmond's point being that one's clothing choices communicate who we are on the inside."

Holding up a rainbow-sequined miniskirt, Mara asked, "What does this skirt say about me? That I'm colorful?"

Cara squinted at her with her brow tensed. "No, it says you're promiscuous, willing to partake in premarital sex and of loose morals."

"Hmm, all that in a single shiny skirt?"

The day continued in an ongoing push and pull on what was appropriate and what reeked of questionable upbringing. Loren wanted to remind Cara that they had indeed been brought up in a questionable environment, but refrained if only to keep the peace.

Fearful of being relegated to wearing support hose and polyester pants with Sketchers, Mercy and Loren offered a compromise. Sunday attire was Cara's call, one hundred percent. But they had free rein to choose clothing for the rest of the week. Cara finally relented, but only after a number of foot stomps and eyerolls.

When Sunday arrived, or D-Day, as Mercy referred to it, the sisters made their way toward the church steps in Cara's chaste clothing selections.

Mercy lifted one side of her knee-length, cleavage shielding, red-and-white-checkered cotton dress. "I can honestly say I've never felt less attractive."

"Trust me, you have," Loren retorted, equally miffed at her attire. Her eyes darted back and forth at the people staring at them. "How do you think I feel? I'm dressed like platinum-blond Barbie in an olive-green muumuu." She'd tried to make the best of it by pulling her hair up in a high ponytail, and applying some fire-red lipstick.

Which Cara made her wipe off with Kleenex before leaving the car.

"Cara, honey," Loren whispered as they walked past members of the congregation wearing capri pants and sleeveless blouses, "tell me again why we're dressed like the Amish?"

"Shit," Mercy groaned, "is this an Amish church? I thought Cara said it was non-denominational? And what does that mean anyway? We believe but refuse to commit?"

The pint-sized prude ignored them as they walked by a group of women closer to her and Mercy's age. They were staring openly at them, wearing stylish sundresses. One even wore jeans.

Cara lifted her chin. "You both look fine. You're just not used to wearing clothes with proper coverage."

Well, Loren considered, she had a point there.

"Proper coverage?" Mercy continued, "I look as though I'm covered in a tablecloth. Not a good look for me."

They followed their small fashion Nazi into the church, who sat them in the middle pews. Which was just fantastic because now the entire congregation could get a good look at their dismal attire.

Upon sitting, Loren and Mercy simultaneously sank lower into their seats as Cara looked around, oblivious to the fact that she and her Pentecostal sisters were the center of attention in a non-Pentecostal house of worship.

Loren thanked the Lord for a quickie service, the message having something to do about predicting your future through faith. The pastor looked to be in his seventies with kind eyes and an engaging voice. His message pulled the congregation toward him, not in fear but more with a sense of hope.

Loren wasn't convinced. At one point in time, the doctor had also seemed kind and well-meaning. His worst offense being the sense of hope he'd instilled in her.

And he'd ended up being a monster.

Finally, the congregation rose from their seats, the noise level in the room increasing a few decibels.

Loren felt her neck tingle. She calmly turned her head to the left and then right, looking for the origin of her discomfort.

Nothing appeared amiss.

Except for him.

She caught him staring back at her, not as much with malcontent but with a barely hidden level of high alert. Like *he* was looking at potential danger. He eyed her while moving with the congregation along the inside aisle, the pews acting as guardrails.

Were those guardrails for his benefit or hers?

Loren followed Mercy toward the outside aisle, her eyes remaining glued to their quarry. He kept walking, a younger girl, close to Cara's age, following.

Despite his wariness, he seemed equally confident. As if he were assessing potential danger and more than able to address it if need be.

He was tall, with a full head of dark, almost black hair and skin that was deeply tanned. Certain areas, like his veined forearms looked to be sun-kissed, as if he'd worked outside the day before and got more sun than intended.

She stared back, and cataloged his attire. A white button-down collared shirt, his wide chest and shoulders testing the seams, his sleeves rolled just below his elbow. He had yet to blink.

He looked at her as if she were his prey.

Oh, how she wanted to be his prey.

Yet, here she was, wearing a forest-green polyester tent.

Alec knew trouble when he saw it. And it had just walked into his house of worship wearing sheep's clothing. Or in this case, a godawful dress that resembled his pup tent when he'd served in the Marines.

"You know them?" Ally whispered as she stared at the three newcomers, along with the rest of the congregation.

"Sure don't."

"They dress funny. Where do you think they're from?"

"The bowels of hell."

"Where?"

Shit, he'd said that out loud. He whispered back, "Bowling Hills."

She seemed satisfied. He was anything but. He didn't need a distraction.

"They don't look trashy to me."

"What?" Alec asked, his head turning toward his little sister.

"Kelly Jeeter's mom heard from Lenore Sterling that these newcomers stopped by the 7-Eleven on their way into town. Said they were nothing better than white trash, the older two, anyway."

"S'at so?" Eyes narrowed further.

"Said the blonde who wore tiny shorts with hooker shoes and the short-haired sister had on a leather bra. Said they were probably prostitutes."

"And how did she know they weren't just driving through town?"

"Kelly Jeeter's mom is a realtor. Said they were renting a house just inside of Wilder."

Inwardly, he congratulated himself on his powers of observation. He could still smell trouble, even when disguised as pious churchgoers. He'd keep his eye on them.

From a distance.

"You shouldn't be gossiping about people you don't know, Ally," he whispered, recognizing how hypocritical that sounded in his head. But it was a teaching opportunity for his little sister.

She looked down and nodded. "Sorry, but you're the only one I've told, and as I said, they don't look trashy to me."

The service concluded, and he was hell-bent on getting back to the farm and the work looming ahead of him.

And that's when she noticed him noticing her.

Surprisingly, she didn't look away in coyness or embarrassment. Oh, no, she blatantly stared right back as if she were daring him to blink.

Oh, hell, did she just lick her lips?

In *fucking* church?

He didn't need this shit.

He needed calm and quiet; he needed an easy life without fucking platinum-blond distractions.

Yet the distraction kept staring.

He finally broke eye contact as they made their way past the pews and through the church doors. He shook Pastor Robert's hand and reached back for Ally's, ready to take control. If he didn't, his sister would be pulling him toward every single female from the church steps to the parking lot.

Ally meant well, but he had no desire to dip his dick into the local pool of pussy. He was fine driving out of town for one-night stands or even a quickie against a bar's back alley wall to address his sexual needs. He didn't need female complications plaguing him in his home town where gossip ran rampant and more men than not ended up at the end of the church aisle saying, "What the fuck just happened?"

He'd made that mistake once, and the pervasive guilt from how that poor decision had affected Ally was a continual unkind reminder.

"Yoo-hoo!" Alec closed his eyes at the familiar voice. Pastor Robert's wife, Emmy Lou. No getting out of this unexpected delay tactic.

He turned with Ally in tow and saw her, his blond nemesis, standing next to Emmy Lou with the two despots-by-association at her side.

Emmy Lou's hand was waving them down, her other arm clenching her pocketbook to her side.

"Alec, you and Ally come meet your new neighbors."

A *frisson* of apprehension speared up the back of his neck. New neighbors?

"They're renting the old Bailey house down by your east field."

Of course, they were. His head fell forward as he chuckled at his bad luck. When he forced his head up, there she was, smiling at him, and not in a neighborly way. He wouldn't have been surprised if she'd sprouted fangs.

"Alec, Ally, this is Loren, Mercy, and Cara. They're sisters and new to the area. And get this, their last name is Ingalls. Isn't that something? The Ingalls girls living in Wilder."

The one with the short dark hair rolled her eyes, nudging the blonde, who almost lost her footing.

He shook each of their hands, leaving Loren's for last, almost buckling at the unexpected strong handshake from such a small woman.

Not normal.

Ally hung back behind him and waved timidly.

"Nice to meet you, Ally," Loren said, peeking around him to his sister.

"Hi." She waved back.

Emmy Lou, ever the welcoming committee, added, "Alec and Ally are direct descendants of this town's founding father, Eubanks Wilder."

The blonde, Loren, returned a subtle smirk. "Wow, so cool. You're like local celebrities."

Was that a tinge of sarcasm? He caught the glint in her eye.

"Hardly," Alec snapped.

Aaannd fuck. He was hard.

The blonde kept endearing herself to the weakest link, Ally. Like a lioness spotting the wounded baby antelope falling back from the herd.

"How old are you, Ally?"

"I turn fourteen next week," Ally replied, her eyes glancing at the younger sister who appeared just as shy as Ally, standing behind and to the side of the she-devil. And what was that sound? Was the younger one humming?

"What a coincidence," Loren said, "Cara is also fourteen. Maybe you can show her around school sometime. Show her the ropes."

His mind took a twisted turn, imagining her arms tied to her sides. Under his control.

Before he could think to soften his tone, he piped up with, "Ally's pretty busy at school. She's taking advanced courses and has very little extra time." A small elbow from Ally found his side, and just as quickly, the smile on the spectacular demon in front of him wavered, the glint in her eye turning into a shard of glass.

"Where do you go to school, Ally?" the demon asked, undaunted.

"Wilder High School."

Emmy Lou added, "The middle school and the high school are in the same building. We're trying to raise money to give the middle schoolers their own location. You can imagine the things they must see walking around all those high school students in the hallways."

The other sister, Mercy, appeared confused. "What things?"

Alec watched the sisters look at Emmy Lou like they seriously couldn't imagine.

"Well, you know, things middle schoolers shouldn't see."

"Like what?" Mercy asked. And she looked dead serious, despite rudely popping her gum.

The demon distraction finally appeared to recognize that Ms. Emmy Lou would rather chew glass than talk about the shit high schoolers got into in the hallways at school.

She chuckled. "You'll have to excuse us. We were home-schooled."

He barely registered her words; he couldn't help but notice how her lips were tinged a soft red. His eyes narrowed, thinking she must have feasted on a small deer on the way to church.

She continued, "I'm afraid we're not well-versed at what goes on in middle or high school, but Cara here will be signing up for classes tomorrow and it sure would be nice if she knew someone." She turned toward Ally again. "What grade are you in?"

Before Ally could answer, Alec stopped the conversation short. "Sorry to interrupt, but I've got to get back to the house. It was nice meeting you." Once again, he grabbed Ally's hand to distance her from the coven.

Unexpectedly, Loren reached out again to shake his hand "Nice meeting you, Alec." Dark brown eyes pinned him down as if daring him not to reciprocate. For Ally's sake and considering he was being scrutinized by the pastor's wife, he reached out. But this time her grip softened, her middle finger running seductively through his palm as they disengaged.

His hand fucking tingled, which made him mad.

And then even more so when it reached his dick.

Fuucckk. How'd she make a handshake seem so filthy?

Loren was livid. Her body literally trembled with rage from that man's unbelievable rudeness toward Cara, not to mention Mercy.

The nerve of that backward-ass Neanderthal.

There were so many ways to incapacitate a man and she visualized Farmer Ted's demise in every one of them.

With the midsummer heat and the blood coursing through her veins, all she could think about was how badly she needed to spar. Had she been at the Center, she'd have a number of muscle-bound morons to work over. But she'd doubt the men of Wilder would be willing to spar and Mercy was no longer an option according to Cara.

Sparring with Alec would deliver the epitome of satisfaction; there were few combat partners in her past who rivaled his size and taking this tree trunk of a man down would be a total turn on.

She opened the driver's door as Mercy and Cara got in on the other side. She leaned down. "Give me a minute, I forgot to get Alec's phone number."

"I don't think he wants—"

Before Mercy could finish, Loren dropped the keys on the seat and made her way through a number of pickup trucks and practical vehicles, until she caught sight of him and his ridiculously large Ford F-450.

She eyed Alec shaking hands with two other men, which must have delayed him from pursuing an escape route.

She waved at Ally and the teenager waved back, just as Alec hoisted his sister into the truck's passenger's seat, avoiding any further pleasantries.

Loren's wide smile masked the pent-up anger that she was about to explode on his fine, sculpted ass.

She stalked his progress as he shut the passenger door and made his way around to the driver's side.

She stepped in his path. "Who do you think you are?"

He kept walking past her as if she wasn't even there.

She stood straight at the direct insult. No fucking way.

She glared at his impossibly large shoulders and then to otherworldly glutes. "Seriously, what crawled up your ass and made a cozy home in your sphincter?"

Hesitation.

And then he turned on her, stalking her direction. She started, as crystal-blue eyes glared down at her.

For a moment, she considered moving into combat stance.

"Those are quite a number of anal references, Ms. Ingalls. You trying to tell me something?"

"That's a ridiculously large truck, Mr. Wilder. You trying to compensate for something?"

His stoic demeanor appeared unruffled, but at the very least, she had his attention.

"Nice, quite the lady."

"You don't know me, or my sisters, for that matter. How dare you treat them as if they were beneath you."

"Is that all you came to say?"

"No," she hissed, her voice low, shaking her head. So close she could smell his minty breath, spicy cologne and heightened testosterone levels. "You are not a nice person." She poked his shoulder and then, entranced at the amount of muscle, poked one outrageously built pec and wondered if he flipped tractor tires as a pastime.

She caught his sardonic glare and regrouped.

"And the next time you see my sisters, you had better treat them with respect because if you don't, I'm going to tear off one of your limbs and shove it up your tight ass."

He was a blank screen. Nothing she said or did seemed to jog any emotion or expression.

"And yes, that was another anal reference but let me make myself perfectly clear when I say you are not welcome to enter *any* orifice in my body."

"Are we done here? As much as I'd like to stay and continue this highly inappropriate dialogue in the church parking lot, I have work to do."

"Just one last thing," she said, stepping back and bringing her voice back to a perky pitch as she smoothed her skirt and pasted a smile on her face. She was going to force herself and him to be neighborly.

Even if it killed her.

"Seeing how we're neighbors, we'd like to invite you and Ally to the house for dinner next week. What night works best for you?"

Stepping up on his running board, he opened the driver-side door to his monster truck. "Well, that would depend on the weather."

"Is that a farming thing? Specific weather conditions for planting crops, herding cattle, violating sheep?"

"No, ma'am, that's a hell thing. Because it would have to be freezing over before I'd allow my sister to step foot in your house."

Chewing her lip, she looked up and smiled. "So, that's a maybe then?"

He ignored her as he swung into the seat, started the engine and pulled out of the parking lot with the expected amount of temperance and reserve considering his cool demeanor during their previous discussion.

Undaunted, she whispered to herself. "Well, that went well."

CHAPTER SIX

"There is geometry in the humming of the strings, there is music in the spacing of the spheres."

—Pythagoras
Ionian Greek philosopher who sought to interpret the entire physical world in terms of numbers

Despite the earlier episode with her condescending neighbor, Loren could hardly contain herself as they pulled into their gravel driveway. She skipped up to the front door, and smiled at the form tacked to the front door. She remained calm as she pulled it from the peeling paint.

"Eviction notice?" Mercy asked with a tinge of hope.

She shook her head. "Bill of Sale."

She opened the door and smiled at what stood in the middle of the front room.

Both Mercy and Cara froze just inside the doorway.

She had expected Cara to squeal or twirl around while humming in pure unadulterated joy. Instead, Cara stood perfectly still, her hand clutching her chest as if she was experiencing some sort of epiphany. And then she took a couple of steps, that same hand reaching out and reverently touching the baby grand piano before her.

Mercy seemed equally speechless but for different reasons. "Um, how did you manage that?"

"It's fine," Loren assured her, reading into what she wasn't asking. "Private sale. Paid cash. Extra to have it professionally tuned by the owner and delivered on a Sunday."

Cara continued to run her fingers along the sides of the black lacquer piano. And then she turned to Loren. "Is she ours?"

"No," Loren answered, "she's yours."

"But it's not even my birthday or Christmas."

Loren held her fingers to her mouth, trying to keep it together.

Cara continued to stare, and then Loren finally took her by the shoulders to guide her to the piano bench. "Well, what are you going to play for us?"

Placing her hands on the keys and closing her eyes, Loren felt like weeping at the visceral response that emanated from every pore of her sister's small body. The simple act of feathering the keys manifesting itself as nothing short of a bodily glow.

And then she began to play. Loren was no musical prodigy, math was her thing, but she instantly recognized Beethoven's Moonlight Sonata. She and Mercy watched in awe as their sister literally became the music she played, her body moving and swaying and delighting in the masterpiece.

"That ought to keep her occupied and out of our hair for a while," Mercy commented, just as enthralled by Cara's music as Loren. "Wanna snort a line of coke?"

"This coming from someone who won't even take a Tylenol."

"I have it on good authority that the kids are always up to

shenanigans when the parents, or in our case, a pint-sized Attila the Hun, is otherwise occupied."

"It's just not the same unless there's a male stripper's ass involved."

The irony that they had never tried drugs or stepped foot in a strip club wasn't lost on either one of them. They spoke euphemistically based on their vast experience with Netflix and On Demand while working outside of the Center while on assignments.

"Just look at her," Loren said, her heart full of joy.

Mercy said with a bump to the shoulder. "You did good."

"Oh, we're not done yet."

Most sisters could easily conjure memories involving stolen makeup, disagreements on the better boy band or fist fights over confiscated clothing. One of Mercy's earlier memories of Loren, or Ava at the time, was her deep-seated, near-obsessive need to protect her sisters.

During one of her first combat training sessions, Mara had taken a size-fifteen boot to the teeth by an overzealous trainer who must have been beaten as a child. Before she could even lift her head to wipe off the offending blood, Ava's protective instincts went into overdrive. Taking full advantage of her trainer's momentary distraction, she rammed her knee into his groin and finished him off with an uppercut to the jaw.

The trainer, who made The Rock appear malnourished, reported the incident to the doctor, who retaliated by giving the sadistic prick permission to take his training with Ava up a notch. After the next day's training, Ava walked away with a bloody nose, two fractured ribs, and a dislocated shoulder.

Ava was sixteen at the time, Mara fourteen.

Mara learned that whenever she fell short of her studies or trainings, the doctor ensured that it was Ava who bore the brunt of her failings. After watching her sister constantly suffering on her behalf, Mara mastered the moves so that Ava didn't have to intervene.

The doctor was a manipulating bastard. He knew full well that she and her sisters would stop at nothing to protect one another, and he made sure they were tested at every turn.

Five years later, Mara was in the process of lifting a priceless Matisse from a trust fund drug addict who'd inherited more money than brain cells from dear old Dad.

Their instructions were to replace the original with the near-mirror image she'd spent months perfecting from the HD photos Ava had shot clandestinely months before.

Forty-two attempts later, she could hardly discern between the two after pulling the original and setting it on the floor next to her copy.

"Someone's coming," Ava hissed, standing at the door of junior's bedroom.

Mara grabbed one of the paintings and slapped it on the wall. She followed Ava to the balcony, closing the doors just as junior and one of his ladies of the evening stumbled into the room and started to tear each other's clothes off.

"Where's the painting?" Ava whispered with wide eyes.

Mara pointed toward the room they'd just exited.

"You left it?"

"I couldn't tell them apart. I panicked."

Ava lifted her eyes to the star-speckled Miami sky. She took a deep breath. "We'll have to wait them out."

Grunts and moans came from inside the room and just as quickly, Ava crammed iPhone earplugs into Mara's ears. She scrolled through her playlist choosing one of Charlotte's personal compositions. She smiled at the memory of her sister searching for something transcendent and uplifting while two drugged-up degenerates went at it on the other side of the sliding glass doors.

Less than five minutes later, Mara grabbed at her ears as Ava yanked out the earbuds, indicating it was go time. She watched over

Ava's shoulder as she slowly reopened the balcony door. Mara tiptoed to the wall as Ava kept an eye over the chalk-nosed, naked bodies.

Mara turned, giving a thumbs-up to Ava, confirming the painting on the wall was, in fact, the copy.

Only by holding them next to each other, with the lights from junior's fish tank spanning the length of one wall, could she see the differing textures.

Not a bad reproduction of the image, but she had failed at mastering some of Matisse's more idiosyncratic brushstrokes. Well, good to know.

Eight hours later they were back at the Center, handing over the masterpiece to the doctor. And as he strode purposely toward his office with the priceless piece of art under one arm and his phone to his ear, Mara wondered if the money generated from her work would go toward more experiments that had created her gift.

The doctor, good ole' stepdad, was nothing more than a mad fucking scientist.

With Cara in an alternate melodic universe, Loren navigated Mercy past the kitchen toward the sunroom. She too sucked in a breath at what was before her.

After cleaning the glass windows, sprinkling the concrete floors with rugs and placing a futon in one corner with bright, colorful pillows, Mercy had been entranced by the natural light that poured into the room, and had even thought about the sunroom as the perfect location in which to paint.

She now stared at the large table holding a brilliant assortment of Windsor & Newton Oils, handmade brushes with Japanese script and dozens of different-sized canvases against the far wall.

Her fingers itched while eyeing the seductive paints. Oh, how she wanted to dip her forefinger in the spicy richness of the cadmium red.

As she sifted through more tubes, her body pined at the thought of swimming in the coastal waters of the cerulean blue.

She picked up a brush and ran her fingers across the feathery feel of the sable bristles. Closing her eyes at the singular touch, she felt her heart clench with longing. Longing that she kept immersed, locked down, compartmentalized.

Art was emotion, emoting. Reaching into the sanctity of your solar plexus and dredging up feelings so deeply seated that it would make your chest ache with both the beauty and darkness of it.

Mercy placed the priceless brush on the table.

What Loren didn't know, was that for Mercy, those feelings came at a price.

Ironic how something that brought her such joy, could also bring her such excruciating pain.

CHAPTER SEVEN

"If you don't work on important problems, it's not likely that you'll do important work."

—Richard Hamming
American mathematician whose work had many implications for computer engineering and telecommunications

"It's official," Loren said, wiping the sweat from the corner of her eye with her work gloves. "Wilder's Hardware Store is my favorite place on earth."

Mercy took a long gulp of her root beer and shook her head. "Dollar Store. As in, everything in it costs a *single dol-lar.*"

Loren thought about that and the fact that her sister had managed to spend two hundred dollars on their first visit.

"I get why we need all the kitchen stuff, and the plastic bins for organization, and the various-sized glass vases and the year's supply of off-brand toothpaste, but tell me again why we need the Mylar balloons?"

Mercy looked at her as if the question were utterly ridiculous. "Because *they only cost a dol-lar.*"

Loren smiled while taking in the fruits of their labor. She couldn't help but feel a deep sense of satisfaction at what a few plants and wood chips did for the front of the house.

After driving through the quaint town of Wilder, both Loren and Mercy had further confirmed their home was an embarrassment compared to the beautifully maintained homes along Main Street. They'd known it was a shithole upon arrival, but after seeing how other people maintained their properties, they were inspired to up their game.

They were seeing homes that had perfectly sod front yards that looked more like wafts of carpet than blades of grass, and exteriors glistening with fresh coats of paint. Some even had decorations on their front doors depicting the current season. Others had window boxes filled with all kinds of plants and flowers that looked straight out of one of those home decorating shows.

That night, during dinner, they'd discussed what they could do to spruce up the outside of their house. Cara piped up that a friend at school said something about the moms always looking at a certain app for house decorating ideas.

And that's when the magic began.

With the magical help of Pinterest.

Loren removed her work gloves, pointing toward the other side of the driveway. "I see purple-blue hydrangeas along the far fence and a bricked walkway trimmed with begonias from the house to the driveway."

She'd also envisioned this in the usual mathematical patterns, but kept that to herself. She picked up her new iPad sitting next to her to search for ideas.

Mercy turned her phone toward Loren. "What about a pale sea green for the exterior of the house?"

"But white trimmed in black is so timeless," Loren said, noting she should check the time. "We should stop. We've got to pick up Cara from band practice in an hour, and there are some things I want to do on the way."

"You go ahead. I'll stay here and finish up," Mercy replied.

"But we are finished, and I want to show you the McAlister House. We'll drive right by it. It's a bed & breakfast, which is kinda like a hotel but with higher rates and fewer amenities."

Mercy shoved her rain boot in the dirt. "I don't want to go. I don't like the way the townspeople look at us."

"What do you mean?"

"Like . . . like they don't like us."

Loren nodded. She noticed it, too. It was like they were the town outcasts. "They just don't know us." She lifted herself from the front porch step and pulled down her cutoffs, and repositioned her silver faux metallic bikini top.

"How are they going to get to know us if they won't even talk to us?" Mercy pulled on the garden hose to wash off her shiny red rain boots, herself wearing a yellow Mumford and Son's tee cut off just below her boobs and black bikini bottoms.

Loren thought about it, "We'll kill 'em with kindness. Say hello to everyone we pass until they have to say hi back."

Mercy cricked her neck back and forth. "I don't think I would even know how to have a conversation with them. I mean, what would I even say?"

Loren picked up the weed eater. "The weather, that's always a good conversation-starter."

Mercy nodded, but Loren could see she remained unconvinced. And then she finally caved. "Just let me put on some shorts and we can go."

After driving by the McAlister House, it was official, home improvement was an important part of living in Wilder. People took pride in their homes and their overall community. If they wanted to fit in, they had to fix up their dingy little house. They agreed they, too, needed an arbor covered in morning glories leading to the backyard like the McAlister home, and started to scope out a list of materials.

"Let's see what Wilder's hardware store can help us with."

Loren pulled into the parking lot of the local hardware shop. A couple of men walked by with small bales of hay as they neared the entrance.

"Afternoon," they said, touching their fitted caps.

And then their wives walked out of the store, laughing, until they saw Loren and Mercy and went quiet, their heads down as they moved past them to catch up with their men.

"Hello," Loren said, despite their less-than-friendly expressions.

But then: Nothing.

They watched as the women all but ushered the men to their trucks, glancing behind them.

"Maybe we should've commented on the weather?" Loren mused thoughtfully. She smiled at Mercy, who looked dejected. "We'll keep trying. Come on, let's get our stuff for the arbor."

She grabbed the door handle to the hardware store and her mood instantly lifted.

In the last week or so, Loren had discovered that walking into an old hardware store was nothing less than a euphoric assault to the olfactory system. She breathed in the aroma of tightly packed bags of potting soil, stacks of freshly cut lumber, and what must have been decades of lingering oil spills.

Dusty rays of sunbeams shone lazily over the dirty black floor mat, which ended as they walked onto the heavily worn, creaky wooden floor. The jingle-jangly door clanged shut behind them.

A man who looked in his mid-fifties with *Henry* embroidered on his gunmetal gray shirt helped them to gather the lumber they would need after showing him a picture on Pinterest.

As Loren paid for their next project and arranged for delivery since they couldn't possibly haul it all home in their Ford Escort, she noticed a Help Wanted sign hanging behind the counter. She couldn't imagine a better place to come to work every day.

"I see you're hiring," she said, doing her best to refrain from waving her hand in the air, and yelling, "Pick me, pick me!"

He hesitated, and scratched behind his ear. "The position's been filled."

Her heart sank, but then her instincts kicked in. "Then why do you have a Help Wanted sign up?"

"Well, lookie there. I guess I forgot to take it down."

He was clearly lying, but then he also looked remorseful.

High road, that's what she decided to take. She held out her hand to shake his. He politely reciprocated. "I'd be interested if anything opens up again. My name's Loren Ingalls."

"Henry Sterling." He smiled. "Nice to meet you."

She started to leave and then hesitated and turned. "You related to Lenore Sterling?" she asked, remembering the woman who worked at the 7-Eleven just outside of town.

"Lenore's the wife," he said, which to Loren, explained everything.

The woman had looked at her and Mercy with outright disapproval the day they arrived into town and stopped by the convenience store to pick up a few things. And then again at church, with the same expression of disdain.

High road. If not for herself, then she had to show Mercy how to take it. "Yes, we've met her," she said, plastering a smile on her face. "Please tell Lenore we said hello."

They walked quietly to the car until Mercy finally broke.

"That woman hates us," she vented, her arms crossed over her stomach. "You should've told him his wife was a judgmental hag."

Loren sighed heavily as she looked at Mercy over the hood of the car. "Kill them with kindness, Mercy, remember?"

Mercy's eyes began to fill, and she looked away. "I told you." She swallowed heavily. "Everyone hates us here."

Loren pulled into the school parking lot, instantly spotting Cara and Ally sitting next to one another on the curb, waiting for their rides. Loren jumped out of the car and walked up to the girls with Mercy following as if she were about to be ambushed by a band of South American terrorists—or some of the local women.

Just as they reached the girls, Mrs. Waterman walked by with her chin in the air and her hand firmly around her daughter's arm. Samantha Waterman was in Cara and Ally's class, but her mother refused to even look at them.

"Hi, Mrs. Waterman, Samantha," Loren said with a meek smile. "Nice weather we're having."

She speed-walked past them as if they were tainted.

And then Loren was so pleased when Mercy also gave it her best shot. "I hear it's going to be perfect bikini weather tomorrow."

Mercy shielded the sun from her eyes. "Look at her go," she said, shaking her head. "It's like a swarm of locusts are about to crest over the hill."

"Why on earth would she not respond to such a great conversation-starter?" Loren asked, almost to herself.

"I told you. Everyone hates us," Mercy said.

"You're competition."

Both Loren and Mercy turned as this pronouncement came from Ally.

"What?" Loren asked.

"You're competition." Ally repeated. "Not only that, you could say you're 'unfair competition.' They're jealous."

"What are we competing for?" Mercy asked, her eyebrows pinched.

Loren sat down on the curb next to Ally. "Wait, why are they jealous? We don't have half the shit they have. Excuse my language."

Cara pulled out a notepad and placed a notch on the page, grimacing at Loren, yet another Sunday in purgatory.

Mercy piped up. "Have you seen the McAlister House? They have a grape orchard and a cute little greenhouse."

Loren added to Mercy's argument. "They have parents and grandparents and bricked driveways."

Cara shook her head as if agitated. "I *told* them they dressed inappropriately."

"No," Mercy corrected, "you told us we dressed like the whores of Babylon. Where the hell is Babylon anyway?"

"It's a borough in New York City," Loren answered.

Ally laughed again and stopped as Loren narrowed her eyes. "I think you're on to something. Please continue."

Loren watched as Ally glanced at Cara, who rolled her eyes, and motioned her to continue. "Please, go on. Now you'll see what I've been dealing with."

Ally leaned toward Cara. "I thought you said they were really smart."

Cara shrugged. "Zero sensitivity to social cues and apparently geographically challenged."

"*Okay*," Ally said with a sigh, turning toward Loren and Mercy. "Well, you're both extremely fit and completely comfortable with your bodies. Wilder's a pretty conservative small town in Texas and the women here, for the most part, are less than pleased with themselves and their bodies. Have you seen any other women in Wilder as fit and as gorgeous as you two?" She went on in a factual manner. "Mercy, look at you. You're cut like some TV ninja warrior, wearing a cutoff tee without a bra, and wearing red rain boots."

"What the hell is sexy about rain boots?" Mercy asked, looking down at her shoe wear.

Ally continued her explanation. "Loren, you're petite with amazing curves but you're also cut. I mean, look at your abs."

Loren glanced at her bare stomach beneath her silver bikini top.

"You're a woman with a six-pack *and* a rack. You look like you could go all *Game of Thrones, Mother of Dragons* on half the men in town."

Loren regarded Ally as if she were working on a puzzle. "No idea what you're talking about. Dragons are fictitious animals. Kinda like unicorns."

Cara lifted her hands as if in vindication. "Now do you see what I'm working with here? They're totally clueless."

"Wow," Ally said, her eyes wide. "They're like superheroes who are completely unaware of their superpowers. Or pop culture."

"Oooh, I can throw a machete and hit the bullseye from twenty yards," Mercy offered up.

Just then Emmy Lou Roberts drove up to the curb and waved to all of them.

Mercy jumped up at the one woman in Wilder who was nice to them. "Hi, Mrs. Roberts, wonderful weather we're having, isn't it?"

"Why, yes, dear, it is."

Mercy grinned from ear-to-ear, looking at Loren and clapping her hands.

"I'm afraid I need your help this evening," Mrs. Roberts said with pursed lips. "I'm pretty desperate. Would you ladies be available?"

Loren grinned. "Why, of course, Mrs. Roberts. Whatever you need, we're here for you."

She patted her chest with a sigh of relief. "Thank goodness, you girls are a godsend. Meet me at the church basement in ten minutes."

CHAPTER EIGHT

"Mathematics is the most beautiful and most powerful creation of the human spirit."

— Stefan Banach
Polish mathematician, founder of modern functional analysis

Five minutes later, they made their way down the basement steps, where Mrs. Roberts began introductions.

To small children.

Some toddlers.

"And this is Emma Jane, she's such an angel," Mrs. Roberts said, and then as if remembering something from the recent past, added, "Unless you give her too much sugar." She placed her hands over the three-year-old's ears. "Let's just say it's nothing short of Armageddon. This is Christina," she said, moving on to the smaller child. "Tina's a bit of a live wire. Don't let her near any light sockets, or small defenseless animals."

Mrs. Roberts kept moving through the basement, grabbing a child and introducing him or her to a mute Loren and Mercy. They were everywhere, a horde of children running around the church's windowless dungeon-like basement.

"And why are we watching them again?" Loren asked, the decibel level of the room making her voice hard to hear.

"Self-defense class," Mrs. Roberts said.

"Aren't they a little young to be learning chokeholds?" Loren inquired, just as one of the four-year-old boys by the name of Tommy gave his younger brother a quite impressive "standing near naked" chokehold. She grimaced as a green line of mucous emerged from the little brother's nose.

"Oh, no," Mrs. Roberts said with a light laugh, "their mothers are taking the self-defense class in the church gymnasium. Cindy Lue Lemming was supposed to watch the children, but came down with acute bronchitis."

"Lucky Cindy Lue," Loren said to herself, counting seven children all under the age of six.

"Thank you again, girls," Mrs. Roberts said, tapping her lip with her finger as she looked them over. She then pulled a *Jesus Slays* tee from a pile sitting on a nearby counter. "Why don't you ladies wear these shirts? They were printed for one of our high school events, and look to be your size." She passed them to Loren and Mercy. "You know how messy children can be."

Mercy and Loren pulled them on in total agreement.

And at that, Mrs. Roberts turned to make her way up the stairs, saying over her shoulder, "I'll be in the gymnasium if you need anything."

Loren turned toward Cara and Ally with nothing short of desperation.

"Don't look at us," Cara said with her hands up. "Ally and I are taking the self-defense class."

Loren turned a skeptical eye toward Ally. "It's true. I just called Alec and he's picking me up afterward."

She then turned to Mercy, who, she was sure, was on the verge of a meltdown and couldn't have been more surprised at what she saw: Mercy, on her knees, with the rapt attention of four little girls. One was sucking her thumb and another seemed to have a panty-in-the-crack issue going on. The other two older girls stared at her as if she wore a Wonder Woman suit.

"Isn't the weather lovely today?" Mercy asked the girls looking at her as if awestruck. They each nodded and Mercy glowed. "How many of you do gymnastics?" They all raised their hands.

Loren was skeptical, given their blatant lack of muscle tone.

"Excellent!" Mercy put two fingers to her mouth and produced an ear-piercing whistle. Miraculously, all the children stopped what they were doing and gave her their full attention. "Everybody line up," she said, pulling mats from a corner to the middle of the room, "we are going to do some gymnastics."

And when the MMA Fighter Wannabe, Tommy, grabbed one of the girls to attempt an American Armlock, Mercy's earsplitting whistle caught his attention. "You," she said, pointing at the derelict, "you have to go the end of the line, but before you do, grab a tissue and take care of your brother's nose. Now, everyone, we're going to begin with an easy forward roll and see if we can get to a back tuck by the end of the night."

The children lined up as commanded.

"Look at you, Tina, you're a natural. . . ."

Loren sat at a nearby table and chairs, completely shocked at her sister's total command of the room.

Mercy laughed as one of the boys performed purposely silly forward rolls. "Okay, funny man, let's see how you fare when we get to the back tuck."

Mercy caught Loren's eye and gave her a thumbs-up. Loren pointed upstairs and Mercy gave her the okay sign with her fingers; the basement was clearly under her command and control.

Loren made her way up the stairs. It took her a while to hunt down the gymnasium as the church grounds were nothing short of a campus.

She counted the backs of fifteen people after opening the doors to the gym, all watching a man in his fifties, wearing what had to be an XXL tee and a pair of gray sweats that barely covered his distended belly. He spoke with an air of assumed authority, continuously pulling the back of his sweatpants up with one hand, the front with the other.

His breathing became labored after a few minutes of asking everyone their skill levels. Loren wondered how he was going to conduct a self-defense class when the intro made him breathless.

Many of the women participating were the same ones who didn't seem to care too much for the Ingalls family, so she decided to lay low, fly under the radar and simply observe.

Alec opened one of the double doors to the church gymnasium and stood quietly to the side. He had showered and was on his way to pick up Ally from school when she'd called, breathless, asking if she could attend the self-defense class at the church.

After a brief interrogation, Alec relented but wanted to see for himself what the class was about. He had offered to show Ally a few moves on a number of occasions, but she seemed embarrassed and reticent. At the time, he wondered if she was uncomfortable grappling with her older brother or just too shy and introverted to attempt such bold moves.

He wanted to protect her, especially after what she'd been through when he'd been overseas. After many attempts, he'd finally resigned himself not to only being her parent and brother but also her personal bodyguard.

"Hello there, Farmer Ted."

His neck turned red at the voice that grated on his nerves at the same time made his body seize up with sexual tension.

The she-devil wore her blond hair in a messy bun, so messy that she looked as if she'd just been thoroughly fucked. She wore an oversized tee not quite long enough to hide the tempting fringe from her much too-short cutoffs. Cutoffs that only served to showcase muscled thighs and highly toned calves. She sported a pair of beat-up Converse with the laces untied, as if she had too much unspent energy to stop and tie them.

He grimaced, lowering the baseball cap on his forehead, hands in his pockets and a leg bent as he leaned against the concrete wall behind him. He couldn't seem to escape the little witch. During the workday, his treacherous mind had bent her over the slats of the horse stall and ruthlessly taken her from behind, cornered her in the tack room, and tied her down with anything resembling a leather strap and used her body in as many filthy ways as his conscience would allow.

He cleared his throat and adjusted his stance. "Miss Loren."

And then watched Officer Tuckus do a piss-poor job of showing how a woman could escape an assailant who grabbed her by the hair in a dark alley.

Yeah, that move would work if your assailant was a ninety-pound woman or a pansy-ass man.

He glanced to the side. Today, she looked adorable, but at the same time lethal. Like one of the feral kittens that roamed his barn searching for prey.

Fluffy and cute.

When you reached out to stroke them, their claws came out of nowhere like a female wolverine, scratching the living shit out of you and then haughtily licking their paws while watching you with unabashed insolence.

Then the porn star of his dirty dreams spoke up, saying with a snort, "Well, that would never work."

His eyes shifted toward her once again, and she was now twisting one of the loose strands of hair with her finger while she openly scoffed at what the officer was failing miserably to demonstrate.

"You an expert on self-defense, Miss Ingalls?"

Her finger ceased teasing the strand of hair as if she had to think about the question. "No, I'm no expert, per se," she relented, and then as if she couldn't hold it in any longer, "but come on. Do you really think a woman who's being dragged around by her hair is going to grab her assailant by the neck, pull him down to the ground, and execute an Arm Bar?"

And then Officer Tuckus noticed his observers.

"Hey, Alec," he called out, jovially waving from the sparring mat.

Alec turned his head toward the class and dipped his baseball cap. "Officer Tuckus."

"Could you help us with this move?" The officer turned to his class. "Alec is a Special Ops Marine. I'm sure he can assist with what we're trying to demonstrate here."

"Former Marine," Alec corrected, but wasn't sure he should intervene, given he also thought the move was for shit. But then he noticed the fluffy kitten's eyes on him and seized on the opportunity. "Happy to help. I'm sure Miss Ingalls would love to help, too."

Her head jerked back, gratuitously large brown eyes now full-on black storms. And then those black storms glanced toward the attendees, and Alec saw that she was looking at her sister, Cara, with indecision. Cara's eyes widened as if telling her older sister to stand down.

"Thanks, I'm just observing," she said, as if chewing rusty nails.

"Ah, Miss Ingalls," Officer Tuckus cajoled her, "please join us. You're new to the community and this will give us all a chance to get to know one another."

Officer Tuckus was an affable fellow, which made him a weak officer. But then, Alec knew there wasn't much to fear here in Wilder, Texas.

He watched her chew on those saucy pink-tinged lips, her eyes silently communicating with her sister, and then finally moved toward the mats.

Fish bowl. Those were the only two words that came to mind as the women of Wilder skeptically watched Loren make her way toward the mat. To her left, Maggie Perkins was whispering to Sue Macy, who openly smirked. Mrs. Roberts had introduced them to Loren after church last week and they didn't appear any more eager to see her now than they did then. To her right, Mrs. Waterman, who had just ignored her and Mercy in the school parking lot, also looked none-too-pleased to see her again.

Regardless of the fine weather they were having.

Ally's words kept hitting her. Competition. Jealousy. In her mind, they were bizarre concepts for the women of Wilder to hold against her when they had lives she'd only dreamed of while growing up in the Center.

Her heart ached at being so summarily shunned, fully aware of her lack of social skills to remedy the situation. And completely at a loss as to how to go about getting other women to like her and her sisters.

She glanced back at Cara after reaching the mat, who looked at her beseechingly. Loren toed the mat with one of her Converse shoes. She knew what Cara was thinking. *Don't hurt anybody. Just do what you're told and don't humiliate me.* Eyes, outside of Ally and her sister's, seemed ready to pounce on any little misstep.

Loren stretched her neck back and forth as a way to ignore all the undivided attention. She flicked her hands with nervous energy, feeling uncommonly vulnerable and unsure how to navigate the situation. Here she was, on a sparring mat similar to the one where she had trained on for years . . . with ruthless intensity.

Taught to fight dirty, with no holds barred.

She uncrossed her arms and dug her fingernails into her palms, refraining from moving into combat position. Reminding herself that she was nothing more than a casual participant who knew nothing about self-defense. Someone who willingly agreed to allow this mountain of a man to touch her as if he were going to attack.

"*Don't hurt him. Don't hurt him,*" she whispered to herself.

Oh my God, this was so outside her comfort zone.

The officer's voice pulled her out of her head. "So, Alec, if you could please hold Loren by the hair . . . don't be messing it up now." He laughed to help lighten the mood.

Alec latched onto her, and it was all Loren could do not to turn and light him up with everything she had. Instead, she followed the ludicrous instructions, putting her arms around Alec's neck and then waiting while Officer Tuckus made some comments on stance and some other shit she couldn't quite follow.

It appeared to be uncommonly warm in the gymnasium and she wondered if it was too expensive to bump up the air conditioning in such an expansive space. Heat moved downward from the curve of her neck, at the same time upward from her unsteady legs to converge in her nether regions.

A strand of hair fell across her face, and touched her lips. She blew at it in a desperate attempt to avoid any unnecessary stimuli.

Loren wondered if the other women in the room could feel the sexual tension as Alec held her by the hair while her arms were wrapped around his neck, the oblivious officer droning on about things that had no real bearing on a situation of this type.

Doing her best to avoid Alec's challenging gaze, her traitorous sense of smell kicked in. She glanced up at the ceiling and inhaled some sort of manly soap alongside what must have been his own personal scent, a unique mixture of freshly turned earth and high levels of testosterone.

She was supposed to be holding him off when all she wanted to do was curl up into a ball and lodge herself into the crook of his neck where she could spend the rest of her days inhaling him.

Jesus, that wasn't at all weird.

Her mantra changed. "*Don't dry hump him. Don't dry hump him.*"

"Did you just smell my neck?"

She pulled back, meeting his accusatory glare. "No. What?"

He grinned. "You did. You were smelling me."

"Don't be ridiculous," she scoffed under her breath. "And if I were, it's because you smell like goat cheese. Like you just came from the barn after milking the goats and doing whatever else you do that would make you smell like cheese."

Loren grimaced. *Nice comeback, you dolt.*

He was openly smirking at her now, and she forced her focus back to Tuckus, who was instructing the women on what to do when grabbed by their scalp. It was utter bullshit and she should know. She'd been dragged around by her hair a number of times by a particularly soulless Israeli instructor, who finally taught her that, in most situations, the best thing to do when you sense danger was to *fucking run.*

She was a mere five foot, two inches, weighing in at a buck ten. But once upon a time, she had been so stubborn. After several fruitless rounds, she'd learned that when you came up against a man twice your weight and the size of a tree, you didn't stop to look for weaknesses in his stance— you *ran.*

Refusing to meet Alec's eyes, which were like crystal-blue lasers boring into her, she glanced at the gymnasium windows and then at the double doors she'd walked through earlier. She then hazarded a look at Cara—who had her hands over her mouth just waiting for Loren to unleash some unholy terror on the man who had snubbed her and her sisters.

"And now pull him toward you as you fall back to the ground," Tuckus instructed.

She followed along, saying in a low voice that only Alec could hear, "And now I'm right where the fucker wants me. Flat on my back."

Tuckus continued, "And then, Loren, you swing your left leg over his right shoulder and pull him into an Arm Bar."

Loren chuckled with disgust. "And now my legs are spread for him, how convenient."

For the next forty-five minutes, Loren and Alec slowly demonstrated moves while the women took turns practicing them on one another.

At the end of the hour, Loren was exhausted, more from the amount of restraint she'd had to exercise than demonstrating what was a completely unrealistic reaction to an attacker.

As everyone began to disburse, Mrs. Roberts thanked Loren and Alec for helping and left to take the petty cash box to the office. Loren turned toward Cara and asked her to fetch Mercy so they could be on their way.

Suddenly, it was only Alec and Loren in the gymnasium, the mats pushed to the side for basketball intramurals that were to begin soon.

"Show me," Alec said, turning his head and wiping his bottom lip with his thumb.

"What?" she asked with a naughty grin. "You wanna play a game of 'Show Me Yours and I'll Show You Mine'?"

Ignoring her flirtatious banter, he clarified, "Show me how you would do it." He moved his head toward the last remaining mat.

Her eyes narrowed, and then her legs felt weak when she looked into his stark blue eyes and then to his full mouth grinning at her with an "I dare you" smirk.

Scoping the gym for witnesses, she looked back at him. "On one condition."

He lifted an eyebrow.

"You hold nothing back."

And with that, he came at her with more speed than she'd anticipated, grabbing a fistful of her hair with ten times the force during class. Her head jerked back as he dragged her along the mat. She moved with instincts that she could no longer deny, turning into him, following the pull of her hair and then just as quickly she went into attack mode, punching every vulnerable point on his body, ending the attack by striking his nose with the palm of her hand.

They both heaved as he touched his nose, his eyes watering.

There now, she had his attention.

Assuming he was distracted by her counter assault, she fought to catch her breath. She was really out of shape and needed to find a way to spar with Mercy to build up her stamina.

Out of nowhere, her arms flew in the air as he undercut her at the legs and before she could react, he had her turned and pinned to the mat with both arms pulled behind her, his knee centered on her back and his body weight bearing down on her.

He bent down, his lips inches from her ear, "Why do you misjudge me?"

Just as he began to pull away, before taking his next breath, he was gasping for it and buckled over in pain. She'd actually head-butted him. In a flash, he saw her face and then that starry black hole one sees when they close their eyes super tight. He rolled off her, holding his nose and forehead as she picked herself up off the mat, graciously extending her arm as a gesture of truce, which he duly ignored, pulling up to one knee and then finally the rest of the way up.

"Why do you continue to underestimate *me*?" she asked, while batting her lashes.

He shook his head with a telling grin that lightened her heart. "Guess I need to stop that," he said, the back of his hand daubing some blood at his nose.

"Oh, my gosh, Alec, what happened?"

It was Ally, rushing to her wounded brother while Loren froze at the expressions on Mercy and Cara's faces. Mercy, with a knowing smile, and Cara with aghast disappointment.

"It's nothing," Alec said, appeasing his sister. "I managed to slip on the mat and hit the bleacher on the way down."

"Are you sure?" Mercy asked with a smug expression, "Sure looks like you got cold-cocked to me."

Loren laughed a little too loud. "Please, like I could do any damage to a Marine." She caught his glance. "Former Marine."

Cara's eyebrows drew together, still highly skeptical and then Loren added, "Besides, would Alec have agreed to dinner at our house if I'd busted his nose?"

Ally's face lit up as did Cara's, while Alec stared at her, his expression revealing nothing.

"Isn't that right, Alec? Tomorrow at six o'clock," she said, looking at him with her hands tucked in her back pockets, daring him to refuse yet another kind invitation.

"That's right." He barely smiled, still staring at her, and she knew that if he could, he would so punish her right now.

Her heart beat wildly in her chest as he swiped up his baseball hat that fell off during their grappling, and repositioned it on his head. "Loren claims to be a gourmet cook. Said she's going to personally make us a real fancy meal. Guess we're in for a treat, Ally."

Loren's face fell while Mercy burst out laughing. "Gourmet cook? Seriously?"

Doing her best to regroup, Loren said, "Let's go, girls, it's getting late. Looks like we have some dinner guests to prepare for."

As they walked toward the gymnasium doors, Loren could feel his eyes boring into her back telepathically saying, "Checkmate."

CHAPTER NINE

"I am interested in mathematics only as a creative art."

—G.H. Hardy
English mathematician,
known for his achievements
in number theory and mathematical analysis

"I'm supposed to be a genius, and I can't even make a decent meal." Loren held her head in her hands as Mercy poked at the disaster on the kitchen table.

In the background, Cara was playing the piano, which had pretty much become a constant during the evenings and weekends.

Mercy picked up Loren's iPad. "Well, hell, Loren, the first time you try cooking a gourmet meal, you may want to start with something a little easier than beef Wellington." She read through the recipe. "What's foy grass?"

Loren lifted her head. "Foie gras. Goose liver paste."

"You were able to find that at the Merchant's Grocery in town?"

"No, I substituted ground chicken livers. They also didn't have prosciutto, so I picked up bacon, instead."

Mercy jabbed the carcass with a serving fork. "Why is the crust so tough?"

Loren lifted her arms in the air. "I don't know, Mercy, I'm a math genius, not a chemistry genius. Apparently, one doesn't guarantee the other."

"Please, you have an IQ of over one-seventy-five. There's nothing you can't master. How about that time you took out that one-eyed Russian?"

"I think the key-word there is 'one-eyed.'"

"Okay, how about when you scaled that skyscraper in Dubai to take photos of the Chagall?"

"That was easy. That's all about the potential fall factor, or the ratio of distance you would fall divided by the length of rope available to absorb the fall. The factor determines—"

"Okay, all I'm hearing right now is blah blah blah. My point is that you don't fail, ever."

"Well, Mercy, beef Wellington appears to be my first fail, and as you can see, I managed to do that *epic*-ally."

Loren lifted her head to check the clock on the stove. It was one o'clock, plenty of time to execute plan B. Problem was, there was no plan B. She was just as shocked to discover her inability to cook a meal as Mercy.

They had done just fine subsisting on frozen foods requiring a short time in the oven or nuked in the microwave. But cooking with pots, pans, and utensils? That was impossible.

Loren leaned on the table and held her face in her hands. "It's our first official dinner party and we have nothing to serve except Hot Pockets and pizza rolls."

How humiliating. After all the ball-busting it took to get Alec to show up, she'd have to serve a frozen pizza from the grocery store.

"Did you make dessert?"

"Baked Alaska."

"How did that turn out?"

"I made the mistake of attempting the French version of the meringue. The eggs didn't fully cook. I thought giving our guests salmonella poisoning might not make a positive first impression."

"Where is it?"

"In the backyard. I shot put the bastard out the back door in a moment of frustration."

"We could always cancel."

"I can't disappoint Cara. You saw how excited she was when she heard they were coming." Besides, there was no way she was going to miss the chance of seeing Alec again, despite her imminent humiliation.

"Well, then, let's go back to the grocery and pick up something fast and easy."

Less than ten minutes later, Mercy pushed a shopping cart, following an indecisive Loren as she combed through the frozen food aisle.

Loren was so disappointed. All she wanted to do was make Alec a gourmet meal and then shove it down his condescending throat.

And then lick it.

As she roamed the aisles, nothing was good enough, special enough.

Gourmet enough.

"Hello, there."

Loren looked up from the frozen bread section to see Mrs. Waterman with her own grocery cart. Instinctively, Loren looked behind her to see who she was saying hello to as Mercy blurted in an overly loud and frantic voice, "Nice weather we're having, isn't it?"

"It is." Mrs. Waterman's eyes widened as if unaccustomed to

being verbally attacked in the frozen food aisle, and she nodded, seeming just as nervous as Loren was shocked.

"I wanted to ask you something, Loren."

Having become a deaf-mute, all Loren was capable of was a quick tilt of her head. This was the first time one of the women from Wilder had willingly spoken to either of them, with the exception of Mrs. Roberts, and now she didn't seem to know what to do. Or say.

And then there was the thing with her hands. Why did they hang so awkwardly? They suddenly seemed overly large and unnatural. And what does one do with them when conversing casually with others?

Mrs. Waterman cleared her throat. "I was wondering what you did for exercise."

Loren couldn't have been more shocked if she'd been hit with a high-voltage stun gun. She leaned her head slightly forward. "For exercise?" She must not have heard correctly.

Mrs. Waterman continued, "Yes, after yesterday's self-defense class some of us were wondering how you and your sister stay . . . so fit."

"Oh," Loren said, "well, we work in the yard a lot."

Mrs. Waterman seemed disappointed in that admission, as if there had to be some deeply held secret to her and Mercy's toned biceps.

Loren struggled with an answer she was safe to share. "And we walk a lot."

She appeared even more disheartened.

"We spar," Mercy verbally vomited.

Loren's eyes went wide, and then she just as quickly squeezed them shut. Mercy was never very good at withholding information. Case in point, one particular assignment in Southeast Asia that went a little sideways, Loren had to intervene when Mercy caved after only two minutes of waterboarding.

And of course, Mrs. Waterman perked up. "Oh, really?"

Mercy nodded with nothing short of glee. "Loren and I have been sparring for years. Tell her, Loren."

Cara was not going to like this. "Yes, well, it's really nothing—"

But Mercy had the woman's rapt attention and wouldn't let it go. "Loren started sparring first and taught me everything I know. I mean, we had . . . instructors, but it was Loren who taught me how to throw a punch." She lifted her shirt. "Check out our abs," She began to lift Loren's tee.

"Mercy!" Loren batted her hands down.

Mrs. Waterman smiled shyly. "Would you be willing to teach us what you do, the sparring? Help us to look like *that*." She continued, "I could speak with Pastor Roberts and his wife about starting a class—"

For the first time since this ludicrous conversation began, Loren's eyes body-checked Mrs. Waterman, and was surprised because she found her to be very attractive. Nothing worth changing in her mind, but it must have taken so much for her to ask for help from someone she hadn't seemed to care too much for just the day before.

"Well, I guess we could consider it," Loren suggested, liking the idea of sparring again and not having to hide it. "I'm not sure the pastor will want to support a class on fighting."

Mrs. Waterman nodded thoughtfully. "Isn't sparring like self-defense?"

"Well, yes, but I don't want to step on Officer Tuckus' toes."

"That was only a one-time class." Mrs. Waterman's eyes started to light up. "Look," she said, glancing behind her as if searching for eavesdroppers, "I love living in Wilder, but sometimes it can seem so stagnant and bland. I don't want to turn into some boring small-town housewife who only knows how to cook and maintain a house. This is a chance to do something out of the ordinary, and maybe even tone up a bit."

"She'll do it," Mercy offered up. "And I'll watch all your kids like I did yesterday."

Mrs. Waterman smiled wide, and Loren just couldn't resist the feeling of helping to put that smile on her face.

"Okay, let's do it."

"Just one more thing," Mercy interjected, "just how good of a cook are you?"

When Mercy explained their dinner dilemma, Mrs. Waterman — who insisted they call her Becky—came to their rescue. She called her husband, informing him she had a philanthropic event to attend that she'd forgotten, told him to order a pizza, and then began filling their grocery cart with food.

According to Becky, gourmet food to a Texan of the male persuasion meant something very different from the recipes Loren researched on the epicurean website.

Gourmet to a man from Wilder meant a thick slab of a perfectly seasoned piece of meat. And, although Beef Wellington was technically a meat dish, Becky was sure Alec would have been less than impressed with the puff pastry that it was wrapped in, not to mention the petite foie gras in the list of ingredients.

"Rex usually wants to grill our steaks," Becky said, placing the platter on the kitchen table, "but I prefer my steak seared in an iron skillet like my grandma used to make."

Which was good because they didn't have a grill, but Mercy was able to fish out an iron skillet that had belonged to the previous renter.

Mercy proudly lifted the skillet for everyone's viewing pleasure as Becky stood in the middle of the kitchen scanning the collateral damage wreaked on the countertops from Loren's previous cooking attempt.

Loren looked around the room as a rosy glow of embarrassment worked its way up her neck. Being completely transparent, Loren and Mercy weren't very good at cleaning. Prior to the initial cooking fiasco, the kitchen sink had already been full of dishes and the trash can overflowing.

Come to think of it, the rest of the house was in no better condition.

Becky finally closed her gaping mouth, and asked, "You're expecting dinner guests?"

Mercy was still proudly holding the iron skillet as Loren worked toward an explanation, "The house kind of got away from us this week."

"O . . . kay," Becky said, nodding her head. "We have a short amount of time to work with, but if we all chip in, we should have this place spick-and-span in no time."

Assuming the role of a drill sergeant, Becky was true to her word. In no time, she had Loren elbow-deep in dishwashing suds while she began to cook. At the same time, she gave Mercy and Cara tasks and instructed them to report back after they were completed, only to be replaced with new ones.

An hour and a half later, Becky pulled her dessert out of the oven. She called it banana pudding, and Loren marveled at the lightly browned meringue that looked like puffy clouds, nothing like the coarse and grainy meringue that was currently drawing some of the less exacting woodland creatures in the backyard.

Becky stood straight, wearing a smile of satisfaction. "There you have it. Skillet-seared rib eyes, Idaho baked potatoes with herbed butter, and my mother's banana pudding, a gourmet meal, according to your typical alpha male from the state of Texas."

"I can't thank you enough, Becky," Loren said with her hands clasped under her chin while Mercy and Cara each slumped in a kitchen chair. "And the house looks great. We couldn't have done this without you."

"You give me a six-pack like yours and teach me to spar, and we'll be even," she said, grabbing her purse from the chair. "I'm also gonna need you to tell me all the details about dinner with Alec Wilder. He lives close to the vest since all that happened with his ex-wife. Rarely leaves the farm unless it's for Ally."

Loren walked with Becky to the front door. "His ex-wife?" she asked, not wanting to sound overly interested.

Becky looked at her with surprise. "No one told you he'd been married?"

Loren didn't want to admit that no one had bothered to strike up a conversation with her or Mercy until today.

"I don't like to spread rumors, but Marisa was a hot mess, as in a *crazy* hot mess. Alec married her after his parents died, and he gained custody of Ally. It was a whirlwind romance, and I guess he thought she'd be a mother figure for Ally while he was stationed overseas. She ended up being loose in the head. Abused that little girl something terrible."

Loren's head jerked back, and she suddenly felt nauseous. "Abused Ally?"

"Beat her, left her in the closet for hours. All sorts of horrible things."

"How did he find out?"

"Came home on leave as a surprise. Found Ally beat and malnourished, locked in her bedroom while his wife was in the kitchen sipping chamomile tea, staring off into space and singing church hymns."

"Nobody in town knew?"

"She wasn't from around here. Showed up out of nowhere. She bolted from her parents' home in Montana along with five grand in cash, landed in Wilder, and set her sights on Alec."

Loren blinked as Cara slipped back behind the piano and began playing. She woodenly opened the front door, trying to absorb the information Becky shared.

Puzzles had fascinated Loren as a child, and she thought she was only a few pieces short from putting Alec Wilder together. She'd assumed all of his pent-up hostility stemmed from some nasty shit that went down while serving abroad, rolling around in the sand with a MK-15 strapped to his back, rather than the horrors inflicted back home on a loved one, by another loved one, who wasn't who she claimed to be.

She swallowed hard and blinked again.

"From what was reported in the news," Becky continued speaking softly, ". . . she'd have stretches of normal behavior and then would slip into psychotic episodes. Her meds ran out a couple of months after Alec was shipped out and her sickness slowly took over."

"How long did the abuse last?" Loren asked, not sure she wanted to know the answer.

Becky tilted her head. "I've said enough. This has upset you. But you've got to understand, the entire town of Wilder feels just awful about what happened to Ally. Feel like we let Alec down and we owe him. I guess that explains why we're so stand-offish with strangers. Just give us all a chance to get to know you and your sisters and everyone will come around."

Loren looked away and nodded. Sure thing. Easy-peasy. We'll give everyone time to get to know us by lying to them and sharing our completely fabricated background. No problem.

Becky paused before walking out the front door. "Cara plays the piano beautifully."

"Yes, she's been playing since she was five."

That is, after the doctor secretly sedated her and wheeled her into an operating room to test out a lifetime of experiments and hypotheses.

"She should consider giving piano lessons to some of the elementary students. I know a number of parents who might be interested."

Loren suddenly felt both heavy and numb.

Great. More people to lie to in order to gain their trust and good standing in the community.

CHAPTER TEN

"Mathematics is the music of reason."

—James Joseph Sylvester
English mathematician; made fundamental contributions to matrix theory, invariant theory, number theory, partition theory, and combinatorics

Alec pulled into the Ingalls' driveway with an overly excited Ally in the passenger seat, and at first, he thought he was at the wrong house.

"They must have hired a contractor," he commented as he switched off the ignition.

Newly planted shrubs landscaped the house, the surrounding ground covered with dark mulch. There appeared to be an arbor in the process of being built to the left of the property, and to the right a half dozen hydrangea plants were peeking up by the fence row.

Several gallons of paint sat on the porch steps with what looked like a new ladder. There was a pile of wooden boards and a new circular saw. The decomposing front steps had been replaced with new ones.

"I told Cara about Pinterest, and they started all these house projects."

Alec's eyes narrowed. "You mean you told them about specific projects on Pinterest."

"No, I mean I told them about the app. They didn't even know Pinterest existed. Can you imagine?"

What woman over the age of fifteen didn't know about Pinterest?

"Wait," Alec said, turning his head, "what is that?"

Ally stopped for a minute, and then smiled. "It's piano music. Cara plays the piano and she's super good at it. But outside of band class, all she plays is stuffy classical stuff so I brought music from some alternative bands."

"Does she only play the piano?"

"No. All of them."

He turned toward her. "What do you mean 'all of them'?"

"Well, she started in the middle of the school year, so for now, she's like a floater. She can literally play any instrument. Even the oboe."

This was interesting. Loren looked like a fitness model and could fight as well as any special ops combat specialist he'd ever come across. Both Loren and Mercy appeared more than able to tackle home improvement projects most men would shy away from. And now he learns the younger one played not only classical music on the piano, but any instrument you put in her hands.

Alec opened his truck door. "Well, let's go see if they can cook."

Before he could take a step, Ally grabbed him by the elbow. "Okay, but please be nice."

"What? I'm always nice."

"No," Ally said, shaking her head, "you're not. You're like the women in town. You snub them and make them feel bad. Which really sucks because they're super nice, and they try really hard to make friends."

"Look, I think it's neighborly that you're being nice to them, Ally, but—"

"And they don't even know how hot they are. I mean, they seriously have no idea. The men in town won't talk to them, either, afraid they'll make their wives mad. And what y'all need to know is that they have feelings, too."

"Okay, message received," he said, a little surprised to hear his sister speak so passionately about how the Ingalls sisters had been wronged by the entire town. But he couldn't help the feeling that they were hiding something, and he'd be damned if he'd ignore his gut ever again.

"But I want to be clear, I'm here to make sure this is a healthy and safe environment for you to visit. I know how quickly you've made friends with Cara, but no matter who her sisters are, I would still insist on making sure I approve of letting you into their home."

Ally tilted her head with a half-smile. "You know I'm okay, right?"

He looked down and nodded. "Yeah, I know."

"You know that you take really good care of me."

Alec didn't move.

"Alec." She lowered her head in an attempt to gain his focus. "You're the best brother I could've ever asked for."

He gave a single nod and cleared his throat as he looked out the window. "Better get inside."

Mercy opened the door for them, and Cara quickly bolted from her piano bench, squealing like middle school girls do while hugging Ally, and then pulling her by the hand to give her a personal tour of the house.

Alec slowly walked deeper inside as Mercy made small talk, mostly about the weather. He looked around, just as surprised to see the inside as he was on the exterior.

The last time he'd been inside the house was when old man

Kramer lived here. He'd become a recluse after losing his wife to cancer twenty years ago. Alec and Ally would visit on Saturdays to bring him groceries and provide some basic human contact. When he passed away last spring, they were two out of about five who attended his funeral, and that included Pastor Roberts and his wife.

Now, the house resembled nothing short of one of those house-renovation shows Ally watched on TV. To the right of the front room was a large piano, the walls painted a stark white with music notes covering the walls. To the left was a small living room, the outdated furniture giving the space a funky twist with new, brightly colored upholstery, patterned pillows and a throw rug.

"What do you think?" Loren asked, walking into the room, drying her hands with a kitchen towel.

He turned toward her and thought seriously about turning around and walking out the front door. She wore a simple white tee that, in his mind, was two sizes too small and showcased breasts that, dear God, weren't receiving any proper support. Her jeans were also snug and looked worn, not from some designer's hands but from her own, as if she'd personally put the hole in the knee and inadvertently splashed some green paint near the pockets.

His body seized up as he felt his blood rush through his veins like a garden hose with a released kink. How did one compact woman make his entire body turn against him, along with his better judgment?

Finding the wherewithal to reply without sounding choked, he said, "Place looks good. You've done a lot of work in a short amount of time."

"Mercy's the visually creative one in the family," Loren said, placing the towel between her legs so she could pull a hair tie from her wrist.

He stood transfixed as he watched her pull her hair up in a quick messy bun, her roots darker from the rest of her hair. A look he typically didn't care for, but on Loren, it looked edgy instead of unkempt.

"She seems to know what colors will create just the right mood for each room," Loren said, flipping the dish towel over one shoulder and slipping her hands into her back pockets, making her nipples strain against the thin fabric.

Alec attempted to refocus on the conversation as Mercy beamed at Loren's compliment.

The conversation lulled, small talk not being his strong suit, but he was resigned to try for Ally's sake. "The notes on the wall are a nice touch," he said, tilting his head toward the other side of the room.

Mercy replied, "They're notes from one of Cara's melodies. I thought it would be nice for her to be surrounded by her music while playing music."

"Come on back and see the rest of the house," Loren suggested, turning to lead the way. "Did you know the previous renter?"

"Owner," he corrected, his eyes honing in on her tight, heart-shaped ass and her trim waist. "Old man Kramer. Lived here all his life. Passed away last spring. House hasn't been lived in since."

Loren suddenly turned to face him, and he lifted his eyes from her jean pockets a millisecond too late.

"Please tell me he didn't pass away in the house."

"Backyard. Sitting in a lawn chair by the big maple tree."

"Thank God." Loren sighed with a chuckle. "Cara would play nothing but dirges if she knew someone died in here."

They were in the dining room. The table-top looked to be a piece of reclaimed wood with a row of cropped sunflowers down the middle, and the mismatched chairs were painted an off-white.

"Something smells good," he said awkwardly, trying to balance between a silent truce, tempering his lust for the little blond vixen and wondering from what planet these hyper-productive women came from.

Truth be told, all this polite conversation made him feel progressively uncomfortable. Like he was wearing a button-down shirt with a too-tight collar. He missed her snark and the way her eyes came alive when she tore into him.

How fucked up was that?

"Hope you're hungry," Mercy said. "Loren's been working on dinner all day."

"It was nothing," Loren scoffed. "Literally."

"Didn't want to put you out," Alec replied with feigned sincerity.

She picked up on the hint of sarcasm and a not-so-subtle reminder of how, in the end, he had gotten the best of her and replied easily, "Oh, I wasn't put out. I was able to spend most of the day defiling the underage male populace of Wilder, with just enough time to throw dinner together."

There she was, there was the little demon he ironically looked forward to verbally sparring with.

"Well, I guess I can't fault you for lack of efficiency." He grinned with a glint in his eye. "Although I can only assume time restraints kept you from working your way through the women."

"O-kay," Mercy interjected, "why don't I go get the girls so we can eat?"

She hightailed it out of the room. Alec did not take his eyes off Loren. He stalked toward her, their eyes tied to one another. And when he'd adequately compromised her personal space, she pulled in a breath at the same time he pulled out her chair.

He watched her eyes slowly slide up to his as she demurely sat down. Each of them acting with the utmost decorum, knowing Ally and Cara would be walking in at any moment.

"Why, thank you. Be sure to let me know if I can help you with that stick," she said, sitting down and gingerly placing her napkin in her lap and then batting her eyes up at him. "Particularly the one permanently lodged up your ass."

He bent down so he was inches from her ear. "There you go again, talking about my backside. If you're into ass-play, then just say so, Miss Ingalls."

She tilted her head with a smirk. "Let's not misinterpret tonight's invitation, Mr. Wilder. Ally and Cara really like spending time together. All I'm trying to do is make it easier for them by being neighborly."

Alec moved across the table and pulled out a chair. "And all I'm trying to do is make sure you and your sisters pass the smell test. Look at it from my perspective, you drive into town inappropriately dressed, eye-fuck me in church, and then head butt me, almost breaking my nose."

"Please," she hiss-whispered, leaning toward him. "I could've done a lot more damage. As a matter of fact, I did you a favor by holding back. I'm pretty sure a single titty-twister would've brought you to your knees."

"So that's the only thing I said that you take exception to?" he asked with a small grin.

"I wasn't done yet," she said demurely, taking a sip of her water as if at high tea. "First of all, there's *nothing* the matter with the way we smell. We shower regularly with flowery scented shit. Secondly, we're not from a sexually repressed backward-ass town like Wilder. Therefore we dress differently. But I wouldn't expect you to understand that since you dress like some throwback to the wild west with your stupid Western shirts and Wrangler jeans."

He leaned back in his chair, undaunted. "I wear t-shirts and Levi's. I don't even own a Western shirt."

"Okay, cowboy boots."

He pointed downward. "Red Wing steel toe work boots."

Ignoring his correction, she forged on. "And lastly, I didn't *eye-fuck* you in church. To be honest, I was instantly repulsed by your troll-like visage and effeminate gait."

"What the hell is a 'visage'? And are you saying I walk like a goddamned woman?"

"If the string bikini on the cowboy fits—"

Laughter made its way from the staircase to the dining room and Alec and Loren instantly sat back in their chairs as if making their way to their corners. The only forces within a fifty-foot radius able to deter their hostility being their two giggling, pint-sized sisters.

CHAPTER ELEVEN

"Pure mathematics, is, in its way, the poetry of logical ideas."

—Albert Einstein
German theoretical physicist

In fear of blurting out a derogative expletive to their lumberjack-sized asshole of a dinner guest, Loren envisioned a metal vise attached to her head, keeping her mouth firmly shut.

On a good note, everyone seemed to be enjoying the meal, particularly Alec. But for reasons unknown, she couldn't care less. She lacked the domestic satisfaction of proving to him once and for all that she was capable of fixing a gourmet meal, despite the fact that she didn't. And, couldn't.

And as she watched him take another bite, it was official.

She hated the way he ate his food.

It was maddening.

Every time he'd pick up his knife and then lift his fork, the stupid muscles in his forearms flexed, and blue veins popped out under tan skin.

And then the food would reach his lips—don't even get her started on that ridiculously stern mouth. She could only imagine the amount of tongue-involved kissing it would take to remove the hard lines and soften them into what was a semblance of a smile.

Stupid, stupid lips.

Far too full.

Smirking all the time.

This man was no gentlemen. And despite the surname, he certainly was no Almanzo Wilder from her beloved books. Almanzo was a quietly courageous, hardworking man who was patient and kind. Alec Wilder was an arrogant, ill-mannered, judgmental prick.

Ally reared back her head, laughing at something Alec said, and guilt prickled Loren's conscience. Of course, he was leery of them. After what his ex-wife did to his sister, how could he not be? Then she thought about Jasper, and those fucked-up comments he made toward Cara, and her blood pressure instantly hiked up several notches.

Maybe she had more in common with Alec than she cared to admit?

Loren did her best to concentrate on her meal and remain quiet. Thankfully, no one seemed to notice as Cara and Ally made up for the lack of conversation with their own constant chatter. Their topics started with a comprehensive discussion on the boys in their class and then switching to antics of some of the mean girls. And as expected, their animated conversation settled on music.

Loren couldn't help but notice how much Ally resembled Alec with her dark brown hair and blue eyes. She had been so shy when they had first met outside the church. It was hard to believe she was the same girl. Her laughter was infectious, and her demeanor soft and gentle. How could anyone ever think to hurt her? It was incomprehensible.

Loren then watched Cara's entire body light up when Ally showed her the sheet music she'd brought with her, wanting to introduce her to a wide array of artists, going on and on about Freddie Mercury, Dave Grohl, and Michael Jackson.

Cara was soaking it all in. She was so much happier here than she'd ever been at the Center. But then, the doctor had never permitted Cara to study music outside that which enhanced her worldwide appeal and ensured the revenue-generating stream established within the realm of classical music.

Loren leaned on her elbows, her chin resting in her hands and prayed no one recognized Cara as the world-renowned Charlotte Halstead.

To that end, the night before arriving in Wilder she had hacked and permanently deleted Charlotte's website as well as any other pictures she could find online. She'd checked the news feeds every night for any reports of a missing piano prodigy, or two escaped maniacal psychotics, and to her relief, she found nothing.

How was that possible, and why wasn't Jasper reporting them to the police or sending his henchmen after them?

"You're serious. You've never heard of any of these artists?" Ally asked, taking a bite of her baked potato.

Cara glanced at Loren, who quickly answered for her. "We were pretty sheltered growing up. Our uncle was highly protective of us."

"Tell me more about your family," Alec said with a glimpse of skepticism.

Mercy bolted out her chair, saying, "I'll get the dessert," as she rounded the table, making a beeline for the kitchen.

As if that wouldn't add to his suspicions.

On a slow exhale, Loren walked him through their fabricated history. She explained how their parents had died in a car crash eight years ago, and they were taken in by a reclusive uncle, and how he had recently died of a heart attack during a late-night dinner. The same story she pounded into Cara and Mercy, staying as close to the truth as was safe, making it easier to remember and recite. All of which could be easily confirmed by searching online documents digitally put into place by Loren herself.

Not all lies, exactly, but strategic moments of omission peppered with a few necessary distortions.

"So, your uncle arranged for piano lessons?" Alec asked Cara as Mercy passed out the small plates for the banana pudding that took center stage on the table.

"Yes, I've been playing since I was five," Cara said. "But Mercy's the real artist in the family; she paints and she's awesome at it. She can paint anything. She can paint near-perfect copies of some of the world's most famous pieces of art."

Loren's eyes widened, and a plate nearly slipped out of Mercy's hands as Cara shared information that was a little too close for comfort.

"I mean," Cara clarified, her eyes bouncing back and forth between Loren and Mercy, "she does it just for fun, of course."

Loren's hand tightened around her spoon as her eyes glanced at Alec who thankfully didn't appear to have picked up on Cara's nervous attempt to detract from her careless faux pas.

Silence followed as Mercy carefully doled out the dessert on plates and passed them around the table.

"After dinner, you'll have to show me some of your paintings, Mercy." He looked pointedly at Loren. "Just because I'm an uncouth smelly farmer doesn't mean I don't appreciate art."

Loren's eyes landed on Mercy, who appeared to want nothing less than to have this conversation.

"I haven't painted anything since I've been here, well, except for the house." Mercy stared at her dessert as if it would escape her plate, picking at the paper napkin. "Too busy working on house projects."

Although not the time, Loren would love to delve more into that comment.

Mercy had yet to pick up an art brush. Whenever Loren

attempted to broach the subject, Mercy would blow it off, saying there were too many other things that needed to be done.

Loren saw Alec's demeanor turn skeptical. "You didn't bring any of your art with you?"

Mercy's eyes locked on Loren as if begging for help.

"Storage," Loren said quickly. "We weren't sure we were going to settle in Wilder for good, so we put a lot of our things in storage."

Mercy picked up her glass of water, swallowing it down in a few gulps as even Cara and Ally sat silent.

Alec was the first to speak. "Ally, finish your dessert. It's getting late."

Ally turned beseeching eyes toward her brother. "Can't we stay just a little longer so we can play some of the music I brought?"

He smiled and then capitulated. "Fifteen minutes. You know I have to get up early."

The girls jumped out of their chairs as if the table were on fire, and Mercy popped out of her seat to clear the dishes.

"Miss Ingalls, may I have a word with you outside?" He moved out of his chair, leading the way.

Loren followed him to the front door, walking past the girls as Ally placed sheet music on the piano and Cara began playing what Ally had called "Bohemian Rhapsody."

Loren mentally cataloged all the missteps taken at dinner and how she could possibly defend them. She knew it wasn't their stories themselves that caused doubt, but rather what guileless liars Mercy and Cara were, their body language making each comment sound false and manufactured. Mercy with her downturned sheepish eyes and Cara with her neurotically flapping hand gestures.

Once the door closed behind them and in a race to get the first word in, she crossed her arms and did her best to mask the tension in her body. "Let me guess—you noticed the pentagram in the backyard?"

His back was to her, his arms leaning on the porch rail as he looked out silently toward the driveway.

"No? The shrunken head draining in the bathtub? I told Mercy to take it to the shed out back, but nooo, she thought it'd make a great ice breaker—"

He turned and stalked toward her, until her back was flush against the door. She fought the urge to raise her arms and move into self-defense mode as his face was unexpectedly full of pent-up rage.

Not rage exactly, but something intense and dark.

Sweet baby Jesus, was he . . . glowering?

"Where's your bra?" he rasped, hands on his hips and the vein in his forehead pulsating at an alarming rate.

Loren looked up into crystal-blue eyes that bore into her, completely blindsided by his question.

"My bra?" she said, pointing at her chest in confusion.

"Yes, the piece of constraining fabric that's used to provide support for a woman's breasts."

Her eyes looked right and then left, still not sure she heard right. "Wellll, since I'm on the short side of a B cup, my *breasts* don't really require support."

He glanced down and her treacherous nipples spiked into painfully hard tips, as if saluting him and confirming his point.

His eyes dragged back up to hers, eyebrows raised.

Her own pulse raged, and cognitive decline ensued. "Okay, you want to get personal. What about you and the stupid way you eat?"

"The way I eat?"

"With the muscles in your arms moving and . . . and veiny things popping out. Then there's your mouth," she said bitterly and as if making perfect sense, "when you put food in that . . . that mouth."

She bit down on her tongue to stop her blathering.

The vice she had imagined clamping her mouth shut at dinner looked to be thrown to the side, mangled, twisted, and useless.

Blood drained from her body as she stared at his lips and calculated the number of lost IQ points only to be matched with the amount of gibberish she'd spewed.

One of those freakishly delicious arms leaned on the door above her head, while the other moved to her waist, sliding farther back and then down, cupping her ass. All while he glared at her, pulling her closer.

"What about your ass?" he asked as if it were also a perfectly rational question. His voice rattled like gravel as his large hands kneaded her as if he were angry, as if her ass was an affront to his senses. His lips hovered over hers, just out of reach. "Heart-shaped and firm, begging me to touch it. Palm it."

She unconsciously pushed her hips toward him as he continued to stroke and knead. She wasn't sure she should or could respond.

Was he angry?

Turned on?

"You think I liked staring at your breasts all through dinner?"

"No ... yes ... I mean ...."

"I don't," he confirmed. But the blatant heat in his eyes said otherwise.

She felt his hot breath on her lips as he continued his verbal assault.

"You think I like watching your ass in those jeans, blatantly inviting me to undo the zipper, reach down and take them in hand? Punish them?"

Sensation robbed her of speech, her hips continuing to search for his as he purposely skirted their intent.

Why was she allowing him to affect her senses to this degree? It was humiliating and, oh, so, fucking hot.

Based on past experiences, she should be immune to his charm.

Moonlight assignations, seductions as a means to an end were executed on a number of occasions as part of an assignment. Thanks to granular timing, there was never a need to push the seduction to the extreme. But out of all those times, not once did her brain fog from just watching a man's bicep perform a mundane task like cutting his freaking meat. Not once did any of the men she'd targeted illicit the hormonal rampage causing her to lose her faculties, namely her jutting hips.

Was she blind from lust or experiencing a grand mal seizure?

His lips, still refusing hers, moved away and landed on the skin just below her ear. At the same time, he blessedly pulled her into his hard-won groin, and she couldn't help but emit an embarrassingly loud moan.

He was so hard and long and . . . and right *there*.

She arched her neck, finding she also took issue with the soap and shampoo he used that made him smell like sex on a stick, and moaned again at the sensation of his lips making small bites along the length of her neck.

All while "Bohemian Rhapsody" pounded out behind them.

She gasped as his lips moved south, latching onto her disloyal nipple, pulling it into his furnace of a mouth to the point of being just short of painful.

She was conflicted, but it seemed to her for all the wrong reasons. Did she want him to give attention to her other nipple or continue to rub her raw with his cock?

He lifted her thigh and wrapped it around his waist, giving him even more sublime access to the softest, most sensitive part of her.

Dear God, she thought the friction good before, but it was nothing compared to this. She shamelessly straddled his waist and he obliged, pinning her against the door, his hands grinding his steel length against her while his mouth ravaged her other nipple.

Finally, his mouth found hers as he continued to gyrate over her. They panted and kissed, their tongues twisting, teeth clashing.

Were they about to have sex against her newly painted front door, or wrestle?

His mouthed untangled from hers, nibbling down the other side of her neck. She reared her head back, trying to pull in some much-needed air as her head was spinning.

She made a paltry attempt to gain control by reciting the digits of the mathematical constant of pi.

But his glorious, unyielding penis kept getting in the way.

"God, I wanna fuck you so hard."

Unable to reply with all the panting she was doing, she cataloged all the nearby places where they could adequately and privately violate one another.

And then, like a couple of feral barn cats drenched with a cold bucket of water, the music stopped.

They both instantly stilled except for the deep inhale and exhale of their chests colliding, their foreheads pressed together.

Her heart sank as his eyes wrenched from hers. His head moved to rest against the door with his eyes firmly shut. He slowly loosened his grip, allowing her legs to slide down alongside his, her hands gripping his biceps for support as she stared at his chest.

She sensed a change in him. A change that came from more than just the ending of the music.

And then the music started again, this time, "Take me to Church," by Hozier.

How apropos, in a lust-killing sorta way.

He stepped back, his hand burrowing through his hair, his eyes squeezed shut.

Shutting her out.

Funny how a minute ago her body was writhing inside an inferno of lust and now she was rubbing her arms to ward off the arctic chill, damp rings from his mouth circling each area of her nipple. The lack of his furnace of a body making them all the more turgid and alert.

He took another step back and turned, once again, to grasp the porch rail. His head hung down between his shoulders.

She hugged her stomach with one arm, her other hand covering her mouth.

What was he thinking? Her mind raced through every rom-com she and Mercy devoured in the past few weeks to give her context and direction. Did he find her too sexually aggressive, or as Cara would say, a woman of loose morals? Or was she just plain bad at kissing?

It *was* her very first kiss, her actions a bit fevered and demanding.

But she couldn't help feeling captivated by him and out of

control. Oh sure, she could take all two hundred pounds of him down with some well-placed pressure to the carotid. But regardless of her discrete combat skills, she still felt dominated by his stature while at the same time indifferent to his strength.

She searched his body language for a hint of what might be going on in his cerebral cortex. The region of the brain vital to a man's sex drive and performance, according to a medical book Mercy had found at the local library.

But as always, he exposed nothing.

Her heart made an audible cracking sound as he turned, and without even a backward glance, he made his way down the front steps.

"Tell Ally I'll be waiting in the truck."

CHAPTER TWELVE

"Progress imposes not only new possibilities for the future, but new restrictions."

—Norbert Wiener
Professor of mathematics at the
Massachusetts Institute of Technology

Winter crept into Wilder, bringing lower temps and above-average rainfall. The Texas prairie was known for its dreary winter weather, never getting quite cold enough to bring forth an uplifting carpet of snow or warm enough for an adequate dose of vitamin D. It did, however, bring about a nice influx of trainees into Loren's self-defense class.

Plagued with cabin fever, the women of Wilder looked for any excuse to get out of the house or office for a few hours of physical distraction.

Informing their husbands, or significant others, that they were attending a self-defense class sounded so much more practical and less self-serving, than say, a Pilates class, or hitting the local tavern for a girl's night out.

The rapid success and bodily results of Loren's first class didn't hurt either, creating a multi-faceted lure for the women in town. First being the noble cause of learning self-defense and the second, getting into the best physical shape of their lives. And with Loren as their vision of perfect physical attainment, it turned out to be a winning combination.

Not to mention a killer marketing plan that drew women outside of Wilder, requiring a wait-list to be implemented to fairly manage the large numbers calling into the church to register for the class.

Loren pulled the mats to the side of the gymnasium for basketball intramurals as her class attendees picked up their gym bags and coats.

"Hey, Loren," Becky called out from the double gym doors. "You going to meet us at Lucky's tonight?"

Lucky's being the local tavern where many of her trainees went to socialize after class, the allure of the establishment having more to do with the owner and full-time bartender, Gus, being quite the hottie, as opposed to a stellar menu.

Much to Loren's surprise, a social life came along with a buzzing clientele. She thought it odd how the town now embraced her. The Ingalls had gone from the town pariahs to Wilder's darlings. It was amazing and a little confusing to think that newly emerging abs among the townswomen were the secret sauce to making friends.

Mercy moved the last mat to the side. "Go to Lucky's. I'll take Cara home."

Despite Mercy's offer, she waved Becky on. "No, thanks. I need to help Cara with homework tonight."

"I could've done that," Mercy argued, picking up the sparring gloves.

"I know. I'm kinda tired and hoping to get to bed early. I also need to pick up the supplies for Cara's science project."

"I can't believe the little shit waited to tell us about her project the day before it was due," Mercy said, running her hands through her sweat-soaked hair.

Even though Mercy preferred being downstairs with her adoring toddler fanbase, Loren convinced her to help with the class, instead. It was so much easier to demonstrate the various moves with a seasoned sparring partner.

To make up for it, she arranged for Mercy to teach an art class to the kids on Saturday mornings. She had hoped it would motivate her to start painting herself, but it had been weeks and the art supplies in the sunroom remained untouched.

"Not sure what's gotten into our once uber-responsible sister," Loren said, putting away the last glove into the bin and shoving it into the supply closet. Cara was on her last nerve with her snide comments and overall disdain for just about everything.

"Have you seen her today?"

"No, why?" Loren asked, grabbing her purse as they walked out the doors.

"I guess you'll find out."

They walked outside, Loren fishing inside her purse for her keys. Mercy nudged her, and she looked up, coming to an abrupt stop. "Why does our little sister look like the girl in the movie *Fifth Element*?"

Mercy shrugged. "Maybe it's because her hair is chopped off and dyed a bright neon orange?"

"Her makeup . . . there's so much of it. When did she do all this?"

Mercy threw her bag into the trunk and slammed it shut. "It had to have been after school. I just happened to see her before your class started. She was standing with some friends. When I called her carrot-top, she gave me the finger."

"The middle one?"

"No, the pinky finger. Come on, Loren, get your head out of your ass. Our sister is turning into a juvenile delinquent."

Cara was standing by the car with Ally, who also appeared to have gone to the dark side, her hair dyed purple and enough eyeliner to share with the rest of the eighth-grade class.

They both had their heads down, gazing into their iPhones, and if their facial expressions were any indication, texting one another rather than having a face-to-face conversation.

"Fair warning," Mercy said, leaning toward Loren with a soft voice, "she asked me to pierce her nose last night."

Loren turned in shock. "What did you tell her?"

"I told her to ask you first."

"And...?"

"And she said, 'No way. Loren's too freaking uptight.'"

"You're kidding me."

"Nope, she's really becoming a little shit. Told me I was a loser because I didn't appreciate some dark emo music she was playing on the piano. Told her if she didn't stop playing her depressing shit-for-music, I was going to snap off the tuning pins."

"I don't understand," Loren said, shaking her head as she stared at her sister's hair that was so thick and beautiful and brunette earlier this morning. "Just yesterday she was the one who was uptight, dissecting the nutritional value of the food we ate and telling us we should all have bedtimes that aligned with the Earth's circadian rhythms."

"Maybe Ally's a bad influence?"

"I don't think so. It's like they both slowly morphed into somber teenage termagents at the same moment in time."

And if things couldn't get any worse, Alec Wilder pulled up in his truck, parking next to her car.

Loren had rarely seen him since the night they both came unhinged on her front porch. And when she did, he made it a point to avoid her. But to his credit, despite having deep issues with her, he still allowed Ally to spend time with Cara. And for that, she was extremely grateful.

That benevolence appeared to be short-lived in light of the fact that he slammed his door shut, and was striding toward his sister. "Ally!"

She looked up, not even a smile.

"What the holy hell did you do to yourself?"

"What? I dyed my hair." She shrugged her face back in her iPhone. "Big deal."

His head jerked back. "Big deal?"

Loren wouldn't have believed it if she hadn't seen and heard it herself. Ally had become just as much of an emo-obsessed dill-hole as Cara.

And then Alec's disapproving eyes landed on Loren, his hands planted on his hips in equal disapproval. "I suppose you had something to do with this?"

Loren's hands shot up in defense. "Whoa, that's a big assumption, Farmer Ted. I'm just as shocked as you are."

His attention refocused on Ally. "When did you do all of this to yourself?"

Ally finally looked up as if it took all her strength to respond. "Cara and I dyed our hair after school in the girl's bathroom. Geez, you would've thought we'd snorted a line of coke."

"You didn't think you should have talked to me first?"

"Why would I? What do you know about hair color?"

"I know there's no such thing as *purple hair*."

She rolled her eyes. "My point exactly, the color's called *Angry Eggplant*."

Loren sucked in at the look on Alec's face and then noticed a crowd of kids moving closer toward the drama.

"Why don't you get your angry eggplant ass in my truck. We'll discuss this at home." He stalked toward the vehicle, but Ally didn't budge.

"In a minute. Gotta send this text."

Whoa, even Loren was growing uncomfortable with her massive level of snark and the kids watching, nodding, smirking in solidarity.

He turned back, pointing his finger to the ground. "Now, Ally."

After sighing and pushing Send, she hugged Cara and then lifted her finger to her ear and thumb to her mouth, her lips saying, "Call me."

Cara smiled, her own head bowing back down to pray at the altar of her iPhone.

Mercy and Loren, along with the band of unmerry teenagers, watched as Ally lugged her body into the truck and Alec slammed his door and drove out of the parking lot.

Only Cara, the orange-coiffed alien aberration smiling at her iPhone, appeared indifferent to her BFF's plight, or for that matter, any potential consequences of her own.

"Cara," Loren said, doing her best to remain calm, "when we get home, you're going to finish your science project while I run to the grocery store. And then when I get back, we're going to dye your hair back to its original color."

Cara glanced up from her phone. "No." Her eyes returned to her screen.

"No?" Loren shook her head and blinked. "Exactly what are you saying 'no' to? Finishing your science project or fixing your hair?"

Cara finally pulled away from her device, one hand on her hip that was jutted to the side. "No, I'm not going to do my science project because I already have an A in the class, and skipping the project will only bring my grade down to an A-minus. And no, I'm not going to change the color of my hair because I happen *to like it.*"

Loren's eyes narrowed. "I suggest you watch your tone of voice with me."

"Why? You're my sister. You're not my mother."

Mercy gasped, and then sang, "Oh, no, she didn't."

Tears welled in Loren's eyes. Mercy had never said those words to her. But then, she and Mercy only had one another, and they were so close in age they usually handled their disagreements with a sound sparring match. But Cara was several years younger and spent far less time with her than Mercy.

But still.

Loren had purposely insulated Cara from the sacrifices she'd made for her, the times she'd finally caved to the doctor and his illegal escapades, all because he'd threatened to take Cara back to the operating room.

How many times had she risked her life? For. Her.

"First of all," Loren said, clearing her throat, "I don't deserve to be spoken to like that. And second, you're right, I'm not Mom. But if she were here, she'd be very disappointed in the way you're behaving."

Mercy sucked in, shaking her head frantically back and forth. "Abort. Abort."

"She'd be disappointed. Mom would be disappointed in me?" Cara repeated, pointing her thumb to her chest. "You two dress like pole dancers and curse like sailors, but it's me who would disappoint her because I chose to color my *own* hair." Cara shook her head. "Unbelievable."

"Hey," Loren protested. "Mercy and I have toned it down. Both with the clothes and our language."

Her response was a condescending snort.

And then, as if the universe recognized they all needed cooling down, the sky opened up with a deluge of rain. Appropriate, given the circumstances.

They each jumped in the car. The ever-watchful band of misfits dispersed like a horde of bees.

As she drove home, quiet derision became a living, tangible thing. Loren was sure the contempt radiating from her sister's body in the back seat was likely to reach out and suffocate her before reaching the house.

Mercy dared not speak, equally as mute by Cara's silent contempt.

Where did all this anger come from? And how did parents know what to do when unleashed by their teenagers?

Loren was grossly unprepared for this, had no idea how to navigate Cara's roller-coaster ride of a disposition. Was it something she did? Was she somehow responsible for her sister's sudden mood change? Should she punish her, ground her? Crush a valium or two in her breakfast smoothie?

Then again, maybe Cara was right, and she wasn't a mom. What gave her the right to parent her? But someone had to do it.

Maybe it was just a phase? And Cara would wake up tomorrow morning her old self, criticizing her sister's cooking and demanding they start recycling like the rest of the civilized world.

What would her mom do?

Then Loren remembered having inexplicable mood swings when she was younger.

She was thirteen when the accident happened. A year younger than Cara. She remembered harboring her own angst-filled melancholy. But no matter how ugly she was to her mom, her mom seemed to know just what to say and do. She knew how to calm her down, encourage a rational conversation rather than spewing hurtful words you could never take back.

More tears welled in her eyes as she drove through the rain. Compartmentalizing memories of her mother into a part of her brain that allowed her to breathe and maintain composure. She concentrated on the lines and shifting angles of the road ahead. Finding comfort in the symmetry of their pure mathematical connections.

After the accident, when she woke from her coma, the lines were just . . . there. She shared what she saw with her doctor, but he'd dismissed it, telling her they would eventually go away. In a way, she hoped they didn't. Discovering inexplicable peace while focusing on objects in front of her moving in stop-action frames helped her from being swallowed up by the soul-gripping grief of losing both her parents.

But the patterns weren't doing their job.

Her chest ached at how much she desperately missed her parents.

They finally reached the house, and as soon as they closed the front door, Cara was at the piano pounding out an angry Chopin's "Revolutionary Etude." Her way of expressing her current state of mind without having to utter a single word.

"I think we should take her out back and beat her smug little ass," Mercy said, sliding into a kitchen chair and holding her head in her hands at the banging of the piano keys that was sure not to stop anytime soon.

"That would certainly make *us* feel better." Loren collapsed into her chair.

"Look at it this way," Mercy reasoned, "with her hair cropped short and the color of a road construction sign, there's very little chance of anyone recognizing her as Charlotte Halstead."

Loren nodded, leaning her forehead onto her clasped hands. "Good point. We should pick our battles." She sighed, feeling so much older than her twenty-two years. "But I can't let her get by with refusing to do her homework."

She pushed her body, which seemed to have gained fifty pounds, out of the chair to face the specter that had inhabited her little sister's body.

"Wish me luck."

"Instead of luck, how 'bout I get you some body armor?"

"These days, Cara doesn't take the body shot," Loren said with a monotone voice. "She uses her words and aims straight for the heart."

Loren stood by the piano, waiting for Cara to finish. "Revolutionary Etude" was a highly complex, violent piece, and Cara was fully committed to playing it to its full emotional potential.

Minutes later, panting after the ominous finale, Cara's eyes shifted to Loren, genuinely unaware of her presence until that moment.

Loren swallowed, searching for resolve. "I don't know what you're going through right now, but I want you to know I'm here if you want to talk. I can't make you talk. All I can do is let you know that I'm here when you're ready."

Cara stared at the piano keys, unmoving except for her chest heaving from the exertion of playing the piece.

"As for your hair, I'm not going to make you change it back. But in the future, I would appreciate it if you'd talk to me first."

Still nothing.

"In regard to your science project, not completing it is certainly your option. But that decision holds consequences. The consequence being that you will be grounded for the next two weeks. On the days I have a class, you will come straight to the gym—alone—and wait for me to finish."

Her eyes finally shot up, wide and argumentative. Still, no words.

"On the other days, I will pick you up from school and bring you straight home. No hanging out with Ally and your other friends."

Cara crossed her arms in agitation, staring at the wall farthest from Loren. "Is that it?"

"Yes, it's your choice."

Cara slammed the piano lid, and Loren jolted at the discordant staccato sound. Pushing her seat back, nearly toppling it over, Cara stalked out of the room.

Loren turned just as Cara's shoulder slammed into Mercy, who was leaning against the wall next to the stairway.

"Brat." Mercy grimaced, rubbing her arm. "It's still early. I swear I can dig a shallow grave in less than thirty minutes."

Loren was about to respond when the doorbell rang.

"I'll get it," Mercy said, walking past a hunch-shouldered Loren.

She peeked through the side window. "Um, it's the sexually repressed soldier-farmer that totally hates our guts."

Loren dropped her head in her hands. "Of course it is."

Mercy turned. "I can always make that grave a double."

Loren reluctantly lifted her head. "How mad does he look?"

Mercy peeked out the window again. "I'd say—furniture throwing mad."

Loren looked up at the ceiling and exhaled slowly. "I'll take care of this."

"Fine, I'll just look for a shovel."

Irreverent humor had always been Loren's go-to. She thrived on shock value. Used it as a coping mechanism to distract from being forced to live in a virtual prison where the staff was convinced she was a textbook psychotic mess.

Living in the conservative Texas town of Wilder, and trying so hard to maintain a semblance of normalcy for her newly formulated family, forced Loren to temper her more inappropriate banter.

To her pleasant surprise, she found that the more she got to know people, and become friends, the easier it was for her to assess whether her saucy sense of humor would be deemed acceptable. More surprising was that she discovered she truly cared about what other people thought about her. Not just about Mercy and Cara, but what they thought of her, too.

That said, she refused to flip a switch and change who she was. It was one thing to read the room and act accordingly, but it was another to become someone else entirely.

That just wasn't happening.

The doctor had tried to change who she was, lied about it to the point where holding true to herself had been the one thing that maintained her sanity.

So, in the small town of Wilder, she struggled for that balance between staying true to herself and being liked by her community.

The one person to which this approach didn't seem to apply was on the other side of her front door with a hot poker up his ass. Despite caring about what he thought of her, she just couldn't seem to squelch certain ribald comments when his eyes latched onto hers.

And let's face it, there was nothing sexier than a hot-tempered Alec Wilder. She'd experienced it firsthand—on the other side of this very door.

But this was a delicate situation. And if she didn't address it maturely, and tone down the sarcasm, it could ultimately threaten Ally and Cara's friendship, and as far as she knew, Cara couldn't afford to lose her best friend.

She took a quick inventory of her attire. Sport bra, check. Ratty old sweatshirt and jeans, check. Nothing he should take exception to.

Up popped that devil on her shoulder as she considered removing her sweatshirt and wearing only her sport bra. She shook off the errant thought and refocused.

Besides, it was cold outside.

Grabbing the doorknob, Loren closed her eyes and took a deep breath. "Behave," she whispered to herself.

CHAPTER THIRTEEN

"Mathematics is not about numbers, equations, computations, or algorithms: it is about understanding."

—William Paul Thurston
American mathematician and
pioneer in the field of low-dimensional topology

Alec stood at the Ingalls' front door, ringing the bell for the third time. He knew they were home. He could hear their muffled voices on the other side.

When he'd pulled into their driveway, he was once again duly impressed. They'd painted the house light green and trimmed it in black.

He wouldn't have thought of that, but it looked good.

Real good.

Not a half-assed job, either. They'd spent the time required to do it right, scraping the old paint off the house and filling in any holes or gaps with wood putty. It wouldn't have surprised him if they'd replaced some boards, too.

Maybe they planned on staying in Wilder? Who spends that much money on a house they didn't even own unless they planned on sticking around for a while?

He noticed the rain had died to a slight drizzle as he turned to lean on the porch rail, waiting on the sketchy sisters to decide if they were going to open the door any time soon and noticed the bricked walkway and flowers along the sides.

Maybe he should think about fixing up his house? Maybe that's just what he and Ally needed? Projects they could do together, to strengthen their relationship.

Fucking couldn't hurt at this point.

He heard the door creak and he turned to see Loren step outside and close the door behind her.

"I'd invite you in," she said, hugging her waist due to the chill, "but we'd have more privacy out here."

He nodded, pissed that she looked so damn good in just a pair of jeans and an oversized sweatshirt. "Your sister as pissy as mine is right now?"

She smirked. "Mercy's digging a shallow grave in our backyard as we speak. So, I'd say that's a definite yes."

Silence. They stood facing each other, not sure what to say next.

"I really had no idea about the whole hair and makeup thing," Loren offered up. "And I swear I don't know what's gotten into Cara; this just isn't like her. It seems like her attitude has been getting progressively worse over the last few weeks."

He shouldn't have been surprised that she assumed he was here to blame Cara for Ally's shitty behavior.

He leaned back on the porch rail with his hands in his pockets. "Despite recent events to the contrary, I'm not here to lay blame."

Hope appeared on her face. And he decided she really was

lovely. Gorgeous, even. The reflection of the moon made her hair glow and her eyes shine. Even her skin appeared luminescent.

Fuck, waxing poetic about a woman who conjured more red flags than a fourth of July parade was not why he was here.

He cleared his throat, getting back on task. "I came here to apologize for my earlier comments and to see if we couldn't stay in touch and help each other out with the girls." He crossed one leg over the other. "This isn't like Ally, either, and I'm hoping if we keep one another informed, we can get to the bottom of this."

She stepped closer, nodding. "I'd appreciate that. I keep asking Cara what's wrong but she just looks at me like I have horns growing out of my head."

Alec's chest tightened as he watched his tough-as-nails neighbor morph into a lost parent. He didn't know how he felt about seeing her so vulnerable.

Lost and vulnerable was his kryptonite. Clearing his throat, he pulled away from the porch railing as he dug into his pants pocket.

"Okay, then." He handed his phone to her. "Put your number in my phone; I'll call you so you'll have mine, too."

Their hands touched with the exchange, and he imagined grabbing her by the wrist and stealing her breath along with her uncertainty. But then he remembered the last time he took a chance on a woman, and then the day he came home for leave.

Witnessing his wife sitting at the kitchen table singing what sounded like a Baptist church hymn, rocking in her chair and looking straight through him was a scene that would be forever etched in his mind. And then searching the house for Ally, and finding her in the upstairs closet. She was gaunt, half-starved, and shaking uncontrollably. Her tear-streaked face looked up at him as if he were a mirage.

He squeezed his eyes shut as his solar plexus caved in on himself. He was supposed to serve and protect. He gave an oath to do so when he joined the service. But the one person who'd needed him most was back home, being beaten and starved by the very woman he'd put in place to care for her.

Not again, not ever again.

He reopened his eyes with renewed resolve as Loren plugged her digits into his phone.

"Feel free to call me anytime and thank you for doing this," she said, handing the phone back, rising up and down on her toes with restless energy.

"Another thing," he said, slipping his phone into the pocket of his jacket. "What happened here—on the porch."

She began to chew on her bottom lip, and nodded.

"It shouldn't have happened. It was a mistake," he said, looking to the side for a moment and then back to her. "It won't happen again."

Loren looked down at her shoes, but not before he caught a glimpse of glassy eyes. She nodded, as if physically unable to dredge up any words.

"Thought I should be clear about that," he said, sliding his hands in his back pockets.

Another nod.

"I better head back." He walked backward toward the steps. "Make sure Ally hasn't started a rave at the house."

An unconvincing half-smile appeared, and she once again nodded mutely.

Alec made his way along the bricked walkway, swung his body up into his truck and pulled away. He glanced in his rearview mirror and watched her slip back inside. He scraped his face with his hand and blew out a breath. Despite the gasket-sized knot in his gut, he needed to do that. Needed to squash any question as to why he showed up at her front door tonight. The more they kept things friendly, the better.

He couldn't afford to get wrapped up with a woman he knew so little about. And what he did know, didn't begin to pass muster. Whatever was going on with Ally required one hundred percent of his focus. God knew he owed it to her.

Driving up to the house, he saw that Ally's bedroom lights were out. He hated to admit it, even to himself, but he was relieved. Their earlier argument was about all he could take for one night, but the thought of sitting in his parents' living room and watching TV by himself was just as unsettling, if for different reasons.

Less than ten minutes later, he pulled into Lucky's Tavern and walked inside. Gus, the owner and friend since high school, was tending bar, so he took off his jacket and sat in one of the barstools, as far away from others as possible.

"Hey, stranger," Gus said with a grin. "You here to drink or troll?"

"Have you ever known me to troll?"

"Not that I can remember. But you might want to rethink that considering there are about a dozen women in here who would gladly oblige."

"Not interested," he said, pulling the bill of his cap lower. "But I will take a Guinness."

"Right up."

A minute later, Gus scooted his drink toward him and leaned on his elbows, taking advantage of the lull. "How's farming treating you?"

"Not too well."

"Still not taking to it?"

Alec sighed. "I don't think it's possible for me to hate anything more."

"So, why the hell are you doing it?"

"Don't have a choice. The only thing I've ever been good at was being a Marine. Those skills don't exactly transfer to civilian life."

"Why don't you talk to O'Malley? He's looking for some extra acreage. Selling the cattle would be easy enough."

Alec shook his head. "Family home; can't do that to Ally. The place is all she's known."

"Well, then stay in the house and lease the land and sell the cattle."

"Not as much profit."

"Not unless you start doing something you can stomach." Gus dried one of the beer mugs. "Look, O'Malley's leasing the acreage at the Old Kramer place, so it makes sense that he take on yours as well."

Alec took a long swallow, the evening taking on a bit of promise. "That's something to consider."

"Hold that thought," Gus said, backing toward a customer who'd called him over.

God, how he hated farming. For as long as he could remember, all his parents had talked about was him taking over the farm so they could retire. He'd joined the Marines in an effort to delay that eventuality, and then his parents were killed in a car accident on their way to their first vacation in over ten years.

Thank God Ally wasn't with them. Alec had agreed to stay home and watch her for the long weekend. Thought it would be a good idea to spend some time with her before being sent to boot camp. The Marines were pretty decent about it. They delayed his being shipped out and allowed him to make arrangements for Ally and his parents.

That's when he'd met Marisa.

He crushed a peanut shell as his mood diminished.

But that actually made him think.

Maybe selling the farm and moving wasn't such a bad idea? Maybe the memories Ally had for the house were those with Marisa instead of their parents. Maybe the old house was a constant reminder of the abuse she'd suffered?

Gus returned, wiping his hands on a towel. "Speaking of the Kramer place, you check out the Ingalls sisters?"

"I know of 'em."

"The middle one, Mercy, haven't seen much of her since she's not drinking age. But the older one comes in a couple of times a week. Teaches a self-defense class out at Pastor Roberts' church."

"I'm sure she causes quite a ruckus when she shows up."

Gus smiled. "She sure is something. Always comes in and orders the Gus Special, steak burger with home fries, then takes it out back to Jimbo."

Jimbo was Wilder's town vagrant who moved about during the

day, but usually spent his nights in the alley behind Lucky's. He was harmless, and had no intention of living anywhere but under the stars. Even during the coldest winter months, he refused to go to a shelter.

During one of their few evenings out, Marisa had told Gus and Alec that they should call the police on him, insisting vagrancy was against the law.

Gus continued, "She puts money in that juke box and gets all the women out on the dance floor. She doesn't care if they're twenty or eighty, little thing manages to get them all to dance. Calls it impromptu cardio."

"You don't have a dance floor, Gus."

"Exactly. She gets them dancing all around the tables, and then the people at the tables can't help themselves and they start dancing. She sure is something to see."

"You sound sweet on her." Alec's eyes narrowed.

Gus leaned closer on one elbow. "Believe me, I'd give it a shot if she were willing, but she's turned down every single able-bodied man within a twenty-mile radius that's made their intentions known. Not sure if she's picky, or prefers the ladies, if you know what I mean."

He left again to pour a beer for another customer and returned. "Couple of weeks ago, Robbie Bennett came in. You know the arrogant ass-wipe. Always acting like he's God's gift because he's a banker's son. He got a little too handsy with her—ended up hunched over, holding his junk as he duck-walked out the door. The entire place went nuts and put her on top of the bar to dance it out."

"Let me guess, she can dance." Alec smirked at the rhetorical question.

Gus grinned as if envisioning her dancing in his mind's-eye. "You ever see the movie *Coyote Ugly*?"

Alec squeezed his eyes shut.

Fucking hell.

Loren looked just like that sweet little blond in the flick, with the fuck-me lips.

He finished his Guinness, knowing where this was going. "I don't think there's a Marine from south Texas that hasn't."

Gus lifted one eyebrow. "Dances better than her."

CHAPTER FOURTEEN

"Choose rather to be strong of soul than strong of body."

—Pythagoras
Greek philosopher who influenced the philosophies of Plato, Aristotle, and, through them, Western philosophy

There were few things in life Mercy felt truly in control of, least of all her desire to paint. That she had managed to refrain from her heart's desire this long had been a Herculean effort. But she could feel herself beginning to cave, could tell she was slowly, and agonizingly, losing her resolve.

She stared out her window from the cocoon of her bed and marveled at the sheer magnitude of the kaleidoscope of stars that swirled in the night sky.

Most artists would choose a Windsor Blue to represent the hues in their skies. She grimaced. There was far too much color in Windsor Blue. In her mind, the sky was darker and more ominous than bright and hopeful. No, she would dip her brush into indigo, affording the sky the deliberate honor of spanning light-years and lifetimes.

Mercy squeezed her eyes shut, and with a heavy heart, she sat up in her bed and pulled on her robe. She couldn't hold back any longer. She wasn't kidding herself; she knew the time would come, but she had prayed every Sunday in Cara's church that she might find a way to delay her bliss and avoid the pain.

She grabbed her phone, slipped down the staircase, and flipped on the single ceiling light illuminating the sunroom. Not the best source of light in which to paint, but ideal situations were never where she found her inner muse. Chaos, indecision, loss of control, fear, those were the emotions that made her pine for a brush, compelled her to do the very thing that would pull her under, take her over, and turn her askew.

She pulled her phone from her robe to check for an answer to her plea. Nothing yet, but she knew it was only a matter of time.

She set up the largest canvas in the room and began to squeeze indigo onto the palette, knowing that within a few hours she would forego the palette, and even her brushes, using only her hands to fully express her innermost emotions.

The sheer euphoria took her breath away as she made her first paint stroke. Tingling goose bumps raised the dark hairs on her arms as if her body were singing hallelujah. She wondered if the feeling was similar to that of an orgasm. Or falling in love. She painted another sweeping stroke and lost herself.

There was just so much to say and feel.

Loren sat up in bed, hearing a noise downstairs, and checked the time on her phone.

Four AM.

And then she heard it again.

She quietly pulled the covers back and made her way to the narrow staircase. She peered down and could see a light coming from the back side of the house. It was probably Cara or Mercy, grabbing a snack since they skipped dinner last night with all the drama that was going on. Just in case, she reached behind her, grabbing the baseball bat that leaned against the wall, a safety precaution that sat benignly until ready for use.

She made her way down the stairs, back against the far wall with her hands in swing position. She peeked inside the sunroom and instantly noticed several canvases leaning against the walls and wondered when Mercy could have painted them.

And then she saw her sister draped over the table, splattered with paint, sitting in a chair with her head resting in the crook of her elbow. She was either taking a break or asleep.

"Psst, Mercy."

She didn't move. Unusual for a light sleeper known to go for the windpipe with a mere nudge to the shoulder.

Another creak, this time from the kitchen. An adrenaline rush drenched Loren's system, her entire body in high alert and ready to swing. Someone was trying to open the side door that opened from the outside into the kitchen.

Thankfully, the lights were out, making it easier to catch the perp unawares. She moved into the pantry to the right of the door and waited for the vandal to make his or her way inside.

She considered rushing toward the bottom kitchen cabinet where three "go bags" were hidden in a hole in the sheetrock. Hers with a loaded 9-millimeter. After a few calculations, she decided she didn't have time and would have to make do with the bat.

The door swung open, and she reacted with a swift swing but instead of connecting with the intruder who had ducked at the last minute, the bat crashed into the door's window.

From the corner of her eye, she caught him scooting under the kitchen table. She turned to stalk him and flipped the table over with one hand. Choking up on the bat, she reared back and suddenly found herself on her back, the bat pulled out of her grasp, the weight of her aggressor pressing her against the floor.

She pulled back a leg, kicking him in the chest with her knee and sending him crashing into a cupboard. She scooted back, opening the drawer just above her, riffled around the contents and pulled out a long kitchen knife. She jumped to her knees in a single motion with the blade at her ear, ready to strike.

"Stop! Loren, stop it."

She hesitated just as Mercy turned on the kitchen light. Loren stayed in combat stance as she took in the figure against the wall, wearing head-to-foot black gear.

Recognition struck and she lowered the knife panting. "Dr. Petrov?"

The man rubbed his bloody lip with the back of his thumb. "Greetings, little Loren," he said with a grin and thick Russian accent. "Quite nice welcome party, no?"

She fought to catch her breath, trying to make sense of who was sitting on her kitchen floor. Her hand shot out to help him up and he hesitated as he considered the risk and then finally obliged.

"What in the hell are you doing here?" Loren asked, lowering the knife to her side.

He once again touched his hand to his bloody lip and then looked at Mercy.

Loren switched her focus to her sister, who looked like shit warmed over. Her face was unusually pale, with dark circles under her eyes.

"I called Vlad."

Not Dr. Petrov. *Vlad.*

Mercy leaned her head against the doorway, clutching her stomach with her arms. "Some time ago."

The knife dropped to the floor, and Loren's eyes went wide. "*You* called Dr. Petrov? Uh, Vlad? Oh my God, do you know what you've done?"

The Russian doctor went straight to Mercy. As his thumb lifted her eyelid, he said, "She had no choice, *padruga.*"

My friend.

"What do you mean, no choice?"

"She suffers, no?" He held Mercy's face in his hands. "How long, *milaya?*"

Loren's head jerked back. She knew several languages, Russian being one of them, and she just heard one of the Center's medical doctors refer to her sister as "sweetheart."

"I have time," Mercy said, avoiding eye contact. "Just a few more paintings."

"Must you?" he asked.

She nodded. "Just a bit longer."

Loren watched with her mouth open as Mercy turned toward the sunroom and Vlad followed. Blinking and finding her bearings, she followed them.

"What's going on, Mercy? Do you not get that you've compromised our cover? A cover that took me months to create?"

Mercy began to pick through her paints with an almost zombie-like expression.

Vlad said, not taking his eyes off Mercy, "You need not concern yourself. Mara tell me what to do. I need new identity, new travel papers. You speak now with Vlad Kushnir, ethnic Russian whose family travel from Ukraine in nineteen fifty-four to southern peninsula of Crimea. I both Ukrainian and Russian. I study in Kyiv at The National Agricultural University of Ukraine. I have expertise in animal husbandry. You find my picture with graduating class twenty-eighteen. New birth documents also available."

Loren's eyebrows lifted. "You're telling me your cover is an Eastern European, with the same name of Vlad, who artificially inseminates livestock for a living?"

"*Tak.*"

Yes. "And you didn't think to change your name from Vlad to say, Oleksander?"

"I both Ukrainian and Russian. Vlad popular name both countries."

She pushed her palms into her eyes and then removed them to glare at Mercy. "And you gave me shit about using the name Ingalls."

Mercy half-shrugged, dabbing a blood burgundy onto her palette. "Lack of judgment from both of you, I'd say."

Loren took a deep breath, torn between shaking her sister and waking Cara to grab their go bags and bolt while they still had time. She crossed her arms and began to pace the room and stopped in front of Vlad, who was completely absorbed in her sister's painting. "I'm still not clear as to why you're here. Care to explain?"

Once again, Vlad deferred to Mercy. She nodded to him, as if giving him unspoken permission, as she pulled another large canvas upright.

Vlad sat on a nearby chair, watching her intently. "Your sister. Her lesions not take well. She suffer greatly, after."

"After?"

"After painting, she suffer migraines. So painful. Beyond comprehension." He hesitated before adding, "She known to lose sight."

Loren, again astonished, said, "How did I not know this?" She then turned to Mercy, who was engrossed in her painting. "Mercy, why didn't you ever tell me this?"

Vlad answered for her. "She say no." He added, "Tell you she paints when she sleeps past pain."

"Painting causes her pain?" Loren asked in disbelief. Thinking she was misinterpreting his accent.

He nodded. "When she complete art, I give injection. Less pain. She does not lose sight."

Mercy spoke, robotically. "I didn't want you to know."

Loren's head turned to her. "Why wouldn't you want me to know? I'm your sister. That's what I'm here for."

Mercy put down the brush, opting to work with her hands.

"There was nothing you could do. I had to paint, either for the doctor or for myself. Either way, I had no choice." She stopped with her paint-covered hands at her sides, head tilted, staring at the painting. "You're a fixer, Loren. And for once, I didn't want to burden you with something you couldn't fix."

The painting had transformed into a man's face, his one eye overly large.

"I see you, *milaya*," Vlad said with blatant adoration. "Always."

Mercy continued to paint, her tearful expression making Loren's throat feel as if a 250-pound man were sitting on her windpipe.

"I know you do," Mercy said.

After a restless night of running through a laundry list of memories, trying to discern where she lacked judgment, why she believed anything Halstead told her and regretting not offing the bastard sooner, Loren finally fell asleep, waking up late the next morning to another gray winter's day. She lay on her side, looking out her window, and began rummaging around the items on her side table. Recognizing the feel of her iPhone, she tilted it up to check the weather app.

Cloudy, eighty percent chance of rain, and fifty-five degrees.

She wondered if the people of Wilder were waking up and having to drag themselves out of bed.

They didn't even know how good they had it.

Try living in a sterile, cold research Center without windows or easy access to the outdoors. A place so dreary and devoid of warmth that going on assignment was nothing short of a treat, no matter the amount of danger they faced. They were given access to limited funds in case of unforeseen events and would spend it all on outrageous outfits just to piss off Jasper and the doctor. Once at the hotel or predetermined safe house, they'd gorge themselves on the local food and Netflix.

Which might explain their current altered sense of normal.

Loren covered her eyes with her elbow and sighed heavily.

Rainstorms, hurricanes, hell, they could've cared less if there was a tsunami as long as they had those few moments of freedom from the bleak confines of the Center and the doctor and his underlings.

Vlad.

She stretched, thinking she wouldn't necessarily file Vlad as one of the doctor's sycophants, but he was certainly part of the medical staff, arriving at the Center well after Mercy's lesions were established and her artistic capabilities were beginning to evolve.

Once again, she sifted through her memories, piecing timelines together. Mercy had to have been at least sixteen when Vlad showed up on the scene. Last night, he appeared to be in his late twenties or early thirties, which would've made him in his early to mid-twenties while working at the Center. That seemed young, though.

She dug her palms in her eyes. Was she completely clueless as to what was going on with her sisters while living at the Center?

She had yet to broach the subject of Jasper to Cara, choosing to wait until Cara came to her senses and re-inhabited her body. There was no way in hell she was going to address that subject with the churlish imposter that was fighting for imminent domain with her sister's soul.

But, if she had missed something sketchy going on between Cara and Jasper, maybe she'd also missed something between Mercy and the young Russian doctor?

But how could she have known? A steady churn of people going in and out of their lives at the Center in the name of scientific research was the norm. Not only doctors but educators, as well.

And like herself, Mercy was inundated with educators.

Mercy had spent years after her surgery working with tutors and highly regarded artists, all at the doctor's orders. All of them are highly compensated, and with one common objective: to hone her artistic skills and turn her into a master.

And they were certainly successful. Regardless of the style, be it

Modernism, Cubism, Expressionism, Neoclassicism, or Renaissance, Mercy could paint near-perfect replicas.

But what was really amazing to watch was when she was in the throes of creating her own art. Art that wasn't coerced for financial gain but that which sprang organically from her soul. Loren would watch mesmerized as Mercy became almost rabid with energy and drenched in emotion. Oftentimes, the pure, intense power of the moment reminded Loren of when Cara played her music. As if the art was pouring out of their bodies in the name of self-preservation.

Loren considered her own inexplicable predilection for all things math-related. She couldn't ever remember having an obsession for her acquired math skills, as her sisters had for art and music, only an inexplicable calm that came with seeing things in a way that made perfect sense. A way that seemed to answer questions that she never even pondered prior to the accident.

Such as the beauty and elegance of pi and how everything, whether man-made or derived from nature, was somehow related to pi.

Which made everything, in her mind, beautiful and elegant.

She remembered the walls in her antiseptic room at the Center covered with calculations, algorithms, and geometric drawings. But she created them not from some innate compulsion but from a dire need for harmony. A specific form of serenity that came in an algorithmic or geometric structure.

Maybe even hope.

CHAPTER FIFTEEN

"Mathematics knows no races or geographic boundaries; for mathematics, the cultural world is one country."

—David Hilbert
German mathematician, and one of the most influential and universal mathematicians of the 19th and early 20th centuries

She sat up in bed and leaned her head on her knees as she looked outside her window. She just couldn't recall Mercy being sick for any period. Tired, but never sick.

After paint-bingeing, Mercy was always exhausted, having been up for days. But she couldn't remember her ever becoming ill or losing her vision. She did recall Dr. Petrov, or Vlad, spending an inordinate amount of time with her, but hell, she assumed he was just another doctor making his daily rounds and doing his fair share of observations. The three of them were like lab rats, constantly being poked, prodded, and experimented on.

She pulled herself out of bed and made her way to the sunroom, wearing her sleep shorts and a T. Peeking around the corner, she eyed Mercy sleeping on the futon and quietly walked inside the room.

Loren's heart warmed. Mercy looked so much better this morning. So peaceful. Vlad must've given her some strong meds after she finished painting last night.

After checking on Mercy, she slowly began to turn in a circle in the middle of the room, and her heart rate picked up speed and her hand came to her chest as she viewed the onslaught of emotions expressed on dozens of canvases, as well as the walls themselves.

Clasping her hands under her chin, she allowed her eyes to light on each individual piece, so struck by their raw beauty. This was when she felt closest to Mercy. When given the rare opportunity to see her sister's true inner-self expressed in explicit brushstrokes and bold swirls of color, depicting compassion, anger, benevolence, and vulnerability.

What would the people of Wilder think of her sister's work if they were to step inside this sunroom? Would they be speechless or fail to appreciate the genius behind the brush?

It would be difficult to blame them if they were unable to appreciate her art. Mercy spent an enormous amount of energy acting as if she were someone else entirely, certainly not the sensitive individual expressed in her paintings.

Yet another coping mechanism meticulously crafted and executed due to their upbringing.

Guilt swirled and, despite her efforts, found its way to her chest. She was supposed to protect her sisters. It was her job to know when they were suffering.

She heard a noise in the kitchen and wondered if Cara was up, but instead found Vlad with a jelly glass and a bottle of vodka. The table had been righted, but for the most part, the room was still askew from their late-night skirmish.

She refrained from smiling as she rounded the table. "You know you're a cliché right now? A Russian drinking vodka at nine a.m. in the morning."

"Cliche's exist for a reason, Ava."

Loren turned toward him. "I'm no longer Ava. You can never call me that, Vlad. My name is Loren, Mara is now Mercy, and Charlotte is Cara. Have you mentioned our prior names to anyone in Wilder?"

He brought the glass to his lips, and hesitated. "If I had, what you do? Kill them?"

"No, but I might kill you for being a liability."

"You not kill me. I love your sister."

Loren stilled as she pulled a box of cereal from the pantry. Finding her bearings, she turned, placing the box on the kitchen table. She grabbed a bowl that was left drying on the countertop next to the sink and then reached into the refrigerator for milk.

She cleared her throat. "For how long?"

"Do not worry, *padruga*; I do nothing to regret."

She snorted. "As much as I hate to pop your vodka-infused bubble, that doesn't make me feel better." She sat in the chair across from him, pouring the cereal into her bowl. "I've met plenty of people who've done some pretty heinous shit and didn't think twice about it."

"I not Doctor Halstead."

"I have no idea who that is." She took a scoop of cereal and stared into her bowl. "Never heard of him."

"I was deported back to Russia after Halstead die. After you escape." He eyeballed her as he ran his finger around the edge of the glass. "I know you kill him."

She stopped chewing.

"You find arsenic?"

She began to chew slowly, remembering that day very well. Finding misplaced or discarded items was like a game to her. But when she found the arsenic, it was as if she'd found the unholy grail.

"You think someone might put vial where you find it?"

She stilled, was he blackmailing her or confessing?

"It took time to place where you find vial before others. I too being watched."

Well, that answered that. She looked up, and swallowed. "Why were *you* being watched?"

"I question your sister symptoms. Her medical information, all fail to, how you say, 'correlate.'"

"Why would you leave a vial of arsenic within reach of a well-documented psychotic?"

"You not psychotic. Mar—Mercy not psychotic."

Her eyes narrowed.

He poured more vodka into the jelly glass and downed it. "I began going through files. Those to which I had access. I find nothing to unmake conclusion."

"So . . . ?"

"So I ask your sister."

"You asked her, an insane person, if she was insane?"

"I ask her why she there."

She picked at a deep scratch in the table-top. "And she told you?"

"*Da.*"

"And you believed her? Why?"

No one else at the Center believed them, or ever spoke to them except when it was necessary. "Breathe in, breathe out"; "Open your mouth and say ah"; or, "This might hurt," just before setting a bone. Let alone cared to ask what brought them to the bucolic state of Utah. Besides, it was all in their files. And if they expressed any pleas to the contrary, the staff dismissed them as part of their delusional psychoses.

"I believe her because what she tell me correlate with gaps in medical information. And because—"

She glanced up, her brow arched. "You love her."

He smiled sadly and nodded. "*Da.*"

"Does she feel the same?"

"I hope, *padruga.*"

"So, what are you saying? That you've never shared your feelings with her?"

"The Center watch everything. Conversation with patients not permitted. I barely manage to find private place to ask her real story." He swiveled the glass on the table. "She young. I wait for her be older. Wait until she understand. To share feelings. I give her time. Now, she older. She knows. She knows my heart."

"How can you be sure?"

"I tell her with eyes." One side of his mouth turned up.

Loren sat back in her chair, openly perusing the handsome Russian sitting across from her. She had to admit, he was charming. It wasn't too much of a stretch to think Mercy could have fallen in love with the only person who cared to have a real conversation with her that just so happened to look like Edward Cullen in that vampire movie they watched last week. "What are you, twenty-eight? Thirty?"

He smirked. "Twenty-seven. I not age well?"

"That would make you, what, twenty-four when you came to the Center? Most physicians begin their careers at thirty, maybe twenty-nine."

He smirked. "For genius, you not see obvious."

She hesitated, then it came to her. Before she could confirm her suspicions, he opened up.

"I too, 'gifted.' Not high as you and sisters. I graduate from university at eighteen. Come to US on student visa, graduate medical school twenty-two."

"Hmm," she clucked with a shrug. "What took so long?"

He smiled. "I need learn English, *padruga*."

She tapped her fingers on her lips, doing her best not to show how impressed she was.

He continued, "Three years internship and residency, I am twenty-five, recruited by most prestigious neuroscientist for Savant Syndrome, Dr. Halstead." He put the stopper back on the bottle. "I was easy choice. Brilliant doctor, easy to deport when services no longer needed."

Suddenly an anxious Mercy was in the kitchen doorway. "Umm . . . we have company. It's either a hulking man posing as a Hemsworth, or our surly neighbor who has the patience of a bomb squad."

"Ally!"

Loren's eyes widened at the familiar voice of her highly suspicious neighbor and then noticed the kitchen, which had suffered from last night's physical altercation.

It could've been worse, considering the element of surprise Vlad bestowed upon her in the middle of the night. But the broken glass, cracked cabinet doors, and kitchen chair with one bent metal leg would tell a different story.

Loren turned to Mercy. "Any chance you noticed a vein pulsating in his neck?"

"Have we ever seen him otherwise?" she asked, leaning in the doorway. "He's convinced Ally's here. He's waiting impatiently in the living room. Told him to give us five minutes to get dressed and we'd establish a search party complete with bloodhounds, the local police—all three of them. And the town psychic."

"How you feel, *milaya*?" Vlad asked Mercy, raw concern in his eyes.

She looked at Vlad and then to her bare feet. "Fine, thanks to you."

As many questions as that generated, Loren couldn't allow their fire-breathing neighbor to see the chaos that was sure to refuel his skepticism and encourage questions she had no intention of answering.

Protecting their newly minted identities had to be the number one priority. And now, a certain love-sick Russian doctor was sitting in their kitchen, belting down 80-proof grain alcohol. And as much as Loren wanted to send him back to the Gulag, she couldn't bring herself to fault him for coming to her sister's aid.

And loving her.

So, if only for the good sense of falling for Mercy, he had to be protected as well.

"Quick," she clipped, grabbing the broom and brushing the broken glass from the kitchen door into the pantry.

Mercy stashed the items that had fallen when Vlad crashed into the cupboard.

They heard Alec's heavy footsteps making their way to the kitchen and they instantly stood straight, acting as nonchalant as their heaving chests would allow.

"Where's Ally?" he asked, reaching the doorway into the kitchen and then came to an abrupt stop. "What happened?" he asked with a raised eyebrow, taking in the kitchen.

Loren took a calming breath not altogether sure what had her more flustered, the state of their kitchen or the testosterone-riddled specimen testing the confines of her doorway, wearing jeans, work boots, and one of those waffle-weave shirts, the sleeves pushed up to his elbows.

"What? Nothing," Loren said, leaning on the kitchen counter and closing the knife drawer behind her.

"Okay, let's try this again. What happened to your kitchen door?"

"We're replacing the windows," Loren explained with an overly wide smile. "A few of them were cracked. You know us, always with the house projects."

He glanced to his side, clearly seeing the baseball bat leaning against the wall. Loren winced, remembering she'd left it there last night. As he bent over to pick it up, Loren and Mercy both eyeballed the butcher knife on the floor. Mercy kicked it toward Loren who stopped it by the handle with the ball of her foot, inches from the sharp blade. Alec glanced up at the scraping sound. She quickly opened the pantry door and kicked it out of sight.

Alec stood with the bat, tapping it into the palm of his other hand, eyes focused on Loren. "You in the habit of using bats during house projects?"

"Don't be silly," Loren huffed, "we just leave that in the kitchen in case we all decide we want to play . . . ball."

Alec's eyes settled on the back of Vlad's head, narrowed, and then eyed Loren as if to say, care to explain?

How does one explain a Russian sitting in their kitchen doing shots of vodka before the noon hour? Not that she had to explain, but she had to be careful and stick to Vlad's, sketchy-at-best, manufactured identity.

Something about being part Crimean and part Russian and assisting farm animals in the act of procreating. . . . "This is our friend, Vlad," she said, deciding to stick as close to the truth as possible. "Vlad, this is our neighbor, Alec Wilder."

Heat began to surface on Loren's face as Alec took in the extra small tee and sleeping shorts that all but showed her lady bits.

Sans bra, no less.

She crossed her arms over her chest.

Thankfully, Alec turned toward Vlad, and they shook hands. Vlad with a shit-eating grin on his face and Alec with expressionless eyes.

"Vlad came for a visit."

Alec cocked his head, his eyes lighting on her tee that shielded very little. "Must be a very good friend. Where you travel from, Vlad?"

"Russia," he replied with his thick accent.

"Russia?" Alec asked with raised eyebrows.

"*Da.*" Realizing his mistake, Vlad over-corrected and blurted. "Ukraine. I come from Ukraine."

Despite looking as if the conflicting answers to his question only conjured more, he turned to Loren. "Where are the girls?"

"The girls?" Loren asked. "Cara's sleeping, but we haven't seen Ally."

Now that she thought about it, how did Cara not hear the commotion in the kitchen last night, or, for that matter, Alec yelling for Ally through the house?

A quick puzzled glance by Loren toward Mercy had her sister moving out of the kitchen and up the staircase.

Alec continued, "Are you telling me Ally didn't spend the night here last night?"

Loren shook her head. "Not that I'm aware of."

He pulled a piece of paper from a pocket and showed it to Loren. "I found this note when I got home last night."

The note advised Alec that Ally was spending the night at Cara's house and would be back in the morning.

"I grounded her when we got home from school yesterday. After stopping by here I went for a beer at Lucky's, came home, and found the note. It was late so I decided to wait to come get her this morning and extend her punishment another week. I've been trying to call her phone, but she's not answering."

Mercy rushed back into the kitchen. "Cara's not here, but look at what I found on her nightstand." She handed a printout to Loren, announcing a concert spotlighting a Queen cover band in Dallas. "Our little sister totally sucks at subterfuge. We're going to have to work with her on how to better hide her tracks—"

"Mercy," Loren interrupted with pursed lips. "Let's focus on finding them."

Mercy nodded rapidly. "Right, I'll get your laptop so you can get inside the network of street cameras and find a match with Cara's profile. I'll hunt down the schematic of the concert hall from the Fire Marshall's database showing the entrances and exits."

Mercy left the room and returned with two laptops and sat beside Loren as they each began to login to their devices.

Alec's eyes moved slowly back and forth between the two women. "Why don't I just go into my Find Friends app"—he raised his phone—"and locate them?"

Loren looked up, realizing theirs was an overzealous approach. "Or, we could do that." She slowly closed her laptop.

"Found them," he said, laying his phone on the table so the others could see. "They're on their way home. Should be back within the hour."

Loren felt a swell of relief, knowing they were safe and on their way home. But then, anger quickly took over.

"What should we do?" Loren asked, looking around the room for answers. "They should be punished, right?"

"Of course, they should be punished," Alec said. "For beginners, I'm going to ground Ally for at least a month. No phone, no iPad, no television, meeting up with friends, or going to after-school events. What they did was reckless. I'm going to make sure she thinks twice the next time one of them comes up with another brilliant idea."

"That's good," Loren nodded. "Put them in virtual and physical lockdown."

Mercy continued to peck on her laptop. "Says here that an effective punishment requires taking away the one thing they love the most."

Loren and Mercy looked at one another, saying what they both were thinking at the same time. "The piano."

Alec continued to watch this strange telepathic interaction with growing interest.

Mercy covered her mouth with her hands and then lowered them. "Cara is going to totally hate you."

Loren closed her eyes at the thought, leaning her elbows on the table. She clasped her hair in both hands. "Why are our strait-laced, rule-abiding sisters turning into future prison inmates?"

"Boys," Vlad said succinctly.

"Boys?" Loren looked from Vlad to Alec. "Cara doesn't hang out with boys, the only friend she has is Ally."

Vlad shrugged. "I have five older sisters. I tell you, girls reach certain age and hormone take over. Boys convince them go on road trip, drink alcohol."

"You think they were drinking?" Mercy blurted, incredulous.

"It is likely," Vlad said.

"Oh my God, Loren," Mercy said, turning to her sister and grabbing her upper arm. "Do you remember the movie *Superbad*? All the drinking and . . . and . . . teenage sex? I knew we should have hit her over the head with the shovel."

Alec continued to gawk at the exchange.

Loren held Mercy by her forearms. "She's fine. You know how I know that?"

"How?"

"She's Emma Stone in *Superbad*. Jonah Hill's love interest? In the movie, Emma was levelheaded and . . . the voice of reason."

Mercy nodded. "You're right. There's no way Cara would drink or have sex. She's too much of a self-righteous do-gooder."

"Exactly, she was probably watching out for her friends, being extra responsible, all while holding everyone in contempt."

Alec cleared his throat to gain their attention. "Tell you what, while you two research parenting skills and talk yourselves into believing our altruistic sisters went to Dallas to look out for their corrupt friends, I'm going home and putting a padlock on Ally's bedroom door and forging a chastity belt out of a piece of steel."

Alec stalked toward the kitchen door and opened it, a loose pane of glass barely missing his hand as it dropped to the floor. He paused, took a deep breath and then stepped outside, closing the door behind him.

Loren stared after him, knowing she'd have some explaining to do, but she also had to prioritize.

"Look up chastity belt," she said to Mercy.

CHAPTER SIXTEEN

"No simplicity of mind, no obscurity of station, can escape the universal duty of questioning all that we believe."

—William Kingdon Clifford
Mathematician and philosopher
who introduced what is now termed geometric algebra

There are few things in life more resolute and impenetrable than two teenage girls who share a common cause.

And a shitty attitude.

Upon their return, neither Cara nor Ally were remotely forthcoming, executing a well-planned united front.

To make matters all the more frustrating, whoever had driven them to Dallas dropped them off at the end of the driveway, which made Loren's list of those to interrogate, outside of Cara and Ally, devoid of names.

She and Mercy cursed themselves for the rookie mistake, acknowledging their little sister had acquired some guile over the last few weeks.

Either that, or they'd lost their edge.

They totally should have staked out the end of the drive.

Instead, they'd ridiculously waited for a car to pull up to the house and were therefore slack-jawed and speechless when the girls walked through the front door as if nothing were amiss.

They rallied, like the highly trained intimidating interrogators that they were, circling the tight-lipped teenagers as they peppered them with questions. The girls responded with one-word answers or even more infuriating, one-shoulder shrugs.

After a few pointed questions concerning drugs and alcohol, the girls rolled their eyes and snorted with outright contempt until Loren was afraid Mercy was going to lose her shit and coldcock both of them.

That's when Loren pulled Mercy into the half bath for a well-deserved break from the interrogation.

Mercy splashed water on her face, pulling a towel from the holder. "I'm this close to committing domestic violence on those little mongrels. How do parents do it? How do they balance wanting to protect their kids with wanting to beat the ever-loving shit out of them?"

"No idea," Loren said, rubbing her eyes while leaning against the back wall. "But I think our cross-examination efforts are futile. Neither one of them is even close to caving."

They switched places. Loren dampened a washcloth, folded it over and laid it on the back of her neck. She glanced at her phone and checked the time.

"Alec should be here any minute to pick up Ally. He gave us an hour to gather facts and all we've managed to get are some pretty snide eye rolls and a number of condescending snorts." A thought came to her. She clicked her fingers. "Maybe separating them will be bring about more intel."

Mercy's head bobbed in contemplation. "Riiight, divide and conquer. Oh, I know, we could separate them and then tell them that the other ratted them out to draw out their confessions."

Resting her arms on the porcelain sink, Loren looked up with squinty eyes. "This isn't an episode of 'NCIS.'"

After binge-watching hundreds of hours on as many social media platforms as possible to better understand culture, slang, appropriate clothing choices, and tasteful home decorating tips, Loren realized Mercy might have gone into overload with the police detective shows.

Mercy checked herself out in the mirror, running her fingers through her chin-length hair. "Disagree. Remember when we separated those two low-level lackeys from the mafia and got them to cough up information on their boss's money laundering scheme?"

Loren's shoulders fell. "Threatening to smash their fingers with a sledgehammer might have been what teased the intel out of them."

"Hey, at this point, I am not opposed to physical threats."

Loren heaved a long sigh, mentally exhausted. "Not sure that's the best approach for two fourteen-year-old girls."

Cara was suffering from multiple personalities and Mercy was keeping secrets regarding their Russian houseguest, who was currently hiding out in one of the upstairs bedrooms.

On top of that, she had a hot-headed, hot-bodied neighbor who made her feel all gooey inside one minute and like a rabid honey badger the next.

All she'd wanted was to give her sisters the family life they'd never had living at the Center and she was failing miserably. Nothing was going right. No one was happy and she was a parental failure.

Loren sat on the toilet lid with her elbows resting on her knees. Their family situation couldn't have been more opposite of that of her beloved Ingalls.

If memory served, only one Ingalls family member at a time went through some sort of personal crisis. Whereby the entire family would come together with outstretched arms, a fair amount of gratuitous crying, and an outpouring of unconditional love.

Loren could do without the waterworks but wouldn't mind if they could agree to take turns with their traumas. Some unconditional love sprinkled here and there would also be nice.

Loren stood, indicating it was time to exit their haven.

Once back into the fray, they re-doubled their efforts. But no amount of threats could compel either teenager to cough up the names of their accomplices or reasons for their sulky behavior.

When Alec showed up at the front door to pick up Ally, he was wearing a threadbare hoodie, an equally worn pair of jeans and an expression that read he was a hair's breadth away from losing his shit.

Loren suddenly felt light-headed.

And aroused.

Ally gathered her overnight bag with the urgency of a drunken snail and turned toward her comrade. They locked arms around one another in an overly dramatic hug.

Loren rolled her eyes.

Ally turned toward the door and faltered a bit once her eyes met those of her livid brother and Loren couldn't help but smirk with satisfaction at the first sign of fear from either girl.

Now if she could only have the same effect on her demonic sister.

Alec glared at Ally and gave a head nod toward the front door, indicating it was time to hit the green mile.

Loren all but lunged in front of them to open the door just so she'd have an excuse to stand inches from Alec's body and verify the scent wafting from his skin was from a bar of Irish Spring soap.

She breathed in with as much discretion as was humanly possible.

Ally walked out first after sending a sullen glance at Cara.

Loren prayed that Alec would, at the very least, look at her, but he simply gave her a head nod and walked out the door, not bothering to meet her eyes.

Loren dug deep and channeled her own inner authoritarian

figure, and within minutes, Cara's eyes filled with tears and her bottom lip trembled as Loren informed her that she would not be playing the piano until further notice.

That was, unless she finally agreed to tell them everything. Where they went, why, and with whom.

The little termagant still refused to cave.

But instead of feeling justified in exacting the brutal punishment, it only made Loren inexplicably sad.

Sad, knowing that Cara considered playing the piano as necessary to her existence as breathing air. But she didn't know what else to do. How was she supposed to protect her if she refused to spill information or failed to show the slightest remorse?

Alec expressed the same amount of frustration with Ally through a few sparse texts. Apparently, the two girls were digging in their heels, despite the indefinite timeframe of each of their punishments.

Two interminable days later, it was Sunday. Loren and Mercy had racked up about six months' worth of church attendances that had compounded due to their inability to spew a curse word without Cara being within hearing range.

Ironic how each of them was undergoing some form of punishment.

And that posed another problem. What should Loren do about Cara attending church?

Cara loved church.

But she was being punished.

Should Loren keep her from attending the morning service and risk missing an important message from Pastor Roberts potentially relative to her punishment? Something along the lines of: "Thou shall not lie to your sisters and disappear to Dallas for a Queen concert?" Or, did they all stay home to make Cara as devoid of happiness as possible, which included policing the piano?

It didn't take long for Loren to realize that Cara's punishment didn't just hamper her little sister's happiness, but hers and Mercy's as well.

All three sisters made their way through the church's parking lot and front grounds, stopping to say hello to each of their friends. Mercy introduced Vlad to a few of the church members, as he had insisted on attending, shadowing every move she made with a reserved commitment.

Mercy whispered to Loren, "Cara's hair doesn't seem to be fading any time soon. And what's with her clothes?"

Loren was just as shocked to see Cara trudge down the stairs that morning wearing black leggings, black tee, combat boots and a leather jacket, her hair still a neon-bright orange.

Loren and Mercy had voluntarily toned down their attire to counterbalance Cara's digression to the dark side, wearing modest hems and necklines and actual colors rather than black-on-black.

"I'm half afraid to check the balance on her credit card," Loren whispered back, referring to the card she gave her for emergencies only. She didn't have the energy to confront her for yet another transgression.

"I don't like that Cara is keeping so many secrets," Mercy commented under her breath.

Loren stopped and looked her straight in the eye. "Pot, let me introduce you to Kettle."

Mercy avoided Loren's eyes.

Loren continued. "You know you can tell me anything."

"Nothing to tell," she said, waving at one of her Saturday morning art students.

"That's not the way Vlad sees it."

"It's a long story," Mercy replied under her breath.

"There's a story? You're telling me that you two have a story?"

Mercy pulled on her arm. "Keep your voice down; he'll hear you. We'll talk later."

Loren seriously doubted that. Mercy was as tight-lipped about her relationship with Vlad as Cara was about her multiple personality complex.

When they entered the narthex, Cara instantly found Ally with

Alec several feet ahead of them, making their way to the pews. The girls nodded clandestinely at one another.

Loren leaned toward Mercy. "Look at them. It's as if they just completed a top-secret mission."

Mercy smirked. "I wouldn't be surprised if they carried a vial of cyanide to ingest under the direst of circumstances— drama queens."

Regardless, Loren was relieved to see that Alec allowed Ally to attend church, too. Maybe she wasn't an abject parental failure after all. One thing was certain, she was going to get to the bottom of what was going on with Cara and Ally, and she would use every trick in the book, and counterintelligence ploy, to do it.

And then she'd attend to Mercy and Vlad.

After the service, which, unfortunately, failed to deliver the custom message Loren had hoped for, she banished Cara to the car while they mingled with the congregation.

Lucky for Loren, it didn't take long for the gossip chain within the small town of Wilder to deliver a snippet of intelligence she could leverage.

Becky Waterman pulled Loren aside as Mercy introduced Vlad to Pastor Roberts. "What's this I hear about you harboring a sexy Russian fugitive?"

Loren chuckled. "If Vlad's a Russian fugitive, I'm a highly trained mercenary capable of bringing a two-hundred-pound man down with my forefingers."

Becky's eyes narrowed. "That was rather ... specific."

"Sorry, just tired of the inaccurate rumors floating around."

"Oh, you mean the one in which he's the wealthy father of your love child, and he's come to Wilder to spirit you back to Moscow?"

"Actually, I was fonder of the one in which he's Russian royalty looking for his long-lost sisters...."

"Let me guess, that makes the three of you Russian princesses? Am I right? Wait, didn't they make a Disney movie about that?"

Loren smiled, thinking of one particular filthy rich wife of a rather unscrupulous Russian politician. A vapid woman who was completely unaware that her painting of the Grand Duchess Anastasia Nikolaevna of Russia, hanging over her gilded fireplace, was nothing more than a worthless fake.

Mercy had *really* outdone herself on that one.

Alec and Ally walked out of the church, and Becky quickly switched conversation gears as they watched Alec make his way down the church steps. "So, how are things going with your neighbor? Has he managed to plow your field?"

"No," Loren hissed. "Trust me, he has no interest in doing anything with my 'field.'"

"Actually, I meant that literally. Rumor is he's considering leasing out his land and taking a town job."

"Why would he do that?"

She shrugged her shoulders. "Apparently, Alec hates farming."

"He does?"

Becky nodded. "And with what's going on at school, I wouldn't blame him for moving into town. He and Ally are just a little too isolated, if you ask me."

Holding Becky by the forearm, Loren forced her attention from Alec. "What do you mean, 'with what's going on at school'?"

Becky pulled her head back. "You don't know? Cara didn't tell you?"

"Tell me what?"

"Ally is being bullied by some of the older girls at school. It's been going on for months."

"Bullied? Why?"

"Because girls are spiteful little bitches, and there's this one girl and her crew who are at the top of the Mean Girl food chain. You remember Susie Mabry from self-defense class? The one who couldn't do a decent push-up to save her soul? She had to move a county over to get her daughter away from the little wretches. Samantha steers clear of them, and I'm afraid that means steering clear of Ally and Cara, too."

"So as not to become collateral damage," Loren mused. She refocused, biting her bottom lip. "I wonder if this has anything to do with the girls going to Dallas last Friday night?"

"Wait, what? Who went to Dallas?"

Loren clued her in on Cara and Ally's jaunt to Dallas, and Becky shook her head and shrugged. "That I know nothing about. I'll ask Samantha and let you know if she knows anything. She did say that since Ally and Cara have become friends, the older girls are starting to pick on your sister, too. I'm sorry, I thought you knew."

Loren began to unconsciously open and close her fists, the blood racing through her veins. She couldn't stand the thought of older girls making Cara and Ally's lives miserable at school.

She refused to allow anyone to mess with her sisters. They might be a highly dysfunctional, barely compatible excuse for a family, but they were all she had in this world, and each of them deserved some level of happiness after what they'd endured over the past several years.

She took a deep breath, cracked her neck on both sides and crossed her arms over her chest. "Names, Becky. I'm gonna need names."

Becky leaned in as if sharing high-security-level secrets, "There's three of them," she said, leaning even closer. "Jenny Morris and Amanda Baker. Amarilla Simmons is the ring leader."

Loren smiled with the same level of satisfaction she felt after uncovering the identity of a low-profile, highly dangerous Venezuelan drug lord. A man both short and hefty who reeked of sweet onions and rather shoddily laundered money through a Hispanic restaurant in downtown Miami. Like Jorge, she'd expose Amarilla Simmons with the same level of ruthless tenacity.

―――

Alec grabbed his jacket from the hook by the front door when the doorbell rang.

A rare occurrence.

Ally wasn't allowed to have friends over since being grounded, and he rarely had solicitors travel out to his place. He looked out the side window to see Loren wearing all black with the exception of a red bandana around her neck. Her hair was tucked up in a black knit beanie and she bounced from one foot to another, probably at the sudden decrease in temperature.

Fucking adorable woman.

Who had a Russian boyfriend. Or was he Ukrainian?

He grasped the doorknob with resolve, whipping it open, and holding on to the top edge as if his life depended on it. "Why are you dressed like a cat burglar from the 'fifty's movie *To Catch a Thief?*"

She shrugged. "Coincidence, I guess. Never saw it." She whisked past him, meandering around the room and honing in on the wall of family pictures. "I only watch contemporary movies to better understand pop culture and certain social cues."

He forced himself to remain rooted at the door, despite his rampant desire to move closer. Her hair was hidden under her beanie, which only enhanced the delicate features of her face. Without makeup she appeared younger, maybe even a little bit innocent. His eyes trailed further down, lingering on the slight curve in her back and then on to her heart-shaped ass.

Wait, why was she wearing all black? Down to her combat boots? "That's why you're dressed like a sniper? Because of being homeschooled, you lack certain social cues, like, how to dress for the occasion?"

She turned her head toward him with a wry smile. "You could say that."

He shifted uncomfortably as she continued to peruse the dozen or so photos he couldn't bring himself to take down. "So, what else did you learn by watching contemporary movies?"

Her eyes moved to a picture of Alec and Ally with his parents, taken a few weeks before the accident.

"*Forest Gump*. Filmed in nineteen ninety-four." She touched the picture with what seemed reverence. "A movie about a mentally impaired man with a heart of gold who transforms the lives of those around him." Her fingers curled inward and then she turned her head toward him, with shadowed eyes.

Those eyes. They were so full of heartache they practically gutted him.

"Let me guess, you learned to never judge a book by its cover?"

"That," she said, "And that character can win out over a high IQ."

She moved on to the next picture to the right. Ally blowing out her candles on her tenth birthday. He and his parents were clapping as if she'd just won a Nobel prize.

Alec watched as she seemed entranced and oddly stricken by the family-oriented photos.

"What other movies gave you profound insights?" Alec asked in an effort to keep her talking, wanting this seemingly rare and emotional side of her to continue. He sensed he was learning more than he was consciously aware from her commentary. Later, when he could better focus, he would connect the pieces of information with her demeanor, hopefully determining who she was, or wasn't. For now, he wanted to concentrate on those nearly imperceptible movements that told you far more about who a person was and the beliefs they held at their core.

Loren moved on to the photo of him and his dad holding up a bass during one of their annual fishing trips.

Two days prior to the picture being taken, Alec had turned sixteen and pitched a fit about having to go on the trip as he was missing an epic party hosted by the football team. He argued with his mother that he was the captain, and therefore obligated to go.

Thank God, she didn't budge.

His dad had been ecstatic.

Alec had acted like an entitled shit the entire time.

But he wouldn't give up the memory of sitting for hours next to his dad in an old fishing boat for the world.

Loren cut into his thoughts. "*Hacksaw Ridge*, twenty-sixteen. A WWII Army medic refuses to kill people and becomes the first person in American history to receive the Medal of Honor without firing a shot."

"And what significance did avoiding indiscriminate killing have in respect to your sheltered life?"

She turned to him, expressionless. "It taught me the importance of having moral courage. Speaking up for others and doing what's right instead of what you're told." She smiled wryly, her eyes moving back to the picture. "But what the movie didn't tell you was that sometimes doing what's right can blur the lines of morality."

She was a conundrum. One minute she came off as trite and sassy, and the next, she was somber and angsty.

He had to remind himself that she was also mysterious and secretive. And probably the sexiest woman he'd ever met. A deadly combination to which he and Ally had fallen victim before. With Ally suffering the majority of the consequences.

"We have something in common, you and I," she whispered. "Both our parents died in car accidents."

"Not common ground I would wish on anybody."

She nodded, her eyes moving along the wall. "Sometimes, when I think about them, I'm not sure if my memories are accurate, or just cloudy, wishful feelings from the past."

"I believe that's true of most people who lose loved ones tragically. They forget the bad times and choose to exaggerate the good."

Even in his own ears, he sounded matter-of-fact and devoid of feeling. An asshole. But he didn't like where the conversation was going. His mission was to learn more about her, not to divulge too much of himself.

"What do you remember?" she asked, pulling herself away from the pictures and moving toward him, her eyes wide and earnest. "What's your favorite memory of your parents?"

CHAPTER SEVENTEEN

"What is mathematics? It is only a systematic effort of solving puzzles posed by nature."

—Shakuntala Devi
Indian writer and mental calculator,
popularly known as the "Human Computer"

The question left Alec feeling exposed. He wasn't a fan of "misery loves company" but found it difficult to knowingly disappoint her. She seemed to be grasping at something, and inexplicably he wanted to help her find it.

Clearing his voice, he complied. "I remember how proud they were when I signed up. Even though my dad wanted me to take over the farm, he was proud of me for wanting to do something more. To serve."

A smile reached her eyes, and his solar plexus turned from feeling tight and fidgety, to warm and satisfied at having something to do with her slight change of expression.

She was now within reach, and he tucked an exposed curl back under her beanie. "Your turn."

Her smile faltered, and he damned himself, clenching the doorframe, as if the door were an anchor keeping him from drifting.

"I remember my mother helping me with homework," she said, looking over his shoulder as if viewing the tableau. "I struggled in math and it came so easily to her. But she never got frustrated or angry. She kept saying that it would come to me. That, in time I would see how math was integral to everything, how it explained everything."

"Was she right? Did it eventually come to you?"

She looked up, tilted her head and nodded morosely. "Prophetically so." She looked up through dark eyelashes and the pain tore at Alec's chest.

And then, shaking her head, she added, "But she was wrong about it explaining everything. Even though I now understand math, it explains nothing. Most of the time, I feel lost and clueless."

He was gutted again by brows that were high and pensive, eyes that turned large and teary. The back of his hand touched her cheek, and moved downward where his thumb found her full bottom lip.

Rather than his usual reaction to Loren, which was wanting to ravish her until she begged for mercy, he felt an intense need to comfort and protect her. How did one small woman encourage so many different feelings? But wasn't that his Achilles heel? The need to protect and defend to the point of losing reason? He couldn't allow his feelings for this woman to compromise his ability to be rational and logical. There were still too many questions unanswered, too many small but important details to be revealed.

Too many unknowns.

Loren stepped back as if reading his internal confusion. "I'm sorry, I digress from the purpose of my visit. I have some intel on our sister situation."

He unclenched the top of the door in relief. "Follow me to the barn. I was about to check on the livestock before going to bed."

He checked himself for mentioning the word "bed." Now, he was envisioning them going upstairs to the first room on the right.

Good thing Ally was brooding in her room.

Who thought his recalcitrant sister could ever make for a convenient cock-blocker?

Not that Loren would be interested, considering her late-night visitor. He wasn't sure what her wrecked kitchen had to do with the Russian, but it was clear she was keeping secrets. He couldn't afford fucking with mysterious women who kept secrets.

She followed him as he walked down the porch steps and toward the barn. "I hear you're going to lease your land." She passed the For Rent sign stuck in the ground. "Is the sign for the land or for the house?"

"House. The land is already leased." He pushed open the barn door and stepped inside, turning on the light switch, which gave the barn no more than murky illumination.

"What made you decide to lease your land? Intolerable neighbors throwing all-night parties and passing out on your front lawn?"

And she was back. Her sadness morphed to cheekiness without blinking an eye.

Ignoring her banter, and peeling his eyes off her, he checked on the calves in their individual stalls to make sure they were fed, and that Ally had completed her chores. She had been less than reliable in the past few weeks.

"Don't like farming."

She moved around, looking inside each of the stalls. "What don't you like about it?"

He leaned on the wooden slats. "Not sure I have to have a list."

She seemed to hesitate at that statement but then started up again. "From what I hear, Alec Wilder is the town darling, and according to popular opinion, you can pretty much do anything you want in this town."

"I don't know about all that."

"Please, I'm sure you'll have no problem picking up a job in town. You practically walk on water around here." She picked up a hay rake and leaned it against the wall.

"Not much time for that as I'm pretty busy kissing babies, and healing leprosy."

A smile crept over her face, and his heart began to pound. It felt odd having her in this longtime familiar space, as the sun was working its way down and the animals were beginning to settle.

She seemed to burn so brightly, like an incandescent light. The internal wire filament heated to such a high temp that it created a glow. But, despite emitting such a warm and comforting light, the filament remained isolated and protected from oxidation.

A light within a sealed vacuum.

So bright but at the same time, very much alone.

She seemed to grow uncomfortable with his scrutiny, as she picked up some twine that was left on the packed floor and began to unravel the twisted end.

"So, what are you going to do? Spend your days spreading all that Wilder charm among the women-folk? Maybe save a baby or two from a burning building when you get bored?" She placed the twine on a hay bale so she could reach inside a stall to stroke the ear of a small calf.

Once again, his eyes lit on her firm ass in the tight-fitting pants.

Maybe a quick fuck was back on the menu?

"Probably sign up with a private security company."

She stopped and turned toward him. "Security company? You've started looking for a job?"

One side of his lip lifted. "No, I've got about half a dozen companies offering me a job."

"So, you're going to be a gun for hire?"

"That's one way of putting it." He checked inside the pen of a calf suffering from a case of pink eye. "The work doesn't always involve firearms. Some people work in the back office, as well."

"Sorry, but it's hard for me to imagine you wearing khakis and a button-down shirt doing accounts receivables in a small cubicle."

He smiled, reaching over the gate and stroking the calf's neck. "You're right. Probably won't be doing that."

"Doesn't that job require quite a bit of travel to obscure and dangerous places around the world?"

He rose, leaning one arm on a gate, and followed protocol on downplaying the details of his new job. "I'm not sure a company that provides security to malls and mom-and-pop shops here in sleepy Wilder is all that dangerous." His eyes narrowed. "You seem to know a lot about the inner workings of private security companies."

"I watch a lot of movies. Have I mentioned that?"

"Yeah." He lifted his chin. "Where did you learn to fight?"

She walked toward him, and just as quickly, a long list of things he fantasized about doing to her in this very barn came to the forefront of his mind.

"Ever see the movie *G.I. Jane?*"

With a sly smile, he said, "I'd bet money you mocked Demi Moore playing a hyper-vigilant Navy SEAL."

She grinned back at him, leaning her head in his direction. "Especially after watching her play a stripper in *Striptease*. Poorly done, I might add."

"And how did you become an expert on strippers?"

She chuckled as if searching for an answer. "*Hustlers?*"

He chuckled, and rubbed his lower lip with his thumb. "Never seen it."

He'd watched it twice. Both times when Ally spent the night with a friend.

He cleared his throat, his words vaulting him back to his original dilemma. She was evasive, which in his mind inferred dishonesty. She had no intention of coming clean and telling him the truth about her and her sisters and what brought them to Wilder.

Her word held as much water as a slotted spoon. He had to remember that when his balls ached and he felt the urge to touch her like she was good and honest and in need of his protection.

Hell, protecting his sister against this potentially duplicitous woman and her sisters had to be his priority until she was able to prove to him otherwise.

He leaned against the stall, crossing one leg over the other and his arms across his chest. "There's some travel to the job. I have to go to D.C. for training. Thinking about renting out the house and moving into town so it's more convenient for neighbors to watch Ally while I'm traveling."

She flinched and he wondered if it was the insinuation that the current neighbors weren't up to snuff.

"Don't you think that will be hard on Ally?" she asked, fingering a rope next to a bale of hay. "Remind her of the time you left —before?"

He took a deep breath.

And then saw red.

His eyes glared into her as she fixated on her boots. No one had ever dared to broach that subject with him. It was a conversation he had never had with anyone, with the exception of Ally and only on rare occasions.

Except for a twitch in his eye, he didn't move. Refused to allow her to see how the question affected him.

"What do you know about that?"

"Not a lot," she admitted, with a single shoulder shrug. "Just what I've heard from others. Look, I don't mean to pry but I'm just worried it will bring up bad memories for her. She seems to be in a difficult place right now."

She was within arm's reach, and it was all he could do not to grab her by the forearm and shake her. If he thought he'd lost all rational thought before, it was nothing compared to the present.

How fucking dare she? How dare she question his protective instincts toward Ally. Most days, that's all he could think about.

Where was she, who was she with? Were they dependable? Did they understand that Ally was all he had left of his family? And how in God's name could he ensure she never had to suffer from his misguided decisions ever again?

He twisted his neck to each side until he heard it crack. Hoping to gain some control and to allow the blood rushing through his veins to settle.

"I'm going to say this one time," he said as calmly as he could manage. "None of this is any of your business and I'd appreciate it if you'd stay out of it."

Her eyes lifted as her shoulders sagged. "What happened to helping each other out and keeping one another informed?"

"That didn't include unsolicited opinions. Poor judgment on my part," he said, pushing off the gate. "I didn't think you'd overstep." He stalked toward the opening of the barn doors.

"Overstep? How is caring about Ally's welfare overstepping?"

Alec turned on her, making her take an uncharacteristic step back.

"You haven't earned the right to worry about my sister's welfare."

"What? Do I have to take some kind of emotional aptitude test to care for Ally?"

"No, you have to be forthcoming and honest about who you are and where you came from."

"I told you," she said, taking yet another step back. "Our parents were killed in a car accident—"

"And you and your sisters were taken in and raised by a reclusive, highly protective uncle. . . . Yes, I've heard the story. Everyone in Wilder has heard your story."

"Look, I've been open and honest with you about Cara and Ally—"

"Where did you learn how to fight, Loren?"

She hesitated, looking around the barn as if for a lifeline.

He stalked her until she was cornered against the barn door. "Where. Did. You. Learn. To. Fight?"

He lifted his arm to lean above her and her arm instinctually raised in a defensive stance across her face as if he were to strike. He watched her reaction as she realized her otherworldly reflexes only further substantiated his skepticism.

Lowering her arm, she cleared her throat, staring into his chest. "Our uncle wanted to make sure we could protect ourselves so he had instructors come to the house for private lessons."

"Where did you live that would make him think that?"

She shook her head, either unable or unwilling to respond.

"A war zone?"

Her dark brown eyes shot up as if in surprise. She shook her head, and then forced a chuckle. "War zone. Funny, but no. My uncle was a peculiar man, conspiracy theorist, actually. He was convinced we were going to be taken over by some rogue country and that we had to be prepared to fight—"

"Stop," Alec said, weary. He pulled his arm down and shook his head. "Just stop, Loren." He slowly turned and made his way through the large doors.

He kept walking as she stood between the barn doors with her arms protectively crossed in front of her.

"You may be considered the second coming to the people of Wilder, but you're a lousy friend."

He stopped and turned, his breath nearly clogged in his throat as he took in her disheveled appearance. If he thought she was beautiful when she was full of sass and fire, she was ethereal and surreal when broken and desperate, her hair peeking out from beneath the ridiculous knit hat, her eyes full and watery. But he had to remember he didn't really know who she was. It could be an act for all he knew.

"I never signed up to be your friend, Loren. Frankly, it doesn't look like you're hurting for friends, considering they travel all the way from Russia to see you."

"Vlad knew my uncle. But you're right. He's just a friend."

"Most people who wake up looking like they've been freshly fucked, are more than friends."

Her arms splayed to the side. "I don't even know Vlad that well."

"So, you always walk around strangers wearing next to nothing?"

"Vlad is here for Mercy. I barely know him."

"You said he was a friend of the family. Was that not true?"

"Yes. No. It's— Complicated." She held her forehead in her hands. "Why do you even care?"

He turned and hung his head for a moment. Taking a deep breath, he said, "You fight like a well-trained assassin, your sisters have remarkable gifts in music and art, you don't have a full-time job and appear not to need one, you don't have a notion as to how to comport yourself unless it's around your fitness minions at the church, or dancing on bar tables. You watch movies to learn social cues. No one knows who you really are, where you came from, or what your real reasons are for coming to Wilder."

She walked closer despite the hostility radiating off him, and he had to admire her for her temerity. "Look, I'm sorry. You're angry. And you're right, that was out of line and none of my business regarding how you raise Ally."

He remained unmoved, his hands on his hips.

Distract, deflect, deter. She was an amazing liar.

"I don't pretend to have all the answers when it comes to parenting. I'm just doing my best, and I know you are, too."

He nodded once and watched her swallow nervously as if she wanted to say more but decided against it. She looked off to the side and into the murky darkness; the only light came from the house.

"Well, I can see I've managed to wear out my welcome," she deadpanned.

"Why did you stop by? You said you had some information?"

———

She made the mistake of looking at his face, to his impassive eyes and stern countenance.

Memories came barging into the forefront of her mind of various staff members at the Center. The ones who believed Dr. Halstead's mock psyche reports.

Nurse Hankowski, who checked her vitals every day and grew increasingly numb and oftentimes irritated at her constant pleas for help.

Professor Myers, her first math tutor who grew insecure as her skills outpaced what he was able to teach her and told the doctor that she was arrogant and unresponsive to his teaching. Lies that earned her her first face slap. She was fifteen.

Doctor Halstead, who told her during a heated argument about Cara's six-hour-long piano lessons, that she and her sisters were nothing more to him than potential revenue-generating lab rats, and at the least, collateral damage for the sake of science.

She remembered the staff's expressions as she begged them to just listen.

Expressions that were turned off and devoid of feeling.

Dismissive.

And once again, she was being dismissed.

After a while, two or three years, she quit trying. Quit asking for help, quit pushing back on her relentless schedule and harsh treatment by her various mentors.

The exception being if it concerned her sisters.

She learned to pick her battles, reserved each one on behalf of Mercy and Cara. But when it came to her, she found it easier to acquiesce.

She pushed those memories into one of her mental compartments and slammed the lid shut.

Shaking her head robotically, she slipped her hands in her back pockets and looked down at the ground. "It was nothing. I mean, it wasn't anything important."

"Are we done here?" he asked, tilting his head toward the house, indicating he was in fact done with her.

"We are."

She waited a minute or two, remaining rooted just outside the barn and digging her boots in the hard-packed dirt. Finally, she couldn't help herself, and glanced up to watch him as he reached the porch steps, the screen door slamming behind him.

Not until then did the tears leak down her cheeks.

Freaking waterworks.

She chastised herself for letting him get to her, wiping them away. She didn't need him. She didn't need anybody. She could take care of her family without anyone's help.

On top of that, she was a good person. Yes, she'd poisoned the doctor, and that certainly left a blemish on her otherwise pristine life. And then there was that poacher in Galapagos she'd knifed. But then, she was pretty sure that was nothing more than a superficial wound. As long as he didn't bleed out.

Closing the barn door, she grasped her arms against the cold, watching her steamy breath waft through the crisp air and marched toward her car.

There was also that goon who'd cornered her in the crime boss's office, while trying her hand at cracking the wall safe. Naturally, she got the precious stones but unfortunately it was at the goon's expense. But come on, he was armed, so it was self-defense. He was the bad guy.

Reaching her car, she turned on the engine and then the heat.

Maybe recounting these past transgressions wasn't a good idea, but one thing was for sure: She was a survivor. She'd made some mistakes, but by God, she was doing her best to correct them. To that end, she would do everything it would take to protect her sister and Ally from Amarilla Simmons and her posse.

She may not be June Cleaver, but she certainly knew how to wield one. Not as well as Mercy—but still.

———

Loren shut the front door behind her and then leaned against it, grateful for the warmth inside her small but cheerful home. The chill outside was nothing compared to Alec's arctic disposition.

She needed to find Mercy, discuss last-minute details for tonight's mission, and get this over with.

Operation Amarilla was well underway.

Without Alec's help.

She and her sister worked better alone anyway.

"Mercy," she called from the bottom of the staircase. "It's colder than a witch's tit outside. You may want to put on an extra layer of clothes. Maybe long underwear."

She waited for a response, looked around, made her way to the sunroom, but Mercy wasn't there. She rerouted to the kitchen where she found her sister at the table, glued to her laptop. She was dressed as instructed in all black but also with a stricken look on her face.

"Hey, what's the deal? Didn't you hear me?"

Mercy looked up, shaking her head. "I think we're in for more than we bargained for."

"What?"

"Mean girls," Mercy explained, pointing at her laptop screen. "I've been doing research on mean girls, like Amarilla Simmons. I'm telling you, Loren, they're no joke."

"What are you talking about? We can totally handle a middle school bully," Loren scoffed, scooting a chair next to hers. "I mean, come on. We've been physically threatened by a radical group from the Russian Foreign Intelligence Service." She sat back in a chair with a sigh. "Speaking of rogue Russians, where's Vlad?"

Mercy waved her hand indiscriminately. "I dunno, somewhere reading Dostoyevsky or carving nesting dolls."

Mercy flipped her screen toward Loren with a serious expression. "Don't discount the intel. We need to better understand what we're up against with Amarilla and her cohorts. Today, I watched *Mean Girls*, *Cruel Intentions*, and *Freaks and Geeks*. These girls are beyond evil and cruel."

"Please, naming your daughter Amarilla is evil and cruel," Loren muttered as she pulled off her beanie, running her fingers through her newly bleached hair. "Besides, I'm not sure we should be assuming Amarilla's character based on mean girls portrayed in Hollywood movies."

"Tell you what," Mercy continued, "you watch the clips I saved and then tell me what you think."

"Fine," Loren said, clicking on the first video. "Go upstairs and put on your long underwear and some black gloves. It's freezing outside. I don't want you catching a cold." Raising her hands, she wiggled her fingers. "But cut the tips off the gloves in case we have to scale a building. I don't want you hurting yourself because you couldn't get a grip on a drain pipe."

"Yes, Grandma," Mercy smirked as she scooted back in her chair and ran up the staircase.

Twenty minutes later, Mercy returned to the kitchen suited up and protected from the elements and slippery rain pipes. She sat next to Loren and crossed her arms in front of her chest.

"Well?"

Loren turned toward her with a stoic expression. "We're going to need your Bushcraft knife." She hesitated and then continued with a sneer and narrowed eyes. "Which we both know is *mine*. I'll grab the crossbow in the garage. We'll need to stop by a pharmacy on the way for a few extra supplies."

Mercy smiled with vindication and then raced back up the stairs.

Loren blinked at the screen. "These girls show no fear; therefore, we have to come at them fully armed."

CHAPTER EIGHTEEN

"A mathematician is a blind man in a dark room looking for a black cat which isn't there."

—Charles Darwin
English naturalist whose scientific theory of evolution by natural selection became the foundation of modern evolutionary studies

The beautifully complex melody wafted through Cara's mind until it was rudely interrupted by the sound of a car door opening and closing outside her bedroom window. She closed her eyes again and picked up where the music left off. It had been dreamy and sweet, the opposite of her current persona, and also the perfect escape to her current situation.

Crud, now she heard voices outside.

Her sisters?

The music continued in the background of her mind, so she hummed along so as not to lose the notes. They were so bright and nostalgic, guiding her back to memories of concert halls, enthralled audiences, and Madame Garmond's rare smile of admiration, and maybe even something like parental pride.

Another sound from outside halted her melody and musings.

She pulled herself from the warmth of her bed and peeked outside.

The front porch Edison bulb gave off just enough light for her to see Loren lift the trunk to the car with Mercy at her side.

Were they leaving?

She moved back, standing just to the side of the curtains.

They looked like they were leaving. "Please leave, please," she whispered with her hands clasped beneath her chin.

Over the last several days, she had composed over a dozen pieces. But her sisters had dogged her every step, policing the baby grand as if it was court evidence.

When submerged in the throes of artistic desperation, she'd play the virtual piano with her fingers on any nearby surface: the new desk they'd bought at IKEA, the scarred kitchen table, or the keyboard cover itself. But running her fingers over the cover, so close to the keys, was almost too painful for her to bear. After a few torturous notes, she'd revert back to the kitchen table.

Not the best acoustics, but whatever.

She pulled the curtain back a smidge and smiled. The mere thought of finally touching those ivory keys made her fingertips hum with anticipation.

If they left, she could play until she was breathless.

The idea had her full-on smiling as she watched Mercy pick up what looked to be . . . a crossbow to place inside the trunk?

Her smile faltered.

And then her eyes moved to Loren, who was loading other highly questionable items into the trunk as well.

A crowbar?

Duct tape?

What?

Memories of when they lived at the Center came to mind.

A mission?

In hindsight, Madame Garmond had done her best to insulate Cara, or rather Charlotte, from her sisters' "trips."

"Your sisters are going on an exciting trip to Copenhagen, where Ava will recite the entire number sequence of pi while Mara attends her first art show at Charlottenborg Palace."

Cara wondered if Madame Garmond knew the truth of her sisters coerced missions. Considering that possibility was as painful to her as being forbidden to touch the ivory keys.

On a few occasions, she had watched Jasper direct Ava and Mara through the halls at the Center, wearing dark clothes that looked more stealthy than fashionable.

Like they were dressed now.

She wasn't sure what they were up to, but whatever it was, it was dangerous. And it had nothing to do with math conventions or art shows.

They could get hurt.

Her hand that was unconsciously strumming on the window sill came up to rub her forehead and then came forward to lean lightly on the windowpane.

They'd *promised*.

Her eyes squeezed shut and then reopened with resounding conviction.

Loren and Mercy were the only family she had left. There was no way she was going to allow them to do something reckless.

Something that could prevent them from returning.

She pictured herself blocking the driveway, like a protestor in an Asian country standing in front of a heavily armed military tank.

She raced down the stairs to first stop them and then question them. They were up for a rude awakening if they thought their interrogation skills could hold a candle to hers.

She turned into the hallway and opened the front door only to watch the car pull out of the driveway.

A frisson of fear ran up her neck and her heart pounded in her chest.

She just couldn't lose them.

And as angry and frustrated as she was with them for grounding her, she knew she had to protect them. Because as brilliant as they were, they were also highly deficient in the art of self-preservation and, to a larger degree, common sense.

What to do?

Find her confiscated cell phone and call them.

Call them out.

It had to be somewhere in the kitchen.

As she raced back toward the kitchen, she noticed Mercy's laptop on the table. She stopped, wondering if she could find information to calm her nerves in the off-chance she was overreacting. Sifting through the history on the device, she scrolled through a list of recent movies she'd watched, looking for clues.

She sat back in her chair, confused.

Just your basic coming-of-age movies?

Again, absolute geniuses in their own right, but deficient in knowing how to behave in ways that the small town of Wilder considered normal.

A notepad sat next to the laptop on the table. Picking it up, she read through the cryptic notes.

- **Evil**
- **Befriend others who are 'like-minded'**
- **Can exhibit violent behavior**
- **Stealthy, know how not to get caught**
- **Cannot address through traditional means**
- **Amarilla = kingpin = first point of contact**

"No." She sucked in a breath as she connected the dots and realization hit. "No, no, no!"

Jetting out of the chair, she ran to the staircase and shouted for Vlad. No answer.

Where was an obtrusive Russian when you needed one?

Okay, back to plan A: cell phone.

The kitchen cabinet.

She lunged at the latched door where Loren had hidden Mercy's brass knuckles after using them to pry off a bottle cap. She flung open the cabinet only to see a white piece of paper folded over with a handwritten note:

"Dearest Cara, aka Devil's Spawn, your cell phone has been buried in a water-tight can in the back yard (at least I think it's water-tight - I always get confused between water-tight and water-resistant). Good luck finding it as we just planted two hundred daffodil bulbs. ~ Mercy"

Cara did her best to summon an expletive and screamed in frustration instead.

She had no choice. She had to run to the neighbor's house and ask for help before her sisters did something they would all regret.

Pulling her coat over one shoulder, she thought of the one person who would know what to do. Who, with absolute resolve, was able to calm her nerves and help her focus. Whether it was stage fright or a post-concert interview in a foreign country, this person had the ability to set her nerves aright and bolster her self-confidence.

Oh, how she missed her.

She wondered if she'd listened to the voicemail yet? It was a desperate move she'd made when she was at an all-time low.

Would Loren be disappointed in her?

Would Mercy lose her ever-loving mind?

She couldn't decide which was worse.

Cara bent over at the waist with her hands on her knees and drew in several breaths. She stifled a sob and stood.

No time for regrets now.

Mercy's black boot smacked Loren in the face as she fell from the perimeter wall.

"What the hell?" Loren spit out a clump of dirt and a leaf as her sister righted herself. "I swear we used to be better at this."

"Well, excuse me. It's been a while since I scaled an eight-foot wall."

"We're getting soft," Loren said. "We've become complacent and ineffectual."

"Jeez, Loren, chill. My foot got caught on a vine."

Loren sat back on her haunches and took a moment to take in the view. They were at the back of the property that overlooked some pretty impressive landscaping, a pool, and a number of entrances to the house itself.

Swanky place. Not a single detail had been overlooked.

According to Becky, Amarilla's mother was the widow of a high-profile and questionably affluent state senator. Since the death of her husband, her mother had become as influential and heavily feared by her neighbors as her daughter was by her peers in high school.

Apparently, the acorn didn't fall far from the genera *Quercus* and *Lithocarpus*.

Mercy sidled up next to Loren, taking in the view as well. "It's like . . . house porn."

Loren refocused and rolled out the schematic of the property she'd found online. The contractor used the high-profile customer as a testimonial on their website, lucky for her. They'd uploaded the CAD drawings along with photos of the finished interior for the multimillion-dollar mansion.

Idiots.

"Ooh, what variety of *hostas* are these?" Mercy asked, fingering a bluish-green leaf.

Loren peeked over the top of her printed schematic. "They look like Canadian Blue."

"Wouldn't they look great on the west side of the house?" Using her hands for illustration purposes, she added, "You know, where there's that empty space between the azaleas?"

Loren tilted her head with wide eyes. "We're trespassing and about to break and enter, and you want to discuss landscaping?"

"Good point," Mercy nodded, circling her hand for Loren to proceed. "Continue."

Loren sighed and pointed at the drawings.

"Amarilla should be here, in the bedroom northeast of the structure. You take the crossbow, and I'll take the duct tape, screwdriver, and crowbar."

"I don't understand the need for the heavy artillery if all we're going to do is scare her. I mean, what's the use of a perfectly good crossbow if it's unarmed?"

"Because the mission is to scare the living piss out her, not go to jail for a felony."

"What makes you think she's not gonna recognize us and rat us out?"

Loren reached into her duffel and pulled out two masks.

"Seriously?" Mercy asked with wide eyes. "Wonder Woman?"

"It's all they had a Walgreens."

Loren pulled her mask on and Mercy grabbed her arm. "Hold on, why do you get to be Iron Man?"

"It doesn't matter," Loren hissed, "this isn't a costume competition."

"Then if it's no big deal, I want Iron Man."

Loren tore the mask off and wrenched the other from Mercy. "Jesus, what are you, ten?"

Mercy put the mask on with a smile and muttered, "Everyone knows Iron Man trumps Wonder Woman."

"I would think you of all people would be pro-female-super-hero."

Her sister shrugged. "I dunno, there's something real about a somewhat broken genius in a homemade badass suit fighting criminal aliens."

"Broken genius," Loren mused, "that's certainly an accurate description."

"Right?"

"Back to the plan," Loren continued, pointing at the document. "We'll enter through these sliding glass doors. Locks are easier to disable. Then we'll go through the living room up the staircase and hang a left to Amarilla's room. I'll wake her up, duct tape her mouth while you point the crossbow at her. I'll tell her we're part of a top secret special forces team put in place to deter bullying in schools."

Mercy snorted. "Oh, that's believable."

"Then," Loren sneered, "I'll tell her she must cease and desist or we'll come back, but this time using force."

"You're kidding me, right? Sounds like a really shitty after-school special."

"Do you have any better ideas?"

"Yeah, we grab the entitled little princess by the hair, shove her skanky ass to the wall and tell her if she doesn't stop terrorizing people, we're going to systematically hunt her and her family down and gut them with a dull spoon. And then, to prove our point, we remove each of her fingernails with steel pliers."

"Good God, Mercy."

"What? It's not like it would be the first time."

"This is a young girl in high school, not a Colombian drug lord." Loren rolled up the schematic. "And besides, we never gutted anybody with a spoon, and as for fingernails, they grow back."

"Did you not *just* say that we were becoming complacent and ineffectual?"

Loren closed her eyes, took a deep cleansing breath, and opened them. "Just follow my lead and let me do the talking."

CHAPTER NINETEEN

"In mathematics, you don't understand things. You just get used to them."

—Johann von Neumann
Child prodigy who at six years old,
could divide two eight-digit numbers
in his head and converse in Ancient Greek

"What do you mean your sisters can sometimes overreact in a crisis?"

Cara felt perched on a slippery slope. One false move and all efforts prior to this moment would be for naught.

She sat in the back seat of Alec's truck with her hands tucked between her knees. She needed to choose her words wisely; this was no time to overshare.

"I wouldn't say this is a crisis, per se, but my sisters can be freakishly overprotective. And I wouldn't want anyone to get hurt, uh, get their feelings hurt because they overreact."

"Overprotective like your uncle?"

Dr. Halstead? That's right, Loren referred to the doctor as their "uncle." *Nothing like that.* "Something like that," she said, glancing forward and to her right.

Ally sat mute in the passenger seat, quiet and resolute in their pact to keep their problems to themselves.

The truth was that Amarilla Simmons and her plastic friends had become a veritable bane to their existence. They were like vultures rummaging for easy prey who set their sights on Ally and started to peck.

Once they found her to be easy fodder, they'd included her sidekick, Cara, and begun to torment her as well. Cafeteria trays were upended, strategically so that the food splattered on their clothes. Notes were sent to popular boys, as if written by Cara and Ally, lamenting to them their unrequited love and adoration. Notes, to their mortification, ending with: "Will you take me to the prom? Please check yes or no in the squares below." Lockers were tampered with and sometimes defaced with spray paint that spelled out "loser" or "poser," or the worst one, which was "pathetic orphan."

Cara and Ally figured they were the chosen ones to persecute because they were comparatively meek and mild. So, they decided to transform their perceived "weak" demeanors.

They would become strong and indifferent.

At the same time, refusing to stoop to Amarilla's level.

The unapproved trip to Dallas was with others who had fallen under Amarilla's sights in the past, and were given temporary reprieve once Ally and Cara became targets.

The girls couldn't have been more surprised when this group of Amarilla-pegged misfits asked them to go to Dallas to watch a cover band for Queen.

Music was their ultimate escape, and this group of potential friends who shared in their passion was just too important to dismiss.

So, in an effort to gain some type of camaraderie within a group that had also been tormented by Amarilla and her comparatively larger group of untouchables, they agreed to go.

Power in numbers and all that.

Unfortunately, their new personas had seeped into their relationships at home. But there was just no way they were going to mess up the chance of having more friends by asking permission to do things they knew would be denied.

And if they told Alec, Loren, and Mercy the truth of their predicament, there was no telling what they'd do. Loren and Alec would probably opt for homeschooling to protect them from a "hostile school environment," but Mercy would go all Helter-Skelter on Amarilla and her friends.

Sister had a thing with gutting people.

Cara continued to navigate her slippery slope solo-style as Ally lost the ability to articulate a complete sentence.

Alec didn't seem equally affected.

He continued with the questioning. "So, we're going to Amarilla Simmons' house, after midnight, because your sisters are overprotective and you're afraid they might hurt her feelings?" His fingers tapped on the steering wheel with what seemed to Cara as barely restrained irritation.

He wasn't even remotely convinced.

Beady and skeptical eyes looked at her through the rearview mirror.

Cara's eyes broke away from his glare and stared at her hands she was now squeezing together. She didn't like to lie, but the truth was too risky. Loren would never forgive her if she told anyone, let alone Alec. And Mercy would eviscerate her. In her sister's favorite words, "... with a dull spoon."

"That's it," she assured him, looking out the side window so he couldn't read the deception in her eyes.

Cara exhaled as Alec's gaze moved to Ally.

"You have anything of value to add to this conversation?"

Cara watched Ally raise her eyebrows as if completely oblivious to the situation. Pointing at herself, she said, blinking her eyes repeatedly with abject innocence, "Me? I don't know anything."

Cara watched the trees and prairie grass along the roadside flit by as she contemplated the multitude of sins she'd amassed in the last few weeks.

What would Madame Garmond say?

She hung her head in shame while her heart ached.

She was lying to Alec and her older sisters about what was going on between herself, Ally, and Amarilla. She was also lying to Alec and Ally about their past, withholding the truth behind her sisters' excessive training in espionage and hand-to-hand combat and missions where very bad things happened that even she wasn't sure about. Not to mention Loren's obsessively protective nature.

Loren wasn't as violent as Mercy, but she had a long history of putting herself at considerable risk to protect her sisters. And they couldn't take the chance of Jasper finding them.

They just couldn't go back to the Center. It was nothing short of hell on earth to watch her older sisters be ignored and even ridiculed by certain staff members who believed Dr. Halstead's false diagnoses.

Not to mention Jasper.

Worst of all her sins, she prayed that Jasper had died in the trunk of his car. Now, she was agonizingly fearful of being found and regretted the compassion she had demanded of her sisters the day they escaped.

Oh, how she prayed he'd suffered a slow, painful death.

And then she prayed for forgiveness for wishing him dead.

Looking back, she and Ally could have handled this whole situation with Amarilla and her goons so much better than they did. But she couldn't turn back now. If she did, she could lose Ally as a friend.

She closed her eyes and prayed they weren't too late and that Amarilla could still draw breath by the time they arrived.

She thought of the one parental figure she'd had in her life.

Madame Garmond.

Who would say, in her vaguely odd Parisian dialect, *"Ah, ma petite cherie, ca c'est la beaute de sagesse rétrospective.* My little darling, that is the beauty of hindsight."

Smoke from the cigarette wafted around Jasper's head as he listened over the phone to the words he had been patiently waiting to hear.

He exhaled another puff of smoke and then snuffed the butt out in the crystal ashtray on his desk. "And you're sure this is where they are?"

"Yes sir, one of the girls reached out to the informant. They confirmed their location."

The voice hesitated, and then continued, "Are we ready to execute the extraction, Dr. Bancroft?"

"Not yet. I have a few obstacles to address before their return. Keep me posted with news from our informant, and I'll let you know when it's time."

He ended the call and sat back in his chair with his hands laced behind his head, his fingers grazing the scar from where he had been struck.

Precisely where he would instruct Dr. Vielle to place his first incision.

The sides of his mouth turned slightly up at the thought of finally besting the great Ava Halstead, aka Loren Wilder.

Yes. He'd gladly give them more time.

Time to get comfortable, maybe a bit more complacent.

Time to relish their newfound, albeit temporary, freedom; it would be all the more devastating for them and satisfying to him, when it all slipped through their fingers.

CHAPTER TWENTY

"Do not worry too much about your difficulties in mathematics, I can assure you that mine are still greater."

Albert Einstein
German-born theoretical physicist best known to the general public for his mass-energy equivalence formula $E=mc^2$

Loren crouched behind the raised hot tub with Mercy close behind. She waited for any unanticipated motion detection alerts.

Nothing.

She predetermined, after some quick hacking, that the home was equipped with a security system, but the service had been recently terminated by the owner.

Unsure whether to find that odd or fortuitous, she decided to assume the owner was in the process of switching security companies.

Certain they remained undetected, she sidled up to the sliding glass door farthest from the master bedroom that led into the spatial living room.

She assessed the expansive glass doors.

Sliding doors were manufactured with two different styles: the slides were either on the inside or the outside of the fixed panel. The latter being the easier to open. She smiled at their good luck as the slider was on the outside. It would have been far more difficult—if not impossible—to pry open, otherwise.

After pulling out a small crowbar and screwdriver from her bag, Mercy clicked on a small penlight from over her right shoulder and Loren went to work.

She inserted the screwdriver between the door and the doorframe, six inches from the corner and diagonal from the latch, and pried it upward. She tilted the door, which lowered the latch, and visibly smiled as she heard it release from the bracket.

Moving the door to the side with just enough room for her and Mercy to slip through, they moved inside. They crept silently toward the staircase which, according to the drawings, was past the front hallway and to the left.

The room was almost pitch-black, as they felt their way past an eight-piece sectional sofa.

And then Loren blinked and had to shield her eyes from the blinding bright light to her right. The light came to her first as the geometrics of an illuminated net, not a usual occurrence when an unexpected sensory hit her retinas.

The source of the light lowered as Mercy ran into her backside, equally addled, but just as quickly raised the crossbow toward the source.

Loren heard the unmistakable sound of a rifle pump as her eyes began to readjust to see an elderly man sitting in a recliner with what looked to be a Winchester 61 perched on his shoulder, pointed directly at them.

"Whoa there, sir," Loren said, taking a step in front of Mercy, with one hand pushing her farther behind her and the other hesitantly raised, "that thing could take an eye out."

"Young lady, I don't think you're in any position to be telling me what to do."

Which was true, considering he was the only one in the room with an armed weapon. A weapon that was typically used for target practice and small game hunting, but a weapon nonetheless.

"Told you we should've armed the crossbow with bolts," Mercy clipped, reading her mind.

The man had to be in his mid seventies. His gray hair was askew and he was decked out in flannel pants and a white tee. Despite his dishevelment, he was spry enough to keep the vintage rifle trained on her.

Behind her, Mercy hissed, "You said the security system was disabled."

The elderly man also had great hearing as he answered for her. "Fired the greedy bastards. They wanted over a hundred bucks a month for their fancy security system. I paid a one-time fee of three hundred dollars to Amazon and put up my own cameras."

Loren forced herself to relax her shoulders and plastered a bright smile on her face, hoping he'd mirror her demeanor. "Wow, we are such dunces. We were staying with friends and must've gotten their house mixed up with yours." She lifted her Iron Man mask and laughed. "See, costume party." She started to move back the direction they came, keeping Mercy behind her. "We'll just be on our way."

The rifle moved up an inch as he got a better grip on the action slide arm. "Did I mention the cameras have audio capabilities? Heard every word you two said."

Loren stopped in her tracks, trying to remember the details of what they'd discussed after scaling the wall.

He lowered his rifle, slightly. "Allow me to refresh your memory. You're here to scare the bejeezus outta my granddaughter, Amarilla."

Loren's shoulders sagged. "Yes, sir."

"Then I suggest you put down that worthless crossbow and tell me what my ornery granddaughter's been up to."

Loren glanced back at Mercy, who was removing her useless mask, and then back to the man. "I'm going to need you to lower your rifle, sir."

"You gonna sit down and work this out like sane and decent human beings?"

His eyes were full of reproach, which made Loren feel like a silly teenager rather than the fighting machine that she was.

She swallowed heavily and nodded. "Yes, sir."

The rifle lowered and then Loren and Mercy sidled toward the sofa, Loren keeping her eyes on the gun until she deemed they were safe.

He finally set it on the arm of his chair, which she estimated would give them enough time to bolt before he could re-aim and cock the Winchester, if and when it became necessary.

"My name is Levi. Why don't you introduce yourselves and then start at the beginning."

It didn't take long to share what Loren knew, as there wasn't much to tell, thanks to her close-mouthed sister and her equally tight-lipped accomplice. Thankfully, it was enough to explain why they were sitting on this man's sofa well past midnight and with unarmed weapons.

Then they heard what sounded like a car pulling into the driveway.

Three heads turned toward the sound of a key unlocking the front entryway and watched as an oblivious Amarilla surreptitiously eased through the door and then froze as she spotted the tableau of faces staring back at her from the living room.

Amarilla attempted a smile as if trying to regroup. "Grandaddy, oh good, you're up."

Loren recognized that the girl was doing her best to calm herself as she absentmindedly shoved the door behind her and woodenly made her way toward them. She knew the feeling.

"Come on in here and sit down, Amarilla. You have some explaining to do."

Loren watched the girl hesitate and purse her lips, pushing a tendril of long blond hair behind her ear. She slowly made her way toward them, as if equally aware as to who was in her living room and to her imminent doom.

"I'm sorry I'm late, Grandad. We were studying and time got away from me."

"Save that conversation for later. I wanna hear why you're being hateful to some of the younger girls at school, namely Cara Ingalls and Ally Wilder."

Loren watched with fascination as she battled between feeling sorry for the girl and wanting to slap her. She was just a wisp of a thing. Beautiful really, but dressed rather inappropriately for her age. That knowledge acquired from the Nazi-style training she'd received from Cara when they went clothes shopping, during the good old days of yore, when her sister chose to move about in human form.

Despite her suggestive attire, the girl's makeup was applied remarkably well.

Still, despite artistically blended contour, her clothes were far too revealing, but Loren had to admit she'd worn similar clothing items; hipster jeans which showed off a taut midriff with a halter top that exposed side and front boobage.

Loren also noticed she didn't carry a backpack that would hold books for studying, but there was a sizable red welt on the side of her neck. Loren took in a breath, catching the strong scent of patchouli as well as an undercurrent of something more woodsy.

Amarilla's demeanor was the opposite of the caricature Loren had imagined while planning her set-down. She'd imagined your typical female bully, someone more ballsy and rife with entitled self-confidence. She pictured a hefty girl dressed in camo, one hand holding a cigarette while the other dunked Cara's head in one of the toilets in the girl's restroom at school.

Instead, the young girl was rather pathetic. She sat hunched over in the chair on the other side of the coffee table opposite her grandfather with nothing less than deep shame.

"This is about your mama," he said matter-of-factly.

Amarilla glanced up, shaking her head as if beseeching him not to continue this line of dialogue.

Levi turned to them, and explained, "My daughter, Amarilla's mother, left six months ago. Ran off with the man who cleans the pool. He's quite a bit younger than my daughter. Closer to Amarilla's age than her mother's. They've been cruisin' along the Mediterranean on a fancy yacht. As you can imagine, my granddaughter hasn't taken it well." His eyes moved to Amarilla. "And she's been taking it out on some of the younger girls at school. You aren't the first ones to show up complaining about my granddaughter's treatment of their kin."

Loren remarked with wide eyes, "Your mom is having an affair with the pool boy?" She shook her head. "That sucks."

Mercy leaned toward Loren and muttered, "In all fairness, we haven't actually *seen* the pool boy."

Loren turned her head toward Mercy and whispered, "How can you be so insensitive? How would you feel if Mom had been screwing someone half Dad's age?"

"You mean rather than getting killed in a car accident?" she asked sarcastically.

"Hypothetically speaking."

"And Dad's gone?"

"Hypothetically."

"I'd say, 'Good for you, you randy cougar. Go get 'im.'"

Amarilla suddenly had tears in her already red-rimmed eyes. "He told me he loved me."

The sisters simultaneously gasped.

"The pool boy? No, he didn't," Loren spat.

At the same time, Mercy blurted, "That mother—"

An obviously still-smitten Amarilla sighed deeply and said, "He prefers to be referred to as an aquatic engineer."

Whereby Mercy said, "Oh, I've got some names for that rotten son of a—"

A loud throat clearing from the entryway interrupted the united commiseration.

They all turned to see Alec, Ally, and Cara standing mute in the doorway, save of course, the throat clearing from Alec. Amarilla had not completely closed the door after realizing she'd been caught coming in past curfew.

Loren sat tall, glaring at her neighbor. "What are you doing here?"

Alec rubbed the back of his neck as he said dryly, "According to Cara, someone was in dire danger of getting her feelings hurt."

Loren felt the heat in the room increase in equal measure to the intense gaze she received from her surly neighbor.

She needed air, as she felt light-headed from just looking at him. Is this what Amarilla felt after she inhaled? Could that be the feeling that seduced people into becoming voluntarily altered?

So why partake in illegal substances when all anyone had to do was stargaze at Alec Wilder?

And could anyone blame her? Those large hands teased her by lightly resting on his hips. Hips that appeared slim due to an abnormally large chest.

As a result of his physique, his light blue polo was tight in the chest with room in the waist, his jeans riding low enough that if he needed to stretch just the tiniest bit, she would have a front row seat to the dusted trail of hair that converged below his belly button and lower to destinations unknown.

But wildly anticipated.

No! Nonononono! She wasn't going to sit here and fantasize about a man who summarily dismissed her not eight hours ago.

That was the epitome of pathetic.

"Hey." Mercy nudged her, yanking her out of her Alec-induced state.

Straightening her spine, she did her best to emulate an emotionally lucid adult. "Why, that's just silly, Mr. Wilder."

Hmm, where did the Southern accent come from?

It earned her upraised brows from her nemesis. She cleared her throat and continued, "No one's feelings are in danger here. Mercy and I just stopped by to have a civil conversation with Levi about what's been going on between Amarilla and our sisters."

"Civil? Who has a civil conversation after midnight?" He nodded his head toward Levi. "How ya doing, Levi? What's the rifle for?"

"I was just showing them my antique Winchester before Amarilla got home. Ain't she a beaut?"

Loren could have kissed the man if he wasn't, you know, a relic.

Her eyes trailed back to Alec and despite the blatant eye-candy before her, reminded herself that she still stung from his earlier treatment.

"So, you're into vintage rifles?" His demeanor all but screamed *liar*.

"I am." Hers whispered, *disprove it*.

"Okay, I'll bite. What do you know about the Winchester 61?"

Her narrowed brown eyes latched onto ocean-blue sardonic ones. "Oh, you mean the model designed by John Moses Browning? The popular pump-action twenty-two rifle that was made from nineteen thirty-two up until nineteen sixty-three? That one?"

Thankfully, her mathematical aptitude came alongside an eidetic memory. There wasn't a single lesson forced upon her by Dr. Halstead that wasn't embedded in her brain.

"Now, why would a woman in her early twenties know the history of the Winchester 61?"

"Did I mention my conspiracy theorist uncle?"

"Once or twice. Maybe three hundred times." His expression communicated he still didn't believe a word of it.

"Mr. Wilder, I tried to talk to you today, but we all know how uncivil you can be. I decided it would be better for Mercy and me to meet with Levi on our own about Amarilla. You know, to stop the behavior before it gets any worse."

Everyone had forgotten the bully at hand until she spoke up. "Great, now everybody will know about mama and Manuelo." Amarilla fell back in her chair and stared resolutely at the ceiling.

"We won't tell anybody," Ally piped up. "We can keep a secret, can't we, Cara?"

"If you only knew," Cara said off-handedly.

Loren widened her eyes, which made Cara blink and attempt to detract from a weighted innuendo. "Which you won't," she stumbled, red-faced, "because I can keep a secret. I'm talking, you know, your typical everyday run-of-the-mill secret. Nothing too . . . dramatic."

Loren slowly closed her eyes at the highly ineffective attempt.

Mercy pursed her lips to the side, "I swear I'm going to gut her."

"So . . . everything is good here?" Alec asked, not quite following the vague conversation.

Levi said, "Before anybody leaves, I want my dear granddaughter to assure Cara and Ally that she's going to stop her shenanigans, call off her gang of female hoodlums, and cope with her wayward mama in a more productive manner."

The elderly man stood and glared at Amarilla, who turned to Cara and Ally, and said, "I promise, what he said." And then she amended with, "As long as you don't tell anybody about Mama and Manuelo."

Cara and Ally both nodded and Amarilla had no choice but to trust them. Quite the benign consequence considering what she had put them through.

Levi reached for the rifle and turned to his unexpected guests. "Now, if you'll excuse me, I have a disreputable aquatic engineer to hunt down and shoot."

CHAPTER TWENTY-ONE

"The moment one gives close attention to anything, even a blade of grass, it becomes a mysterious, awesome, indescribably magnificent world in itself."

—Henry Miller
American writer and artist whose
work was banned in the United States until 1961

Over the next couple of weeks life seemed to finally settle for the Ingalls sisters. Despite the calm, Loren felt antsy and somewhat neurotic. She couldn't shake the feeling that their idyllic life in Wilder was too good to be true.

She imagined a mean-spirited god, like the ones you see in those superhero movies, watching from above and waiting for that unsuspecting moment to once again agitate their world and wreak havoc.

Worse, she imagined Jasper tracking them down and bringing them back to the Center.

But not today.

Today she was going to set her neuroses aside and have some fun.

For today was Mercy's birthday, and she was turning twenty-one.

Loren wanted this day to make the list of "All-time favorite memories" for her sister. The day started with breakfast in bed, featuring a waffle with the numerical twenty-one candle perched in the center. It took several attempts and a wrecked kitchen, but she and Cara were able to create the perfect Belgian confection to begin Mercy's special day.

After inhaling the first couple of bites, the deluge of birthday presents began. First, she opened a picture from Cara of the three of them taken on the day Cara dyed her hair back to its original color. She also received a bracelet from Cara where the ends came together with tips that resembled the twisty sections of barbed wire. Cara called it "Edgy jewelry for her edgy sister."

Loren handed Mercy a full set of new paints to replenish those she'd used over the past few months, thanks to Vlad's assistance in mitigating her pain.

Vlad peeked his head in Mercy's bedroom door to hand her his own gift. Loren's eyebrows rose as Mercy slowly opened the tissue paper and sucked in a breath. She held up a portrait of herself. Rather crude compared to the art Mercy was able to put to canvas, but nevertheless a heartfelt attempt to capture her likeness.

"Vlad," she said as her fingertips lightly touched the canvas, barely concealing a forlorn smile. "I don't know what to say."

Loren watched the interaction with nothing short of fascination. The palpable longing that filled the handsome, and ever-patient Russian's eyes and the guilt-ridden gratitude reflected in Mercy's.

It was no secret to Loren that during the numerous all-night painting sprees, Vlad would stay up for hours waiting for Mercy to exhaust her pent-up stores of creative angst, until she'd collapse in a nearby chair. He'd then administer the medicine that would stem the migraines that were soon to follow.

Loren still couldn't quite figure out what was going on between her sister and the young doctor. Vlad spent his days at a distance from the girls yet never too far from Mercy, in case she needed his assistance. Content to be at her beck and call while remaining at arm's length.

Whereas Mercy appeared romantically unaffected but always close enough to appease what appeared to Loren as nothing short of tormented yearning in Vlad.

Mercy hugged the canvas to her chest with watery eyes as Vlad hung his head with a sheepish smile.

Awkward.

Lightening the mood, Cara pulled Mercy to the piano and played her a light and comical song she made in her sister's honor titled, "Oh, How You Gut Me."

Now, Loren and Mercy were on their way to Lucky's Tavern to celebrate with friends.

Loren, quite pleased with her efforts, billed it as the perfect ending to a perfect birthday.

Mercy grinned, bouncing in her seat. "What do you think I should order? A Guinness or a Cosmopolitan?"

Pulling into the gravel parking lot, Loren parked the car and turned to her. "Let's take it slow. Maybe try a lighter beer, like a Corona or Stella."

"Maybe I'll have a glass of wine. So sophisticated."

"Worst. Hangovers. Ever," Loren cautioned, and then thought about how the alcohol could possibly induce Mercy's migraines. "Is Vlad coming?"

"He said he'd check in later."

Loren hesitated and then blurted out, "Are you in love with him?"

Mercy gave her the side-eye. "Um . . . no."

"Sometimes you seem like you are."

"We're close friends. That's all." She glued her eyes to the window.

"Does *he* think you're just close friends?" Loren asked, knowing the answer to the question, but wondering if she did.

Mercy lifted a shoulder. "For the most part."

"For the most part? What does that even mean?"

"It means it's my birthday and I don't want to talk about Vlad. I want to celebrate my big day by having my first legal sip of an alcoholic beverage."

"Are you saying you've had your first illegal sip?"

"Ugh! No. I've never had any alcohol. I've never done drugs. I've never been on a date. Jesus Mercy, I've never been kissed. I'm about as inexperienced as it comes for a girl on her twenty-first birthday."

"Woman," Loren corrected. "You're not a girl anymore. You're a twenty-one-year-old woman."

"It takes more than a number to make you a woman," Mercy huffed, her hands shooting forward in agitation. "It takes years of decision-making. Some right, some wrong, hopefully learning from the wrong ones. It takes human interaction and thousands of normal, everyday experiences."

Loren's throat tightened at hearing Mercy echo her own feelings of inadequacy. Mercy clutched her hands in her lap as if to regain control of her emotions.

"Hey," Loren said with a soft voice. "Look at me."

Mercy turned her head toward Loren without making eye contact.

"You'll do all those things. I promise. Let's not worry so much about what we haven't done but get excited about all the things we get to do."

Mercy gave a slight nod.

Loren nudged her shoulder. "Like drink too much alcohol on your twenty-first birthday."

Mercy agreed with a tentative smile, "Let's do this."

Two hours and three Corona's later, Mercy was having a great time laughing and dancing around the tables with their friends.

Loren remained lucid enough to ensure her sister did nothing she'd regret while drinking just enough to enjoy a healthy buzz.

Checking her watch, she made her way to the bar, getting Gus' attention despite the packed seats.

"My order ready?" she yelled over the din of the crowd.

He lifted his finger, and skirted to the back, emerging with a white plastic sack. "One Gus' Special with extra sauce."

"Thanks," she said, taking the sack.

Gus yelled back, "Tell Jimbo I said hi."

She smiled over her shoulder. "Will do."

CHAPTER TWENTY-TWO

"It is not certain that everything is uncertain."

—Blaise Pascal
French child prodigy who became a mathematician, physicist, inventor, philosopher, writer, and Catholic theologian

Very few things surprised Alec.

And to a degree, he was okay with that.

Prime example: When Booger Williams left the sleepy town of Wilder to join a cult out west, Alec didn't bat an eye. And when rumors circulated that Larissa Haynes' prize Holstein gave birth to a two-headed calf, again, no uptick in the surprise factor.

Which was to be expected, pretty typical for ex-soldiers to regard civilians' perception of drama with detached cynicism. There was no doubt in Alec's mind that the sick and twisted shit that he'd witnessed in the desert had irreversibly affected him.

But it wasn't the atrocities of war that robbed him of the ability to become truly shocked.

Not even close.

Rather, it was coming home early on leave and witnessing his wife in all her whacked-out glory. So out of it mentally, she didn't even acknowledge him standing in front of her, grabbing her arms, shaking her as he yelled, "Marissa, look at me. Where the fuck is Ally?" She just continued to rock back and forth, singing some jacked-up children's rhyme.

She had reminded him of the insurgency-worn women of Afghanistan. Women who had finally lost it after seeing their families decimated, husbands executed, and their children slaughtered in the name of collateral damage.

And then his heart tanked. Where was Ally?

Racing up the staircase with his heart beating out of his chest, he swung the door open to Ally's bedroom, only to find it empty. Just as quickly, his head reared back as he picked up the stench of urine and human feces. And then saw the puddle from beneath the closet door at the same time he heard whimpering.

He nearly pulled the door off its hinges, but what he found inside literally brought him to his knees. Ally huddled in the far corner with her stick-thin arms hugging her knees with tears rolling down her face.

Leaning his elbow on bent knee, he scrubbed his face and then held his hand over his mouth as he witnessed the gut-wrenching fear in his little sister's eyes as she hugged the back wall, too panicked to notice who had opened the door.

He coaxed her out of the closet with soft words, repeating over and over, "It's okay, Ally. It's me, Alec. Everything's okay now." She finally looked up, suddenly hopeful at hearing his voice, and lifted her arms out to him. He held her tight to him as she sobbed into his shoulder and nearly lost it himself when he found the bruises and lacerations littered all over her small frame.

It wasn't much later when he learned that Marissa didn't witness atrocities but rather, she was the one who executed them.

That day pretty much drained him of any future astonishment for what he was sure would be the remainder of his life.

His reaction to the number of people dancing and singing at Lucky's Tavern tonight was mild, but it was enough to arch his eyebrows, which was still a rare thing for Alec Wilder.

Case in point, it was a weeknight. The people of Wilder didn't party on the weekends, let alone the weeknights. They didn't party as much as celebrate with reserved, pious dignity.

Second point, he walked inside to see that the crowd had pushed all the tables and chairs to the sides of the room. To see this many of his friends and neighbors dancing with their hands in the air, and in unison, bordered on . . . well, surprising.

The bar was packed, and he was forced to turn sideways to work his way through the bodies before he could get to the bar and flag Gus down.

"What's up with the crowd?" Alec asked with a raised voice, as Gus made his way toward him.

"Birthday," Gus yelled back. "Mercy Ingalls'."

Alec looked over his shoulder and found Mercy with Becky Waterman dancing and laughing together to the song "Down to the Honkytonk" with a half dozen other women. Becky appeared to be teaching her to line dance.

Sitting in the corner booth was Sue Ellen Whalen doing a shot of tequila with Edgar Mason. Sue had been love-sick for Edgar since middle school but too painfully shy to approach him. But there she was, tossing her mousy brown hair over her shoulder and laughing at whatever came out of Edgar's mouth and then out of nowhere, they began to arm wrestle.

And Edgar clearly liked it.

It seemed as if a number of the women of Wilder had morphed

into their alter-egos. They walked with their backs straighter, chins up, and skirts shorter.

He knew who'd prompted this change in this once lackadaisical community, as well as this evening's events. A certain smart-mouthed bleach-blonde. And this impromptu party must be the reason Cara was spending the night with Ally, so Loren and Mercy could hit the town without the risk of coming home hammered in front of their younger sister.

Pretty responsible strategy, as long as they were safe and circumspect.

His eyes scanned the room.

He didn't see the Russian.

Interesting.

Loren wasn't in the bar, either.

His jaw ticked. He was annoyed.

He turned back to Gus, who was handing a beer to the guy next to him. "Surprised her sister isn't here."

Gus jerked his thumb over his shoulder. "Out back with Jimbo." He wiped his hands on a bar towel. "Guinness?"

"Hold that thought. I'm gonna go check on Jimbo."

Gus returned a knowing smile, which Alec ignored as he shifted his body back through the crowd and out the front doors.

The noise level decreased significantly as the door latched behind him. He jammed his hands into his front pockets relieved for Jimbo's sake that they were having a mild winter, but thinking tonight might be the exception.

He followed the path to the back alley, past the large metal trash bins where he found his longtime homeless friend sitting on top of several woolen blankets, eating what looked to be a double-decker hamburger dubbed "The Gus Special."

Loren was sitting cross-legged on top of a wooden crate, laughing at something Jimbo said. "So, you told the little girl you were a Bedouin?"

Jimbo swallowed and grinned. "What? That's what I am. A nomad traveling the prairie as opposed to the desert."

"I guess it's all about perspective." She shrugged.

"How 'bout you, Miss Loren? Travel much?"

Alec remained in the shadows just outside of the lamplight next to the back door of the bar. He kept his presence unknown. There was no way he was going to miss an opportunity to learn more about this woman's elusive past.

He noticed she'd pulled her hair up in one of those messy buns. Platinum-blond wisps framed her face, and his chest warmed at overly large eyes that looked the color of rare whiskey. He watched her head dip as she repeatedly pulled at one of the zippers on her tall suede boots. "Yes and no."

Jimbo swallowed another bite. "What? You either do, or you don't."

She shrugged her shoulder. "I traveled a lot. All three of us did. But our schedules were tight. Not much time to explore or check out museums."

"I'm assuming that's because of that overprotective uncle of yours?"

She smirked and then with a sad turn of her head, smiled at Jimbo. "He didn't like for us to wander too much."

"What's the point of traveling if you can't wander?"

"I guess you could say he had his own agenda, and time to ourselves didn't serve it."

"Sounds like he wasn't very much fun to travel with."

She readjusted her weight, sitting up a little straighter. "He didn't travel with us per se; he sent us on trips with hired help. They were to keep an eye on us at all times. But don't you worry, Mercy and I found ways to fly under the radar and enjoy ourselves."

"Went into stealth mode, huh?"

"You could say that," she said with a wry grin. "During a . . . trip to Paris, we took the wrong line on the Metro and came out at Place de Pigalle, known for being one of the seedier parts of the city. Mercy was only seventeen at the time, and the first person we passed was a man dressed as a woman in six-inch metallic heels walking his fuchsia-dyed poodle down the street."

"What'd Mercy do?" Jimbo asked, sipping on his straw.

"She walked right up to him and politely asked for directions to where we were headed." She shook her head with a nostalgic half-smile on her lips. "And where she could find those same pair of heels."

They laughed together, and Alec's chest tightened at the sound.

And then Loren added, "That's when I realized that Mercy had been isolated for so long, that she didn't have any preconceived ideas as to those things that should take her by surprise."

"You wanted her to be shocked and outraged by Parisian transvestites with great taste in shoes?"

"No, of course not," she said with a smile that turned somber. "I just never want her to feel insecure because she doesn't know the first thing about fitting in."

"She's a good young lady, Miss Loren. You've raised her well, despite your uncle."

Alec watched her grin sheepishly at Jimbo's compliment. She said softly, making Alec strain to hear what she said.

"Sometimes I get so confused as to what's normal and what's the exception. It's exhausting to be constantly on the search for cues and clues. The best I can do is learn from movie scenes, books, and plain old every day observations, so that when the time is right, I can be sure to act accordingly in the right way at the right time. But to be honest, I miss the mark more often than not. And then I worry about what example I'm setting for Mercy and Cara."

Jimbo also got quiet. "You know what I wish for you and your sisters, Miss Loren?"

"An online discount for stripper footwear?" she panned cheekily.

"No, ma'am," he said with a tilt of his head and a slight smile. "My wish, for you and your sisters, is that each of you gets so comfortable in your own skin that you no longer need to mimic other people or worry about what other people think." Jimbo closed the plastic container and set it to the side, giving Loren time to marinate in his words. He smiled and clapped his hands together as if to change the mood. "So, did you and Mercy ever get to where you were going?"

She tilted her head in question.

"In Paris."

Loren shook her head and with a forced smile, she said, "No, our uncle's . . . staff found us before we made it to our destination."

As if the memory turned sour, she picked at a loose piece of wood on the crate and then chucked the sliver at the light. It ricocheted off the building's brick wall, landing next to Alec's boot.

Jimbo and Loren's attention turned his direction, so he felt compelled to move out of the shadows and into the glow of the security light.

CHAPTER TWENTY-THREE

"Arithmetic is numbers you squeeze from your head to your hand to your pencil to your paper 'til you get the answer."

—Carl Sandburg
Swedish-American poet, biographer, journalist, and editor who won three Pulitzer prizes: two for his poetry and one for his biography of Abraham Lincoln

"Evening, Jimbo," Alec said to break the silence.

"Well, hey there, Alec. Come on and join us. Plenty of room." Jimbo grinned.

Alec nodded, moving closer to the light. His hands moved to his front pockets as he leaned on the brick wall. For whatever reason, nerves started to settle in. "Nice weather we're having."

Oh, perfect. Now he sounded like Mercy with her repetitive tagline when greeting people. These days the entire town was greeting one another with, "Nice weather, isn't it?" in some sort of homage to the Ingalls sisters and the unexpected level of enthusiasm they instilled in everyone they came in contact with.

"Yes, sir." Jimbo nodded as he took another bite. "Mighty fine weather."

Alec finally lifted his gaze toward Loren. "Evening, Loren."

"Hey, Alec," she greeted, with her hands on her knees. "Are Cara and Ally still at your place writing the soundtrack to next year's box office hit?"

He smiled and nodded, but not before noticing that her green knit sweater fell to one side exposing a creamy white shoulder, the lamplight making her skin appear translucent.

He cleared his throat as he worked a rogue weed with the toe of his boot. "They'd moved on to a scary movie by the time I left."

"Nice," she said, her smile competing with the sexy roll of her whiskey-brown eyes. "Tonight, *you* get neurotic little sister duty." She turned toward Jimbo to further explain. "That's when Ally and Cara squeal at all hours, convinced that every sound they hear is someone coming to hack them with a chainsaw." Loren turned back toward Alec and smiled knowingly. "But they're happy and safe and that's what matters."

Alec nodded. "So true." He cleared his throat as the conversation started to lag. This was the longest non-confrontational conversation he'd had with his enigmatic neighbor and he didn't want it to end. "Thanks for letting Ally spend the night while I was out of town last week."

Lord, he was grasping for straws and Jimbo appeared just as confused, his head bobbing back and forth between them.

"Oh, yeah, not a problem. How did orientation go?"

Alec nodded. "Went well." Not sure what to add to that as details of his job weren't to be discussed due to the nature of his profession.

"They teach you the QWERTY keyboard and how to send and receive email?"

Alec nodded with a chuckle. "Something like that."

More like department protocol for how to remotely infiltrate city-wide video cams and hack into VPN's set up by targets. As a Raider he was usually the boots and brawn, not the one sitting behind the computer, but what they taught him he could have taught and then some.

Alec had asked for a low-key position as compared to his career with the Marines. He had a sister to raise, and until she graduated, he needed a job that would keep him home most nights. He could do that by pulling intel to track targets as opposed to securing them. He agreed to fieldwork only when his particular expertise was required and didn't require weeks of travel.

When and if that project came about and he was called out, he would ask if she could stay with the Ingalls. Which reminded him, he was to have his last debriefing next week and needed to ask if Ally could hang with them after school and maybe stay the night. When it came down to it, despite holes in their stories, the Ingalls' home base was as safe as a fortress of Amazonian warriors.

And one Russian.

Fucking Russian.

More conversation lag.

"So," Loren piped up, as if she too was working to revive a dying conversation, "the girls seem to be doing much better at school. Even made friends with Amarilla Simmons."

"Yeah, I've been checking in on Amarilla and her grandpa lately. Cara and Ally tag along. Soon as we get there, they run into Amarilla's room, giggle at high decibels and then I have to drag them out with wet nails and repetitive girl hugs."

"Like they won't all see each other the next day at school."

"Right." He nodded, kicked a brick embedded in dirt.

Again with the crickets.

Jesus Christ.

Okay, now he was pissed. Why was the conversation so easy and fluid between her and Jimbo, but shooting the shit with him seemed like a chore? Despite the not-so-distant past, when he preferred superficial convos with his lady friends, this wasn't going to cut it. Not even close. Maybe if he could talk to her alone, without Jimbo staring at them like they were alien transplants that just showed up out of nowhere and landed on his side of the sidewalk.

He sighed and rubbed his bottom lip with his thumb. He glanced up at Jimbo. "I came back to check on my friend here. You need anything, Jimbo?"

"Nah," his old friend replied, patting the lid of the Styrofoam container. "Loren here took care of me tonight. Gave me plenty of blankets and a hot meal. Can't ask for more than that. That'd just be greedy."

Jimbo was anything but. He appreciated all the kindness people gave him and ignored them when they acted otherwise.

"Well," Loren said, stretching her legs out in front of her. "I guess I better go check on Mercy. Make sure she's having fun but not so much that she'll regret it in the morning. 'Night, Jim." She popped off the crate, dusting off her pants.

"Night, Half-Pint. Thanks again."

She grinned at the nickname and threw her hand up as if it was nothing as she walked toward Alec and away from the light. Before she could get past him, he touched her arm. "I'll walk you back."

"That's okay," she said, pointing toward her chest, "no fear of chainsaws here."

His eyes remained glued to hers, but it was a Herculean effort to keep them from following the path of her finger. "Wanted to talk, if you have a minute."

"Okay," she said with a shrug as she moved past him. God, she smelled so fucking good, an exotic mixture of vanilla and honeysuckle.

Jesus, now he was sniffing her hair. And he, of all people, hated it when he read a book and they said shit like that. Like a woman could actually smell like a flower.

Alec gave Jimbo a quick wave before following Loren through the alley, catching the older man's cheeky grin.

She stopped before reaching the parking area and turned toward him with her arms crossed over her chest. He watched her defenses shoot up like a spring-loaded rifle target.

It was his experience that when women were nervous they got tongue-tied, but not Loren. No sir, Loren would erupt with words.

She didn't disappoint.

"So, what did you want to talk about? Let me guess, the NASDAQ? Identity politics? The plight of baby seals in certain remote Asian countries?"

She was so damned beautiful. He wanted nothing more than to touch the curve of her collarbone and then maybe kiss some of her nervous sass away.

His eyes snagged onto her creamy shoulder and he recalled how sweet that particular part of her body tasted.

"I'm wearing a bra."

His eyes shot up at the unexpected comment.

And deadpan delivery.

"Come again?"

"You've expressed your concern about my underclothing in the past." She cleared her throat. "Or, lack thereof." She tightened her arms in front of her chest and his resolve weakened as his disloyal eyes moved toward the B cups in question. "I didn't want you to think that I would walk around in public braless. Not that I haven't. I have . . . gone braless, I mean. And in public. But I know I need to be more circumspect around Cara and her friends."

The more she rambled, the more a blush of embarrassment slowly progressed up her neck, landing on her cheeks.

His eyes narrowed, remembering the way she reacted to his five o'clock shadow on her soft skin. And then he blinked slowly and became momentarily dizzy at the thought of his beard on those tender peaks, and then biting them.

He scratched his jaw to forcibly pull his thoughts and eyes from their less-than-honorable pursuits.

He needed to ask a favor as it pertained to Ally, not ruminate on the after-effects of stubble on rock-hard nipples that he could see regardless of her aforementioned support garment.

His voice came out hoarse and gravelly, "Wanna get dinner sometime?"

Ah. Fuck. Where in the hell did that come from?

She appeared equally shocked as she ducked her chin as if doing a sound check on what she'd heard. And then glanced up, blinking with slow exaggeration. "Um ... what?"

He planned on asking her about Ally staying with them while he went through more training and babbled something else entirely. He looked to the ground, searching for his fucking balls. He shoved his hands back in his front pockets and honed in on the front door to Lucky's. "Forget I asked."

"No," she blurted out, grabbing his arm. "No way are you taking that back. You asked *me* out. You actually asked *me out*. On. A. Date."

"Okay, let's not make a big deal out of it." He fidgeted, his arm feeling singed by her touch. He yanked his hands out of his pockets and placed them on his hips. Feeling awkward as hell, he rubbed an eyebrow with the pad of his thumb and then to the back of his neck.

He bristled as she stared up at him, slack-jawed. "Is that a yes, or just your irritating way of stretching this moment out only to say no?"

"Yes!" she said with a raised voice. "I mean . . . ." She subtly shook her head with an eye roll. "It depends. I have a pretty busy schedule."

"Do you now?"

"I do."

"Okay." He shrugged.

Fuck this shit. This was too hard. He started to make his way back to the bar.

"No . . . wait," she said, stumbling after him and grabbing his bicep.

He paused and took a deep breath, trying not to cave to that goddamned flowery smell. Honeysuckle.

"I might be able to work something in."

"Yeah?"

"I mean, I've got classes. And of course, I'll have to color my roots and polish my fingernails." She looked at them as if offended.

Not breaking eye contact, he lifted her hand to inspect the evidence. His eyes shifted to her delicate hand and then back to those whiskey eyes that intoxicated him. "You polish *these* nails?" he asked, raising the hand toward the light. "These chewed-up nails?"

"I can't help it," she replied with drawn brows. "When there's polish on them they remind me of Skittles, and I can't keep them out of my mouth."

Closing his eyes, he momentarily blanked at the thought of the things he could put there. Things that were long and hard and raging below his belt.

"And then, I have to polish them all over again. It's a rather vicious cycle."

Subconsciously, he rubbed her manicure-less fingers between his.

"What plans are reserved for Friday night?"

"I'm watching *A Star is Born* with Mercy, Cara, and Becky. And Becky's teaching me how to make pancakes."

"Which one?"

"Blueberry."

"No, which version of *A Star is Born*? I think Ally told me there were three."

"I have no idea. But now my vote will be for a three-movie marathon."

"While eating blueberry pancakes."

"Yeah, the homemade kind. Not the kind you stick in a toaster."

Alec nodded with narrowed eyes. "You *are* busy."

She lifted an eyebrow and shrugged the opposite shoulder.

"What are you doing tomorrow night?"

"I have a self-defense class and then I'm helping Cara study for a math test."

His mind conjured the memory of Loren in his living room. "Like your mom used to help you?"

He watched her swallow.

"Yes, like that," she whispered. He'd hit a nerve and she subconsciously moved closer.

"Maybe you could also find time to eat." He continued to hold her hand and was now kneading his fingers into her palm. The fronts of their bodies were touching and he kept staring at her lips.

"I think I could manage that."

"I do have one contingency."

"What's that?" she asked with a glint in her eye. "Does it involve ropes or gags?"

Ropes and . . .? Where did that come from? "Oh yes, those are definitely on the table," he said comically, but instead of chuckling she nodded as if in contemplation.

"So, no cow-tipping or late-night toilet paper raids?"

"Good Lord, woman, you went from ropes and gags to barnyard antics. What kind of men have you dated?"

"None," she replied softly, as they both stared at his fingers intertwined with her much smaller ones.

He turned his head in confusion. "None?"

She slowly shook her head.

"Are you saying . . . you've taken a break from dating?"

"No," she said as Alec's fingers paused.

"Wait, you're not saying . . .? Are you saying you've never . . .?"

He watched her swallow and meet his gaze. "Remember? Over protective uncle."

He bristled at the repetitive story, which he knew to a degree was just that. A story with more holes than he could keep up with. "Okay, that takes us back to my contingency."

"What's that?"

"No lies."

He watched for her reaction. Brown eyes hooded as she watched their fingers no longer having their own make-out session. "That . . . shouldn't be a problem."

"Good."

"But to be clear. I don't have sex on the first date."

His eyes narrowed. "It's not an expectation. But if it happens, I'm willing to roll with it. Statistically, I'd say that's pretty typical." He hesitated and cocked his head. "But to be clear, ropes and gags are still on the table?"

"Sure," she said, "you can show me how to rope a steer. I'm game. Not sure what we're gagging, but I'm open."

He gave her a side-eyed glance. Was this another one of her jokes? Her brown eyes didn't reveal an ounce of guile, not a smidgen of pretense.

How did this woman come off so blatantly seductive, at the same time so seemingly innocent? Could he have been wrong about her? Could she be telling the truth about an overprotective uncle with radical conspiracy theories . . . who hired staff to teach her to fight and possibly run her down in Paris?

Who home-schooled her and her radically artistic sisters?

To the point where they had to watch movies and read books to learn social cues?

What did that even mean? Could they have been that isolated growing up? They all seemed so innately honest in their obliviousness.

In for a penny, in for a pound, he might as well test his theory.

"Where, exactly, did you hear about ropes and gags?"

"Lucinda Packett. She mentioned going out with a rancher who lives east of Newberry. Said she hoped her first date involved ropes and gags."

He chuckled, "Maybe you should refrain from using terms before they're fully defined?"

It was her turn to narrow her eyes. "What do *you* think it means?

And while you're at it, maybe you could explain why Cara is always saying 'Bye, Felicia' or 'Damn, Gina' with a snarky grin?"

Alec chewed his lip to refrain from laughing. He was not considered "in the know" when it came to pop culture trends, but even he knew what those terms meant merely from being a brother to a teenaged sister.

"And what does it mean to spill the tea or to be 'shook'? And why would the girls tell me my eyebrows are the opposite of 'on fleek'?" she continued, clearly on a roll. "And at Eli's Diner the other day, Cara said she was ordering the salad, but she was 'low-key cravin' the pasta.' And Ally said with one single word, 'Totes.'"

Alec shifted his stance. "I don't think I'm qualified—"

"So," she continued, "I grab your sister's book bag sitting next to me in the booth and hand it over to her. *After which,*" she said dramatically and with a flip of her hand, "she and Cara laughed at me so hard they cried." She raised her arms in frustration. "What the hell does a tote bag have to do with eating pasta?" She looked up at him, waiting for an explanation.

Alec smiled, despite his efforts to remain serious. One thing was for certain, a date with Loren Ingalls was going to be anything but predictable. What was uncertain, was whether to believe a word coming out of her delicious mouth.

Alec reached up to hold her shoulders. His right hand tingled a bit as it touched bare skin next to a barely noticeable bra strap. "Your mission, if you choose to accept it, is to research your questions before our date tomorrow night after you help Cara with math and do whatever you feel is necessary with your hair and nails. If you still have questions, then I'll do my best to answer them."

"Can I find the answers on Pinterest?"

"You may have to expand your search options."

"Instagram? I just discovered that one."

"Why not ask one of your girlfriends?"

She grinned, her smile and whiskey-brown eyes captivating him.

"Mission and date accepted. I'll just"—she waved toward the entrance to the bar—"get Mercy and drive her home."

She walked backward a couple of steps, clasped her hands, and turned awkwardly.

Jimbo had found his way next to Alec, just as a very drunk Arnie Feller collided with Loren and made the mistake of attempting to cop a feel. Jimbo and Alec sucked-in simultaneously as she stunned Arnie with a roundhouse kick to the head.

Arnie grabbed his cheek in pain as Loren barely lost her stride.

"Gosh darn it, Arnie, sober up and go home to Byrdie."

"Jeezus, Loren, did you have to go and bust my lip?" He looked down at his hands and his eyes grew large. "Jesus H. Christ, woman! You clean broke off my front tooth!"

"You better be grateful I'm not calling your wife," Loren retorted as she swung open the door to Lucky's and slammed it behind her.

For the second time that night, Alec was surprised at what he had witnessed.

"Jimbo," he said, as he watched Arnie spit blood onto the parking lot, "mark my words, where that woman is concerned, there's more to the story. And I highly suspect, I'm not going to like the ending."

Jimbo chuckled. "Maybe so, but won't it be a hoot gettin' to it?"

CHAPTER TWENTY-FOUR

"Perfect numbers, like perfect men, are very rare."

—Rene Descartes
French-born philosopher, mathematician, and scientist

Loren worked her way to the bar and waved Gus down.

"Hey, Loren, what can I get ya?" Gus asked.

"I'm good," Loren said doing her best to talk over the din of inebriated voices. "But could you ring Byrdie and tell her to get an ice pack ready for Arnie?" She looked down at the time on her phone. "He should be home in about eight minutes with a broken tooth and busted lip."

He grinned as he picked up his phone. "You have anything to do with that?"

She squinted her face. "Yeah . . . about that, the heel of my boot got caught on his tooth. Could happen to anybody."

"I'm sure he had it coming to him. He's been known to get handsy after a few drinks," he said as he picked up his phone. "I'll call her."

"Thanks." She jerked her thumb toward the front doors. "Mercy and I are heading out. Thanks for everything."

"Didn't do anything but provide a venue, and quench some thirsts."

She gave him a knowing smile. "You know this place is special."

"Largely because of you, and now your sister."

"Please keep an eye on Mercy if she's ever here without me. Oh, and don't hesitate to call me if you think she needs a ride home."

"Will do."

Loren gave a final wave, found Mercy, and coaxed her toward the front door. Everyone yelled their alcohol-enhanced goodbyes and simultaneous "Happy Birthdays!", and Mercy waved back with thank you's and blowing kisses.

The chill took Loren's breath away. "A cold front must be coming in."

"Feels good," Mercy said. "It was really hot in there."

Suddenly, Vlad was at Mercy's side and Loren wondered how the hell he did that. Just popped up out of nowhere.

"You good, *milaya?*" he asked, bending his head slightly so he could look at her eyes.

"Oh, hey, Vlad. Yes! I'm great. I'm wonderful. That was the best birthday party ever!" Mercy stumbled a bit, and the Russian was there to grab her by the upper arm and help her regain her footing.

Her lack of equilibrium did little to dampen her enthusiasm. "Did you see my cake? It had candles and *everything*. It had my name written on it! And did you see all of my friends there? All the people who like me? It was awesome."

"I am glad," he said with a small smile. "You deserve to be happy, *milaya.*"

Suddenly she stopped, causing both Loren and Vlad to suffer the biting wind. "Are *you* happy, Vlad?" she asked, searching his face.

Loren remained silent, not wanting to interfere during this rare communication between Mercy and her doctor? Lover? BFF? She opened the passenger door, but Mercy remained standing, now in a staring contest with Vlad.

"How can you be happy just waiting around for my headaches to hit? What kind of life is that, Vlad?"

His eyes avoided hers. "I am happy when you are happy and well." He looked up at Loren, clearly wanting to halt this line of communication. "I will follow you home."

She nodded, suddenly feeling very sad for the Russian, but not altogether sure as to why.

Loren drove slowly even though she had had her last drink hours ago. But she wanted to give a now silent Mercy every opportunity to share details concerning her relationship with Vlad.

"He never once did anything inappropriate," Mercy said out of nowhere as they made their way up the driveway. "I knew he cared for me. But he never did anything he shouldn't have."

"That's good, Mercy." Loren glanced her way. "Because if he had, it would have been wrong."

"You know, other than you, he's the only person who's fought for me. Who believed in me. Who was there for me when I told him the truth and asked for help."

Loren pulled into their driveway and turned off the engine, neither one willing to move.

Loren cautiously took that as a sign that Mercy was willing to open up. "This medicine he gives you, is he the only one who can administer it?"

Mercy shook her head. "No, any doctor could. But he doesn't want anyone to know about the reason for needing the drug. He said it will encourage too many questions. My condition is rare, and if the details surrounding it got out, Jasper would be sure to find me. Find all of us."

"So, he's willing to subjugate his life to being there if and when you need him?"

"Pretty much."

"He must really love you."

Her eyes turned glassy. "And what does that say about me? He loves me so much he's willing to leave his homeland, give up his medical career, and live in this dusty prairie town to simply administer drugs to me when I get a headache. And me? I can't even manage to return his feelings."

"Those feelings are somewhat out of your control. You can't help it if you don't share them. And you shouldn't feel guilty about that."

"So, what do I do? Do I keep leading him along so I get my injections and protect my family? Or, do I stop painting, stop the headaches, and let him go?"

Loren watched the golden hue of the lights in the front living room. "What if he left the medicine with me? What if I gave you the injections?"

Mercy shrugged. "We haven't had that conversation. But you do enough, Loren. You shouldn't have to babysit me anymore than Vlad." She pushed open her car door, and Loren knew that the rare moment of sharing was over.

She followed Mercy up the steps and into the house when Mercy stopped abruptly inside the doorway, causing Loren to bounce off her back.

"What the hell, Mercy?"

Mercy finally moved to the side and what Loren saw made her stop in her tracks.

Cara was standing awkwardly next to a prim and buttoned-up woman with a stern, reproachful look on her face.

Madame Garmond.

Loren winced as Mercy whispered, "Is it me, or is she silently judging us?" Unfortunately, the alcohol had affected Mercy's inner volume, making her loud enough for everyone to hear, including the judgmental woman wearing a string of pearls, a black crepe suit, and patent leather heels that were so shiny, she need only look down to check her lipstick.

Cara cleared her throat, sounding as if she'd just swallowed glass. "Mercy, Loren, you remember Madame Garmond?"

Taking a deep breath, Loren did her best to gather herself. She blinked more slowly this time, trying to make sense of the prim woman standing ramrod straight in their living room.

"Good evening, Ms. Garmond. You'll have to forgive our shock as we really aren't in the habit of greeting people showing up from . . . our past."

Before the last word was uttered, the front door blew open, and Vlad entered the foyer, creating a small gust of wind and discrediting Loren's statement. And just as quickly, came to an abrupt stop, staring openly at the woman with pursed lips and narrowed eyes.

"Madame Garmond." He removed his knitted beanie and bowed his head slightly in greeting. "*Quelle surprise.*"

"Charlotte," Ms./Madame, or whatever they were calling her, turned toward Cara. "You did not mention *Le Docteur Russe* was here, as well."

Mercy mumbled, "Evidently, there are a number of things our sister has failed to mention."

Ignoring Mercy's comment, Loren took control, motioning toward the living room. "Why don't we all sit down and discuss . . . recent events."

Madame Garmond led the way, primly hooking her equally shiny purse over her elbow and making her way into the living room to the sofa. Before sitting, she lifted an empty bag of potato chips from the cushion and placed it on the coffee table with a look of utter revulsion.

Mercy plopped down in the chair facing the sofa next to Loren, as Cara sat quietly next to the elderly woman. Vlad remained standing in the doorway as if berating himself for failing to make one of his signature covert exits.

Loren began to feel the red tinge of embarrassment creep up her neck.

Even though the outside of the house was Pinterest-worthy, the Ingalls sisters and their elusive Russian guest weren't known for keeping a tidy house. Magazines and paper plates with remnants of Hot Pockets were strewn all over the coffee table. The side tables littered with upended Coke cans—the last-minute vestiges of running late for Mercy's birthday party and scarfing down food before leaving for Lucky's.

Loren didn't even want to think about what the kitchen looked like. But, despite the current state of their home, she couldn't allow this woman to usurp her authority. This was her home, her turf, and this woman needed to know that.

"Ms. Garmond, you can no longer refer to Cara as Charlotte. Her name is Cara."

"I see, then I would ask that you kindly address me as *Madame* Garmond."

Loren's eyebrows rose as the small woman tilted her head and crossed her arms in front of her. She might have been slight, but her larger-than-life persona was no less than an MMA fighter jacked-up on steroids while wearing an exquisite strand of pearls.

Loren swallowed. "All right, *Madame* Garmond, her name is Cara now, so you can't call her by any other name. It's for her protection."

"I see." The woman's smile appeared manufactured. "Tell me, do you consider yourself her protector?"

How did she manage to lace so much disdain in such a succinct question? Loren took a deep breath. "I am her protector and her older sister."

"And do you find yourself doing an adequate job?" She scanned the room and lifted a can of hair spray stuck to a paper plate on the side table. Madame continued, "This room is a disgrace. And the kitchen, a germ-riddled nightmare." She reset the hairspray and paper plate on the table and wiped her hands together.

"Despite that, my charge did offer me a lovely assortment of Hot Pockets and Corn Dogs upon my arrival. Apparently, that was all that she could find that was edible. There was a container of tuna salad, but upon further inspection it appeared more similar to a horticulture project than a viable food source."

Okay, she had a point. But honestly, how rude. Loren took another calming breath, and said, "Today is Mercy's birthday. We were rushing to get to her party, and Cara," she widened her eyes at her younger sister, "was supposed to be spending the night with a friend."

She gave Cara a withering look. "Cara, why aren't you at Ally's?"

"I was, until Madame Garmond called. Letting me know she was here."

Madame Garmond interjected, "Letting her know that I had arrived, as she had requested."

The elderly woman, closing in on seventy, turned toward Cara. "Please inform your sisters that you called me, insisting that I travel to this backwoods part of the country because you were in crisis and in desperate need of my counsel."

Loren turned hot eyes toward Cara. Counsel?

Cara sucked in a shaky breath as if her betrayal had hijacked her voice.

Loren couldn't manage to hold back. "Seriously, Cara? I thought everything was settled with Amarilla and that things were going back to normal at school?"

Cara hunched one shoulder, a pitiful half-shrug. "I kinda missed her. Before . . . leaving, Madame Garmond had been the only person I could talk to about stuff when you and Mercy were at . . . math conventions and art shows."

Mercy huffed while slinging her leg over the arm of the overstuffed chair. Never one to mince words, even when sober, she said, "You missed this . . . this . . . geriatric fem-bot posing as a human capable of emotion?"

Cara lashed back. "Oh, like you're capable of emoting."

"At least I have a heartbeat."

"She has a heart," Cara said defensively. "It kind of shows up when you least expect it and need it the most."

"But we were doing so well." The confusion and disappointment ripped from Loren's gut. Not to mention her brain. She was conflicted between Cara's blatant disregard for their safety and her little sister's need to send out an SOS. Why would she do that? Loren had tried everything to get through to her during what she and Mercy referred to as Cara's crazy-ass bitch phase. But Cara had stubbornly refused to share what was going on, even lied to them and snuck out of the house. She'd come home from school and go straight to her room to play some of the most depressing music known to mankind.

The matronly woman piped up. "Yes, I can see how well you've been doing. Imagine my dismay as I discover my charge at a neighbor's home, unchaperoned, while her sisters, her protectors, are spending an intoxicated evening at the local *brasserie*."

Mercy's dilated eyes turned beady. "Wait, are you French or English?"

Loren elbowed Mercy in the side. "You're not helping."

It was clear that Loren suffered greatly in Madame's esteem, but now wasn't the time to spew. Rather, it was time to think and assess their level of risk. At least until she could come up with ideas on how to address the visceral contempt sitting before her.

Mercy leaned toward her, and whispered, "How do we know she's not a spy? How do we know Jasper didn't send her to surveil us?"

Hmmm, good point. Switching her focus from Madame Garmond's unkind opinion to their current situation in terms of safety, Loren asked, "Cara, how exactly did you make contact with Madame Garmond?"

Ms./Madame Garmond reacted to the question by reaching into her purse and pulling out what looked to be a flip phone from the '90s. "I purchased a set of disposable phones once we began to travel extensively. I never trusted Doctor Halstead, let alone that halfwit

Jasper Bancroft, and made sure Cara was able to reach me at a moment's notice. That said, prepaid phones can be tracked using the traditional, albeit less accurate, method of cellular. Therefore, I was sure to change phones every two weeks."

Loren's eyes widened as she stared at Cara. "You've had a burner phone this entire time?"

Again with a pitiful half-shrug. ". . . Yes." Her eyes lifted suddenly. "But I only used it once, to ask Madame Garmond to . . . to come for a visit."

"This is absurd," the woman said, "Please show me to my quarters so that I might retire. It's quite late, and Charlotte, errr, Cara, should be in bed. We can readdress the situation in the morning when we're all a bit more rested" she glanced at Mercy—". . . and sober."

Cara sheepishly said, "She can take my bed, and I'll use the sleeping bag."

Rubbing her eyes, Loren began to weigh their risks given the circumstances and the current number of houseguests.

"Okay, everyone, just wait a minute," Loren said, standing with her hands out in front of her, stalling everyone's dissent. "Going to bed with the delayed strategy of addressing all this in the morning makes no sense. We now have two people from the Center who have been communicating with us, know where we live, and are now standing in our living room. Let's not kid ourselves. The chances of Jasper knowing we're in Wilder are extremely high."

"Dr. Bancroft?" Madame Garmond smirked. "Dr. Jasper Bancroft is nothing more than an incompetent menace."

"A menace who has taken over the Center and has access to all of Dr. Halstead's resources. Over the years, Halstead amassed a sizable network of underground groups and individuals who are more than capable of hunting us down. And Jasper has free rein to commandeer them toward his cause.

"Despite everything I've done to alter and create information online, there's still only so much one person can do with a stolen laptop." She turned to Mercy, praying she was sober enough to recognize their level of risk. "Remember when we were working a job? We always had to act on the worst-case scenario. And as of right now, that would be that Jasper knows where we are and is arranging for us to be returned to the Center."

Madame Garmond spoke up. "Why would Dr. Bancroft go to such great lengths to find you and Mercy? I understand why he would want to find Cara. Her musical talent garnered the Center a considerable amount of revenue. But why would he want you and your sister to return?"

Hmm, something didn't smell right.

Did she really know nothing of Dr. Halstead's less-than-honorable side hustle and the millions of dollars it generated?

Nope, Loren wasn't buying it. The woman had bought burner phones for crying out loud. The real question was, did she know that Cara's musical acumen was created by Dr. Vielle and his scalpel? She certainly had everything to gain by being a willing accomplice. She traveled the world, ate at five-star restaurants, stayed in the nicest hotels. And all she had to do was ensure that Cara was playing at peak performance levels.

Not a bad gig.

Loren made a mental note to come up with a strategy to expose the older woman's duplicity and figure out what game she was playing.

Loren resumed her earlier appeal. "I don't think any of us should assume we're safe given the amount of communication that's gone on between us now. I get it. Jasper's not the sharpest tool in the shed, but believe me, he knows how to subcontract brain power."

And how to capture it.

Vlad cleared his throat, his hands still clenching his beanie. "I can assure you, if Jasper Bancroft knew I was here, he would have sent his henchmen already."

"I have little concern as well," Madame Garmond added. "After you three escaped and I was sacked, I gained employment with a university in Connecticut. While speaking at a conference in Austin, I received Cara's call. After listening to her desperate request, I purchased a car with cash and drove to this dismal prairie town. In the meantime, I gave my credit card to a colleague with permission to use it for necessities in order to create a virtual paper trail of my returning to Connecticut."

She pulled a rolling suitcase from the hallway and parked it in front of Vlad. Apparently, he would have to make do as an impromptu bellboy.

Mercy eyes narrowed once again, "So you're an Englishwoman, claiming to be French, living in Connecticut."

Madame was less than amused. "My mother was an artisan from the French village of Montbazen, and my father, a stoic English duke. Suffice it to say, my father insisted we live in London.

"My mother instilled in me a deep love for the arts. My artistic preference became music. My father, a blue-bloodied descendant of centuries of monarchs tasked with ruling over a duchy, insisted I also have a mind for how one makes money . . . with music. Due to my broad knowledge of the subject matter, I came to the United States upon invitation of Dr. Halstead to become Charlo—Cara's caregiver and business manager. It didn't take long for me to realize that Cara's situation was nothing short of extreme. I've loved and protected her for the past several years as if she were my own. And I will continue to do so until the day I die."

Silence. The whole . . . you could hear a pin drop, thing.

As Madame Garmond turned toward the staircase, Mercy called out, "You smell really nice."

Whiplash. Loren was sure she suffered from an acute case as she gaped at her sister.

The woman turned and gave Mercy, what had been as of yet, a rare and genuine smile. "Why, thank you, dear. I have a bottle of L'Air du Temps that I think would be perfect for you." She looked her up and down. "Considering you reek of low-shelf spirits."

Vlad quickly followed her up the staircase, toting her suitcase behind him with Cara close behind.

Loren rubbed her forehead and turned to Mercy. "It sounds like they covered their tracks."

"Jasper's too busy lording over the Center and coming up with new diabolical schemes to worry about us. I'm telling you, he has no intention of hunting us down."

"No, he'd hire it out. I can think of half a dozen less than savory mercenaries who'd love nothing more than to see us apprehended and punished."

"You worry too much. We're fine. We got out. Escaped. Let's enjoy our freedom rather than live the rest of our lives looking over our shoulder."

"I think that's the delusional haze of alcohol talking."

"Maybe," Mercy said with a yawn as she pulled Loren in for a hug. "Thank you for the awesome birthday party. Now, go to bed and we'll worry about all of this in the morning."

CHAPTER TWENTY-FIVE

"God used beautiful mathematics in creating the world."

—Paul Dirac
English theoretical physicist, regarded
as one of the most significant physicists of the 20th century

"What do you mean he puts the gag on the woman's mouth? And how does that include a ball? Omigod, where does the ball go?" Loren stood stock-still in the middle of washing a plate and stared wide-eyed at Mercy. The dishes could wait, but the answer to these questions had to be addressed and stat. She had a date that night with her ridiculously sexy neighbor and needed to know what she'd unwittingly signed up for.

Mercy continued to dry a mason jar, unaware of Loren's palpitating heartbeat. "Becky said the ball goes into the mouth and then the gag ties over it."

"That *cannot* be true. That's what you do to stifle a prisoner, not your . . . lover."

Mercy shrugged as she slid the dry plate on top of the others in the cabinet. "That's how Becky explained it. Said there's a lot of content on the Internet out there that's all about rough sex. She told me to Google 'submissive,' 'dominatrix,' and *Fifty Shades of Grey*."

Loren stared out the window to the backyard, and wondered if she left now, could she make it to the state line before Alec pulled into the driveway.

Her mind was racing with memories of their discussion while standing outside of Lucky's.

"So, what are the ropes for?"

Mercy leaned against the kitchen counter and slung the dishrag over her shoulder. "The man uses a rope to tie the woman's hands behind her back. Or vice versa. Becky said sometimes the woman ties the man up."

"So . . . you're completely at their mercy? You have no control over what they do to you?"

"Apparently, that's the point, to let go of all control. Thus, the word 'submissive.' Look at you. Why are you freaking out?" She chuckled. "Like you could ever be submissive."

But what if you had inadvertently given your date the impression that you could be?

Loren slowly shook her head back and forth. "What made you ask Becky about all this sex stuff?"

"Lucinda Packett was going on about it last night, talking about her date with some rancher out in Newberry. I was just as shocked as you are, so I asked Becky some questions." She placed the jar in the cupboard. "That woman is such a wealth of knowledge."

What in the world?

"Lucinda's going to allow him to do that?" Loren asked, staring at Mercy. "After all these months teaching the women of Wilder our most effective self-defense moves, they're just gonna throw themselves at the will of their assailants, hold up their hands and ask them to please tie them up while batting their eyelashes?" She held her wrists out toward Mercy, "Excuse me, sir, would be so kind as to truss me up, stick a ball in my mouth, and attack me sexually?"

"If it's consensual, you can't call it an attack."

"What do you call it then? Temporary insanity?"

"What are you so riled up about? Just because other people are into whips and chains, doesn't mean we have to be."

Whips and chains? Now there's *whips* and *chains*?

Loren continued to stare at prairie grass wafting in the wind outside. "Whatever happened to a nice first date, like when Alonzo gave Laura a scarf and kissed her? Without tongue?"

"First of all, that sounds like an awful first date. And second, you do know the book and TV series are fictitious? Like, they never ever happened?"

"That's not altogether true. The books are based on real events—it's just that the events are largely fictitious."

"Okay, let's not pretend that I care or what you said makes sense. You need to start reading books written in the last decade, at least. Books that educate you on what a date in the modern era looks like."

Loren felt her Toaster Strudel working its way up her esophagus. What had she gotten herself into?

"Keep washing, Loren. If we're going to get this house clean before Madame Garmond and Cara get back from the grocery, you need to kick it into high gear."

Loren just kept shaking her head, looking out the window.

"Hey, Earth to Loren, what's the matter? Hand me a plate."

Loren turned from the window and stared at Mercy, feeling the blood drain from her face. She hugged her stomach and began to chew on her thumb. "I may have agreed to be sexually assaulted by Alec on our first date tonight."

Mercy's eyes turned confused and then deer in the headlights. "Wait. What? You have a date with our perpetually perturbed neighbor?" She lowered her head to look straight into Loren's eyes. "And you told him you would have sex with him?"

Loren nodded her head, and squeezed her eyes shut, and then opened them. "The kind with ball gags and ropes."

"Why? Why would you tell him that?"

"I thought ropes and gags had to do with roping a steer or something." Although now that she said it out loud, it did sound absurd.

"Hold on, you thought you were telling him you would rope and gag a steer with him on your date?"

Loren dug her palms into eye sockets. "Stop talking. You're making it worse."

Mercy grabbed her hands and pulled them down. "Just call him and explain. He'll think it's funny, you know, in a totally batshit crazy kinda clueless sorta way."

Loren's eyes shot up with hope. "That's what I'll do. I'll call him and tell him something came up, and I can't go on our date. Oh!" She snapped her fingers. "I'll tell him we have an unexpected houseguest and it would be rude to leave."

Loren snatched her phone from the kitchen table, and just as quickly, Mercy grabbed it out of her hands. "Don't you dare cancel your date."

Loren scowled and grabbed it back, her fingers going to Farmer Ted in her Favorites. "Excuse me, I'm not going out with someone who plans to hog-tie me and then violate my body."

Mercy snatched the phone again and held it up high over her head. Loren jumped, trying to grab it. "Seriously, I should stay home and find ways to counter the damage caused by our irresponsible houseguests."

"Let me repeat." Mercy said, using her extra height as leverage. "DO. NOT. CANCEL. THE. DATE." And with that, she reached up and pushed the End Call button.

"Why not?"

"Because I need my big sister to go on her first date so that I know what to expect when and if I ever get to go on one."

Loren's shoulders took a nose dive. "Oh, that was a low blow."

Mercy's right eyebrow shot up as she smirked. "It had to be done."

Loren sighed heavily. "You totally pulled the little sister card."

"Yep."

"A card I *have* never and *will* never be able to pull."

"That's because you're older than Cara and me. It's called math, math genius."

"If Cara would allow for us to settle our differences through physical force, I would totally pull the big sister card, kick your feet out from under you, and feed you dirty socks."

"Like you even know where the laundry room is."

"I know where it is. I just don't use it on a regular basis."

Mercy crossed her arms and leaned back on the counter. "So what are you going to tell our surly neighbor when he instructs you to bend over for him while throwing a small, hopefully sanitized ball in the air?"

"I'll sweep his feet out from under him and stuff the ball in *his* mouth."

"Oh, so you want *him* to be *your* submissive."

"No! I don't want him to be my . . . . Tell you what, we're done with this conversation. You're making me go on this date for educational purposes, so suffice it to say, I'll be returning with intel."

Mercy smirked and picked up her dish towel. "Well, according to our new houseguest, we have to do a better job of cleaning said house. I believe her words this morning were: 'How one cares for her home is a direct reflection of what is transpiring in one's life. And your lives are chaotic, slovenly and discordant.'"

Loren rolled her eyes as she stuck her hands back into the dishwater. "What does discordant even mean?"

"I looked it up. It seems our lives are 'harsh and jarring due to a lack of harmony.' You know, in addition to being slovenly and chaotic."

"The outside of the house is nice," Loren countered, handing off another plate to Mercy.

Mercy nodded. "I mentioned that, and she told me that it was a dysfunctional attempt to appear centered and polished on the outside when on the inside we suffered from deep-seated emotional turmoil."

"That's total bullshit. What nerve," Loren huffed, while scrubbing the Velveeta cheese that had dried on the last plate. It must have been from last week's toasted cheese sandwiches.

Mercy shrugged. "I dunno, she might have a point."

Loren's eye shot to Mercy. "You called her a geriatric fem-bot last night."

"Yeah, but this morning she told me I had vast potential and gave me a bottle of fancy French perfume." Mercy paused. "And then she handed me a pair of rubber gloves and told me to start illustrating that potential with elbow grease."

"Did you tell her to kiss your ass?"

Mercy side-eyed her sister. "Geez, calm down, you little maniac. I put the rubber gloves on and cleaned out the refrigerator. She told me my work was quite impressive."

What the hell? When had Mercy become so tolerant? Loren could remember a time when she had to restrain her from clocking a passerby on the streets of Copenhagen for gawking at her red corset, denim shorts, and fishnets.

Loren fished for remnants of dishware in the tepid water and found another plate with caked on remnants of loaded nachos from a few days ago. "How convenient that she goes to the grocery and Cara leaves for school while we're left here to clean the entire house."

Mercy turned sheepish. "Before they left, she asked me what I wanted to eat for dinner and I told her that sometimes I dreamed of Mom's chicken and broccoli casserole."

"What?" The indignation in Loren's voice trumped all other emotion. "I would've made it for you."

Mercy gave her a look that read, "Like that would ever happen."

"I'm serious. I could've figured it out. I would have at least tried had I known it was that important to you." Loren pursed her lips and scrubbed like her life depended upon the eradication of all cheese from every plate in the house.

She should be making mom's casserole, not some pretentious, overbearing, well-dressed stranger. Well, practically a stranger to her and Mercy. Her shoulders fell as she wondered why she'd never thought to ask Mercy or Cara what foods they missed, or liked, or wanted to fling across the table in a food fight for fuck-sake?

And why did Mercy suddenly take to Madame whatever-her-name-was after a single backhanded compliment? Was she that starved for validation and a home-cooked meal?

Despite all her efforts, Mercy and Cara continued to reach out to others for their emotional needs rather than her. What was she lacking? Would she ever be enough? She worked so hard to get them to Wilder, yet outside forces kept creeping their way in, disrupting what she was trying to build with their fledgling family.

"Hey, Cujo with a scrub brush," Mercy said, stopping Loren's hand from scrubbing furiously, "you're going to scratch the laminated design off the plastic plate."

Loren dropped the plate in the soapy water and turned to Mercy. "From now on, you come to *me* if you want Mom's casserole." She stabbed a soapy finger toward her own chest. "Come to *me* if you need perfume recommendations, or . . . or . . . dating advice."

"Hey, hey," Mercy said, giving her sister a light punch to the shoulder, "take a chill pill, sis. No one is replacing you. No one is betraying you."

Loren sniffed while leaning her elbows on the counter, refusing to look at her sister.

Mercy's voice softened as she bumped her with her shoulder. "You've got to come to terms with the fact that other people are going to come in and out of our lives. Some are going to be good influences and others are going to be mistakes. You can't control every aspect of our lives and frankly, you shouldn't want to. You have to let us live our own lives on our terms. Even allow us to make a mistake or two . . . hundred."

Struggling to hide the tears pooling in her eyes Loren leaned on her elbows, stared at her feet, and nodded. She swiped at a tear with her bicep before it dropped.

"But don't doubt the bond between us," Mercy added. "You are my big sister, my best friend, and not to mention a critically important pain in my ass."

Loren nodded. But then the tears kept springing up and . . . yup, there was snot. Crap, it was running down her face. She pulled her sleeve across her eyes and under her nose. Madame Douche-Canoe would grab her pearls and suffer an apoplectic fit had she witnessed such a poor display of restraint.

Loren's voice was raspy as she stood straight and pulled her shoulders back. "When did you get so smart?"

Mercy grinned wide. "Since I turned twenty-one. One more thing, so get ready to stem the water-works."

"Okay."

"You ready?"

Loren grimaced with a half-smile. "Girding my loins here."

Mercy cleared her throat. "You have proven on many occasions that you would die for us. I know for a fact that you came close a time or two . . . hundred. I also think that you've kept some really bad shit from us. I can't speak for the other pain in my ass, but I can make an educated guess that both she and I would die for you, too."

Loren shook her head, squeezing her eyes shut. "Don't say that. Don't *ever do* that."

Mercy smiled wryly. "Ah, just one more thing you have no control over, sista." Loren yelped as Mercy smacked her on the ass with her damp dish towel. "Now, help me finish cleaning the house so you can get out there on your first date and become the sexual submissive we all know you can be."

Loren rubbed her backside with a frown. "That was unnecessary."

"Better get used to the rough stuff. By the way, what are you going to wear? How are you going to do your makeup?"

Hmm, she hadn't thought too much about all that.

"I dunno. I guess I'm going to wear a sweater and a pair of jeans." She pulled out the drain to let out the dishwater. "And the only makeup tips I have are for changing identities in the middle of an operation. Makeup for non-mission purposes is supposed to enhance your facial strengths and hide your imperfections. I have no idea how to do that."

"No problem. I'll do it. There're all these YouTube channels on how to apply makeup. I'm an artist, how hard can it be?"

Loren started wiping down the rest of the counter. "Okay, but let's not get crazy. I don't want to look like I'm trying too hard."

"You mean thirsty." Mercy said, picking up a carton of milk and a Twinkie wrapper so Loren could finish with the countertops.

"I'll be sure to drink plenty of water before Alec picks me up."

"Not what I mean. 'Thirsty' is slang for trying too hard. You know, like, being 'thirsty' for attention."

Loren rolled her eyes. "Fine, don't make me look 'thirsty.' Make me look fully hydrated and ready for a bland, non-threatening first date."

CHAPTER TWENTY-SIX

"Life is a math equation. In order to gain the most, you have to know how to convert negatives into positives."

—Anonymous

Alec looked up from his new company laptop as Ally came through the front door with her book bag hanging off one shoulder and a duffel over the other. Both items took turns sliding to the floor as she twisted her body from side to side.

Her small frame fell onto the couch in a teenage slump.

"Hey," Alec said as his screen lit up, "glad it's Friday?"

"Omigod, yes."

"Big plans this weekend?" he asked, typing in his new passcode.

"Not really," she said and then shot out of her slump to sit upright with a cheesy smile. "Apparently not as big as yours."

He glanced up and raised a single eyebrow. "Oh, yeah?"

Chin resting in hand with a cheeky smile, she said, "Cara told me you asked Loren on a date tonight."

He sighed. That's just what he needed, estrogen-rich assumptions about what tonight was and was not. To be honest, he wasn't even sure what it was about. "Just dinner. No big deal."

"No big deal, huh? Where are you gonna take her?"

"Lucky's."

"Lucky's? You're taking Loren to the local bar on your first date?"

God, he didn't need this. He didn't need Ally and Cara making this more complicated than it was because of some adolescent wishful thinking.

Second thought, maybe this was a mistake. Loren Ingalls was a thorn in his side. A gorgeous, enigmatic, irreverent, unavoidable vision that he was having enormous difficulties not jacking off to every night. Taking her to dinner and having one-on-one time might only exacerbate the masturbating problem.

And frankly, he was pretty fucking chafed.

"Look," he said, his typing becoming more like stabs than pecking, "... don't start making tonight into something it's not."

"Like what? A date?"

"No, like something ... romantic leading to ... other things ... romantic."

"Okay, so you're taking Loren on a romance-free date at the local bar."

"That's exactly right."

"That's not a date, Alec. That's shooting the shit with friends."

"Watch your language. But yes, that's it. That's exactly what we're doing. Just two friends meeting at the local bar to discuss current events in their community."

"So, it's not a date. It's a city council meeting consisting of two attendees."

"With food and alcohol," he added.

"Uh-huh, just so you know, you're really bad at dating."

"Well, just so you know, the ladies aren't complaining."

She reared back, staring at him with a furrowed brow. He needed to defuse the situation. He wasn't going to get strong-armed into making tonight a romantic interlude by his fourteen-year-old sister who would love nothing more than for him and her best friend's sister to become a couple.

He closed his laptop without properly shutting it down and turned toward his tenacious sibling, who continued to stare daggers at him.

"Look, I don't want you to get your hopes up. This is more of a truce than the beginnings of a relationship. It's important that you understand that."

"You like her."

"I do." He nodded. "I also like fried okra but I'm not having a relationship with it."

"You *like* her, like her."

"Are you not listening to me?"

The smug teenager was overriding sexually deprived brother, and it irked him that she knew it.

"You know that all the single guys in Wilder and the neighboring counties would give anything to be in your shoes tonight?"

"Oh, trust me, I'm well aware of her vast and growing fan club."

"Yeah, but do you know she *never* goes out on dates?"

"Just because a woman doesn't date doesn't mean she's not . . . socially active."

"I'm not a baby, I know what you're implying and you're wrong about Ms. Loren."

He smirked. Such naïveté.

"Ask me how I know," she insisted.

Alec dropped his head. "Do we have to do this?"

"Yes."

"Okay, Ally, how do you know that Ms. Loren isn't promiscuous?"

She moved to the edge of the sofa. "Because she's always

lecturing me, Cara, and Amarilla on being selective when it comes to boys. She also says that the greatest thing you'll ever learn is just to love, and to be loved in return."

"You do realize that's a direct quote from *Moulin Rouge*?"

Ignoring him, she continued. "Loren says you'll know it's love when you realize you want to spend the rest of your life with someone, and you want the rest of your life to start as soon as possible."

Pinching his eyes with frustration, he said, "*When Harry Met Sally*."

"She tells us not to settle but to be patient and wait. And we'll know it's right because, at that moment, it's as if the whole universe exists just to bring the two of us together."

"*Serendipity*. Okay, that's enough." Alec raised his hand as she took a breath. "Do you not see that she knows nothing on this subject? Good Lord, she has to draw on some of the sappiest movie quotes known to mankind to give you advice." He ran his fingers through his hair. "Movies, by the way, that you forced me to watch and are now indelibly etched in my brain because of their saccharine aftertaste." His rant continued. "The woman spouts movie quotes because she has no frame of reference when it comes to the subject matter."

"That's my point, Alec." Ally reached out to hold his hand. He was instantly silenced by her earnest expression. "She honestly and truly knows nothing about the subject matter. But she pulls from the only references she has in a heartfelt attempt to set us on the right path." Her smile turned impish. "Think about it. She's just a girl, standing in front of a boy, asking him to love her."

"Okay, we're done here."

Ally sat back against the sofa, chuckling, now in full-on irritating smart-ass teenager mode.

"Get this through that adorable thick skull of yours. This is a truce-dinner. Nothing more. Now, if you'll excuse me, I have a city council meeting to get ready for."

As he stomped up the stairs, she yelled, "Be sure to tell her she had you at hello!"

CHAPTER TWENTY-SEVEN

"The important thing to remember about mathematics is not to be frightened."

—Richard Dawkins
British ethologist, evolutionary biologist, and author

Loren slumped over the kitchen table, her head in her hand, strumming her fingers on the cracked Formica tabletop.

Mercy had texted Cara while she was still at school and told her to pull a dating guide from the local library, one preferably written within the last decade.

Everyone seemed to think it was their place to insert their opinions regarding her date, when all she wanted to do was find a bunker and wait it out until Alec gave up knocking on the front door and went back home.

Cara walked into the kitchen with a book in one hand and a triumphant smile on her face. She claimed it was written last year and received rave reviews.

Loren scooted over and gave Cara room to sit in between herself and Vlad.

"Okay, let's get started," Cara said as she turned the page to her book with a wide grin. Loren noticed Cara had dressed more Amish than usual and had to credit the elderly woman cooking a dish she called Coq au Vin in their kitchen for the knee-length skirt and white blouse with a Peter Pan collar rather than the usual jeans and graphic t-shirt her little sister wore. Didn't take long for her influence over Cara to set in.

Loren wasn't sure that was a good thing.

Cara cleared her throat. "The author says that men are attracted to women who have what is called *Jay_nay_sez_koi*."

"That's *Je ne sais quois*," Madame Garmond corrected her.

"What's that mean?" Cara asked her mentor.

"*Ma petite*, did you not say that you were attending French class?" Madame countered with an uplifted brow.

"Well, yeah."

"Then perhaps you should tell me the proper translation."

Loren rolled her eyes and let her little sister off the evil woman's virtual meat hook. "It translates to: 'I don't know what,' which in this context means that men are attracted to women with an appealing quality that cannot be adequately described or expressed."

Cara nodded her head as Madame Garmond poked at what smelled like chicken browning in bacon.

"Oh, listen to this," Cara added, squirming in her seat, "she goes on to say that it isn't about looks. She says, 'Gorgeous women get dumped every day. It's about mystery and learning how to create intrigue.'"

"I've definitely nailed that intrigue thing."

All the trash talk didn't help, either. Giving him the impression that she was worldly and sexually active and then doing a one-eighty by telling him she had never been on a date before. As it stood, he either thought she was sexually repressed, or that she was only interested in sleazy one-night stands.

She squeezed her eyes shut. Why, oh why, did she do that?

Because that had been her job for the last several years. Lying to people about who she was so she and Mercy could take something from them. They were like military-trained grifters.

Women who knew a lot about how to effectively use a tactical knife but had no idea which fork to use at the dinner table. They could steal your multimillion-dollar David Hockney painting while you took a private phone call but didn't have the first clue on how to set up a profile on a dating site.

"But that explains why he finally asked you on a date," Cara insisted. "The intrigue must have won him over."

"And here I thought it was because I was gorgeous."

Vlad pulled out nail clippers from his pants pocket and stretched out his thumb. Madame Garmond cleared her throat in reproach, stopping him in his tracks and looking at him as if he was about to spit a loogie on her shiny patent leather purse.

He hunched his shoulders and slipped the clippers in his pocket. "For what it is worth," Vlad commented, "I think you pretty woman, Miss Loren."

"Thank you, Vlad," she said with a genuine smile.

A sudden cascade of tubes, bottles, and other makeup-related paraphernalia was dumped in front of Loren as Mercy sat down and scooted her chair closer to her, setting up a standing mirror.

"She's going to be drop-dead gorgeous after I'm through with her," she said with what Loren thought to be a high degree of confidence since her sister didn't even wear makeup. At least not since moving to Wilder and all things fun and frivolous censored by Cara.

Loren riffled through the various contents and picked up a tube of lipstick the color of the truck parked in the town's fire station. "How do you even know how to apply this stuff?"

"Please," Mercy replied with a wave of her hand. "I'm an artist. How hard can it be? But just in case, I watched a few makeup tutorials on YouTube. I got this."

Cara continued to read from her book. "She also goes on to say that you have to maintain your independence." She leaned the book down as if scrutinizing Loren and found her acceptable. "You've definitely got that covered."

Freed her sisters from a sinister doctor and set them up in a home in the remote prairie land of Texas. Yep, they could check that one off the list.

Loren grabbed the side of her chair as Mercy began to apply what she said was a thin layer of primer on her skin.

"Hold up," Cara piped up with her finger in the air. "It says you can, under no uncertain terms, pursue him." Cara's eyes narrowed, now pointing her accusing finger at Loren. "Have you been pursuing Alec?"

Mercy piped up. "No, she avoided him like the plague except when she thought he wasn't looking and made sexy eyes at him."

Loren's head pulled back. "What are you talking about? I never made sexy eyes at Alec Wilder."

"Please, you did, and you do . . . when you think he's not looking." To illustrate, she tilted her head toward Vlad and narrowed her eyes while batting them slowly.

Vlad shook his head. "That is not it. It is more like this." And then he held his head high and raised an eyebrow.

Mercy grimaced. "You look more like a cartoon villain than Loren pining over Tractor Bob."

Cara continued reading down the list. "Never let him see you sweat." Lowering her book, she patted her finger against her lips. "Has he seen you all gross and sweaty? I have and it's not a good look."

Loren was unable to respond as Mercy began to apply copious

amounts of foundation on her face, answering on her behalf. "She was sweating buckets all over him during that first self-defense class in the church gymnasium. She clocked him, too, although she claims she didn't."

"You hit him?" Cara cried in disbelief. And then as if in realization, she squealed in a higher pitch. "Oh my gosh, you lied. You said he fell and hit his head or something. We should never lie. Tell her, Madame Garmond. Tell her it's a mortal sin."

Before the elderly woman could respond, Loren said to Cara, "Let's just say that I'll probably be foregoing the Pearly Gates."

Cara's face fell. "That's not the least bit funny." And then said with more sass, "Do you want to go to hell?"

Loren squinted her eyes as Mercy was getting a little carried away with what appeared to be a tube of concealer.

"Of course not, I was just kidding, but before you get all snippy with me on the evils of lying you might want to remember that trip you made to Dallas recently." Loren said, doing her best to make eye contact with her younger sister. Difficult to do as Mercy's application process was similar to that of some of her more aggressive artistic brushstrokes. "But to answer your question, yes, he has seen me gross and sweaty."

Cara twisted her lips as she glanced at Madame Garmond, and read on, "Oh, this one more than makes up for you being sweaty and physically accosting him. She says here that you should always 'treat your body like a finely tuned machine.'"

"She is that," Vlad concurred.

"Her body's a lethal weapon," Mercy chimed in. "She's like that bad as—" Mercy glanced up at Madame Garmond. "Um, that really cool chick in that old Terminator movie who wouldn't die no matter what or who you threw at her." Mercy leaned toward Loren with an ominous-looking black-tipped brush. "Quit being a baby and hold still while I apply the liquid eyeliner."

After what seemed an interminable amount of time suffering through more layers of makeup and Mercy's insistence that she remain still, Mercy sprayed her face with something she called "setting spray" that smelled more like a bathroom trash can that had been out in the sun too long.

She coughed a couple of times as Mercy looked over her face as if it were a Horchow therapy sketch.

"Done!" she said with a wide grin. "New and improved Loren Ingalls."

For a millisecond, three sets of eyes took in Mercy's work. Loren's face began to feel warm with all the mute scrutiny.

Until Cara finally said, "She looks quite glamorous."

"Doesn't she?" Mercy said. "It's called 'red-carpet' face."

"The red lipstick is quite dramatic," Vlad remarked.

"Are her cheeks supposed to be sunken-in like that?" Cara asked, physically sucking in her own cheeks.

"It's called contouring," Mercy explained. "Makes her cheekbones pop."

Cara leaned in closer. "Are those fake eyelashes?"

"Aren't they beautiful? I picked them up at the local drugstore. They're magnetic."

Loren was getting nervous as everyone kept staring at her, the mirror situated in a way that wouldn't allow her to view Mercy's efforts.

Apparently, Mercy felt the reticence from her viewers as well. "Well, what do you think?" She turned toward Mrs. Garmond.

"Oh, well, Miss Mercy, I find her to be quite chiseled and red-carpet worthy."

Mercy smiled and turned to Cara and Vlad.

Vlad nodded and chewed his bottom lip. "I must agree with Madame." He looked up at Mercy. "Where is date?"

Mercy shrugged and looked to Loren for an answer.

Loren shrugged hers as well. "I dunno."

Cara smiled weakly and squeezed Loren's shoulder with encouragement. "You look ... unreal."

They all continued to stare at her face with narrowed eyes while

Mercy grabbed her various tubes and palettes and turned to her with a stern face. "You've got just enough time to get dressed, don't smudge anything. I'll run this stuff upstairs."

Mercy jetted through the hall and upstairs, and just as quickly, all three began to talk at once.

"She doesn't look like herself. It's like she's plastic." Cara said, shaking her head and getting a closer look.

"We have words in Russia for woman look such as this. Not good ones," Vlad added sternly.

Madame Garmond took Mercy's place in the chair in front of Loren and began to call out orders. "Cara, tell Mercy I need her to go back to the grocery to pick up a spice I had forgotten. Do not allow her back into the kitchen. Vlad, stand by the living room window and let us know when Loren's gentleman friend pulls into the driveway."

Loren finally grabbed the mirror to look at what had everyone moving into crisis-mode. What she saw made her inhale sharply.

"Oh, my God! This is too . . . too much," she said. "I'm either going to a movie premier or hitting the pole at Girls Gone Wild down in Newport."

Her lips were not just red, but a lacquer-red and her contoured cheeks could literally cut glass. Her eyelashes looked more like huge fluffy spiders that mated and gave birth to more fluffy spiders. Her eyebrows were oddly perfect.

No one had perfect eyebrows.

"I can't go out looking like this." She glanced at the time on her phone. "I have to call and cancel."

But then what would she tell Mercy? It would only hurt her feelings. And there was the stupid sister card, irrevocably pulled. As much as she hated it, it was Loren's responsibility to follow through. Even under the worst of circumstances.

Her head jerked up as she heard Cara shepherding Mercy down the stairs to the front door. "Madame said we have to pick up some . . . ."

"Cardamom!" Madame blurted.

"Okay, quit pulling my arm. I'm going as fast as I can." Mercy's voice rang through the hallway, "We'll be right back, Madame. Have fun tonight, Loren."

Vlad leveraged the opportunity to make a hasty exit. "I go with girls. Delay return."

Madame shook her head. "No, you wait on the porch and advise Master Wilder that Loren is running a smidge behind and will meet him at the local brasserie."

A woman on a mission, Madame Garmond grabbed one of the teardrop-shaped makeup sponges Mercy had left behind and turned Loren's face toward her. "This just needs some toning down. Hold still, and I'll have you looking more like yourself in no time."

For an elderly woman, Loren was shocked at how quickly she went to work, patting the damp sponge over her face and rinsing it several times in the sink. Removing much of the excess product, she began to blend, making Loren wonder if Mercy had used a trowel during application.

Madame then grabbed a clean dish towel from one of the drawers, pulling it gently along Loren's lips, making the towel appear as if it were cleaning up a murder scene as opposed to an overly enthusiastic makeover.

During the process, Loren breathed in Madame's light perfume and noticed her hair was a soft, salt and pepper color.

Her hands were small, the skin crepey from years of, what? Did she wash dishes? Scrub floors? She seemed too regal and put together to do something so mundane. Although she did know her way around the kitchen. The chicken smelled wonderful.

Without warning, Madame tugged at one set of the magnetic eyelashes, and then the other, causing Loren to yelp. Loren's fingers went to each eyelid to stem the stinging. Humming a tune Loren didn't recognize, Madame pulled out a mauve-colored lipstick from inside her shiny black purse and gingerly dabbed it across Loren's lips.

"There," she said, moving the mirror so that Loren could assess her work.

Loren sighed with relief as she recognized her face, the makeup now giving her a pretty glow as opposed to the look Mercy had delivered with such a heavy hand.

"How did you know how to do that?" Loren asked, gripping the sides of the mirror.

"A lifetime of practice," Madame said with a slight nod of her head.

"Thank you." Loren was amazed at how quickly she'd gone from grossly over-done to a slightly improved version of herself.

"You're most welcome," Madame replied, matter-of-factly. "I'm sure your beau will find you quite beautiful with or without makeup."

"Thanks for the encouragement. To be honest, I have no idea what the criteria for success is when it comes to dating."

Madame shifted in her seat. "When you attended your seminars and conventions, did you not have the opportunity to meet and enjoy the company of men your age with similar interests?"

Lies. Loren always seemed to be either propagating or defending them. What would life be like if she could be completely forthright and honest?

But who was to say that Madame wasn't also well-versed in subterfuge?

"Madame," she said with a sigh, wishing she could go to her room and pull the covers over her head as opposed to going on a fact-finding date. "All those years at the Center, did you really believe I attended math conventions and seminars, and Mercy was strolling around art shows? Did it really make sense to you that we would be allowed such privileges when we were also supposedly diagnosed as dangerous psychopaths? Did you, or anyone else for that matter, ever question anything Dr. Halstead did to us at the Center?"

Madame clasped her hands in front of her, sitting tall and refined in the midst of their shabby kitchen.

"Would it surprise you to know that I was fully aware of what was going on at the Center as it pertained to you and your sisters?"

Both blood and anger raced through her veins in a dead heat as she contemplated Madame knowing the truth and allowing them to be abused, their skills leveraged in the most dangerous, dishonest, and devious of ways. All in the name of profit, thereby funding the Center and making the doctor a very rich man.

Loren raised an eyebrow. "I guess I shouldn't be surprised that you were on the take as well."

"Oh, Dr. Halstead had no idea that I was aware of his countless criminal activities."

"But you said nothing. You did nothing to help us. To help Cara."

"An understandable assumption; inaccurate, but understandable."

"Funny, I don't recall you playing a role in our escape."

"No? Did you honestly think it an accident when you so conveniently came across a vial of poison?"

Loren froze at Madame Garmond's insinuation. The same insinuation made by Vlad within days of his unexpected arrival.

Could they have been working together? Vlad never once mentioned Madame Garmond as an accomplice when it came to Dr. Halstead's death.

And now Madame was claiming to be aware of their missions when she was supposedly clueless yesterday. Charlotte wasn't even aware of why they had left for days, sometimes weeks, at a time.

Could Vlad and/or Madame be lying about why they were here?

Maybe Mercy's intuition about Madame was spot-on before turning into the old lady's personal sycophant, that is. Maybe she was here spying on them and reporting into Jasper.

Now that Loren thought about it didn't seem so farfetched. Cara, Madame, and Jasper traveled all over the world together. Could have Madame and Jasper been partners in crime despite Madame's insistence that she didn't like or trust Jasper around her "charge"?

Loren sat back in her chair and clasped her hands over her

stomach in an attempt to appear unaffected. "I think you have more to tell me. Please continue."

"We don't have time to go through all the details." Madame stood from the table to check on her simmering chicken. "We can discuss them later. Until then, you have a nice young man coming to pick you up for an evening out. Just be yourself and I'm sure he will find you utterly charming."

She gave Loren's clothing a once-over, which consisted of cutoffs and a shirt printed with a large tongue hanging out of a mouth on her chest. "That is, assuming you own presentable clothing."

Loren glanced down at her shirt. "I think I can find something that doesn't scream 'sex dungeon' or 'daddy issues.'"

Madame then reached behind her neck to unclasp the string of pearls that lay there and re-closed the clasp once it encircled Loren's slender neckline. "These pearls belonged to my mother. Allow me to loan them to you for this evening. She claimed they could provide any outfit a hint of refinement and good taste."

Loren glanced up, still not sure what to think of Madame's stilted, but kind gesture. "Think they'll clash with my red satin bustier and fish nets?"

Madame's prim demeanor softened the slightest. Loren felt herself becoming uncomfortable with a look from the elderly woman that tinged on the side of pity.

"I think you use cavalier and inappropriate humor when you feel frightened and unsure of yourself."

Loren straightened her spine. "The only thing I'm unsure of is why you're here. And the *only* thing that frightens me is the prospect of my family being sent back to the Center."

Madame tilted her head and nodded slowly. "We have more in common than you realize, my dear. That too is my greatest fear *and* the very reason I am here."

CHAPTER TWENTY-EIGHT

"Truth is ever to be found in the simplicity, and not in the multiplicity and confusion of things."

—Sir Isaac Newton
English mathematician, physicist, astronomer, theologian, and author. Widely recognized as one of the most influential scientists of all time

Alec had just pulled into Lucky's parking lot at the same time Loren arrived.

He descended from his truck to meet her by the entrance door. They made their stiff and awkward hellos, only to be surpassed with a stiff and awkward hug.

"You look, nice." Alec said, feeling oddly and uncomfortably pleased that she had made an effort with her clothing and makeup.

"Oh," she said, looking down at her dress as if embarrassed. "This old thing."

As Alec held the front door open, Loren noticed that the bar had quite a different vibe compared to the night of Mercy's birthday party. No dancing, no lines two-people-deep behind the bar, several people trying to grab Gus' attention to place a drink order.

Tonight, the music on the jukebox was slow and moody, and the tables spread out with couples sidled up next to one another.

"This is unusually . . . cozy," Alec said with what appeared to be a bit of discomfort.

"What is this? Couple's night?" Loren's eyes scanned the room and then she sucked in. "Sweet baby Jesus, is that Henry and Lenore Sterling canoodling in the corner?"

At that moment, Henry whispered something in his wife's ear and she giggled like a teenager as she swatted his arm. The typically thorny woman looked to have just come from The Hair House with a fresh perm and wearing lipstick, no less.

Henry returned the arm swat with a naughty pinch to her rather large thigh.

"Yeah, I didn't need to see that," Alec said, as he turned away from the visual train wreck.

"Nobody needs to see that." Loren grimaced.

"Doesn't their daughter attend your self-defense class?"

"Used to. She got a job offer in a nearby town. Told me she wasn't sure she was going to take it because she liked living at home."

"Isn't she in her late twenties?"

"Thirty-two."

"What made her change her mind?"

Loren glanced down, suddenly infatuated with her new, red, embroidered cowboy boots. "Someone may have told her that it was time she had an adventure. Spread her wings a bit."

Alec smirked. "No wonder they're all over each other. They're empty-nesters."

"Aren't they a little old to . . . you know."

"Canoodle?" Alec asked with a chuckle. "I don't think there's an age limit, Loren."

Turning her head in the other direction, she spotted Becky Waterman giggling at something her husband said and then toss a straw at him as they shared a private joke.

She was pleased to see her friend out of her house and having a good time with a spouse who, more often than not, preferred to sit in his recliner and game with strangers online.

On their other side was Sue Ellen Whalen, who worked at the local feed store and attended Loren's self-defense class twice a week. She was sitting next to Edgar Mason, with a huge smile on her face. Things seemed to be progressing nicely for the terribly shy couple. Loren gave her a discreet thumbs-up when Edgar wasn't looking, and Sue Ellen smiled back as her face turned an alarming scarlet red.

Loren had soon learned the physically fit Amazonian woman didn't attend her classes to learn self-defense but rather to acquire a sense of womanly self-confidence, confiding to Loren a deep and abiding love for Edgar as early as second grade.

However, Sue Ellen was more accustomed to lifting feed bags and dealing with local farmers while working at the feed store than knowing the first thing about how to capture Edgar's attention with her womanly wiles.

Edgar was a math teacher at the high school. He was skinny and nerdy and just as oblivious as to how to engage with the opposite sex as Sue Ellen.

After one particularly aggressive class, Sue Ellen pulled Loren to the side, whispering that it was common knowledge that the two older Ingalls sisters were highly regarded by the male population of Wilder and asked her to teach her the secret to attracting the opposite sex.

Thankfully, Becky Waterman was close by.

Because Loren hadn't the faintest idea.

In a state of panic, she grabbed Becky by the forearm and pulled her into the conversation, having no idea how to give this woman advice on how to turn on the sex appeal. To her relief, Becky was able to share with Sue Ellen some basic tips on how to garner a man's attention. And right now, Loren wished she had paid closer attention.

Something about making lingering eye contact.

Whatever advice Becky told Sue Ellen seemed to have worked, considering how close the couple they were sitting to one another and how Edgar had his arm awkwardly hanging off the back of her chair.

Loren narrowed her eyes, wondering if they were going to engage in any kinky stuff tonight. For the life of her, she just couldn't picture it and then cringed as she envisioned Edgar throwing a small ball into the air and telling Sue Ellen to go fetch it.

"This okay?"

Loren jumped a little as Alec nodded toward a table close to the back as he removed his jacket.

"Oh, yeah. Perfect."

"You okay?"

"Sure, I'm fine." She removed her own jacket, second-guessing the black, button-down shirt dress she wore with her new cowboy boots. She touched the pearls at her throat, wondering if they made her look ridiculous or provided an element of sophistication to her outfit.

After the makeover debacle, she literally threw on the closest items she could find in her closet that didn't have stains or wrinkles. She didn't make it all the way down the stairs with the first two outfits, as Madame Garmond stood waiting for her, shaking her head and pointing for her to turn around and try again.

Funny how Madame Garmond's critical eye and mannerisms mirrored Cara's. Or was it vice versa?

Honestly, it was as if Cara was standing at the foot of the stairs, judging her clothing choices as opposed to distracting Mercy with an impromptu grocery run.

For that matter, why exactly was Loren so tolerant of Madame's scrutiny? She had no more resilience to the older woman than Mercy and Cara, and she wasn't sure why.

Madame deemed the first outfit unacceptable as the cropped top exposed her midriff.

Madame sighed heavily. "*Mon Dieu*, it's forty degrees outside and you're dressed as if you're about to visit the beach. What message does that send a young gentleman?" Madame asked, her arms folded, one over the other, with one set of fingers thrumming against her bicep.

Loren's finger shot in the air, "Oh, I know this one. That I just got fitted with an IUD?"

Madame was less than amused.

Loren stomped back up the stairs, contemplating trouncing down the steps in a red corset and booty shorts. But decided she didn't have time for shenanigans and chose what she thought was a much more subdued option: an electric blue bodycon dress she'd picked up at clothing store in Waymore.

She only made it to the first step when Madame said in a stern voice, "Please explain how a circumspect young lady exits a vehicle in such a dress without exposing her lady bits?"

"Underwear?"

Madame's eyebrow shot up, unimpressed.

Loren ran her hands down the side of her dress admiring how it clung to her body. "I believe I'm agile enough to descend from a pickup truck without embarrassing myself."

"Not in that indecent ensemble. Do you not watch TMZ?"

"Yeessss." No, but Loren was going to google it as soon as she got back home.

Finally, when she descended the staircase in her shirt dress and cowboy boots, Madame pursed her lips. "I guess that will have to do. It's a bit short, but not as short as the prior atrocity."

And just when Loren was about to make another snarky comment, the strangest thing happened. Madame cleared her throat, and said, "You're a lovely young woman with vast potential. That needs to be recognized, most of all by you."

Loren swallowed hard as she made it to the bottom of the

stairs. Feeling self-conscious, she began to straighten her perfectly straight skirt in order to avoid looking the woman in the eye. "You think I have potential?" Oh, God, now she sounded like Mercy, all warm and gooey over a random compliment from a near stranger.

Mercy, the bullshit-meter-detector, who could spot subtle manipulation in the form of empty platitudes with pinpoint accuracy. Yet after only one thinly veiled compliment from Madame, Mercy was scrubbing the refrigerator while humming a tune with an earnest look on her face.

And here was Loren, unable to deny the warmth that spread through her solar plexus and into her heart at the older woman's kind words.

There was an ever so slight softening in the older woman's eyes. "*Certainement, ma chère.* You are a lovely young woman who has the opportunity to prove her worth by the way she comports herself."

Loren's confidence in her attire returned at the memory of the conversation and instead of hopping up in her seat at the high-top table, she gingerly stepped up, while pulling her dress down to ensure she wasn't giving anyone a glimpse of her panties. Or lady bits.

"You're awfully quiet," Alec said, resting his elbows on the table.

"Just a lot on my mind."

"Anything you want to talk about?" He began to roll up the sleeves of his navy-blue shirt and Loren watched in fascination at the veins that ran up his forearms.

Were men even remotely aware of the mystical power of the forearm? Lord knew she'd caught plenty of them staring at her cleavage and wondered if they understood that forearm porn was ten times more seductive. Of course, you had to have the right forearms.

Aware she was staring, she glanced away. Then remembered Cara's dating tip to "be mysterious and create intrigue." "Nothing to be concerned about. Just some international concerns that I'm working through."

That was good. The reference to international affairs had an air of mystery and intrigue.

Alec smiled at her and she thought she'd lose her mind while gazing at his dimples. How weird might it be for her to lick one of them?

"Oh yeah? Espionage for an underground spy agency?"

Loren's eyebrows rose. Whoa. Not a perfect hit, but still too close to home.

"Funny." Loren forcefully chuckled. "No, I have a new houseguest, she's of French descent, raised in England, and I'm just working through her idiosyncrasies."

There. No lies. Maybe not so mysterious, but whatever.

"Short visit, or will she be languishing at the house for a while like Vlad?"

He seemed agitated.

Loren shrugged. "I'm not sure. Cara is quite close to Madame Garmond. She was her primary caregiver when we lived with my uncle."

Before he could dredge up any questions about Dr. Halstead that would only lead to more lies, she jumped out of her chair, tugging her skirt down as a nervous afterthought.

"I'll order our drinks. What'll ya have?"

"I can order our drinks; I'm not a total Neanderthal. Sit down and let me grab Gus."

"Nope, I'm already up. Name your poison."

Alec seemed unsure, but conceded with his shoulders lowering. "Guinness, and tell Gus we'll be ordering food, too."

"Wow, you're actually going to feed me. Big spender."

"Thought I'd splurge on some appetizers as long as you don't order one of the fancier wines."

"My," Loren said with her hand to her chest, "you certainly know how to woo a lady."

He gave her a slight grin which made her little heart zing. They were exchanging banter rather than hurling insults at one another. That was a good sign, right?

Then she remembered another dating pro-tip her dear little sister had imparted; "Do Not Pursue Him." She immediately dropped her saucy smile. She wasn't pursuing him. She was just getting him a drink. Making sure a person was hydrated was not pursuing him. She made it to the bar as she argued the point to herself and felt a nudge at her side.

Becky was standing next to her with a huge Cheshire cat grin. "So, you and Farmer Ted? And you said he didn't want to plow your field."

"Trust me, there are no sweaty farm chores going on here. Just two people on a casual date."

"So, he literally asked you on a date. I mean, he specifically used the word 'date'?"

"Yes, he used the word 'date.'" Loren eyebrows raised. "Why? Are we not on a date? Is the word 'date' some sort of euphemism for something strange and kinky?"

"Oh no, a date is a date," Becky assured her, her eyes jutting back and forth between Alec and Loren. "But a date with Alec Wilder is more akin to an urban legend. You've heard about it but haven't actually seen it with your own eyes."

"That's being a bit dramatic." Loren tried to capture Gus' attention.

"Do you not understand the significance of Alec Wilder asking *anyone* on a date that takes place in Wilder? You've broken through his proverbial testosterone ceiling. You're the first woman he's asked out on a real date since his wife dropped her basket."

"Ex-wife," Loren corrected. "What do mean 'dropped her basket'?"

Becky took a sip from her cocktail. "It's a Southern term for when someone loses their ever lovin' mind."

"That makes no sense."

"It's supposedly less crass than coming right out and calling someone batshit crazy."

"Huh, I guess it is more amenable than saying that someone is psychotic, diagnosed with delusional disorder, or even schizophrenic with homicidal tendencies."

"Once again, rather specific examples, but yes, people from the South are all about preserving one's delicate sensibilities."

"That's kinda nice."

"So, are you going to let him plow your field tonight?"

"Ew, and no, and could we discuss sex without involving farm references?"

Becky turned slightly to glance at Alec. "If I were you, I'd have dirty barnyard sex with him. Who knows if you'll get another chance?"

"What? You don't think I'll get a second date?"

"I didn't say that."

"You implied it. You said I better have sex with him because it's the only chance I'll get." Loren pointed at her neck. "It's the pearls isn't it? I look ridiculous wearing pearls in a bar."

"Puleeze. You're in Texas. You can ride a mechanical bull clutching your pearls wearing a string bikini and no one would think twice about it."

"Well, since you seem to know everything about everyone in this town, do you happen to know if Alec's . . . you know . . . kinky?"

"Kinky?" Becky's voice rose, and then she chuckled.

"Shh, keep your voice down. Yes, kinky. Does he like to do weird stuff during sexy time?"

"Okay, if I can't discuss sex without using farming references then you can't refer to it as 'sexy time.' But to answer your question, no idea. Marisa and I weren't friends." She tilted her head. "But when I think back to before he enlisted, during high school, I don't recall rumors of any sexually deviant behavior."

"Mercy told me that you said that some men like rough sex."

"Oh, you're talking about Lucinda Packett and that Newberry guy."

"So, it's true. Mercy said something about gags and ropes . . . and other stuff."

"What? You thinking Farmer Ted is going to ask you to get freaky with him?" Becky smirked and then barked out a belly laugh.

"Stop laughing," Loren said, glancing back at Alec, who was now in conversation with someone sitting in her chair. And that someone was a female, laughing at something he said and wearing the very same electric blue bodycon dress Madame had deemed inappropriate.

Loren grabbed Becky by her forearm and twisted her so they were both facing the bar with their backs to the offensive scene.

"Who's that woman?"

Becky started to turn and Loren yanked her arm. "Don't look."

"How am I supposed to tell you who she is if I can't look?"

"Okay, you can look but don't be obvious."

Becky sipped on her drink as she turned slightly while Loren remained ramrod straight, facing the bar.

Becky turned ever so slowly back around. "That woman, my dear friend, is nothing but trouble."

"What do you mean?"

"That is Marybell Simmons."

"Amarilla's mother?" Loren gasped. "I thought she was having an illicit affair with her pool boy."

Becky's eyebrows shot up. "What? Marybell is screwing the help? Where did you hear that?"

Loren squeezed her eyes shut, angry with herself for revealing the secret. "You can't tell anyone, Becky."

Becky scoffed. "Just because I know a lot doesn't mean I blab a lot."

"Promise you will not repeat what I'm about to tell you."

"Girl Scout's honor." Becky sipped on her drink, again peeking behind her. "But you'd better hurry up because Marybell's running her coffin-shaped fingernails up and down your date's arm."

Loren glanced back just as Marybell laughed and grabbed Alec's forearm.

Oh, hell no.

That was *her* forearm.

She'd called dibs.

Loren's eyes narrowed to slits.

"That dress is doing her no favors," Becky snarked as she took another sip of her drink.

"It's indecent," Loren sneered. "How does she expect to get in and out of her car without flashing someone?"

"Think that was her intent." Becky nudged Loren. "So, whatcha gonna do?"

Loren stared at her target. "Right now, I'm counting kill zones."

Becky chuckled, assuming she was joking, "Where you at?"

"Two hundred and thirty-four. Nine of which are less invasive with little to no blood. The others would be considered sloppy, but oh, so gratifying."

"Remember," Becky said, "the objective is to score a second date with Farmer Ted. Dismembering Marybell, the mother of Cara and Ally's newfound friend, Amarilla, might not be conducive to that goal."

"She'll never know what hit her," Loren said as she made her way back to her date, laser-focused despite the haze of anger welling up in her chest. As her pace remained steadfast her vision changed from 3-D objects to geometric patterns and shapes. A common occurrence when scoping the kill shot.

Becky hissed loudly before she was out of hearing range, "Just remember, nobody looks good in an orange jumpsuit."

CHAPTER TWENTY-NINE

"It is not knowledge, but the act of learning, not possession but the act of getting there, which grants the greatest enjoyment."

—Carl Friedrich Gauss
German mathematician and physicist who made significant contributions to many fields in mathematics and science

"Oh, hey, Miss Loren!"

So close. She was literally seconds away from confronting her quarry when Lenore Sterling began waving her over to her and Henry's corner of the bar.

Loren wasn't sure which was more disconcerting. The fact that she'd have to slip her knife back into her cowboy boot or that Lenore Sterling was actually smiling as opposed to sneering at her.

Visions of Marybell Simmons gasping for breath while wearing her bodycon dress, that if she were honest, looked better on the promiscuous whore than her, would have to be put on the back burner.

After all, she was now a delicate Southern gentlewoman. And it would be rude to dismiss Lenore's waves, regardless of past slights.

Diverting her path to destruction toward the opposite corner of the bar, Loren pasted a smile on her face. "Well, hello there, Lenore, Henry. Isn't the weather lovely tonight?"

Lenore clung to Henry's arm as if it were a life raft. "Why, yes, it is. And you're looking beautiful tonight."

It was all Loren could do to refrain from looking shocked at the woman who made their initial move to Wilder a difficult one, letting everyone know of their revealing attire during their visit at the 7-Eleven and rudely contemplating their questionable career choices. Not to mention ensuring she never worked at Henry's magical hardware store.

"Th-thank you, Lenore. I see you've been to the hair salon today. It looks lovely."

The woman lifted a jiggly arm to pat her hair. "I splurged at The Hair House for date night with my handsome husband here," she said, winking at Henry as he smiled back and patted her arm.

Henry gave his wife a nudge which made Lenore squirm in her chair and Loren increasingly uncomfortable before Lenore said, "I owe you and your sister an apology."

Loren's eyebrows lifted.

Lenore took a sip of liquid courage and continued under Henry's watchful eye. "I made some assumptions about you and your sister before getting to know you. And for that, I am sorry. The next time I see Mercy, I will be sure to tell her the same."

Curiosity just about killed Loren, and before she could ask why the change of heart, Henry offered up an explanation. "You've been a good friend to our daughter, Savannah. Gave her good advice. She's doing great at her new job, and Lenore and I have the house all to ourselves."

He gave Lenore a suggestive grin.

Loren struggled to find adequate words. "Well . . . that's . . . great news. I'm glad it worked out for everybody."

Lenore seemed to have more to get off her chest. "I thought you were nothing but trouble that first time we met at the 7-Eleven, based purely on how you were dressed, but Henry helped me realize that it's wrong to assume someone's character on very little information." Lenore seemed encouraged by Henry's smile directed at her. "I've promised to get to know people better before making insensitive comments about them and assuming the worst."

Henry lovingly squeezed Lenore's hand and then turned to Loren. "If it's not too late, we'd love for you to work for us at Wilder's Hardware. Lenore's been busy managing the 7-Eleven. We'd certainly understand if you're no longer interested, but wanted to put it out there."

Loren felt her heart expand, as if an entire lifetime of condescension toward her had been lifted from her chest. Her eyes began to fill and she subconsciously touched her pearls.

And just like that, the curvy brunette undressing *her* date with her eyes and molesting him with her Halloween nails, was no longer an issue.

What filled her senses was the prospect of going to work and smelling paint thinner, fertilizer, and the chemical off-gassing of the PVC garden hoses on a daily basis. Not to mention the grainy feel of sawdust on virtually every surface, and the warmth of the mid afternoon sun wafting through the industrial steel plated glass windows.

What job could be more satisfying and irrefutably normal than working at a local hardware store?

None, that's what.

Yanking herself out of her self-imposed reverie, she cleared her throat. "I would love to work for you. My evenings are busy with my self defense classes and helping Cara with homework, but my days are completely free."

Henry slapped the table with a grin and then reached over Lenore to shake Loren's hand. "It's a deal, come in Monday morning and we'll start the paperwork and get you started, little lady."

Her smile faded slightly. "What should I wear?"

Lenore eagerly answered for her husband. "Just what you would normally wear. There's no uniform."

"Okay," Loren said with a renewed smile and a slow nod. "I'll be sure to wear something work-appropriate."

"I've no doubt that whatever you choose will be just fine. By the way," Lenore added with a wink, "love the pearls."

Loren made her goodbyes, feeling like she'd just been awarded a Nobel prize, and turned toward her table only to be reminded of the trashy MALF (mother Alec ((would no doubt)) like to fuck) and re-found her pulsing heart rate.

Like the stealthy assassin she was, she lifted her boot as if to scratch a difficult spot and gripped her knife, no one the wiser.

As she meandered through the throng of tables, her mission re-established, she slowed as Lenore's confessions connected with her conscience.

"... it's wrong to assume someone's character based on very little information..."

She faltered and sighed. What did she really know about Marybell Simmons? Maybe there was more to the story, just like there was more to her and her sisters' story.

"... get to know people better before assuming the worst."

Crap, Marybell was just given a stay of execution by the town's most malicious gossip and here she was, clutching a knife recently sharpened with a leather strop with diabolical plans to terrorize, at the very least, Amarilla's mother because she was making eyes on her fuck-worthy neighbor.

Seriously, look at him. Who wouldn't want to take that home and do dirty things to him?

Not that she planned to. Oh no, tonight she was going to be polite and circumspect.

She was on a first date, and nice girls didn't get down and dirty on the first date. She didn't need to watch movies to know that, for crying out loud.

But come on. How could she blame Marybell for being attracted to Alec? With those lickable dimples and porn-worthy biceps . . .

Maybe she should gather more intel before coming to a conclusion as it pertains to— She came to a complete halt. Jesus fuck, that woman was nearly clenching his balls.

CHAPTER THIRTY

"Mathematics is not a deductive science—that's a cliché. When you try to prove a theorem, you don't just list the hypotheses, and then start to reason. What you do is trial and error, experimentation, guesswork."

—Paul Halmos
Hungarian-born American mathematician and statistician who made fundamental advances in the areas of mathematical logic, probability theory, statistics, operator theory, ergodic theory, and functional analysis

Alec politely removed Marybell's fingers, along with her creepy-as-fuck fingernails, from his arm.

But no sooner than when he extricated himself from potential bloodletting, she leaned against him using his arm as a scratching post and whispered in his ear. "You sure are looking mighty fine tonight, Alec."

"Appreciate the compliment, Marybell." He refrained from rearing back from her sugary sweet perfume.

"Why don't you be a gentleman and buy me a drink? Or are you gonna play hard to get tonight?"

"Ah, now, I wouldn't be much of a gentleman if I bought you a drink while on a date."

Which, by the way, where was his date? He had watched her saunter to the bar with hooded eyes and had to remind himself that tonight was to re-establish a truce. Nothing more. And suddenly, he caught Gus' shit-eating grin at his dilemma as he leaned against the back of the bar while drying his hands with a bar towel.

Maybe she went to the restroom. He looked over Marybell's shoulder and finally found her mid-discussion with Lenore and Henry.

He suddenly flinched as those nails found their way to his thigh.

"Everyone knows you don't date." Leaning closer to him, she said, "You only do hook-ups."

"I'm here with someone, Marybell."

"Where is she, then?" She looked around the bar, failing to find what she deemed as viable competition, smirked, "I don't see anyone here."

While her fingers worked their way higher, he saw his pint-sized date making her way toward them. And if looks could kill, she looked no less than a trained assassin holding a grudge and something sketchy behind her back.

Once again, he yanked on the talons securing his thigh. Good Lord, the woman had some upper-body strength. Nothing compared to his date, but enough to make him hiss as her nails scraped against his jeans, refusing to release.

"Well, hey, y'all."

Alec's eyes widened at Loren's change of demeanor, and impromptu Southern accent. She stood directly in front of them with a strange smile on her face as a clueless Marybell continued to sit in his date's chair.

Loren reached out to shake the woman's hand that had been holding his thigh hostage.

"I'm so glad to finally meet you. I'm Loren Ingalls. Your daughter and my sister, Cara, are friends."

"Oh, yes," Marybell purred, giving her a quick once-over. "I remember seeing her new little friends at the house the other day."

"How is Levi?"

Marybell's eyes narrowed. "You know my father?"

"I do. He's dropped Amarilla off at the house a couple times."

"He's doing just fine. Ornery as ever and far too involved in my life but doing fine."

Alec watched in fascination as his date expressed the epitome of southern gentility.

Loren continued, "Would you like to have dinner with us? I know you've been out of town for past couple of months, but I would love the chance to get to know you better."

"Oh, you're with Alec?" Marybell's eyes once again scanned her competition, her smirk indicating she found her inferior.

Loren continued to smile without responding, and to Alec's amazement, without giving the offensive woman an upper-cut to the jaw.

Marybell began to languidly disentangle herself from Alec's side. "That's such a kind invitation, but I've got plans, just dropped by to catch up with some friends and pass some time."

"Well, that's just too bad." Loren lied, "Maybe next time."

Marybell draped herself over the table to grab her purse that sat on the other side of Alec, managing to rub her tits against his arm, before standing straight and placing the strap over her shoulder. "I'm sure I'll be seeing you later, Alec," she said with a wink. Then, turning her back to Loren, she leaned down and gave him a kiss on the cheek and whispered, "Call me." She exited behind Alec's chair toward the front doors, not giving Loren a backward glance.

Alec's focus remained on his date. "I must say, that was alarmingly civil of you."

Loren's grin became wider and a bit scarier as she continued to look over his shoulder.

Alec turned to see what had her attention just in time to watch Marybell open the door, unaware that her thong was in clear view due to a clean split from her waist to the bottom of her gaping dress.

Alec turned back, squared his elbows on the table and fisted his hands over his mouth, watching Loren look everywhere in the room except at him.

"Loren, did you do that?"

Moving to the now empty chair to the left of Alec, she sat in her seat with what looked to be smug satisfaction.

"Do what?"

"You know what."

His hand moved below the table, landing lightly on her knee. Alec heard and felt her intake of breath as his hand made a torturous path down a well-toned right leg and into her boot, lifting the weapon from its hiding place and tossing it on the table in front of her.

"You carry this with you on dates?"

"You never know if things will get weird," she explained, gingerly placing her napkin in her lap. "Or if you need a dining utensil."

Her eyes began darting around the room, as if looking for a swift diversion.

Alec also made a quick sweep of the room. Those sitting nearby were busy snickering at Marybell's grand exit, missing the tactical knife spinning in a circular motion on the table.

Alec continued to glower, knowing it was making her all the more uncomfortable. "You're gonna tell me that you use a Zero Tolerance combat knife to cut your food?"

"Sometimes," she shrugged, waving for Gus, as she slid the knife from the table into her lap. "When there's a lot of gristle."

Gus appeared and she visibly relaxed and smiled wide as he wrote down their long-awaited drink orders and dropped off menus.

Alec side-eyed his date as she leveraged the slight disruption, slipping the knife back into her boot.

"Oh," Loren popped up with a wide grin, "I almost forgot, I just got a job."

Being with this woman was like riding a rogue roller coaster and white-knuckling the safety bar. Frankly, he was barely hanging on.

"Today?" he asked.

"No, just now." She motioned behind her. "I start work Monday morning working for Henry."

"At the hardware store?" Now that was a surprise. Lenore Sterling had made it her life's mission to discredit the moral compass of the Ingalls sisters.

She nodded enthusiastically.

"And Lenore was okay with that?"

"I know, right? She apologized to me," she said, sitting tall. "Can you believe it? She said she shouldn't have made assumptions regarding our character based on our attire."

He nodded, thinking how he was guilty of the same and how Loren and Mercy had slowly wormed their way into the hearts of the townspeople.

Even into the heart of Lenore-the-town-gossip Sterling.

And if he was honest, he, too, was getting sucked into their mysterious yet pleasant orb.

He rubbed at his own chest.

"How 'bout you?"

"Me?"

"Yeah, how's the new job?"

"Oh," he said, nodding. "Going well." His turn to be elusive and non-forthcoming.

"What is it you do, exactly?"

"Back office admin stuff." He responded, looking down as he unfolded his napkin.

"For a private security firm." She added.

"A private security firm slash collection agency."

Her eyes narrowed. "So, your company provides mall cops as well as payment collection services. What an odd combination."

An astute observation, as he'd just signed up as a private security contractor for M2M.

"What back office stuff do you do for them?" she asked as Gus dropped off their drinks and moved on to the next table. "Accounts receivable, payables?"

"I.T."

Actually, Alec's area of expertise was in exposing weaknesses in communications systems. A skill set honed while he was part of MARSOC.

But that specific job description was only to be given on a need-to-know basis. And the individual deemed "in need" had to be approved by his supervisor.

She took a sip of her drink. "And you can do that remotely?"

"I can." For now, anyway. Thanks to a widely respected expertise while enlisted, he was able to negotiate working undercover from home. The plan was to eventually lead a tactical team once Ally graduated high school and started college. But for now he was going to lay low, work on gathering intel and soak up all the information he could while keeping a close eye on Ally.

"Are you still planning to move closer to town?"

At that moment Gus showed up with his order pad, and grabbed the pen resting on his ear. "Sorry, guys. Busy night. It's like someone crop-dusted pheromones all over town. I swear the sexual tension in here could etch glass." He pointed his pen toward Edgar who was making his way to the jukebox and raised his voice. "Edgar, you play another Marvin Gaye song, and I'm gonna break your fingers." Shaking his head, he looked up. "What would y'all like?"

Alec also felt uncomfortable thanks to the local bar turned sex dungeon environment. Not to mention that his nerves were strung tight with the feelings he had for his date.

One minute she was light and disarming; the next, she was brandishing a knife he'd only seen used during a particularly unexpected and brutal skirmish in an Afghani village.

Despite his efforts, Lucky's didn't appear to be the place to keep a clear head and have a friendly dinner.

He turned to Loren, lifting the napkin from his lap. "How 'bout we take dinner to go?"

"Where are we going?" she asked. "Cara is out with Ally and Amarilla, but I have two houseguests and one nosy sister at the house."

"My place."

She smiled tentatively. "Okay."

He rubbed his thumb along his lower lip in doubt. Maybe going back to his place wasn't such a good idea.

They placed their orders, and while waiting, made their way around the room saying their goodbyes, a life-long habit for Alec who lived in such a small town that bore his last name.

While shaking hands, Alec would glance at Loren, who was hugging people and owning the room with her sweet smile and red embroidered cowboy boots.

His mayoral trek was out of obligation. Hers was because she was, simply put, a people magnet. And the fact that the townsfolk's regard for this sinewy bleach-blond was the result of a hard-won victory made her appeal all the more heartfelt.

Shrouded in mystery, ridiculously fit, and intrinsically kind, with a side of crazy.

He was totally fucked.

Finally, Gus brought out their order, which included a Gus's Special that Loren quietly placed next to a sleeping Jimbo before heading out of town.

CHAPTER THIRTY-ONE

"A mathematician, like a painter or poet, is a maker of patterns. If his patterns are more permanent than theirs, it is because they are made with ideas."

—G.H. Hardy
English mathematician, known for his achievements in number theory and mathematical analysis

Loren removed her coat and placed it on the hook next to the door where remnants of Alec's and Ally's outerwear rested.

Searching for inner bravado and feeling as sexually savvy and as painfully horny as a reluctant nun who never got to sow any wild oats, she began to recite some of her favorite mathematical functions to temper her libido.

It didn't help that Alec smelled like *eau de homme* with notes of testosterone-infused pheromones.

She followed him into the kitchen as he turned on the lights and set the bag of Styrofoam containers on the counter.

"Would you like a drink?" he asked while opening one of the cabinet doors and setting a couple glasses on the counter.

She soaked him in, finally getting a good look at him as he was no longer veiled by the dim lights of the bar but rather starkly lit by the light fixture over the kitchen table.

His curly dark hair was getting a bit long, and she twisted her fingers together to keep them from reaching up and wrapping them around her index finger. He was his usual stoic self, with crystal-blue eyes edged with a color of indigo she couldn't quite recall ever seeing in Mercy's paint lineup.

"Loren?"

Oh right . . . drink.

"Yes, please," she said, adverting her eyes from his physical goodness, to the elements of the old-fashioned kitchen that hadn't ever been updated. Nothing like the contemporary farmhouse styles that were all the rage on Pinterest.

"All I've got is scotch, but it's good."

"That's fine," she said, barely turning his direction as she took in the white refrigerator with the curved lines and the walls covered with an old-time strawberry print.

Her body felt strung tight and hyper-sensitive as well as inexplicably drawn to Alec. In an effort to dampen the electrical arcs coursing through her body, she focused on her physical surroundings. A trick she learned to ground herself and, as a result, avoid drowning in sensory overload.

Slowly, her vision began to blur and then return with a distinct clarity as the lines of the refrigerator moved into the familiar fractals and lines that distracted her.

Sighing, she took in the room with a different perspective, seeing how all the lines came together and meshed, making it crisp and clear and relatable. She promised herself to remember each line and curve and later transpose it onto paper when she reached the sanctity of her bedroom.

A cold brush on her arm yanked her back, and she realized Alec had merely touched her with the glass of brown liquid and ice cubes.

"Thank you," she breathed taking the glass from his hand and feeling that undeniable spark when their fingers made contact.

Beneath an invisible shroud of self-preservation, Loren's body hummed with a visceral need to be touched. The ice cubes clinked as she stared into her glass, willing herself to slow her heartbeat and calm the fuck down.

Just take it slow. All in due time. They would get to the sexy part later. For now she needed to hold onto her glass and refrain from jumping him.

Conversely, Alec leaned back against the kitchen counter with his ankles crossed, assessing her while taking a slow drink. It was as if the more anxious she became, the more calmness he exuded.

He took a sip, and his Adam's apple bobbed, and she felt her lady parts swoon and then weep. And just like that, she was wet.

Nothing weird about that.

He glanced down at his drink, blocking the view of his Adam's apple, and she almost objected.

"I'm glad that Lenore Sterling apologized to you."

Taken slightly off guard, she didn't respond but sipped her drink instead, wondering where she might find the closest bathroom.

He continued. "I wanted to do the same. Tonight, I mean."

She looked at him, her drenched panties an afterthought. "You wanted to apologize?"

He moved his wrist in a circle, sloshing the ice around in his drink. "I haven't been very open-minded as it pertains to you and your sisters and I thought taking you to dinner tonight might be a good way to let you know that I was wrong."

Her heart stopped and then inconveniently lodged in her throat.

She rubbed her forehead, doing her best not to over react or misinterpret what tonight was about.

He took another sip of his drink, which, this time, she failed to notice as she focused on how to cough up the pulsating organ beating inside her esophagus.

Her life had conditioned her for disappointment. When you had zero expectations, you were rarely disappointed.

But she'd had expectations. For tonight.

He nodded. "I was wrong in making character assumptions about you without getting to know you first."

She felt her heart making a downward spiral from her throat to her stomach. Was this a date or a pathetic excuse for an apology?

He confirmed her suspicions. "I'm sorry, Loren. I was hoping we could start over tonight. Establish a truce."

A truce.

Funny how his apology didn't render the same satisfaction as Lenore's.

Instead, she felt silly.

Humiliated.

She smirked at her clueless self. She'd actually thought he might have feelings for her. Well, enough for a date anyway. But the only feelings she managed to pull out of him were regret and guilt.

Fucking expectations.

Walls erupted around her. Her inner voice could hear them lock into place. Concrete and impenetrable.

She took a long drink, winced from the burn and set the empty glass on the counter.

"Apology accepted," she said, pushing off from the refrigerator to grab her purse she'd placed on the kitchen table. "It's late," she said with a forced smile. "Thanks for getting me out of the house. It's been crazy lately, what with all of our visitors, but I need to get back."

"It's not even ten o'clock."

"It's late for me. Early to bed early to rise, you know the drill."

She hated herself for the tears welling in her eyes.

So stupid.

So gullible.

Her head down, she made her way to the coat hooks by the front door.

He didn't want to date her; he didn't want to do kinky stuff with her. He just wanted to apologize.

Here, she thought she was would to recite a list of "no-goes" for tonight's sexcapades and deliver worthwhile dating tips for Mercy while skipping over the more intimate parts of the evening.

So much for that plan. Her new objective was self-preservation and maintaining what was left of her dignity.

Just as she reached for her coat, a large hand grabbed her bicep. Highly distracted and registering an attack, she instinctively reared back and rotated her arm and palm to set up for a joint lock.

Before completing the move and snapping his wrist, he wrenched himself from her grip causing her to stumble. Momentarily confused she looked up to see Alec holding up both hands in supplication and breathing hard.

"Jesus Christ," he fumed. "What the fuck, Loren?"

Oh shit, fuck, hell.

What was she doing?

Both of them were panting, and equally discombobulated. But he was now looking at her like she was unstable.

Out of her mind.

One hand covered her mouth, followed by the other one. She stared at him, transfixed, shaking her head; she couldn't believe it herself. Clasping her hands together in front of her mouth, she said, "I'm so sorry."

Alec ran his hands through his hair as if trying to make sense of her over-reaction.

She remained ramrod straight, in praying mode, waiting for him to kick her out of his house.

But instead of escorting her to the door, his gaze shifted from confused to soft. "Can I touch you?"

She nodded briskly not daring to speak.

He walked up to her cautiously and wrapped his arms around her.

She melted at his touch.

And then she breathed in the wool from his shirt and the smokiness of the scotch. She buried her face in his neck and inhaled a fragrance she couldn't pinpoint but made her knees go weak all the same. He needed to stop wearing that cologne or using that soap, or whatever it was that made her have such an insatiable craving for him.

She melted more. Fused her entire length against his body. He felt so perfect. Like stability and goodness wrapped up in a beguiling, manly package. And she had attacked him.

"You know I would never hurt you." He said into her hair.

Physically? Like she would ever let him. Emotionally? She was defenseless. He could decimate her. Regardless, she nodded, not willing to disengage and content to just breathe him in.

Like stubborn Velcro, he pulled her far enough away to bend down slightly, holding her face in his hands. "I was just trying to slow you down. Stop you from leaving." He was shaking his head. "What made you want to leave?"

His hands moved to her shoulders, lightly massaging them, waiting for her answer.

Loren felt so tired. Tired of being chronically alert, perpetually skeptical, and consistently heartbroken. The concrete battlements fell away, crumbling around her until she felt vulnerable and exposed. But she was just too tired to do a damn thing about it.

"I thought this was a real date. That we were going to have sex, and I was going to have to lay out some ground rules because I gave the impression that I was promiscuous and maybe a little kinky." Loren swallowed, laying it all out. "But you just took me to dinner to apologize."

So much for being mysterious and not pursuing him. At least she wasn't sweating. If you didn't count the arousal pooling in her underwear earlier.

She continued, her tone more forceful. "I don't want nor do I need your apology, or pity for that matter. I need a date, a real date with no hidden agendas. I want to have sex with you on this date, not because I'm promiscuous, but because I deserve it. I've waited a long time for this and you don't get to turn my night into some sort of self-righteous, grand gesture apology. That. I. Don't. Want."

"Okay, okay." He said nodding his head. "It *was* a real date. *Is* a real date," he said with a slight smile. "Can't a guy apologize and ravage a woman at the same time? Does that go against some sort of intrinsic Ingalls' woman-code?"

She was who she was and that was perpetually skeptical. "Are you sure you're not just saying that to make me feel better?"

His eyebrows furrowed. "You think I'm spewing a line so that I can"—he searched for the words—"pity-fuck you?"

She rubbed at her temple. "At this point, I really hope so."

Dimples sprouted on both sides of his upturned mouth, and she felt intense satisfaction in being the cause.

"All right, then," he said, letting go of her arms and clapping his hands, "let's get this bedding business out of the way."

He took her hand, walking backward, and leading her toward the staircase. "Just so you know, if you're bound and determined to set ground rules, now's the time to do it."

"Funny you should mention 'bound,'" she said, following him without question. "That's not going to happen."

He nodded, working his way up the staircase. "Agreed. No tying one another up."

He was full-on smiling at her and she had to hold herself back from doing a happy dance. Because that wasn't sexy. And she was going to have sex. With Alec Wilder.

She perked up. "And no rubber balls."

He hesitated, glancing at her. "Rubber balls?"

"Gag balls."

"Why would you think . . .? Are you serious?"

"As a heart attack."

They reached the doorway, and he pulled her deeper into his room and she took in the sparse surroundings that looked circa farmhouse 1990s. On the left was an outdated bedroom suite, the wallpaper printed with mauve flowers and faded greenery.

"Alright then. No gags, no bondage. Anything else that's a hard stop for you?"

"That's a good question. I'll let you know as we go."

"Should we establish a safe word?" He asked with a grin.

"What's a safe word?"

"I thought you watched a lot of movies."

"Apparently not the same ones you do," she murmured as she began to unbutton her dress. "Can we just go easy? Do some normal, everyday sex stuff and maybe work our way into things one might classify as more adventurous?"

"Start with vanilla schnapps and work our way up to Fireball?"

"Something like that."

"I can work with that." He nodded solemnly, watching her fingers working their way down the row of buttons of her dress.

"But don't be timid," she added as she shimmied out of her dress and pulled off her boots, kicking them to the side. "I want you to bring your A game."

"Wow, no pressure."

Loren stood tall with her hands on her hips in a pair of white cotton panties and a matching bra. "Okay, your turn. Show me what you got."

Grabbing the back of his shirt with one hand, he pulled it over his head. "This is the strangest conversation I've ever had during sex."

"Shhh," Loren said, taking in his perfect chest and abs that resembled corrugated steel. "Let me take this in."

Alec raised his eyes as if embarrassed by her perusal. She didn't care. Becky foretold that this would be a one-and-done date, further solidified by the fact that she failed nearly every dating tip Cara had cited from her all-knowing book of dating.

Of course, there was also the counter-attack in the man's living room. Another potential contraindication for a second date.

If this was going to be her one and only date with her ridiculously attractive neighbor, she wasn't going to waste a minute of it.

She slowly walked around him. "Take off your pants."

"I'm feeling a bit objectified here," he said, unbuckling his belt.

"Sorry, not sorry." She finally went mute as he shucked his dark jeans and stood straight.

He wore black cotton fitted briefs, the brand displayed on the waistband.

As if possessed by a severely undersexed spirit, her fingers reached out to touch one perfect glute, gliding along as she walked around to face him.

He looked straight ahead, standing at attention and looking over her shoulder. She bit her lip as she just couldn't resist moving her fingertips over his rippled abs and into his briefs.

He jumped as her hand wrapped around his length. "Jesus, Loren, how about some warning?"

"Sure. I'm going to feel your penis now."

His eyes arched. "What happened to starting out slow?"

She moved her hand up and down, mesmerized by how unique it felt. So hard, like it was standing at attention. But then again, so smooth and malleable, like it was incapable of remaining still.

She was feeling a bit overwhelmed, her nipples tightening and her breathing labored. She needed a game plan to help establish goals and gather her wits.

"We'll go slow during the sex act, but fast-track the foreplay," she asserted, spinning her forefinger in a circle, indicating the need to move things along.

"Got it," Alec responded, mimicking her with his own forefinger. "Fast-tracking."

"We'll move past the part where you slowly remove my clothes."

She rolled her eyes. "So lame. . . and past where you lay me down on the bed like I'm a delicate flower." She added with sarcasm, "Because that isn't stupid."

"I thought you said you were inexperienced?" he said hoarsely as she was now gliding her fingers across the indent at the tip.

"Do you have any idea how many contemporary romance novels Mercy has read to me?" She bobbed her head side to side. "Well, the sexy parts, anyway."

She noticed his shoulders hunch as her hands continued to work him.

"My bad," he said with a gravelly voice. "Carry on."

"Thank you. We can also skip where you look at me as if you've never seen a naked woman before. Which we both know is false. So really, why bother?"

"Right, I mean, I am thirty-two." He sucked in as she held him in her hand. He was becoming progressively engorged and she felt torn between wanting to give his cock more attention and getting through her list to ensure a successful sexual experience.

"And let's not feel the need to recite one another's names. Please, I already know my name. And hopefully, you'll have my full attention. So, just don't."

"Do I need to write this down?" he choked out.

She continued, while stroking him. "Skip past you mentioning how wet and unbelievably tight I am. And where I declare yours the biggest cock I've ever seen in my life." She thought for a minute. "That's it. Instead of all that, I say we get right to the good part."

His eyes caught hers. "Some might argue those are the good parts," he hissed as her grip inadvertently tightened. Realizing she was fisting him, she loosened her grip.

"Please, it's just a waste of time."

"So, the men you've been with were good with you . . . fast-tracking?"

She took a deep breath and removed her hand from his cock, his big, beautiful cock, to make a long overdue point. "At the risk of being overly-transparent and lacking in 'mystery,' I'm not a virgin."

She bit her lip and forced herself to muster through. "But I might have misled you on my level of experience. That said, if this is going to be good for both of us, we should agree that all of that extraneous stuff is superfluous and kind of silly when the end goal for both of us is to get to the—"

"Good part," Alec finished for her.

"Exactly." She grinned. He was going to be a great sex partner. She just knew it.

"So," Alec said, resting the back of his hand on her cheek. "If I were to touch you like this, it would be a waste of time?"

He moved closer gazing down at her, turning his hand until his palm was cupping her face, his thumb moving languidly along her bottom lip.

She cleared her throat, suddenly aware of how good it felt to have Alec Wilder touching her so damn softly and looking into her eyes with such reverence. "I mean, I guess that would be okay."

His pupils appeared fixated on her lips until she became progressively agitated and began to squirm. It felt as if her lady bits were pulsating in rhythm with her heart.

Speaking of which, was that moisture dripping down her leg? She might need to make a doctor's appointment. That couldn't be normal.

Still holding her face in his palm, his lips touched hers, distracting her from her potential medical condition, while he slowly pulled down the strap to her bra. Before she knew it, the kiss ended as he gazed down at her bare breast. His thumb now making the same movement against her nipple that he made to her lip.

"Is this a waste of time?" he asked, before taking the now distended nipple into his warm mouth.

"Um . . ." Her eyes rolled back in her head, making it impossible to finish a sentence. Then his other hand made its way to her ass, kneading and pulling her against that lovely length of steel pipe hiding beneath his boxers.

She admired his level of stealth as he managed to move and manipulate her body until she was lined up perfectly against him. A moan escaped her lips as he simultaneously sucked on her nipple while kneading her ass and undulating that beautiful steel rod against her clit.

"You want me to stop?" he asked between flicks of his tongue. "So we can fast-track to the good part?"

"No . . . yes." She was confused, her mind trying to navigate the pulse points between her ass, nipple, and clit. He was turning her into an unintelligible mass of nerve endings.

"Yes or no, Loren."

To her disappointment, his hand had relinquished her ass cheek. Before she could object, his long, tanned fingers inched their way down the front of her panties, and he was now using her embarrassing amount of arousal as his personal slip and slide.

"Mmm . . . so wet and wild."

"Oh, my, God," she said holding his shoulders and doing her very best to climb his torso despite him keeping her firmly where he wanted her, moving her this way and that so that all her important pieces and parts were mindlessly rubbing against his.

Lips and then teeth nipped at her collarbone as slick fingers plucked at her swollen clit as she tried in vain to perform a military crawl all over his body.

"Alec," she said breathlessly, not sure what she wanted to say or feel.

"Loren," he responded, and she blushed at how much she liked hearing him say her name. "Baby, what do you need?"

Her jumbled mind landed on the endearment. It was funny how ridiculous they sounded in the sex scenes she read, yet when Alec called her "baby" it was like she was someone special.

Someone to be revered and protected.

"Don't stop," she panted.

"What do you want?"

"More."

Before she could instruct him as to more of what, he made a sinuous path down her body, kissing and nipping along her ribs and over the front of her panties until he sat back on his haunches. Mortification set in as lidded indigo eyes never left hers as he worked the soaked blend of spandex and cotton down her legs.

She blurted, "I'm . . . getting checked for that."

He halted all movement, holding her panties at knee-level and looking up at her. "Checked for what?"

One hand leaned on his shoulder as the other waved over her private parts. "For whatever's going on down there."

He looked up with squinty eyes. "Could you elaborate?"

Oh, God.

She face-planted into her hands. Now he thought she had some sort of sexually transmitted disease.

"It's nothing. I mean, other than the preponderance of sweatiness, down below." She said swishing her hands in the area of question. A beet-red flush heated her face.

She watched him grin and mumble something unintelligible.

He touched her calf, and at his non-verbal command, she stepped out of her panties. As soon as they hit the floor, he lifted her thigh until it was over one shoulder, and he was looking at her most private area until she was blushing from head to toe.

"Are you talking about all of this?" His tongue lashed out as if he couldn't hold back any longer and she thought she was going to pass out at the way her entire body hummed with electrical currents. Before catching her breath, his mouth was full on her.

Licking.

Sucking.

Wet and filthy.

Mercy had read about this in a couple of books. But Loren had doubted seriously that this level of intimacy would happen tonight, or ever. It seemed so personal and somewhat unsanitary. Like, it would take a year of first, second, and third bases before making this physical leap of faith with a man. Not to mention a long hot shower beforehand.

Losing her grip, not to mention her mind, she clung to his shoulders, trying to maintain balance while writhing against his mouth.

Mother, Mary, and Joseph. His teeth were now a part of the process. How much longer could she take this? And what degree of bodily harm would she exact if he were to stop?

Tongue, then teeth. Both taking turns working her clit.

As if having a mind of their own, her palms moved to touch her now sensitive nipples that were full and distended, as if impatiently awaiting his attention. Her fingers moved on to his unusually soft hair, and she wondered for a nano-second if he used a high-end conditioner.

As if sensing her distraction he nipped at her swollen nub and growled.

"Oh, God, Alec."

Her body seized as his mouth continued to work its magic.

A wave of electrical charges pulsated through her body. She trembled and moaned at the feel of muscles enlarging and contracting, followed by an onslaught of aftershocks cascading through the rest of her body.

Thankfully, he caught her as she crumpled to the floor, grateful for an area rug that she noticed for the first time since entering the room.

Alec easily picked her up from the floor as if she were a throw pillow as opposed to a ridiculously toned woman gladiator and slowly lowered her to the bed.

His chest tightened as he gazed down at the perfectly sated woman who was smiling back at him.

Chewing the inside of his lip, he focused on seeing her for the first time outside of her usual habitat: in his bed without her guard up or sporting a side of snark. Rather, she lay before him entangled in her own blond wisps of hair with her arms lying above her head on each side of the pillow. A rather vulnerable pose for a woman with a hair-trigger temper and deep sense of distrust.

Despite her languid demeanor, he knew she withheld secrets from him and the rest of Wilder, but the more time he spent with this enigma of a woman-child-warrior, the less her secrets seemed to matter.

He wasn't deluding himself. He knew she was standing on some sort of figurative ledge, teetering along the precipice and in danger of losing her footing.

But he was all in. And his job, moving forward, was to hold on tight and to be there to pick her up if and when she fell. Because he knew, without a moment's hesitation, that this was so much more than an attempt to get her out of his system.

Not even close.

This feral nymph of a woman had robbed him of all reason and self-preservation. And he was both excited and terrified at the possible outcomes.

Standing up, he pushed down his briefs, not taking his eyes off her.

She lifted onto her elbows. "I hope this means we're getting to the good part." The glint in her eye betrayed her.

He threw his boxers over his shoulder. "Not yet. You haven't complimented me on the size of my cock."

He straddled her as she tilted her head as if to check out the goods. She shrugged one shoulder. "It'll do."

He settled between her legs and leaned his head a breath from hers. "Do I need a condom?"

"No," she whispered, suddenly shy, and then added, "I test negative for Chlamydia, Gonorrhea, Syphilis, Trichomonas …"

"Loren," he interrupted. "Did you test positive for any STD's?"

She shook her head.

"I'm clean as well."

He lifted one of her hands, kissed the inside of her palm and placed it on his neck and plunged into her.

She clenched his neck as she stifled her moans beside where Alec was sure she left nail marks. He gave her a minute to catch her breath and plunged again.

She cried out.

He slowly repeated the cycle of thrust and retreat, then began to pick up the pace. Her legs wrapped around him as she moaned and licked his neck.

He could feel her breath next to his ear as she spoke, "Isn't this where you tell me how tight I am?"

God, he was going to enjoy this woman.

Without losing momentum, he moved both hands under her ass and pulled her up until they were facing one another. "I wouldn't say tight. But then again, not necessarily cavernous. It'll do."

He tried to contain a grin but was sure he failed.

She bit his ear and then stiffened as it earned her several impaling thrusts. Not an easy feat as she was tight as fuck.

Alec loved the way she clung to him, meeting his pace at the same time as surrendering to him. Her muscles tightened more, contracting around him, before she began to chant, "Oh God . . . Alec . . . yes . . . yes . . . yes."

Giving her a moment, he held her upright, aware of her sudden lack of energy, and then he continued to find his own ending.

Finally, he groaned and then stilled after his final thrust. He felt physically depleted, emotionally exhausted and ready for round two.

He gently lay her on her back and grinned to himself at her earlier eye roll alongside the analogy of "like a delicate flower."

If Loren Ingalls was a delicate flower, it was of the Venus Mantrap variety.

He lay beside her wondering what manic thoughts were worming their way through her stubborn brain.

Food. It was his experience that sustenance could tame the wild beast in his little sister. After a long day of Ally tackling middle school, to distract her from fixating on the drama *du jour*, he'd throw a bag of Cheetos at her.

She hadn't eaten yet.

On a mission, he jumped up, pulled on his boxers and made his way downstairs. Grabbing some plates and silverware, he grabbed the bags of Styrofoam containers and took the staircase back to his bedroom two steps at a time.

At first, he smiled wide at seeing two gorgeous globes bending over in front of him and thought of what positions he was going to put her in come round two. And just as quickly he frowned, when she began pulling on her panties with a grimace and then her dress.

"What are you doing?" he asked, holding the bags up in one hand, the dinnerware in the other. "I thought we could have a picnic in bed?"

Goddammit, he was trying to be helpful, maybe even a little bit romantic, and here she was in escape mode again.

He bitched at himself for leaving her alone, even if was for like two whole minutes.

"Thanks for everything tonight." She was looking for her boots. "Gotta get home."

"Would you please let me feed you?" He put the items on the bed and grabbed her by the forearms, sure to let her see his intent before putting his hands on her. A reactive punch to his junk would impair his plans for the rest of the evening.

He bent down to make her look him in the eye. "What's going on in that beautiful head of yours?"

"Nothing." She looked to the right, avoiding him. "I'm sure you have things to do. Just like I do."

She pulled away and hopped on one foot and then the other to put on her boots. "Thanks for dinner, even though we didn't get around to it. And thanks for the sex."

Alec turned his head in confusion. "The sex?"

And then she did the most unexpected thing he could imagine, after having the hottest sex of his life. She jutted out her arm. "Yes, thanks for everything. I had a great time."

His head reared back.

Was she seriously looking to shake his hand as if he helped her with a faulty wiring system or a plumbing problem?

What the fuck?

He glared, refusing to accommodate her. She choked out a nervous chuckle, and retracted her hand, wiping her palm on her skirt.

"I guess I'll see you later." She skirted around him. "You know, small town and such."

Before he could demand that she remove her clothes and get back in the bed so he could spoon-feed her, she was through the doorway and running down the stairs.

The front door slammed shut, and he wondered if she even took the time to put on her coat. He marched to the window just in time to catch her sprinting to her car wearing nothing more than her thin cotton dress, red embroidered cowboy boots, wet underwear and a strand of pearls.

CHAPTER THIRTY-TWO

"Where there is matter, there is geometry."

—Johannes Kepler
German astronomer, mathematician,
and astrologer, best known for his laws of planetary motion

Driving home, Loren couldn't help but grin wide and shake her head in complete disbelief at what had just occurred.

She had sex.

SHE HAD SEX WITH ALEC WILDER.

And it was *glorious*.

Her limbs felt like goo as she wiggled in her seat with unrestrained delight.

Alec Wilder was everything and more than she had ever imagined and God knew she had amassed thousands of dirty thoughts as it pertained to sex with her grumpy neighbor.

Sex with Alec easily made the top of her Best-Things-EVER list.

It was better than hacking into a highly secure government site after months of poking until finally discovering that elusive way in.

It was better than the ultimate thrill when swapping a piece of art valued at multimillions of dollars for one of Mercy's dupes, while the owner was Still. In. The. Room.

Sex with her neighbor ranked right up there with the anticipation of having their first Thanksgiving dinner as a family outside of the Center, without the ever-present security cameras monitoring their every move and conversation.

Sex with Alec Wilder was better than Pi.

And, oh, how she loved Pi.

The simple calculation was everything. Encompassed everything.

Pi was life.

But sex with Alec Wilder was *living*.

She brought her hand to her chest, the other remaining on the steering wheel, contemplating how nice it would be if it could be more.

What would it be like to have many nights lying in his ridiculously strong arms exchanging inappropriate banter and discovering one another's nooks and crannies?

Not just the physical ones, but also those hidden and cradled in their souls. Deeply protected, hard-won secrets that no one else knew, discovered bit by bit.

Day by day.

Night by night.

Shaking her head, she smiled sadly to herself. She was in no position to be greedy. She wouldn't allow it. By God, she was going to be grateful that her first time, or at the least the first time she was a willing participant, was with Alec Wilder.

Life was too short and unpredictable to hold out for fairy tales.

And Mercy was right. She was far too old to imagine herself as her beloved Laura Ingalls, with parents that loved unconditionally, sisters that shared their every secret and a life-altering romance with her next-door neighbor, who lived with his sister.

Nah. She'd trade the fairy tale for the dirty one-night stand and run with it.

Because as she saw it, she could either spend her time being sad for what tonight wasn't, or she could choose to be blissfully happy for what it was.

A wonderful night of sex with a dreamy man.

On her terms, and in complete control.

Never again would she allow herself to be placed in a position for it to be otherwise.

Findling, Utah
 Halstead Labs and Research Center
 Five Years Ago

Crying didn't help. Yelling was a useless endeavor. Despite this knowledge, Ava's throat was raw and her face perpetually damp, as she was physically unable to wipe her tears due to the straps holding her arms immobile.

After days of hearing excuses as to why she couldn't see her sisters, responses from the staff had morphed from denials of any knowledge of their whereabouts to outright avoidance.

Desperate for answers, Ava went into a frenzy, screaming and ranting and pounding on doors. She would do whatever it took to get Halstead's attention, because she knew that he alone held the answers to her questions.

Her efforts landed her in solitary confinement. She'd lost count of how many days she'd spent in the padded room. Four, maybe five? She couldn't be sure as she'd also been tranq'd by a gigantic orderly named Milo who acted more a mute prison guard than a medical assistant.

Apparently, Halstead had grown tired of complaints from Bancroft and the staff. Complaints of delusional episodes resulting in her pounding on restricted doorways and numerous attempts to destroy biometric devices with hair brushes and forks left on untouched dinner trays. All the while insisting on seeing her sisters.

The staff was beside themselves.

Dr. Halstead assured them that her behavior was a result of manic paranoia recently diagnosed by the doctor himself.

Banging on yet another door she was unable to enter, she had turned to see Bancroft entering the hallway with the creepy orderly the size of a cattle barn lumbering close behind.

Before she could think to move within range of a security camera, Dr. Bancroft allowed the orderly to pass by him, giving him plenty of room to grab her by the back of the shirt and around her thigh and slam her onto the cold floor.

Blindsided first by the shock and then the pain of unnecessary force, she struggled for air as she attempted to pull herself up. Making it to her knees, she watched blood hit the floor below her and swiped at her nose. She was bleeding.

Again, before she could gather herself, the orderly picked her up by one arm and dragged her down another hallway with Bancroft now leading the way, pressing his finger on the door's device and allowing the orderly to force her into a room she had never seen before.

Basically, a padded cell.

Bancroft stood in the corner with his iPad at the ready, as the orderly grabbed the hem of her shirt and yanked it over her head. Her arms instinctively covered herself as she hadn't taken the time to put on a bra in her quest to find her sisters this morning.

At seventeen, and virtually isolated from society for three years, no one had seen her body since she began to develop. Her mortification was only further heightened as the orderly pushed her sweats down her legs, causing her to lose her balance and fall to the floor still holding her breasts. Now naked, one hand doing its best to cover her breasts, the other her pubic area, her arms were wrenched free as the orderly shoved them into an open-back tear-proof smock, forcing them through the arms of a straitjacket. She winced as he relentlessly yanked at the bindings in the back, making her shoulders feel as though they were being pulled from their sockets.

She didn't bother to struggle, her focus bent on finding her breath and remaining lucid. Besides, based on the size of the orderly manhandling her, her efforts would be futile. No, the best strategy was to be still and continue to breathe.

After rendering her under control by the bindings, the orderly stood behind her, his arms pinning her to his chest, his tree-trunk legs wrapped around hers, leaving her defenseless. Dr. Bancroft finally lifted his head from his iPad and pulled a syringe from his pocket.

Ava awoke hours later on the cold, tiled floor with a canvas-covered throw pillow and some sort of thin aluminized thermal blanket that served no purpose at all in light of her body shaking from the frigid temperatures of the room.

Slowly pulling herself into a sitting position, a difficult process without the use of one's arms, she analyzed her surroundings.

The walls were a gridwork of padded squares. She turned to the right and spotted a toilet without toilet paper and pushed to the side was the meager blanket and coarse pillow. Nothing to lend her comfort.

She turned her body to see what was behind her and spotted the camera mounted at least eight feet high. Too far for her to reach but angled in a way she would be unable to hide from its lens unless directly beneath it.

She scooted to that very spot, the sole act of defiance affording her some small sense of control. It wasn't much, but it was something. And she sat there waiting and yelling, insisting she see her sisters.

And here she was, day four or maybe five, with no human contact besides a new orderly she had never seen before, bringing her water in the morning and then again in the evening. She shamefully lapped it up, like a cornered dog looking for any type of sustenance.

He ignored her questions about the whereabouts of Mara and Charlotte, refused to even look at her, and then walked out the door, the clicking sound of the door closing bringing her to a new level of desolation.

To the orderly, she was nothing more than a task to cross off for the day.

She forced herself to stand, mindful she was naked from the waist down, and slowly dragged herself to the door and began pounding, yelling through the barred window.

"Mara!" she screamed, although her voice was weakening. "Charlotte!" She pounded again. "What have you done with my sisters?"

Her head jerked back as she heard the biometric device make its ever-fateful pinging noise. She scrambled to the corner of the room, as it was past feeding time.

Maybe it was Halstead.

To her disappointment, in walked Bancroft, and drowning out the light from the hallway, with his beefy arms crossed over his chest dressed in white scrubs, was the menacing orderly who'd roughed her up and shoved her in the straitjacket.

The skinny orderly who brought her water refused to look at her as if she were a crazed lunatic, but this one kept his soulless eyes trained on her.

Naked from the waist down, she didn't like the way he looked at her, like she was his next meal.

Bancroft walked languidly toward her, looking down at her with a bored blink and heavy sigh. He bent down on one knee next to where she was sitting underneath the camera.

She refused to cower from him. She needed to stay strong and determined if she was ever to see Mara and Charlotte again.

"So obstinate. So disobedient. You are trying my patience, Miss Ava."

"Where are my sisters?" Her voice cracked and she hated herself for sounding weak.

"They are exactly where they should be, aiding Dr. Halstead by furthering scientific discoveries."

"I want to see them. Now." She swapped fear for tenacity.

"Dr. Halstead has given me orders to leave you in this room until you agree to comply and cease harassing the staff and orderlies."

Anger diffused her body. The old man who had promised to protect her and her sisters was nothing less than a monster.

"I have a message for dear old dad."

Surprising herself as much as Bancroft, she spit in his face.

His anger turned palpable, his visage morphing into a mottled red with veins bulging from his neck. She instinctively backed up against the wall.

He slowly pulled a neat, white, square handkerchief from his back pocket and slowly wiped the spittle as he chuckled without a bit of humor. "That will cost you dearly, Miss Ava."

He stood, glaring down at her, and motioned to the goon at the door.

"Milo," he barked as the orderly in starched white scrubs moved toward them. "I'm going to step into the hallway and disable the room's camera. It will take the security guards ten minutes to troubleshoot the alert and re-enable the feed. You have ten minutes to do whatever it takes to convince Miss Ava that behavior modification is in her best interest."

He moved toward the door, a disturbing half-smile dominating his face as his eyes bore into Ava's. "Anything."

Ava had begun her combat training at fifteen, but a couple of years of Krav Maga wouldn't make up for being starved and bound by a straitjacket. Despite this, she wrenched helplessly at her arms, completely immobile and ineffective.

The instant the camera's alert began to resonate throughout the room and hallway, meaty fingers grabbed her by her hair, turned her to face the corner and slammed her forehead into the wall. He let go and she fell to her knees. She leaned against the cornered walls for support.

Dazed, she gasped as he grabbed her by the hair again, and turned her around to face him. Reading his next move, she reacted by the only means available to her, the use of her legs. As he moved one leg forward, placing his weight on it, she easily swept his back leg, sending his lumberjack-sized body crashing onto the floor.

Her Krav Maga instructor's words echoed in her befuddled head: "The bigger they are, the harder they fall."

But he wasn't staying down.

What her instructor had failed to teach her, was how to defend herself when the assailant three times her size got back up, while she still modeled the latest in upper-body restraint apparel.

She kicked and flailed, but was no match against his dead eyes and brute strength. He grabbed the straps at the back of her jacket and flipped her onto her stomach as if she weighed no more than a bag of chips.

Anchored to the floor between steroid-enhanced thighs, depleted of strength and running out of options, she forced herself to think. What was her next move? What could she leverage?

She could hear him fumbling with the ties on his scrubs and gasped at the pain of him yanking her up and onto her knees. One side of her face lay flat against the ice-cold tile floor, so she tried to move her weight to her shoulder but couldn't find her balance.

She squeezed her eyes shut and thought she might vomit when she felt him poking and prodding against her.

Realizing her fate and lack of options, she rested her cheek onto the floor and let the tears flow.

And then fingers bore into one hip while his other hand latched onto the ties at her back and she screamed at the indescribable pain.

Unable to move her arms, she was as useless as a trussed puppet as he violently yanked her back by the knot, keeping her hands restrained and immobile. She tried rolling her weight to her forehead which only earned her more pain.

With each thrust she screamed and swore he was ripping her from the inside out as the tears flowed and the pain gripped her over and over.

He didn't make a sound, save a hefty grunt with each thrust.

Couldn't Bancroft hear her? How could he not know what was happening to her?

Reality was a cold bitch as she realized that he had to know and didn't care.

She had no one.

There was no one to protect her.

She felt a bloody slickness between her legs that ebbed some of the pain but did little to stem the mortification of being unprotected and powerless.

She winched her eyes shut and willed herself to breathe in and out, despite the repetitive onslaught of flesh against wounded flesh.

And then, *forty-three*.

Her eyes flew open and closed just as quickly, as in her mind's eye she could suddenly see the number forty-three: A prime number that, since the accident, she'd found inexplicably reverent and soothing.

Ava couldn't explain why she felt this way about a certain prime number, but forty-three had become a safe beacon in a stormy sky keeping her safe and providing her focus outside of herself when she was scared or couldn't sleep.

Then, just as suddenly, her mind shifted, and she began to draft spheres based solely on primes and their elegant patterns. Shifting again, she began reciting prime numbers, almost as a mantra, and could feel herself further disconnecting from her body.

Her ever-present prime numbers held strong.

So soothing and rare.

Like faithful sentinels protecting her.

And as if her mind were an old-time television switching channels, she could see herself sitting between her parents on their sectional sofa, eating popcorn while watching Pixar movies. Mara was playing with a fluffy stuffed rabbit as Charlotte slept in her makeshift bed, which was no more than an overstuffed chair, her small body held captive behind strategically placed throw pillows.

Her mother laughed at a particularly absurd part of the cartoon while her dad did his best to hold back a chuckle, asking if there was a chase scene he could look forward to.

Between her slight body weight and her assailants frantically increased effort, her head met the corner of the wall. And after a few head-splitting thrusts she finally found . . . silence.

Ava winced at the pain as she craned her neck, and stretched her lower limbs. Pain so evenly distributed she couldn't pinpoint exactly where she hurt the most.

She tried to move her legs underneath her to sit up, and gasped, then it all came back. Turning her face to the floor, she sobbed.

Just as quickly she cursed herself for the tears spilling down her cheeks. An unnecessary waste of resources.

She tried getting past the pain, knowing she should stand and move her body around the room in order to warm herself, but it was a little late for that revelation, considering her current condition.

Hanging her head and closing her eyes, she knew she'd arrived at the moment she'd been avoiding.

Leveraging the use of the corner wall, she inched her way up until she was standing. Turning her body so she could rest her head against the wall, she took a moment to close her eyes, catch her breath, and find her balance.

She opened them, glanced down and gasped at all the blood. Her blood, dried and running down the padded wall like red-soaked tears. Her hair draped across her face from what must have been a head wound. She turned to see more blood on the floor and then noticed the stickiness between her legs.

Her body trembled uncontrollably, wishing she could reach the metallic blanket, more to cover the blood on her body than to warm herself.

Ava looked up at the glowing green light indicating a now operational camera.

She knew what Halstead wanted and she would give it to him. She would give him the appearance of obedience until she could find a better way. Because the ugly truth was, he held all the power.

Slowly, she made her way to the center of the room, turned and looked directly into the eye of the camera. "I apologize for my behavior, Dr. Halstead. I promise that, moving forward, you will have my full cooperation."

Losing her balance from her weakened state, she fell to her knees. She didn't know what hurt more, the impact of her knees hitting the unforgiving floor or the impact on her pride. Nevertheless, she knew her lack of balance only painted her as more contrite.

Submissive.

It took what felt like two minutes before the door opened and Halstead himself entered the room, pulling her up to standing and holding her steady.

He didn't care to comment on what looked to be a murder scene before him or her obvious injuries.

Without a smidge of emotion, he said, "Follow me."

He walked toward the door, but she didn't move. Couldn't move. He turned his head toward her with an upturned brow.

"I'm not sure I can walk," she said, wobbling.

"You will if you want to see your sisters."

Without waiting for an affirmation, he continued through the door. Adrenaline coursed through her body, and she learned that with the right motivation, she could do anything.

CHAPTER THIRTY-THREE

"What science can there be more noble, more excellent, more useful for men, more admirably high and demonstrative, than this of mathematics?"

—Benjamin Franklin
As a scientist, he was a major figure in the American Enlightenment and the history of physics for his discoveries and theories regarding electricity

Loren pulled into the driveway, her previous state of sexually induced euphoria having been trampled by memories from her past.

She drove past the house into the side drive on the left, admiring the Blue Angel hostas she and Mercy planted a couple weeks ago.

Turning off the engine was much easier than blocking the memories.

She had finally found her sisters that fateful day.

After instructing staff members to wash her down in a nearby shower room and handing her a set of clean scrubs, Halstead had personally led her to Mara's room, where she lay unconscious and hooked to an IV.

He explained that Mara shared the same blood type as Charlotte, and was to be her standby blood donor, if need be.

He then took her to Charlotte's room, who was also sedated post-surgery. Dr. Halstead expressed that he was quite eager to discover over time if the surgical lesions performed by Dr. Vielle would garner the same results as they had with Mara.

Loren rubbed her forehead and rested her head on the steering wheel. It wasn't long before Charlotte's genius was discovered: She was a musical prodigy and Dr. Halstead couldn't have been more pleased.

Like a proud father who had just unleashed some pretty hefty revenue potential.

Of course, the doctor pontificated that it was all in the name of science. And that Loren needed to honor the sacrifice made by her sisters in the benevolent quest to further his life's work.

As if their participation was voluntary, despite being strapped to their hospital beds and sedated.

But she knew who was truly at fault as she reached down to cradle Charlotte's hand.

She was.

The old man had promised to protect them and she believed him. He had promised to give them a real home, and she convinced her sisters that he was the answer to their prayers.

And they believed her.

But promises were flighty things, made with vigor one day and easily discounted the next. It would serve her well to remember that no one, save her sisters, could be fully trusted. And despite feelings of goodwill toward Madame Garmond and Vlad Petrov, she needed to take their words and intentions with a grain of salt.

Because everyone lied and used and manipulated everyone else.

Loren sighed at the kind reminder that it was better to compartmentalize the past and live in the present. And most importantly, to rely solely on herself.

Now was not the time for maudlin thoughts of the Center. Tonight, she had afforded endless hours of graphic playtime imagery of a certain neighbor who resembled Thor from the Avengers and fucked like that guy in that Gray something . . . something Shades movie Mercy had shown her clips of . . . what was that movie called again?

Loren sat back in her car seat and let down her window to listen to the sound of the male prairie cicadas doing their musical best to attract a mate. She thought of Alec and how she felt magnetically pulled toward him.

Like a touchstone.

Like a prime number.

Like forty-three.

She would never, as long as she lived, forget the way he looked into her eyes while moving inside her. Like she was beautiful and someone special.

She placed her hands on her reddened cheeks and closed her eyes to relive the look in his eyes and the feeling of being swept into something surreal and perfect.

Ah, what would one do without a momentary delusion or two to fall back on?

She would grant herself the luxury of holding onto that delusion for tonight and face reality tomorrow. She'd give herself that much time to dream of a gravelly voice and overly confident strong hands.

Her eyes widened at the sudden sound of piano playing from inside the house. And then there was laughter. Laughter that sounded as if it were coming from a number of people.

She glanced behind her seat, out the back window of the car to see several vehicles parked close to the front of the house that she had failed to notice.

It was a moonless night, so she couldn't make out the makes or models of the cars and identify the people inside. A small-town skill that came in handy while living in Wilder but gained her no leverage tonight.

Opening the kitchen door, she blew into her ice-cold hands and admonished herself for forgetting her coat in a mad dash to avoid Alec's imminent rejection. Her stomach growled and then did a happy dance as she took in the food on the table before her.

There were so many bowls and containers they barely fit onto the small table, one or two sitting precariously close to the edge. Loren moved them toward safety and picked up a plate while sporting a wide smile and huge appetite.

"Ohmigodyouhadsex." Mercy stood in the doorway with huge eyes, an empty plate in her hands and a spoon in the other.

"Keep it down." Loren shook her head toward the ceiling and then at Mercy. "People can hear you."

A saucy grin dominated Mercy's face. "So, you're not denying it." She lowered her voice and set her dirty dishes in the sink. "You had dirty sex with our crotchety neighbor."

Before Loren could deny, deny, deny . . . Becky Waterman walked in the kitchen and came to an abrupt stop when spotting Loren. "Oh, my," she said, covering her mouth with her hand.

Loren held her hands out to the side, waving her empty plate around. "What?"

"*You* got your field plowed."

Loren lowered her hands, suddenly self-conscious and touched her forehead, wondering if Alec had branded her with a Sharpie while she was basking in post-coital glow.

"No, I didn't get anything plowed—"

"You did!" Becky said with an unusually low voice as if Loren hadn't just stated the opposite.

"Oh, yeah, she did," Mercy confirmed.

Loren grabbed a spoon and began poking at food as opposed to convincing her gleeful accusers. "I . . . I said I didn't."

Becky answered for her. "Oh, it's obvious. You did the dirty with Farmer Ted aka Alec *freakin'* Wilder."

To Loren's utter dismay, she heard the voice of a small English woman of questionable French descent, from the living room.

"Levi, I forbid you from leaving before having a second healthy platter of food."

It was Loren's turn to be shocked. Madame Garmond was laughing . . . no, she was giggling like a schoolgirl as she rounded the corner. Like a comedic scene in a B-rated movie, Madame came to a full stop when she spied Loren.

Loren smiled and waved her fingers, doing her best to inspire a non-freshly fucked demeanor.

Despite her efforts, Madame lifted a single eyebrow and announced with a hushed voice. "Dear heaven above. You have been compromised."

Loren's face turned beet red. "I wouldn't say that, exactly," she hem-hawed.

From what must have been the living room turned community center came Cara. "Ally, you play the next stanza for Amarilla, and I'll fix Mr. Simmons another plate."

Before she could more than lay eyes on Loren, Madame Garmond blocked her view. "You sit with Mr. Simmons and Amarilla while I plate another serving of Coq au Vin."

Cara barely caught sight of Loren as Madame turned her by the shoulders to shoo her back into the living room. Before turning the corner, Cara yelled out, "You didn't let him see you sweat, did you?"

Mercy chuckled. "I think she let him see a lot of things."

Loren's eyebrows furrowed. "You're all acting like I frequented a seedy sex dungeon."

"Wilder has a sex dungeon?" Mercy's brows shot up and then

toward Becky for confirmation as she dipped into what appeared to be a food-blogging-worthy trifle dessert.

Loren grabbed her own spoon as Mercy took a bite directly from the bowl before Madame returned from redirecting Cara.

"No sex dungeon," Becky said with a shake of her head, "although I do know a couple who have a room strictly for s.e.x," she spelled, "and it has a swing."

Madame returned to a wide-eyed Mercy, an all-knowing Becky, and a guilt-ridden Loren.

Her hands placed on insubstantial hips, Madame said, "Please tell me you thought to employ protection."

Annddd . . . Loren lost her appetite, set her plate on the table, took a fortifying breath, and admitted defeat. "We did."

"When do you see him again?" Mercy asked, assuming the most romantic of outcomes.

"I don't think there's going to be a next time."

Madame turned her head to the side. "Oh, bollocks, he was a disappointment in the sack."

"Oh, my God, no," Loren said, clutching at the pearls Madame had loaned her, not sure if she were more offended by the conversation or the prim and proper woman who seemed completely at ease instigating it.

Madame waved a bejeweled hand. "It's quite acceptable to move on when the relationship is bereft of chemistry, my dear."

"Yeah," echoed Becky. "You have to try a number of cock . . . tails before finding the one that gives you just the right zing."

"Discretion is key, however," Madame intoned.

Mercy nodded. "Exactly. You don't want to get a reputation for being easy." She glanced at Madame for validation.

"So true, but you mustn't act indifferent in that someone else shags your man."

"Okay," Loren interrupted, raising her hands in the air. "That's enough about my one-night stand."

Suddenly, a male voice captured their attention. "Um . . . Miss Loren, you've got company."

Three heads turned toward the kitchen entrance at an embarrassed Levi Simmons.

And if things couldn't get any worse, Alec Wilder himself moved beside Levi with his signature face, the one lacking any and all expression, looking absolutely yummy in a washed-out dark-blue hoodie and ratty sweats.

Her abandoned coat looked the size of doll clothes clasped in such large hands.

"I'd like to talk to you about that, Loren."

Simultaneously four heads, a couple with open mouths, moved toward his deep voice and then swung in her direction.

Loren felt the blood inch up her neck until it reached the top peaks of her forehead. She wiped her clammy hands together and then straightened her skirt as she cleared her throat.

"Hello, Alec. Are you here for Ally?"

"No." He shook his head once as his eyes shuttered. "I'm here for you."

"My dear," Madame commented, "why don't you escort Master Wilder upstairs where you may have a touch of privacy."

"Okay." Loren swallowed self-consciously, scooting herself between the table overflowing with food, and Mercy, Becky, Madame Garmond, and Levi Simmons.

Levi scooted next to Madame, allowing Loren to stand next to a stoic but determined Alec.

"Follow me," she instructed as she entered the hallway and up the stairs.

Alec squeezed at the back of his neck.

Despite harboring a rather unhealthy dose of self-awareness, his eyes continued to greedily follow Loren's sweet ass as she climbed the stairs.

Of course, she had great tits, too.

But God almighty, that ass.

Harder than a tire iron, he adjusted himself.

He dipped his head, still allowing for his preferred view, but hiding his slight grin in case she was to glance over her shoulder and catch him leering at her.

Each step she made was an exaggerated thud as if she were walking the last green mile as opposed to searching out a room with some privacy.

Reaching the top of the stairs, she passed a door to her left, turned to face him, and motioned for him to follow as she turned the knob. Instead, he eyed a sticky note on the door directly to his right, which read: DO NOT GO TO BED BEFORE TELLING ME EVERYTHING, OR ELSE YOU'RE DEAD TO ME.

It was signed Mercy, and he instantly knew this had to be the door to Loren's room.

Her private sanctum.

The woman was surprisingly skilled at spewing her emotions, while at the same time, maintaining and withholding an impenetrable vault of information. He felt an inexplicable need to learn everything about her as quickly as possible. And he'd bet money he could learn far more from behind curtain B as opposed to A.

That said, curtain A looked to be a bathroom, a venue far more amenable to make-up sex, not that they had had an argument but he could certainly conjure one up. Then again, based on her ramrod straight back and exaggerated foot stomps he may be in store for some angry sex.

He looked to his left and then to the right, and at the risk of sporting a perpetual hard on for the next couple of hours, he reached for the knob to the opposite door she had indicated and walked in.

"No, no! Not in there."

Ignoring the two hands pulling on his arm, he strode inside. He stopped short, standing in the middle of her bedroom and staring at what he saw before him. His eyes moved all the way down to the floorboards and back up to the crown molding.

There had to be hundreds of them. Maybe even thousands. Pieces of papers tacked to the wall, overlapping one another and covered with odd drafts and sketches.

Not taking his eyes off them, he tossed her coat onto the bed and turned her direction to see if the walls behind him held the same drawings.

They did.

So many sketches of what appeared to be the most meticulous of drawings made little sense to him but were impressive regardless.

He walked past her to touch one tacked next to her light switch. It looked like one of those pictures of a snowflake magnified to the point they became more than a speck of frozen water, but a beautiful, ornate sculpture with definition and structure.

He turned toward her to gauge her reaction to his discovery. She was shaking her head, covering her hand against her mouth and avoiding eye contact.

Then he noticed the small table next to her, covered with a pile of the very same papers with dozens of more sketches.

"What is all this?" he asked.

She looked down at the floor as she crossed her arms over her chest. "They're nothing. Doodles."

"Doodles?" His eyes moved around the room. "You have layers of doodles covering your walls."

Mute, he watched her work her bottom lip with her teeth. "I need you to tell me the truth, Loren. Could I finally get something real from you? Please."

"They're . . . how I see things sometimes."

He remained quiet for a moment, taking it all in. "What things?"

She finally raised her eyes to his and swallowed as if trying to make a decision. "Everything."

He ran a hand through his hair as he made another turn of the room.

"Everything?" he asked and turned back toward her. His eyes searched hers as he reached out his hand to lightly touch a finger, compelling her to continue.

She nodded. "When I look at things and really focus on them, my mind cuts them into slices, kind of like a grid or a spiderweb."

Alec reached down and picked up the paper sitting on the top of the stack. "What's this?"

"That's a shell," she explained, taking the paper. "I drafted it in a three-dimensional spiral applying the Pythagorean theorem. It was super easy. I mean, you could learn this in early Algebra." Her voice seemed to grow with anxiety as she pointed at the design. "I drew the first triangle using a simple equation, $a2 + b2 = c2$, and then I put c back in the equation as a, kept b as one, and built it out, placing each new triangle at a right angle to the first."

She became quiet again. Alec watched her as she remained focused on her sketch. As if waiting for his next reaction.

He picked up another drawing. "And this?"

Pointing at a particular circle, she said, "This circle is pi, and that design is wave-particle duality."

He had no idea what any of that meant.

"Believe me, these are rudimentary geometric sketches." She pointed at the stack. "The ones on the wall are things that have caught my attention during the day that I drew later. Sometimes I have trouble sleeping, and drawing them can be therapeutic."

Her eyes looked at him earnestly. "I'm also super interested in the images of sine, cosine, as well as tangent waves, and how their reflections vibrate due to the speed of light making a space-time grid and potentially representing one fractal fusion. I mean, wouldn't it be cool if we could find a way to capture the potential energy of geometry?"

As she continued to speak in a language he failed to comprehend, a realization came to him. "All three of you," he said, dropping the paper onto the table and staring at her. "How is it that you and both your sisters have such . . . gifts? I'm no mathematician, but it seems highly improbable that one sister would be born a musical genius, the other an artistic genius, and you, a mathematical . . ."

"Genius."

Confirming to Alec that she was one of three siblings possessing DNA that was mathematically improbable if not impossible.

One eyebrow raised in question, causing her to fidget.

"How?"

"Good genes?" she replied with a shrug.

"Loren," he said, wanting to learn more about what papered her walls but also determined to address what he came here to say. "We need to talk."

"Nope." She popped the P and shook her head frantically. "No. We. Do. Not. I'm totally good. No need to discuss anything. Don't need an apology, an explanation—"

"Hey." He pulled her toward him as he sat on the edge of her bed, holding her hips captive. "We need to talk about what happened tonight."

"I know what happened. I was there."

She attempted to pull away, but he also knew she had the skills to easily incapacitate him if she really wanted to. "Look at me, Loren."

Conceding with a huff, she met his eyes and it just about killed him to see the raw vulnerability in them.

"You need to know that what we did tonight meant something." He lifted a fist to his chest, not taking his eyes off her. "To me."

"You don't have to say that." She shook her head.

"I'm not just saying words, Loren. I mean them. I don't want what happened tonight to be a one-time thing. I want to explore this. See where it goes."

Alec's eyes held hers as hers narrowed.

"What does that mean?"

"What don't you understand about what I just said?"

She chewed on her bottom lip, and he found it adorable and also frustrating.

"Are you saying you want to *date* me?"

He smiled, astounded that she could discuss and draft such lofty mathematical concepts but be totally clueless to the obvious.

"You do know that's the second time you've asked me that."

"All things considered, it bears repeating."

"Yes, Loren Ingalls. I'm saying I want to *date* you. Again."

"One more date?"

"No, many more dates." This was becoming ridiculous.

"Will we be having sex?"

"Preferably."

"Will you be having sex with other women?"

Now he wondered if he'd misread her. "Why? Do you want to have sex with other men?"

"Oh, God, no. I'm pretty much ruined for all other men. I mean, really, what's the point?"

"Okaaay," he replied, nodding his head while suppressing a grin. "That's both highly flattering and . . . forthcoming. But to answer your question, no, I will not be having sex with other women while we date."

"So, we're a thing?" she asked with a burgeoning smile.

He nodded, extremely full of himself that he put it there.

Once again, he fully recognized she was teetering on some sort of metaphorical ledge. Like a starving bird on a wire, food within reach but too full of distrust to go for it. He didn't know what happened to her to make her so mistrustful and suspicious, but he was going to feed her if it fucking killed him.

"And all this?" she asked, her eyes lifting toward the wall behind his shoulder.

"A surprise," he replied, "but I have a feeling that being with you is going to be full of surprises."

Their moment of bliss was shattered by a knock on the door.

"Yes?" Loren called out.

A woman with what sounded like an English accent said. "We have two impressionable young ladies in the living room, not to mention a number of guests, asking questions about your *petite tête-a-tête*."

Loren grimaced as Alec stood, kissing her on the cheek and leading her toward the door while holding her hand.

"Oh, *today's* she's French," she complained. "Cooking Coq au Vin and using terms like *tête-a-tête*. Just you wait, tomorrow she'll go all English dowager, asking us if we want a spot of tea and throwing a good old-fashioned Edwardian conniption if it's not her beloved Earl Grey."

Alec opened the door to the small woman with her nose in the air. "I trust you've both come to an understanding."

"We have." Alec nodded once.

"Might I make a suggestion for future consideration?"

Loren groaned, and said, "No!"

While Alec replied, "Please do."

"The next time you partake in activities of a more pagan nature, please see that you are a gentleman and take the time to ensure the lady is properly buttoned up."

Loren inhaled sharply and darted to the mirror over her dresser.

Alec pulled his lips together in a straight line as he heard her gasp, as she discovered that in her haste to escape his bedroom, she had inserted the first button at the nape of her dress into the third buttonhole, exposing a good bit of chest and cleavage, leaving little doubt as to their "pagan" activities.

Alec turned to Madame, meeting her stoic expression with his own. "I will do my best to be more hands-on in the future."

Madame said with an exaggerated side-eye, "I do believe that is precisely what got you into trouble in the first place."

CHAPTER THIRTY-FOUR

"One of the endlessly alluring aspects of mathematics is that its thorniest paradoxes have a way of blooming into beautiful theories."

—Philip J Davis
American academic applied mathematician
known for his work in numerical analysis
and approximation theory

Sunday couldn't come soon enough for Loren.

"Come on, come on, come on!" she shouted, holding the front door open while waiting impatiently on the porch.

Vlad was the first to make it to the door, tying a woolen scarf around the collar of his peacoat.

"You are in quite a hurry, *mi padruga*."

"Yeah, yeah . . . keep it moving, my self-proclaimed Ukrainian Ruskie. We've got souls to save and potlucks to plan."

Mercy emerged behind Vlad, holding her hand to her eyes to ward off the bright midmorning sunlight.

"Trust me, she's in no hurry to get to church to save souls. She's eager to get to church to see our grumpy neighbor and fantasize about doing dirty things with him in the back pews."

Loren's smile felt a mile wide. "He's not just my grumpy neighbor. He's my grumpy boyfriend." She skipped down the steps to the car and turned back to the slowpokes behind her. "But I need to get there early because the Thanksgiving potluck committee is meeting today, and I'm the chairperson."

Mercy hesitated. "*You're* chairing the Thanksgiving potluck committee?"

"What?"

Vlad and Mercy looked at one another over the hood of the vehicle.

"My friend," Vlad said with a look of extreme concern, "you cannot cook."

"I can cook," Loren said, rolling her eyes theatrically.

"No," Mercy said emphatically, "no, you cannot."

"It's not like I'm doing the cooking. I'm managing the event."

"You know nothing about Thanksgiving food."

"Okay, point taken. But last night, Madame agreed to join the committee, and she's going to help me."

"Thank God," Vlad said, opening the car door for Loren.

Both Mercy and Vlad smiled at one another, before Mercy slipped into the back seat beside Loren.

Loren checked out their ride. It looked to be a brand-new Range Rover with the new car smell and everything. "Vlad, is this a new rental?"

He cleared his throat. "I purchase yesterday. Not make sense to rent."

Loren shot a glance at Mercy, who avoided her as Vlad closed the car door.

Cara bounced out the front door and down the steps as Madame closed the door behind them.

Ten minutes later, they spilled out of the Rover and made their way to the church's main doors, closed due to the unusually cold November temperature.

Loren made her way down to the basement with Madame Garmond behind her. Everyone was there ahead of her, watching her intently with knowing smiles on their faces.

"We just heard a rumor. Is it true?" Lucinda Packet asked.

Before Loren could ask about what, Emmy Lou Roberts said, "Now Lucinda, the Lord's house is not the place to spread gossip." She squirmed in her chair, fluffing her hair. "Unless of course Loren wants to dispel any rumors."

Loren moved to the front of the table and assisted Madame with removing her coat. "Yes," her eyebrows shot up as she smiled at Madame. "I am chairing the Thanksgiving potluck committee this year, but the good news is, I brought reinforcements."

"I'm not talking about this year's potluck," Lucinda stated, undeterred. "Is it true that you and Alec Wilder are dating?"

Loren caught Becky's attention at the opposite end of the table with an expression that asked: "Really?"

"What? Don't look at me," Becky said, pointing at herself. "I didn't have to tell them anything. You showed up together at Lucky's, and now it's all over Wilder that you're a couple."

Loren felt self-conscious as she placed her coat on the back of her chair and sat down. "It's true," she said pulling a notebook from her purse. "We are . . . exploring the possibility of a relationship."

Sue Ellen popped up with: "I saw them at Lucky's; they are the cutest!"

"I heard he hand-fed her grapes."

Loren protested. "We didn't even—"

"I heard he couldn't keep his hands off her."

She turned to Madame. "It was all very circumspect."

Another woman, maybe in her early twenties who had recently attended one of Loren's self-defense classes, but for the life of her, Loren couldn't recall her name, piped up with, "I heard Marybell Simmons showed up," capturing everyone's attention, "and started coming on to Alec right in front of Loren."

Everyone in the room gasped at the affront and turned to Loren for confirmation. Remembering Amarilla, and the look of devastation at her mother's antics with the pool boy, Loren played it down. "Well, I wouldn't say—"

The woman continued, "And that Loren took her dinner knife and split her skirt right up the back, past her skanky thong and everything!"

Madame regally turned her head toward Loren, her expression indicating that she was less than amused. Loren's face turned a deep shade of shame. "Now that's obviously a gross exagg—"

"And then they fought in the parking lot and Marybell grabbed Loren by the hair and pushed her to the ground—"

Loren shot out of her chair. "Now, *that* is an outright lie."

The room quieted at Loren's over-the-top reaction to being bested by the town skank. But come on, talk about blasphemy! Marybell probably possessed the sparring skills of a third grader.

She pursed her lips together and could actually feel Madame's recrimination from less than two feet away. "What I meant to say," she gingerly rearranged her skirt as she sat back down with as much Madame-approved ladylike aplomb as she could muster, "is that is all just nonsense."

Lenore Sterling came to her defense, sort of. "That's true. Nothing but nonsense. Why, I saw them leave early, with their food boxed up to go."

Her face was on fire, knowing what that implied to the stern woman who had inspected her clothing choices for her first date.

"None of that happened . . ." She glanced at Madame, who seemed to look right through her. "Exactly like that."

Sue Ellen then asked, with a bit of disappointment, "Then are you saying it's a rumor that you showed up at your house later that night with your dress unbuttoned to the waist and your hair all bed-head crazy?"

"No," she said emphatically, and then with less vigor, "not to the waist."

Becky pasted a guilty smile on her face. "Okay, I might have mentioned that, but for the record, all I said was that there were a few buttons 'askew.'" She emphasized with an eye roll and finger quotes.

Loren's embarrassment was hijacked by Madame standing up and leaning authoritatively on her fingertips.

"Allow me to introduce myself to the ladies at the table who have yet to make my acquaintance." Loren shrank back in her chair. "My name is Madame Garmond. I am Loren, Mercy, and Cara's English grandmother of French descent. It is a pleasure to meet each one of you. Without further delay, and in anticipation of what I am sure to be a rousing sermon, please take a sheet of paper and list those dishes you would like to prepare for this year's Thanksgiving . . . potluck. I must admit, the concept of a gathering where each person brings a pot of food in a questionably sanitized dish, is foreign to me. Regardless, I am determined to embrace the cultural and hygienic anomaly. After you have made your food preparation selection, I will peruse the list, categorize them in the proper food groups and advise if your choice is permissible. If not, you will be instructed to choose a dish in the category that I find to be lacking."

Loren was equally subdued by Madame's assumed authority, and her outright lie, in a church basement no less, that she was their grandmother from over the pond.

Emmy Lou jumped up to grab a notepad and some pens in one of the cabinet drawers and began to pass them out.

Madame continued her monologue, "I have no doubt that with the proper administration and adherence to personal hygiene, this Thanksgiving's . . . potluck . . . will be a grand success."

Sue Ellen raised her hand. "What do you call a person of both English and French descent?"

"Exceptional," Madame intoned.

Loren covered her smile with her hand as the geriatric pit bull with unimpeachable manners single-handedly wrangled the discussion toward the matter at hand and shut down conversations trending toward illicit rumors.

Madame gathered her shiny purse and cardigan. "Ladies, shall we rise to the narthex?"

Without another word, Madame turned toward the staircase as Loren and the others scrambled to grab their coats and purses.

The young woman of the forgotten name, whispered, "Is she, like, from royalty?"

Loren shook her head, despite the contrived story Madame shared upon her arrival. But she still felt the need to come to her defense. "She's really quite nice once you get to know her. It kind of shows up when you least expect it and need it the most."

CHAPTER THIRTY-FIVE

"The good Christian should beware the mathematician and all those who make empty prophecies. The danger already exists that the mathematicians have made a covenant with the devil to darken the spirit and to confine man in the bonds of hell."

—Saint Augustine
One of the Latin Fathers of the Church and perhaps one of the most significant Christian thinkers after St. Paul. Augustine created a theological system of great power and lasting influence

To Loren, the service wasn't exactly rousing but did the trick in terms of helping her to be a better person. For another week anyway.

She sat obediently beside Madame as they listened to Henry

Sterling sing a solo, and then Emmy Lou provide an update on upcoming events.

Loren had a great side view of her new boyfriend sitting several pews in front of her. He wore a dark-blue, button-down shirt and listened intently to each individual no matter the level of mind-numbing boredom.

Loren fidgeted, contemplated if the quantized structure of energy and space-time actually required that the structure at the smallest level would be represented as a lattice shape. She then tried to remember if she applied deodorant in her rush to get ready this morning and then did her level best at discreetly sniffing one pit.

Madame caught her odd head angle and lifted a single eyebrow, and then blinked slowly.

Loren pulled herself together by sitting on her hands and then pulling one out to check the time on her phone again. She took a deep sigh at how much time she still had to endure and began to play with her hair, pulling the front wisps over her eyes, wondering what she'd look like with bangs.

Then she wondered what Jesus would look like with bangs.

She blew the hair out of her face, and then after another scathing look from Madame, self-consciously tucked it back behind her ears.

Ally sat in the pew directly in front of Loren and Madame, apparently preferring to sit with Amarilla, Cara, and Samantha rather than her brother.

Amarilla leaned her head toward Ally and whispered loud enough for Loren to hear, "Your brother is so stinkin' hot."

"Ew," Ally said with a grimace. "Shut. Up."

"No, seriously, Alec's even cuter than Marco," Amarilla whispered, "And Marco was hotter than fuck."

Obviously unaware that Loren and Madame Garmond had taken seats directly behind them, Amarilla continued. "I just turned fifteen. Alec's what, thirty?"

"He's thirty-two, you pervert."

"Nice. An older man."

"That's a fifteen-year age difference. That's not nice. That's illegal."

"In two years, it won't be. The legal age for consensual sex is seventeen in the state of Texas." She sighed heavily. "I can be patient."

"For your information, Alec is in a committed relationship with Loren Ingalls, you know, the sister of one of your best friends."

"Hey, I'm not my mother." Amarilla seemed genuinely offended. "But a lot can happen in two years, I'm just saying."

"In two years, they'll be married with babies by the time you're *legal*. And then he'll be an old man with a paunch and two kids wrapped around each leg."

"Hey, Loren," Cara whispered, turning to the side with a little finger wave, oblivious to the conversation and the two now unusually straight torsos sitting to her left. "Madame, do you have any those mints?"

Madame lifted the clasp to her purse, opened the tin, and deftly offered one first to Ally and Amarilla.

"Ladies first," Madame said. Cara, as if on cue, plucked one from the tin and popped it in her mouth.

"Ladies . . ." Madame repeated, with an unmistakable skeptical tone.

"No, thank you," Ally said, looking straight ahead.

"No, thank you, ma'am," Amarilla echoed.

Loren watched as Madame leaned back against the pew, slowly placing the tin of Altoids into her shiny patent leather purse with a look of pure disdain on her face.

After Pastor Roberts wished everyone a blessed Sunday, Ally and Amarilla gave a quick goodbye hug to Cara and Samantha and skedaddled out of the holy building like two guilty nuns at a Planned Parenthood pep rally.

Alec found Loren outside the front doors and down the front church steps as he gave her a chaste kiss.

"You're going to have to do better than that if we're going to have two kids over the next two years," Loren said with a saucy smile.

"I believe we agreed to explore, not procreate," Alec whispered. She could feel his grin against her earlobe. "There is a chronology to a relationship, not always followed but, if I recall, strongly recommended by my mother."

"Hey, I can slow my roll, but I can't speak for the others in this town. And just so you're not blindsided, it's been foretold that you will not age well in the next couple of years. While I will continue to maintain my youthful glow." Okay, that last part was a lie but, when it came to her boyfriend, she had control issues.

Loren couldn't contain her smile or the strange satisfaction in feeling Alec's hand possessively touch her back as they said their first hellos as a couple.

It wasn't long before Becky found her in the crowd and waved her down. "So, Madame Garmond is your grandmother? Why didn't you ever tell me?"

Loren winced, knowing Alec was standing next to her now, wondering the same thing. "Adopted grandmother," Loren blurted out, "but unofficial. No documentation. Actually, it's more wishful thinking on her part than anything concrete."

"Like a fairy godmother?" Becky said, nudging her shoulder.

"Something like that," Loren said, forcing a chuckle, thinking it was time for a sisterly discussion about boundaries, who was in charge of their fabricated backstories, and their houseguest's presumed extended stay.

Her chest squeezed as once again she felt to be losing control. The last thing she was willing to do was to allow others to make decisions and unexpected announcements that could affect their safety and meticulously documented aliases.

It was then that Madame Garmond caught her attention. "Oh, hello dear, I've invited a few people over for a small post-sermon luncheon."

"How many are a few?"

"Oh, just a few close friends," she waved, "Pastor Roberts and his wife, Mrs. Waterman and her charming daughter, Samantha, and Mr. Simmons and his granddaughter, Amarilla."

"Really?" Loren said, genuinely shocked. "I thought for sure you would have forbidden Cara from ever spending time again with Amarilla, after," she lowered her voice, "the conversation we just overheard."

"Oh, that," Madame Garmond huffed, "Quite the contrary, we all need to keep a keen eye on that young lady."

"Right . . . because . . . she can't be trusted?"

"Oh my no," she said, as if affronted, "because she is a lost soul, pining for authority and establishment of boundaries. Now is not the time to forsake the girl but rather to nurture her along, considering her mother is failing miserably." Her lecture continued. "Mr. Simmons is well aware of his daughter's philandering nature and is quite beside himself as to how to guide his granddaughter. It is our duty, as women possessing a strong moral aptitude, to rally behind Miss Amarilla Simmons as positive female influences and support his grand-parental efforts."

Well, crap. Just when she was about to boot the old woman on her fake English keester for upsetting their familial balance, she goes and says something like this.

Madame Garmond was bossy, arrogant, and enviably well put together. Attributes she and Mercy struggled with, having been raised in a sterile environment consisting of a strange mixture of lab coats and combat gear. Loren couldn't help but wish she and Mercy had had a Madame to influence them when they had first arrived at the Center.

Madame seemed to just be getting her second wind. "Now, as for *le Docteur Russe*." Madame guided Loren to the side, away from Alec even though he seemed adequately distracted by a conversation with Gus. "He is completely smitten by our girl, and frankly," she said, pulling Loren closer, "I don't trust him as far as I could heave him over a stacked stoned balustrade."

Loren turned to her wide-eyed. "You believe he's a mole on the verge of turning us into the Center for the bounty Jasper must have hanging over our heads?"

"Good heavens, no," Madame said with a dismissive head shake. "He's biding his time, hoping our girl finally sees the light and falls head over heels in love with him. He's obviously love-drunk and daft as a mad hatter."

"I don't think that's a real English or French term . . . or thing . . . for that matter."

"Pay attention," Madame continued, undaunted. "We must introduce him to some of the women of Wilder. Help him to fall for a nice young woman who shares his affection."

"I was thinking more along the lines of kicking him out of the house."

"Whatever for? He's a love-sick menace, not a criminal, for goodness sakes."

"I'm not a hundred percent sure who anybody is anymore," Loren said, almost to herself, as she rubbed her forehead.

Madame ignored her. "Which is why I invited that brash young woman, Daniela Harris, to our luncheon."

"Who?"

"The young woman in the undercroft during the committee meeting."

"Undercroft?"

"Beneath the chancel and nave."

"Wait, are you speaking English or English, English?"

"For a genius, you lack the proper language of religious architecture." The elderly woman seemed to be on a tangent and took a breath. "Nevertheless, I have invited Daniela as she seems to be of the proper age and snarky nature as our girl."

Daniela must have been the name of the woman in the committee meeting she couldn't quite place. "So, you're planning to get rid of Vlad by introducing him to Daniela?"

"Exactly," Madame preened. "The poor man is never going to alter his attention for Mercy until another woman captures it."

"You are quite the meddler, Madame."

"My dear, it's never meddling when one merely looks out for the people for which one cares." As if an afterthought, Madame added, "Please feel free to invite Alec and Ally as well."

As Madame strode away, with a regal wave to another Wilder acquaintance, Loren muttered, "Gee, thanks for letting me invite people to my own house."

Loren speculated if Madame was as innocent and oblivious as she let on. Loren had learned never to believe what someone revealed of themselves but to rely only on information she was able to unearth through data mining and good, old-fashion Google.

She watched Madame converse with a smitten Emmy Lou, who treated her like a celebrity. Why, it wouldn't surprise Loren in the least if the elderly woman turned out to be a two-bit fraud from Hoboken with a long rap sheet of scam artists on her Ancestry.com account.

Tonight, she would pull out her dusty laptop and do some sleuthing as it pertained to Madame Garmond and *le Docteur Russe*, aka Vlad Petrov, dispelling any skepticism she harbored for the two people she feared could cause her family the most harm.

Intentionally or unintentionally.

And then tomorrow she would start her new job with a fresh attitude and clear mind.

Loren was so relieved when the Thanksgiving potluck turned out to be a monumental success. Largely due to Madame Garmond and her iron fist when negotiating with the women of Wilder on those dishes she deemed "Thanksgiving potluck-worthy."

Madame vetted each listing, ensuring they passed the veracity test. Which was basically comprised of Mercy texting Becky Waterman, who gave it either a thumbs-up or thumbs down.

Loren didn't dare tell Madame that Becky allowed a few to slide as they were longtime favorites. Case in point: She seriously doubted the pilgrims fed on "beans and weenies" during the first Thanksgiving.

That said, it was touch and go on a few questionable casseroles and side dishes. Madame and Lenore Sterling nearly came to fisticuffs when the English woman turned up her nose and lip to Lenore's description of a mint Jell-O shrimp mold garnished with apple slices tossed in a mayo-based dressing.

Madame countered that the dish did not align with the Thanksgiving theme.

Lenore insisted it was a staple on her mother's Thanksgiving table, and she had brought the shrimp mold to the potluck every year since her passing.

Madame delicately inquired if her passing were at all related to the shrimp mold.

After getting Emmy Lou Roberts involved as a mediator of sorts, neither Lenore nor the pastor's wife proved to be a match for the Ingalls' pretend, adopted-in-spirit-only grandmother.

The shrimp mold was out, and homemade gingerbread was the strongly recommended substitute which fell under the category of dessert as opposed to where the shrimp mold landed, which Madame had named Gastronomic Atrocities.

During the potluck, Madame sat at a checkered-cloth-covered foldout table with Cara, Ally, Samantha, and Amarilla.

Loren sat at the adjacent table, surprised that the teenagers seemed more than okay with the seating arrangement as Madame regaled them with stories of American terms that drove the English, in her words, "Utterly mad."

"What's the matter with the word 'burglarized'?" Cara asked as she took a bite of the turkey roasted by Emmy Lou.

Madame swallowed a bite of stuffing with a frown. "A home gets 'burgled.' Whereas getting burglarized," she said, butchering the pronunciation, "sounds more like a chemical reaction."

"Sorry," Ally said, squeezing ketchup on her plate. "But getting 'burgled' sounds a lot weirder to me."

"And then there is the word 'jelly,'" Madame said before taking a bite of turkey.

"What's the matter with jelly?" Samantha asked. "Like, peanut butter and jelly."

"Jelly refers to a mold of sorts. That jiggles."

Amarilla piped up with, "Like Mrs. Sterling's disgusting shrimp and apple mold." She shuddered.

"Well, yes, that is the proper use of jelly in a somewhat improper and forgettable dish. But it's jam that you spoon out of a jar, not jelly."

"But we have jam. It's like preserves," Ally said.

"That would be marmalade," Madame said with an all-knowing tilt of her perfectly coiffed head.

Levi sat directly across from Madame. "Well, I like how you say things," he stated, wearing a freshly ironed shirt with what looked to be copious amounts of pomade to slick down what little hair he had. "Everything sounds prettier when you say it."

Madame twittered and Loren smiled as she eavesdropped on their conversation, content that all was going so well at their table, not to mention the potluck as a whole.

Mercy, Vlad, and none other than Daniela, sat across from Loren and Alec, with Gus on Alec's other side.

Loren pointed with her fork at the amount of food on Mercy's plate. "You going to eat all of that?"

"No," Mercy said, unfolding the napkin and pulling out the utensils wrapped inside. "I'm going to eat as much as I can and take home whatever's left."

"Did you ask per-mis-sion?" Loren asked with a grin, referring to their most recent long-term authoritarian houseguest.

"Noooo," Mercy said, her expression that of one of the children

LIVING WILDER

sitting at the smaller table on the farthest side of the church basement, exhibiting more commitment to horseplay than eating. "She's not the boss of me." She looked up at Loren. "But if she asks, I totally never said that."

At that moment, one of the more aggressive boys at the children's table began giving a fake series of uppercut punches to the boy sitting next to him.

"Hey, Henry Calhoun!" Mercy yelled with her hands wrapped around her mouth, "Don't make me make your mother call child protective services on me."

The room let out a communal chuckle as Henry's hands flew to his sides with a theatrical grin that was missing a front tooth.

Mercy was considered Wilder's child whisperer, not so much because of her ability to nurture, but her capacity to bring the town's feral children to heel.

And the children loved her.

Alec squeezed Loren's leg, and she turned to him as he whispered in her ear. "You did a great job."

"Thanks," she said. "Madame was the henchman for the food, so the rest was just logistics."

He kept looking into her eyes until she began to fidget. "What?" she asked with a nudge to his shoulder, a great excuse for getting closer to his neck and panty-melting scent.

"You happy?" he asked, with his usual stoic self.

"Yes."

And then he kissed her on the forehead which she had learned translated as deep adoration from one of Mercy's love-language books.

She wasn't sure he adored her per se, but he appeared to be in heavy "like."

CHAPTER THIRTY-SIX

"But mathematics is the sister, as well as the servant of the arts and is touched with the same madness and genius."

—Harold Marston Morse
American mathematician best known for his work on the calculus of "variation in the large," a subject in which he introduced the technique of differential topology now known as Morse theory

A few days later, on a beautiful Sunday afternoon, they celebrated Thanksgiving at the Ingalls' home.

Loren stood on the front porch in a spice-colored skirt, a white, long-sleeved sweater and wearing knee-high gray suede boots. She crossed her arms loosely in front of her chest as she waited for Alec to pull into the drive. He'd just texted that he and Ally and their special guest were on their way.

The weather was warmer than usual at sixty-plus degrees. Loren raised her eyes skyward and swore she could smell the bright colors of the cumulus, a surreal mixture of bright blue, warm yellow, and a tinge of pink.

Thanks to her new job at the hardware store, an inviting brick walkway led to the front porch, a vast improvement from the cracked concrete path from before.

The elaborate wooden arbor to her right led to a flower garden with a long row of fencing with vines entangled that would hopefully bloom next spring with grapes.

She turned to her right and smiled at the half dozen hydrangeas that had grown twice their size since planting them with Mercy's help, their gorgeous blooms providing a waft of fragrant air as you moved to and fro on the front porch swing. Earlier in the fall, they'd transitioned from milky white to soft pink and were now taking on a gorgeous red-wine tint. Soon the plants would go dormant for the winter, but for now, she'd enjoy every minute of them.

She heard before she could see the four wheel-drive truck as it rounded the curve to the driveway. Her heart beat faster at the prospect of seeing Alec and their first-time guest.

The instant the truck came to a stop, Ally jumped out of the back seat, gave Loren a quick hug and ran into the house as if she hadn't just seen Cara the day prior.

And then Alec erupted from the driver's side, giving her a lazy sexy grin. She waved at him, bouncing on her tiptoes as the passenger door opened and Jimbo's head popped out.

"Hey there, Half-Pint," he said with a smile and a wave.

"Hi, Jimbo," Loren said. "Happy Thanksgiving. So glad you could come."

As he made his way up the brick pathway with his usual slight limp, Loren could see that he looked to have showered, wearing clean clothes and a light coat.

He stopped at the foot of the steps. "You look pretty as sunshine, Half-Pint."

"Thank you, I'm so glad you could join us. And you're looking quite spiffy yourself."

Alec reached Jimbo's side, carrying a Pyrex dish.

Jimbo lifted his thumb toward Alec. "Your beau here was kind enough to let me use his bathroom. Couldn't come to Thanksgiving smelling like a goat."

Alec clutched the older man's shoulder. "We're just happy you're here."

Thanksgiving at the Ingalls turned out to be a community event, a good bit smaller than the potluck but just as loud and boisterous. Madame, once again the faithful party planner, had invited Levi and Amarilla (Marybell was off on another tryst), Becky and Samantha (Becky's husband, once again incognito, gaming becoming more and more of a priority, even during holidays).

Daniela showed up, and Madame shrugged her shoulders at a suspicious Loren, causing them both to glance at a grinning Vlad, who kissed Daniela on the cheek and took her coat.

And of course, Mercy, Alec, Ally, and Jimbo rounded out the guest list.

A couple of times during the meal, Mercy would catch Loren's attention, soft eyes communicating to one another how grateful they were without uttering a single word.

While Madame and Mercy began to set aside the main dishes and pull out the various desserts, Alec looked at Loren and tilted his head to the side, indicating "follow me." Loren moved her napkin to her chair and gladly followed his lead past the living room and through the front door.

Loren was sure he would be sitting on the front porch swing, but caught him just as he was turning the corner. He seemed to be in a hurry, based on his relentless pace, and then she frowned as he stepped inside the new tool shed.

Excellent. She was eager to show off the newly constructed structure. A steal with the company discount she got at the hardware store.

She turned the door handle, but before she could shut it, Alec's arm reached past her and slammed it shut, grabbing her by the arms and pushing her against the work-bench.

She could feel her entire body tense at the perceived assault. But then a miraculous thing happened. Just when she hit that edge of no return, and was about to unleash her wrath, his signature scent held her sense of self-preservation hostage. And instead of reacting to a potential threat, melted against him and inhaled.

"What?" she croaked as his mouth found her neck, and his hands were already making their way up her skirt.

Once again, she breathed him in and then out.

And. She. Melted.

Like warm butter in a hot iron skillet, the heat wearing down her defenses while the hot liquid pooled mercilessly downward, reaching the sensitive area of her lady bits.

"Alec," she moaned, self-conscious of sounding like those hormone-addled women in Mercy's romance novels. But honestly, his hands were everywhere, and just when she thought he was honing in on a single erogenous zone, he'd moved to another area of her body as his mouth licked and nipped its way down her neck and shoulders.

"It's the boots," he stated matter-of-factly, as he twisted her around so his chest was against her back, and she had to grab onto the shelf just at eye level for leverage.

"Boots?" she croaked as his mouth latched onto the back of her neck while his octopus hands multitasked, one dipping into the front of her panties, finding her clit as if assisted by a homing device, the other staking claim to her ass.

His lips were now tugging at her ear. "You wore fuck-me boots for the sole purpose of teasing the fuck out of me."

"I wore boots to stay warm," she argued, at the same time secretly promising to purchase the high-heeled, knee-high suede boots in every color as soon as she could find her breath and sanity.

His hand pulled away from her happy place and undid the top snap on her skirt and then the second, the sound a sexy prelude of things to come. He slowly pulled the silky skirt down along with her panties, until he was on his knees.

She looked over her shoulder as he worked her garments to the floor, lifting one boot at a time to free them and tossing them to the side to land on a stack of potting soil bags.

He sat back on his haunches with nothing less than reverence on his face.

Her body trembled as his eyes, full of naughty intentions, looked up at her through ridiculously long lashes that she knew the women of Wilder would pay good money for.

"You ready to be punished for what you did?"

Amazed at her pooling desire, with no concerns at all to her overall safety, she gave him a slight shrug. "I have no regrets." And with what was pure instinct alongside sexual intent, she licked her lips.

"Oh, now you're just asking for it." His eyes blinked slowly, never leaving hers. "Move back," he instructed.

She hesitated, as he moved to the side with one hand on her calf directing her stance.

Aware she was naked from the waist down with the exception of her libido-inducing boots, she felt heat rise up her neck, landing on her face as she faced forward.

"Open your legs."

Resting her forehead on her hands gripping the shelf, she felt him pull at her calf and she stepped to the side, conflicted at feeling both vulnerable and wildly excited.

She glanced down between her arms, just as he sat on his haunches, his hand inching their way up her thigh and then sliding through her folds.

"So wet for me." He nipped her ass cheek, and she yelped.

"According to online health sites, that's perfectly normal."

"That's . . . good to know." His fingers moved her juices toward the front and over her clit.

She swallowed as he moved painstakingly slow, coming up on his knees. She loosened one hand, grabbing the edge of the workbench at her waist to accommodate the awkward but oh, so satisfying position.

She heard a guttural moan and then realized it came from her. "Alec," she said, not sure what she needed but desperate to get to it.

"Don't move," he warned, his fingers now moving not only forward but now back toward toward what she considered uncharted territory.

"Is this normal?" he taunted.

"I . . . I . . . don't know."

"Do you like how that feels?"

"Oh, God, yes."

"Well then, you're going to love this." She felt his hands spread her folds open.

And then his mouth, Was. There.

What this man could do with his lips, tongue, and teeth was quite literally obscene. And where he moved his fingers, back and forth, he mirrored those same movements but with his mouth.

And she loved it.

He pinned the back of her legs against his chest, allowing her to lean back more, giving him better access for more licking and sucking and ravishing.

She totally got what the word "ravish" meant now. She'd read it in books and would roll her eyes at what she thought was romance novel hyperbole. But as of today, she got it. Because the man was eating her like an overly anticipated holiday dessert and *ravishing* her.

Her heart raced, the blood surging in places of her body she didn't know existed, as his animalistic assault heightened. Clutching the shelf above and the workbench below, she could feel the pressure reach an untenable point.

And then suddenly Alec stood, one arm wrapped around her waist as she heard a snap and then a wrenched zipper. And before she could even look over her shoulder, he covered her mouth with one hand, the other on her hip, and thrust inside her.

Before catching her breath, she came. Screaming into his calloused palm, acutely aware of handing over all physical control as he relentlessly pumped inside her body.

She continued to hold on tight to both the shelf and the workbench. And without warning, the shelf began to tilt from the additional weight, along with the contents. Several small containers of screws and some paper towels came tumbling down, her quick reflexes deflecting them from doing any bodily damage.

Alec continued his relentless thrusts, unaware of the shed carnage surrounding them.

Alec's moan followed, both hands clutching her at the waist, the pressure of his fingers sure to cause bruising.

He jerked once, and then again, as her body milked him to the end.

After taking a moment to catch their breath, Alec pulled away, giving her neck a last nip.

She rose from her forearms and did her best to dust off the wood shavings and leftover potting soil from the surface of the workbench. One side of the shelving support was intact, the other bent and resting on the bench.

"What happened?" Alec asked, pressed to her back and now conscious of his surroundings.

"Collateral damage," she quipped.

"You okay?" He pulled her up, handing her the discarded garments.

She grabbed one of the rolls of paper towels that was once on the shelf, removed an inner strip and handed it to a suddenly mute Alec. Then she took another strip and cleaned herself as well.

She pointed at the plastic trash bin in the far corner, where Alec disposed of the evidence of their shed tryst, and she did the same.

Silently they pulled their clothes back on. Loren found it difficult to look him in the eye. When she finally did, he stood before her, his eyes pensive.

"That was . . . unexpected," she said with a forced laugh.

He rubbed the back of his neck. "I didn't intend to take it so far." He hesitated, his eyes looking sheepish and unsure. "I shouldn't have done that."

She took a step toward him. "It was my fault."

He shook his head. "No, it wasn't. Here we are at a family holiday meal, and I take you in the backyard shed."

He appeared embarrassed and regretful. The last thing she wanted was Alec Wilder to ever regret her.

"It was the boots," she said, with a saucy smile.

He smiled back, rubbing his bottom lip with his thumb. "They taunted me."

"We should throw them away for being so . . . naughty."

"Or," he said, lifting an eyebrow, "you could wear them every day. Maybe even sleep in them."

Her arms went around his neck as she stared up into crystal-blue eyes. "Thank you for making my first Thanksgiving in Wilder so much better than I could have ever imagined."

His eyebrows furrowed once again. "We didn't use protection."

"Becky took me to her OB-GYN. I'm on the pill. I was supposed to wait another week before . . . indulging . . . but I'm sure it's fine."

She kissed him, and he hugged her and gave her a small slap on her ass. "We need to work our way back inside. You go first while I clean up with the garden hose."

She turned her head to the side in question.

"I'd love to spend the rest of the day smelling you on me, but I'm not sure the rest of your guests would feel the same way when it came time to hug-out our goodbyes."

"Ooh," she returned with a grimace. "Good call." She patted his shoulder. "You go clean up and I'll cover for you."

To Loren's relief, they both managed to make their way back to the festivities with none the wiser. When asked where they had gone from a cheeky Mercy, Loren glared combat knives at her while Alec remained completely unaffected, stating they were sitting on the front porch swing enjoying the weather.

Madame fixed Alec a piece of pumpkin pie and then skirted out of the dining room to enjoy the rest of her guests who had decided to enjoy the weather on the front porch as well.

Loren began to scoot behind Alec's chair when he grabbed her by the arm. "Where are you going?"

"To get a piece of the pie. Apparently, only our guests get served."

He tugged on her arm. "Madame gave me what looks to be half of a pie. We have plenty." He pulled her from the back of his chair, situating her on his leg with one arm holding her to him.

Never. Absolutely never had Loren felt such unreserved joy. They took turns taking bites while the adults sat on the front porch, and the younger girls took turns playing music on the piano in the front room.

After giving Loren the last bite, they continued to sit there quietly, enjoying the music and laughter in the other room, and in no hurry to move apart.

Loren mused about how their lives had changed so dramatically in less than a year. They lived in a nice home, with worn-in couches, scuffed furniture, and a number of quilts to cuddle in during cold winter mornings.

She had the best job ever on the planet, helping other people improve their homes, not to mention the pure joy of keeping track of inventory. And then there were her evening classes, now her side hustle, training women to defend themselves while at the same time improving their confidence and overall self-worth.

But most importantly of all, giving Mercy and Cara the life they deserved. The life she owed them.

A life that at one time seemed impossible. All because of one single monumental mistake of judgment.

Deep down, she knew she needed to dig deeper into Madame and Vlad's backgrounds. Check their bank accounts to see where money was coming in and where it was going out. And, at the very least, go over their own individual efforts at hiding themselves in the small town of Wilder, Texas.

Maybe she put it off because she was afraid of what she'd find. But was it really wrong to trust them? Maybe it was okay not to question their stories, but trust in their motives. God knew she and her sisters had garnered their own laundry list of lies. Each and every one of them necessary to ensure their protection.

But then there was Alec. She knew she was falling for him. When she would spot him from across a room, her heart pounded like a newly adopted puppy, the sound of his voice alone causing her have to change her panties on the reg. But was it right to hide her past from him? Could she honestly expect to create a longterm relationship with this man after so much deception?

Alec finally broke the silence. "You happy?" he asked, kissing her below the ear.

Unable to form words for fear of spewing the guilt brewing inside, Loren merely nodded and then rested her head in the crook of his neck. She finally got hold of herself and said, "So, so, happy."

CHAPTER THIRTY-SEVEN

"Measure what is measurable, and make measurable what is not so."

—Galileo Galilei
Italian from Pisa; astronomer, physicist,
and engineer, sometimes described as a polymath

Alec arrived at the M2M headquarters and main training compound in Greenville, South Carolina for an impromptu meeting at 0800 hours Monday morning. He had hoped to receive his first assignment by now, but the company seemed more interested in extending background check efforts than leveraging a newly acquired asset.

Which was why he was surprised they had called him in, providing little information and insisting that he take the next plane to the Greenville-Spartanburg International Airport.

He had followed orders. And was now sitting in his director's office. Your typical hurry-up-and-wait scenario. Yet he couldn't deny the comfort of finding himself once again in a military-esque environment despite being a contracted civilian.

MARSOC had been the right fit for Alec, as opposed to managing a farm, and he hoped he'd find the same compatibility straddling his home life responsibilities alongside a career with M2M.

M2M was an obscure operation with a website that indicated your typical private or event security services.

But as with many private security companies, the lines between security and quasi-military operations had become blurred, their contracts falling more in line with military-style assignments, further evident by these companies hiring staff with former Special Forces backgrounds for their skills in combat.

He checked the time on his phone. Loren should be well into her day at Wilder's Hardware. In his mind, he pictured her bent over the workbench in the shed wearing those fucking unforgettable boots, licking her puffy lips.

He began to send her a good morning text, when Director Birch entered the office with two coffees. Another man who also looked to be military, based on his rigid demeanor but wearing civilian clothes, followed him into the room.

Alec stood out of habit.

"No need for all that saluting and genuflecting bullshit," Director Birch assured Alec. Birch was an older man; some might call distinguished with salt-and-pepper hair and an unusually fit body for a man of his age.

"Alec Wilder, meet Trevor Forrest. Ex-Navy Seal and the lead on your first assignment."

Alec shook the other man's hand who was just short of reaching his own six-feet, two-inch stature, but of the same build and presence as if he, too, came from a boots-on-the-ground military background.

Director Birch continued, "Forrest is working on a lengthy assignment that has begun to show progress. For geographical reasons, we would like for you to get involved."

"Geographical reasons?" Alec asked.

Forrest took over the explanation as Birch blew on his coffee.

"We've been contracted to infiltrate a facility as part of a much larger crime ring. Leads on various high-profile assignments keep pointing us to a medical facility in Findling, Utah, namely Halstead Labs and Research Center. For years, getting inside or collecting any useful information has been near to impossible."

"Until recently," Birch added, as Forrest opened a file and set it on the desk, lifting a photo of an elderly man and placing it on the top of the stack of papers.

"We've suspected the founder and namesake of the facility to be part of numerous unsolved crimes spanning every continent but having few similarities."

Birch took over. "We're talking drug deals in Venezuela, Mexico and Peru, art heists in Austria and France, money laundering and financially lucrative intel sweeps on dozens of very bad people in some very dangerous parts of the world."

"Sounds compelling, but I don't live in Findling, Utah, nor have I ever been."

Forrest continued, "Since Halstead died several months ago, things have changed. They've gotten lazy, messy. Two months ago, they were facilitating the movement of cartel combat vehicles into Mexico, which turned into a shit-show. They lost a number of men. We think they lost some valuable brain trust."

"Halstead, you mean?" Alec asked.

"And others."

"Defectors?"

"Correct."

"Who contracted our services?"

"Irrelevant."

Alec grew pensive. "Does this . . . fall under our jurisdiction?"

"If you're asking if we have the power to make legal decisions as it pertains to this assignment, yes," Forrest provided. "What you need to know is that we have been contracted to perform a small part of a much greater effort. We've been instructed to surveil the facility and infiltrate it. Once inside, we gather the sufficient intel so other groups can do their jobs, bringing down those within the facility but more importantly, those criminal factions outside of the facility."

Birch spoke up. "You'll soon learn that jurisdiction is a flimsy concept when working for M2M. There's rarely an assignment where our involvement can't be construed as critical to the success of the mission. There's more," Birch stated matter-of-factly, "but we provide information on a need-to-know basis. For your safety and others."

Birch set his empty coffee cup down and picked up the full one. "By the way, your background check has been completed, so you're good to go."

"But I don't warrant additional information?"

"That was the additional information."

"I'm still not connecting the dots on the geographical part of this assignment."

Forrest connected them. "We've learned that one of the defectors is hiding out in Wilder."

Alec eyebrows shot up. "Wilder?"

"Those at the Center have been working toward bringing them back into the fold. Back to Utah."

"Involuntarily?"

"Correct. We're going to load up with surveillance tech and follow them in."

"Have we confirmed consent?"

Birch and Forrest looked at one another.

Birch broke the silence. "We've been instructed to keep the target in the dark."

"We can't be sure they'll work in our favor, knowing our complicity," Forrest explained. "And we don't have the time to talk them into it."

"Couldn't we shoot them a deal? Seems like they'd be more amenable if they knew they had a vested interest."

"I appreciate your interest in the overall success of this mission," Birch said, taking another sip, "but you have an inch of intel, where those above you have mounds of information extracted over numerous years."

Forrest further explained. "Ours is a small cog in a very complex wheel. We get the parameters of our contract, and we follow them."

Alec sat back in his chair, contemplating what this meant. There wasn't a soul he didn't know in Wilder. Eventually someone was going to be betrayed.

By him.

His mind ran through a Rolodex of names.

The hair on his neck began to rise as Forrest pulled out an 8x12 photo.

Loren.

Sitting in the carpool line at school. Probably waiting to pick up Cara, maybe even Ally, at the end of the school day.

He thought he might pass out from lack of oxygen while performing a Herculean effort at appearing unmoved.

"You know this woman?" Forrest asked.

Alec glanced at him and took a long breath. "I think you already know the answer to that question."

Birch asked, "Is this going to be a problem?"

"No, sir."

Yes, it was.

He added, "But I can tell you that based on my personal knowledge of the target, she'd be far more productive as a Trojan horse than a sacrificial lamb."

Not to mention safer.

"She's your neighbor," stated Forrest.

"She is."

"Her younger sister is close friends with your sister, Ally."

"That's true." And then Alec wondered if those at the Utah

research facility were pulling in Cara and Mercy as well. Were her sisters even aware of Loren's criminal involvement? Were they involved?

But he didn't want to ask questions that would divulge information that could potentially hurt, more than help.

He weighed his next question. "Do we know of any others they might be pulling back in?"

Forrest shook his head. "Intel shows they're only coming for her."

Alec didn't bat an eye, despite the need to upend the desk in front of him.

She was a sitting duck.

They were coming after her.

Birch sat back in his chair, assessing Alec. "Have you witnessed any . . . irregularities?"

"Sir?"

He leaned forward, pointing at Loren's photo. Her hair was much shorter in this picture than the bleached-blond mane just past her shoulders. No telling how long they'd been watching her.

"With the target," Birch added.

Hundreds of sketches littering her walls came to mind as he stared at her picture, remaining as expressionless as humanly possible.

Forrest seemed anxious. "Would you classify her behavior as sporadic or manic?"

He and Loren's intimate relationship was a recent event. There was a chance they only viewed their connection as it pertained to Ally and Cara. "She's the sister of my sister's best friend. I don't think that necessarily warrants personal knowledge of Miss Ingalls' behavior."

Forrest pulled another photo from the stack. Alec instantly recognized the picture of the two of them. It was recent. Had to have been taken last weekend among a throng of friends and family outside the church. He had his arm around Loren, trying to keep her warm, looking down at her as she looked up at him with complete trust.

Forrest cleared his throat. "We don't have a lot of time. We've been instructed to allow the target to be taken due to her . . . unpredictable nature."

"Go on," Alec remained expressionless.

Birch and Forrest shared another glance as if communicating their common struggle. Birch offered up the last piece of information. "She's a documented genius with a Mensa score of over one seventy, trained to the equivalency of a lethal weapon, and diagnosed as criminally insane."

And there it was.

Alec was once again in his lifetime, shocked.

And gutted.

He raked his fingers through his hair, as if gouging deep grooves into his scalp.

He leaned his elbows onto his knees and covered his mouth with clasped hands to hold it together.

The two men remained silent as if allowing him to ruminate in the information provided.

He couldn't begin to contemplate Loren as insane.

Of course, he thought the same about Marisa.

But still, Loren?

Unpredictable?

Of course.

Fought like a trained assassin?

He'd witnessed it firsthand.

Criminally insane?

His eyes bore into Director Birch's. "If we've been instructed to let them take her, why do you need me? What value does my connection to Miss Ingalls bring if we aren't going to leverage it?"

Forrest answered him. "You're considered on standby, due to her mental unpredictability."

Birch added, "And for your safety."

Alec blinked slowly, processing the information before him. "Did you recruit me into M2M because of my skillset and background with MARSOC, or my geographic location to the target?"

Director Birch answered as Forrest looked down. "I think you know the answer to that question."

Birch advised Alec that as project lead for M2M, Forrest would debrief him on further details regarding their department's role in the NSA-CIA mission.

They were dismissed.

As soon as they were outside of Birch's office, Forrest was on his phone arranging for helicopter transport to Wilder, Texas.

After ending the call, he turned to Alec. "There's more I can tell you, and more I can't. You're ex-military. You should get that. But don't assume that as a contracted civilian operator, that there aren't severe, life-altering consequences for going rogue." He stopped in the middle of the corridor. "Do we understand each other?"

Alec nodded. He understood. Didn't mean he was going to comply. "What's the plan?"

"I've been working on getting inside the research center by posing as a gun for hire. They've already got someone inside informing them of the target's location. My mock team was to perform the extraction."

"Who's the inside informant?"

Forrest blinked slowly. "Classified."

Jesus H. Christ.

How in the fuck was he going to determine next steps based on such spotty information?

"So, we're going to bring her in?"

"We were," he said, leaning against the wall. "My contact at the research facility, a Dr. Bancroft, decided at the last minute that he needed to be there for the extraction. Apparently, he specializes in tempering her clinically diagnosed condition when it turns volatile. He left Utah for the pick-up point earlier this morning and is en route. He's taken a flight to a small airfield that caters to private planes, Holict Airport."

"That's about six miles from Wilder," Alec offered.

"We need to reach the target before he does and to ensure we are in charge of manning the extraction. If he gets to her first and takes her in without us, we've basically failed your first mission with SCS. If we don't get inside the research facility, we can't surveil the premises."

"So, how exactly will I assist?"

"You're part of the extraction team."

"I thought we were keeping the target in the dark in regard to my role."

"Correct, she's to think you are part of my team."

"How exactly is that undercover profile going to keep me safe from her volatile nature?"

"It's not," he said, reaching into his pocket and popping what looked to be a breath mint in his mouth.

Alec leaned his head against the wall. "Could you just cut the fucking undercover-lingo-bullshit and spell it out for me?"

"As far as she will know, you work for me, a gun for hire who has been contracted by Bancroft. You have been keeping tabs on her to aid in her extraction from Wilder, to the research facility in Findling, Utah."

"So, I'm selling her out. Where's the rest of our team?"

"You're looking at 'im."

"Just the two of us?" Alec chuckled. Unless this guy had a titanium suit underneath that button-down, they were up shit's creek. "If we're going to beat Bancroft to Holict Airport we need to leave A-SAP."

"Well, that's the thing. We won't make it in time if we go to Holict. You wouldn't happen to know of a large field in Wilder where we could land a helicopter?"

CHAPTER THIRTY-EIGHT

"'Obvious' is the most dangerous word in mathematics."

—Eric Temple Bell
Scottish-born mathematician, and science fiction writer

Mercy pulled into the driveway. She loved driving Vlad's smokin' new Land Rover. It still had that new car smell, and it was a far cry nicer than Madame's Mini Cooper that she bought as a cash purchase from what she called "A rather questionable source that reeked of bangers and mash."

Whatever the hell that was.

Madame's phone rang. From what Mercy could tell from the conversation, Cara had forgotten that today was a half day at school.

Madame turned to Mercy with the burner phone at her ear.

"Mercy, love, can we pick up Cara and Ally from the secondary school?"

"Are they out now?"

Madame asked Cara and confirmed they were indeed standing outside the school doors.

"Tell her that's what school buses are for," Mercy said.

Madame advised the bus as an obvious mode of transportation, and said back to Mercy, "She contends that riding the bus is totally lame and akin to social suicide amongst her peers."

"Freakin' little divas," Mercy muttered. "Tell her to go park her royal backside with Loren at the hardware store, and I'll pick them up after dropping off the groceries."

Madame communicated the message, ended the call, pulling down the sun visor to touch up her lipstick.

"Why are you checking your lipstick? We're home."

She pursed her lips and patted her shiny gray hair. "Levi mentioned stopping by today."

Mercy smiled as she stepped out of the SUV and opened the back passenger door to grab handfuls of grocery bags.

"So, you two are spending a lot of time together."

"Hmm," she answered with what might have been a small smile. Mercy couldn't be sure, looking at her reflection in the visor's mirror from the back seat.

Mercy said with her best British accent that sounded more cockney than the Queen's English, "You seem a bit dodgy at the moment."

Madame caught Mercy's reflection. "I see you've made an unsuccessful attempt at improving your knowledge of British slang."

Mercy emerged from the back, carrying about four plastic bags in each hand and managed to shut the door with her hip.

Madame made her way gracefully up the steps with just her purse.

"You go on," Mercy said with one side of her lip upturned, "I'm sure you're quite knackered after making that long sojourn to the grocer."

Madame's eyes looked up with an exaggerated sigh. "Only because I had to spend my time with a veritable knobhead."

Mercy stopped midway up the steps. "Madame Garmond! Did you just call me a ... a ... dickhead?"

"Don't be ridiculous. That would be crass," she said, opening the door and waving Mercy in. "Please do hurry before you find yourself arse over tits."

Mercy could barely contain the laughter. "What would your duke of a father say if he heard you right now?"

"Well, he'd probably say that the acorn didn't fall far from the tree."

Mercy hesitated, not expecting that.

Madame continued. "And he would only say so privately. Lord knows he would never sully his reputation by acknowledging my existence in public."

Mercy's head shook side-to-side as her eyes widened. "What?"

Madame heaved another sigh. "I was what is called a by-blow," she said, folding her arms, still holding the door as Mercy stood there with her mouth open and her hands drooping with plastic bags. "A love child, or one of my all-time favorites from my father: a rather unfortunate outcome."

"But I thought he insisted that you and your mother live with him in England rather than France?"

"Not together, but within a controllable distance. You see, he was never one to shirk his responsibilities, only to ignore them."

"He and your mother never married?"

"Goodness, no. That would have been quite the scandal considering he was already married when I was conceived."

Mercy scooched through the door sideways to make room for the bags while trying to make sense of this new information. "I hope you know my mind is totally blown right now."

Madame followed her. "It's not something one likes to talk about despite the begetting of illegitimate children amongst the peerage a rather common occurrence. Nevertheless, it was difficult to watch your father, who was no less than British royalty, raise his legitimate children in utter luxury while you were raised by a ruined single parent in a sublet, openly ridiculed and shunned by the neighbors and townsfolk."

Mercy imagined the rigid woman as a small, vulnerable child being bullied by the other children of the local gentry, and it made her chest cave.

She finally made it to the kitchen where Vlad sat at the table and she plunked the bags down. "Oh no, I don't need help," she said, full of sarcasm. "I can totally wrestle twenty bags of groceries all by myself."

And then she noticed the near-empty bottle of vodka, and the jelly jar he was tipping back and forth on the table.

"It's kinda early to be sipping the sauce, isn't it?"

He didn't look up but moved his head slowly from side to side. "I have failed you, *milaya*."

Madame entered the kitchen, placing her purse on the table. Mercy caught her attention as she looked just as confused. This wasn't like Vlad. He certainly enjoyed his drink of choice but not before noon nor to such an extent.

"What? I'm good," she said, slowly pulling a carton of milk out of a plastic bag. "No migraines for some time now." But then again, she wasn't painting. Trying to see if she could quit cold turkey so she wouldn't have to be babysat for the rest of her life.

He continued to shake his head, and then Mercy noticed his shoulders shaking. As if he were sobbing. She instantly placed the milk on the table and crouched down to his side. "Vlad? What's the matter?"

Bloodshot eyes and reeking of alcohol, he finally looked at her with tears running down his face. "They . . . they promise they take care of you."

"Who?" she asked, shaking her head.

"They promise that I bring you back, they do surgery, and . . . and make you well again."

Fear sliced through Mercy's body as she went to her knees and grabbed his arm. "What did you do, Vlad?"

"They said you have little time. That misplaced lesion only get worse and you lose sight and then die." His face crumpled as his other hand moved from his lap, drunkenly slapping a pistol on the table. "They are coming."

Mercy stared at the gun and then looked up at Madame, who was holding her hand to her mouth.

"Who is coming, Vlad?" But she already knew.

Dear God.

"They not come for you. They betray us."

With a stronger voice, Mercy squeezed his arm. "When Vlad, when are they coming?"

And then a shot fired out of nowhere, shattering the window over the kitchen sink. She ducked her head as shards of glass continued to drop into the porcelain basin. She yanked on his arm to pull him to safety as Madame crouched by the table with her head between her hands.

But he was limp, and pinned in by the chair. And then she noticed the blood splattered across her chest, his upper body draped over the table.

"Mercy, get down!" Madame screamed.

She blinked and hunched down deeper, trying to gather herself.

She needed a gun.

Mercy reached up with one hand, scrambling for Vlad's gun on the table. She felt the textured gunmetal handle, pulling it under the table and, checking that it was loaded, she unlatched the safety as she pointed it away and scooted beside a shaking Madame.

All they could hear was their heavy breathing as they waited. Mercy worked through the kill shot details, as she listened intently for any incriminating noise. The shot had to have been from high and from a distance, as it came through the window and hit him in the temple area in order for the blood to splatter onto her chest. She wiped the blood on her cheek, confirming the hypothesis.

Several painstaking minutes passed as she held her finger alongside the trigger, waiting for someone to burst through the kitchen door to their right or from the hall entrance to the left.

Nothing.

Madame gently pulled on Mercy's arm. "What did he mean, they weren't coming for you? Who are they coming for?"

Mercy ran through his last words, trying to make sense of them.

"Jasper must have found us. They convinced Vlad I was going to die if they didn't operate, so he outed us."

She also knew that Jasper despised Loren on an almost visceral level and implied a fucked-up affection for Cara.

"Let's think this through," Mercy said, leaning against the kitchen cabinet, her chest heaving while continuing to support her pistol stance with both hands. "They'll assume Cara's at school, and that Loren's at the hardware store."

Madame's hand went to her throat. "But Cara and Ally are on their way to Loren. They're all together."

Mercy pulled her phone from her back pocket, calling her sister.

Loren didn't pick up.

She then tried calling the store phone, but got an automated message.

"We've got to move fast if we're going to get to them in time."

If it wasn't too late.

They moved from under the table, Mercy helping Madame to her knees and to standing. They inched their way to the front door just as they heard a vehicle pull into the driveway.

Mercy yanked Madame to the side wall beside the door, her own back flat against the wall. She squatted and then crab-walked to peer through the blinds at the window. It was a fire-red 1950s Ford F1 truck. "It's Levi." She heaved a sigh and then tensed as she realized he could be in the sniper's crosshairs.

Mercy threw open the front door and jumped back to the side, yelling at Levi to stay down as he opened the truck door.

He ducked, having spotted Mercy holding a gun.

They waited again, but nothing.

She yelled out to Levi, "Vlad's been shot. He's . . . gone. I need you to take Madame while I get Loren and Cara at the hardware store. But let us come to you."

"Hold up!" he yelled, moving inside the vintage truck and pulling something from behind the seat. He ducked behind the door again, holding up what looked to Mercy to be a .220 Swift rifle. Better for taking down varmints as opposed to a crack-shot sniper.

But it was better than nothing.

She crept out the door with Madame clenched to her side, her gun moving at no apparent target, as Levi did his best to cover her. When she reached him, his arms went around Madame protectively.

"Go on," he said. "I'll call the sheriff while you get Loren and Cara."

He held Madame closely as he helped her inside the truck through the driver's seat side.

"You can't do that, Levi," Mercy said, fear gripping her insides.

He turned to her with a confused scowl, his bushy eyebrows furrowed.

Mercy swallowed. "You have to trust me on this. Please, I'm begging you. Take her to your house and lock the doors . . . and stay clear of any windows."

He nodded as if unsure.

"Promise me," she said, "promise me you will not go to the police."

He nodded more firmly. "Go on and get. I'll take her to the house." And finally, "I swear."

CHAPTER THIRTY-NINE

"I would not dare to say that there is a direct relation between mathematics and madness, but there is no doubt that great mathematicians suffer from maniacal characteristics, delirium, and symptoms of schizophrenia."

—John Forbes Nash, Jr.
American mathematician
who made fundamental contributions to game theory,
differential geometry, and the study of differential equations

Alec turned just as the chopper rose vertically to a skid height of about three feet and then remained motionless, hovering, with a slight tilt to the left.

Forrest gave the sign for clearance, and the helicopter began its northeast ascent back to Greenville.

Gus waited by the designated roadside, leaning against Alec's truck. Alec gave his friend a man hug, clapping him on the back.

"Thanks for doing this at the last minute."

Gus dropped back with his hands in his pockets. "You would've done the same for me."

"Look," Alec said, "We're in a hurry, and it's important."

Gus waved him off. "Go ahead and do your James Bond shit. I can walk home. Won't be the first time."

Alec clasped in on the shoulder. "Thanks, man."

He jumped in the driver's seat and fired up the engine as Forrest slammed the other door shut.

They made their way down the road, speeding past all the familiar road signs he'd seen for as long as he could remember. But today everything seemed foreign to him, surreal.

Thank God Ally was in school. He checked the time on his dashboard. She should be in World History. He needed to find a place for her to stay until he got past this fucked-up mess of a mission. She certainly couldn't stay with the Ingalls.

He squeezed his eyes shut and then opened them to take the next turn toward town.

Of course, that wasn't their names. Cara, Loren, and Mercy Ingalls wasn't some absurd accident. He had always known that, but chose to ignore it along with all of the red flags because of his attraction to one long-legged supposed head case.

But criminally insane?

He had made peace with the signs that Marisa wasn't in her right mind. Erratic behavior consisting of zoned-out moments and then uncontrollable rage. But then she'd apologize, even said she was bipolar and admitted to not taking her meds as she should. But her diagnosis was far more severe and her behavior more dangerous than anyone could've imagined.

During the chopper ride, Forrest gave Alec the background information gathered from his contact at the research center through the communication devices embedded in their flight gear.

Forrest advised the girls, at a young age, were in a car accident that killed both parents. That Bancroft's father, a Dr. Halstead, had adopted the three sisters after learning of Loren's sporadic issues in the foster care system. Your typical pre-serial-killer behavior: obsessed with killing small animals and dissecting them and then later going after one of the foster parents with a kitchen knife.

Halstead's reasoning for adopting the sisters sounded suspicious to Alec. Supposedly, in order to keep the three girls together and due to his profession, he felt he would be the perfect adopted parent.

But then Ava, now Loren, began to show signs of significant mathematical acumen. Testing confirmed she was nothing short of a mathematical prodigy. Additional testing proved she was also a borderline psychopath.

"So, you're telling me that Halstead outsourced Loren as the brains behind a number of criminal activities?" Alec said through the microphone in his headgear over the roar of the rotors.

"Affirmative. She leveraged her genius to hone her hacking skills, estimated to be in the one percentile of the Black Hat community."

Alec was now maneuvering the truck at breakneck speeds. "Talk to me about the sisters," Alec asked, "Are they innocent in all this or complicit?"

"According to Bancroft, the younger sister, Charlotte who you know as Cara, has no idea of Ava's criminal activities. And has been protected from details regarding her medical diagnosis. The girls were permitted to spend time together when Ava was medically subdued. Those times were rare, as Charlotte had been traveling the world performing concerts as a piano prodigy."

"And Mercy?" Alec asked.

"Mara," Forrest corrected. "Bancroft didn't share much information regarding the middle sister. Apparently, she's also considered behaviorally altered, but to what extent, we don't know. Intel shows her complicit on a number of art heists where priceless originals were swapped for near to flawless dupes."

"Why leave?" Alec asked, slowing down as he neared town and Wilder's Hardware.

"We don't know," Forrest admitted, loosening his grip on the overhead strap. "Maybe when Halstead died there was a power struggle. Maybe Ava lost that fight and convinced her sisters to leave? What we do know is that Ava and Mara were involved in a number of crimes, and not in a small way."

CHAPTER FORTY

"Mathematics, rightly viewed, possesses not only truth, but supreme beauty—a beauty cold and austere, like that of sculpture."

—Bertrand Russell
British polymath, philosopher, logician, mathematician, historian, writer, social critic, political activist and Nobel Laureate

Loren finished helping her customer load the last bag of potting soil into the back of her SUV. "Thanks, Elsie," she said, shutting the back hatch as the elderly woman made her way to the door. "Drive safe."

Elsie opened the car door. "By the way, tell Henry I just love the new shirts."

Loren glanced down at the black polo with "Wilder's Hardware" printed on the upper left.

"He'll like hearing that," she said, knowing that she was the one who picked them out and ordered them for herself.

More professional.

When Henry saw her wearing it for the first time, he said, "Well, hell. Now everyone will want one."

Elsie wedged herself in her seat, shut the door, and pushed the button to roll her window down. "Tell Mad that I'll see her at Ladies Night at the church. She's promised to teach us how to play Whist."

Loren chuckled at the nickname the women of Wilder gave Madame. Of course, neither she, Mercy, nor Cara was permitted to utter the moniker, but Loren knew the old woman secretly loved having her own special nickname among her lady friends.

"Sure will, but beware, she's a card shark. Don't take your eyes off her, especially if she comes in wearing a white blouse with suspiciously long sleeves."

Elsie laughed and Loren waved and quickly made her way back into the store. She didn't want to leave it unattended, as Henry had been called out for an emergency run to the Holict Airport, but Elsie was in her nineties and had no business hauling the potting soil on her own.

As she walked inside, she saw Cara and Ally checking out the bird feeders.

"I didn't see you two come in. Why aren't you in school?"

"Half day," Cara said, hopping on the counter by the cash register. "I forgot. Mercy's on her way to pick us up."

Loren gave her a dubious look. "You have quite the selective memory."

"It's understandable," she said with a shrug. "I'm a teenager, which means my prefrontal lobe isn't yet fully developed."

They shared a glance and the irony of the brain-related statement.

Loren responded, "Nice try, buuttt, not pickin' up what you're puttin' down."

"Ugh," Cara said with an exaggerated eye roll. "Nobody says that anymore. You are so lame."

Loren turned her attention to Ally. "Hey, Al, have you heard from your brother?"

"Nope," she said, sorting through the breath mints. "He said he'd call later tonight when he got to his hotel."

Loren smiled, as he'd told her the same.

"Crapola," Cara said, rummaging in her book bag, "I totally forgot my pre-Algebra book."

"Bet you didn't forget your sheet music," Loren said.

Cara pulled out what looked to be reams of sheet music from her bag with a toothy grin. "Ravel's 'Bolero.'"

"My point exactly."

"Well," Cara said, chewing her lip and zipping her bag. "I'll just have to go to school early in the morning and study for my test."

"Oh, no, you're not," Loren said, "you're going to march right back to the school, get your book, and come back."

"Says who?"

"Says Madame Garmond when I call her."

Cara's eyes narrowed, but she knew she was bested.

"Fine," Cara said with a scowl. "Come on, Ally."

"I'm not going," Ally replied, pointing her thumb toward her bag next to a display of beef jerky. "I didn't forget *my* books."

Cara pulled her backpack over her shoulder with a huff. "I'll be back."

Her dramatic exit was tempered by the twinkling sound of the door chimes as she stomped outside.

Loren checked her next pick-up order as Ally went back to perusing the bird feeders.

"Hey, Ally, I have to go to the back to grab some polyurethane pipe to go with these fittings. Could you keep an eye on the front and let me know if a customer comes in? Shouldn't take but a minute."

Ally nodded as she lifted the roof of one of the feeders and peered inside.

Loren jogged to the back lot straight to the pile of pipe sitting next to several palettes of fertilizer. She made a mental note to reorganize the yard, so that more of the related items could be found in proximity to one another.

She pulled her work gloves from the back of her cutoff jean shorts, understanding now why Cara didn't want to walk all the way back to the school as the sun was particularly hot today despite the season. She bent to check the model number inked on the side of one of the stacks of pipe.

"Hello, Ava."

She stilled. First at the name, and second, at the voice saying it.

"I do believe it's time to go home."

She stood straight to see Jasper no more than twenty feet away. Six so-called orderlies, some tatted on the neck and face, wearing green scrubs, stood close behind him.

She assessed each one in terms of flexibility, which wouldn't be much. Muscles of their magnitude could be a significant detriment when fighting someone with agility and speed.

She made a quick sweep of her surroundings and in seconds she tallied everything within range that could be used as a weapon.

And then she remembered Mercy.

"Where's Mercy?" she asked.

"Mara," Jasper corrected, taking a step closer, "is safe and sound at your hovel of a farmhouse. She will remain so, if you cooperate."

And then the sound of door chimes. "Hey, Loren."

Ally.

Loren shut her eyes for a millisecond.

"Mrs. Crannick said she'd come back for her . . . or-der."

Ally went quiet, probably sensing something was very wrong based on the scary men and Loren not taking her eyes off them.

"Thanks. Ally. Go on home."

She heard the sound of the door chimes again and knew instinctively that someone was guarding the door so that Ally couldn't get back inside.

They were trapped.

Per design.

"Um, Loren...?" Ally said with a shaky breath.

"Stay where you are," Loren said over her shoulder, slowly moving a few steps, so she was between the goon at the door and the men in the yard. She then saw the ambulance sitting outside the open chain-link fence.

Jasper said, "There is no reason this young woman should come to any harm. As a matter of fact, she can come with us, and we will see her safely home. What do you say, gentlemen, shall we make room?"

They didn't make a sound.

No surprise to Loren.

Their job was to attack and subdue, not to engage in light conversation.

Loren glanced to her right at the man who stood between Ally and the door, also built like a tank. There was no doubt they had her beat in terms of numbers, but she'd bet good money they couldn't come close to her fighting ability.

But she didn't want Ally to see that.

If she went with them, she'd eventually figure out a way to escape and avoid Ally witnessing some pretty gruesome combat. Protect some of her innocence.

"I will go voluntarily, if you let her go."

"Don't be silly, Ava," Jasper said, as if speaking with a child. "We are here to protect her. From you. There's no telling what maniacal stories you've told her."

"She knows nothing," Loren argued, getting desperate, fully aware that nothing she said would matter.

Jasper shook his head as if saddened by such an unfortunate set of circumstances. "She shouldn't be left alone. If you'll just come along with us and allow us to take her home, no one will get hurt."

Jasper stepped to the side as one of the green Hulks came toward her. She instantly moved into an attack stance.

"You'll have to kill me first."

———

Alec pumped on the brakes and skidded to a stop directly behind an ambulance parked behind the back lot of the hardware store.

He jumped out of the truck, Forrest moving with the same level of urgency.

Alec, because he wanted to get to Loren.

Forrest because he didn't want to miss the extraction.

Before they could get through the open gate, a skinny little dude in a lab coat stopped them.

"Mr. Forrest, right on time."

Alec could hear the familiar sounds of a skirmish in the backlot, but the lab coat dude was holding them back.

"I assume this man is part of your team?"

Forrest nodded, "Dr. Bancroft, this is Alec Wilder. Per our discussion, Alec has been surveilling the target for the past several months."

The man seemed to assess Alec and then nodded his head. "Yes, thank you for the intel. I'm afraid we have an unexpected situation involving a member of your family."

"Ally?" Alec asked, his heart rate rising.

He nodded as if troubled. "Miss Ava has threatened to kill her if we make any attempt to return her back to the research center. She's quite agitated and our team is doing their best to subdue her. I'm afraid she's completely unmanageable at this point. I'm going to have to ask you to allow us to handle this until we can sedate her and then hand her over for transport. I took the liberty of arranging for an ambulance for ease of transport and medical attention."

Alec pushed past the man and as soon as he got through the gate, with Forrest close behind, he began his search for Ally. No sign of her.

He turned toward the white coat. "Where's Ally?"

"She's in the far corner, to the right. Miss Ava won't allow us to come to her aid. She insists she'll kill her before going back to her home at the research facility."

And then his eyes moved to Loren, her hair wild even though it was pulled back, her body covered with prairie dust, blood dripping from her nose and forehead.

Four men lay on the ground, incapacitated but alive, while three others did their best to overpower her.

Forrest stood beside him, watching with the same level of fascination.

"Notice something?" Alec asked, so only Forrest could hear.

They watched side by side as she moved from a V Armlock to a Bow and Arrow Choke. A Ju-Jitsu move she could easily transition for the kill.

But she didn't.

Forrest said back, "She's not going for the kill."

"Something doesn't add up." Alec started to move to her aid, as he watched her lose her balance and stumble before reasserting herself. Forrest's hand reached out to stop him. "Do not blow our cover. We aren't here to rescue her. We're here to transport her."

Alec held back, but only because she was wiping the floor with these idiots.

"It's like . . . she's playing cat and mouse with them . . . slowly wearing them down."

Alec took a step forward, torn between seeing Ally with his own eyes and throwing Loren over his shoulder and taking her somewhere safe.

Forrest continued to hold Alec back, not taking his eyes off Loren and with an expression that held the same level of confusion as Alec.

Alec fumed, "This is fucking horseshit."

"Do not go rogue on me, Wilder. Do your fucking job."

Bancroft had moved toward the back of the ambulance and opened the back doors. Forrest caught Alec's attention, nodding toward the ambulance. Alec followed his gaze to see a man the size of one of his farm silos emerge from the back. His head was shaven, his neck the size of one of Alec's thighs.

The man's arms were so huge, they hung at a V, unable to touch the sides of his body. He also wore the same ridiculous blue-green scrubs, so tight the seams threatened to burst.

The silo looked more like a steroid-riddled prison mate than an orderly.

Bancroft explained, "Let me introduce you to Milo."

Alec huffed. No fucking way. Milo the Silo.

"He and Miss Ava go way back. He has had exceptional luck in subduing her in the past."

Alec's fists opened and closed, he leaned toward Forrest. "I swear to God, if he hurts her, I will personally destroy you before tearing his oversized head off his body."

The giant walked onto the lot, the three other meatheads moving to the side, more than happy to make way for him.

But something very odd happened. As soon as Loren saw Milo the Silo, she stumbled and then stood as if in recognition. And then, with her chest heaving and blood dripping down her chin, an unexpected smile lit her face.

"Yes, they're old friends," Dr. Bancroft assured with a thin smile.

Loren didn't know what game Jasper was playing, but she couldn't take the chance of any harm coming to Ally. She could never live with herself if it did. Ally had been through enough in her short life, having lost her parents and then suffering abuse from someone she should have trusted.

But this was absurd.

The so-called orderlies Jasper brought with him were pathetic. Easy to overpower and seven clowns short of a circus.

An utter waste of time.

And somehow Jasper knew it.

She was self-taught to train slow. A lesson learned after a number of hard knocks when attempting to replicate certain moves, not fully engrained, at top speeds. She soon recognized that the tactic wasn't conducive to learning how to do anything effectively and precisely.

The physical motion required calm, a full understanding of each step of the movement, practicing each of them until programmed into muscle memory. Then when the time came, you could replicate the moves, leveraging the adrenaline surge as opposed to suffering from it.

White belt fundamentals executed at black belt speeds.

These guys performed at speeds of napping slugs.

Her sub-par sparring partners lay on the ground. Some holding broken or fractured bones, others scooting toward the perimeter of the lot.

She stumbled from a moment of fatigue when she saw him. Her mind jumbled, as she stood straighter.

Thoughts of Jasper and his fucked-up machinations were obliterated as she gazed at the man who stole her innocence.

Oh, how she had dreamed of killing him.

A wicked smile grew on her face, wiping blood from her chin. Everyone around her dissolved into the background.

It was just her and the man who raped her.

She had learned a thing or two since that day in the padded room. And would use every ounce of fight-mode adrenaline to painfully kill this mindless tree of a man.

"Looking good there, Milo," she said, taunting him. "I see you've *not* done something different with your hair."

He moved forward another step, too short of brain cells to anticipate the danger.

"You think you can take me . . . again?" she asked, pointing the toe of her Chuck's and drawing a line in the prairie dust in front of her. "Just so you're know, 'cause you're not the sharpest tool in the shed, if you cross this line, I will kill you. And it's gonna hurt." She glanced around the lot. "I might even shove a steel pipe or two up your ass for good measure." She shrugged theatrically. "I mean, fair's fair."

Not a word. Just like before.

She backed up a couple of steps, slowly looking down at her line in the dust and then back up at dead eyes, silently daring him with giddy anticipation.

"Red Rover, Red Rover...." she sing-songed.

He moved and everything morphed into lines and fractals. The hulking movement of his body translating into slow motion like an old-time movie reel, but instead of a body, she saw kill points.

It took but a few seconds, and with lightning speed-moves he was nothing more than a lifeless body mass at her feet, his stump of a neck twisted awkwardly to the side.

Crouching beside him, she whispered, "The pleasure was all mine, you sick fucker."

Alec held Ally in his arms as she sobbed.

Loren appeared so absorbed in the wreckage she had caused she hadn't noticed Ally breaking away and running straight into Alec's arms.

Forrest seemed equally taken aback at having witnessed Loren easily manhandle the first set of attackers with what seemed painstaking patience and then swiftly murder the last assailant with psychotic glee.

And that song....

When Alec heard Loren singing while taunting the so-called orderly, his heart sank. Memories struck of Marisa weaving back and forth, singing children's rhymes while Ally was locked in her upstairs closet, beaten and starved.

Dr. Bancroft moved toward Loren with his hands in the air as if in appeal. "Ava," he cajoled her, "that is quite enough."

Loren raised her eyes, shielding the sun with her hand. Her breath lodged in her chest as she saw Alec holding a distraught Ally.

"Omigod, Ally," she said, and then her hand moved to her mouth in horror.

She glanced down at the prone body at her feet, realizing that the satisfaction of ending the life of the man who took her innocence was nothing close to the self-loathing from stealing a piece of Ally's.

What had she done?

Ally had seen everything.

Had seen her take a life.

The very innocence she committed to protecting, she'd sullied.

Ally would never be the same. There were no take-backs or do-overs. She would be irrevocably damaged. Another piece of her soul was robbed, but this time, by Loren.

To her right she heard a commotion. Mercy and Cara. They were forcing their way to her and being held back by her early attackers.

Mercy could take each one of them down without nicking her nail polish or mussing her hair.

She had to put an end to this. "Mercy!" she yelled.

Her sister stopped just short of shoving one of the orderlies' heads against the concrete brick building.

"Avatar!" she yelled.

Mercy instantly released the man, who stumbled to his knees, and stepped forward, shaking her head a half dozen times.

Loren remained firm with a nod.

"No, no, no, no," Mercy begged, her eyes wide.

Loren nodded again, this time with tears in her eyes. She repeated with a broken voice, "Ava . . . tar."

Mercy's body caved into itself as if Loren had just pulled her life support. Just as Loren knew it would. But really, she had no choice.

Cara yanked her arm from one of the orderlies, but Mercy grabbed her by the wrist before she could go to Loren. Mercy wouldn't like it, but she would never disobey her command. There were just some directives they both knew as unavoidable.

Painful realities.

Jasper moved toward her, hands in the air as if she were a grenade about to blow. But she knew him so much better than those watching with bated breath. He had won, and of that he was well aware. This was all a stage show and he was the lead.

"I have to give you credit. That was quite something," Jasper said with a low voice. "You have managed to provide indisputable evidence of your psychopathic tendencies." He pulled paperwork from an inner pocket of his white coat. "With this paperwork, chronicling your history of psychosis, we should have little trouble getting your friends here to take you home. Are you ready to negotiate now that you see what little leverage you have?"

She caught Alec's profile. For the first time that she could remember, he appeared shaken and confused. She just needed to get to him and explain. But what was the point?

After what she had done.

Because if there was one thing of which she was certain, the world was a balance of right and wrongs. Good and bad. And even though this wasn't her first kill, it was the first one executed without remorse or the batting of an eyelash.

According to the many sermons by Pastor Roberts that she'd listened to over the last year of Sundays, she knew the balance had to be restored.

The Lord giveth, the Lord taketh away.

"Begin," she said, refusing to look Jasper in the eye.

"You go willingly, and I will allow Mercy and Cara to remain." He bent his knees, forcing her to meet his eyes. "And when I say willingly, that means you follow my direction implicitly. Which includes admitting to all of this." He lifted the paperwork for emphasis. "And you travel back to the Center without any arguments, the dismembering of body parts, or bringing any doubt to the veracity of my work."

"And you actually expect me to believe that you will allow Mercy and Cara to stay here? Forever?"

He shrugged. "That depends on you now, doesn't it? As long as you comply, they get to have the happy, carefree life you will now only dream of. That alone is well worth walking away from their revenue potential."

She didn't believe a word of it.

But to his point, and she truly hated him for it, she had run out of leverage and options.

She glanced over his shoulder, noticing a few of the orderlies climbing into a nondescript white van. How appropriate.

And also an unfamiliar man standing next to Alec and Ally.

"How did you find us?" she asked, near her breaking point.

"Well, that is an interesting story," Jasper said, holding his finger to his lip in contemplation and then turned his head as if counseling her through her crisis. "Mercy's fucktoy, Vlad, has been in touch with me for months. But he won't be giving you anymore trouble. Oh, and you know that nice fellow that's been courting you here in Walnut Grove?"

He pointed his thumb over his shoulder.

Loren's eyes narrowed.

Jasper continued, "He works for me. Oh, and you're going to love this. I mean the irony. His mission? To gather intel on you and your sisters and assist in your abduction."

And she broke.

Her chest heaved on a sob, and her eyes began to pool, unable to look at Alec. She ditched her head and stared at her feet. Doing her best to get herself together. She lifted her eyes to the sky and took a breath and made the mistake of looking his way again.

He stared back at her, holding Ally. Looking at her with doubt and mistrust, as if he had never seen her before.

As if she were out of her mind.

She thought of the way he touched her as if she were someone special when, all along, she was the mark. A mark he got to fuck.

Once again, she had placed her trust in someone, only to have it thrown in her face.

She glanced down at the inert body at her feet.

But then again, did she deserve any better?

The Lord giveth, the Lord taketh away.

Loren's focus moved to her Chucks, chewing her lip in order to refrain from breaking down completely.

"Deal."

"That's my girl. Good choice."

"I ask one thing."

He sighed. "Don't push me."

"I want to talk to him." Her eyes shot up toward Alec.

"For what purpose?" His eyes narrowed.

"Closure."

"You understand our deal? If you lay one hand on him, or worse, if you tell him anything to discredit me in hopes of getting some sort of revenge or misguided romantic closure, your sisters will also be going back to the Center."

"The closure's not for me."

He blinked slowly, motioning for one of the orderlies that had yet to jump into the van.

Jasper held out his hand as the terrified man placed the canvas bundle in it.

Loren's chest concaved further. "Is that necessary?"

"Oh, my, yes," he said, holding it up to her as if he were dressing a child. "Do as you're told."

She obediently slid her arms into the sleeves as he crossed her arms, turning her around and tying the straitjacket in the back.

Before Jasper could turn her back around, she made the mistake of looking at Mercy and Cara and wondered if this would be the last time she would ever see them.

They held one another, doing nothing to come to her aid.

They knew better.

Alec held Ally tight to his side as Jasper waved him toward the lot.

He looked at Forrest, who gave him a head nod, communicating he'd stay close to Ally.

"Ally," Alec said, "This is Trevor Forrest. Stay with him while I speak with Loren."

"Why is she wearing that?" Ally asked, looking up at him with confusion as she swiped at her eyes. Alec gently transferred her over to his partner.

"It's to protect us, and to protect Loren from herself."

Ally grabbed his arm. "But she didn't do anything wrong. She was trying to protect me," she said, patting her chest.

"Ally, please just give me a minute."

He guided her toward Forrest and made his way into the yard, as Jasper blocked him once again.

"She's distraught but having a moment of lucidity. She wants to talk to you."

Alec didn't spare him a glance as he made his way to Loren. He would be lying to himself if he didn't feel completely at odds with her standing there wrapped in a straitjacket, tears streaming, her hair a wild halo around her face.

He needed to hold her.

He needed to tell her he was going find a way to help her, somehow, some way.

But right now was not the time. And until that time came, he needed to maintain his cover and play along with the prescribed assignment.

He also needed to make sense of the man she just brutally assaulted and killed in record time. It's not that he was immune to brutality, having seen so many atrocities while serving in Afghanistan.

But this wasn't the Middle East or a military zone. This was the small town of Wilder, Texas, where the most danger you had to face was the sketchy stoplight in the middle of town.

Or a crazy fucking wife, who tortured your sister.

He blinked at the unlikely similarities of his past and present.

Fuck.

Still, nothing made sense relative to this jacked-up mess of a mission, where there were more questions than information. In all his years in the military, he didn't know of a single assignment where everyone involved wasn't deeply entrenched and fully aware of all the details and ultimate remedy.

Trying to piece together the sparse information he was given against what he knew from spending time with this enigmatic woman made him feel confused and off-kilter.

Of course, having fallen for her might have had something to do with that.

But if she were truly criminally insane, why did her sisters willingly leave with her and escape the facility?

How could she care so much for Jimbo and the people of Wilder, and then murder a man in front of witnesses without a second thought?

How could she threaten to kill Ally when she had been nothing short of a sister to her over the last several months?

And why did Ally seem to be the only person unaware of the threat?

He walked within a few feet of her and stopped.

"I hear congratulations are in order," she said, her tears and blood moving in converged rivulets down her face. "Good work. You had me totally convinced."

He pulled a bandana from his back pocket to wipe her cheeks, and push the hair out of her eyes, but she reared her head back, her eyes violent.

"Don't. Touch. Me."

"Loren," he hesitated, working through what he wanted to say as opposed to what was dictated. Afraid that if he didn't toe the line, he'd get pulled from the mission, and be unable to keep her safe during transport and while inside the research facility.

Remaining mute and fucking hating himself for it, she spoke again, "I want you to know that Mercy and Cara are completely innocent. No matter what they tell you, you have to believe that. I know you might not trust me," she chuckled to herself, "can't say I'll be doing any 'trust fall' exercises with you anytime soon, but I swear to you, on my parents' graves, they are innocent."

"What about you, Loren? Are you innocent?" He needed something, anything to help him make sense of the past few hours.

She glanced over his shoulder, her eyes narrowing. "No," she said with a slight shake of her head. "I'm anything but."

He lowered his head toward hers, hell-bent on getting more answers.

Something.

"Lab coat over there," he said, nodding his head toward Bancroft, "says you used Ally as a pawn, that you refused to be taken." He finally looked up, but he was too much of a coward to look her in the eye. "That you said you'd kill her before going back."

He found the balls to glance at her to catch her reaction, which was simply a weaving pause and intake of breath.

He knew her answer would be a defining moment and wasn't sure he was prepared for it.

She turned toward him, her eyes now steady and sure. "Collateral damage. Isn't that what you military types call it?" She turned her eyes away as if searching for something in the distance. With a shrug, she said, "It was unfortunate that she was all I had to leverage."

He bowed his head with his hands on his hips, his chest tight, finding it difficult to swallow.

Jasper interrupted them, standing with his goons by the fence. "We need to leave. We'll clean up the mess, but it's time to take her home."

Alec moved his hand to her back, and she jerked her torso away from him.

He froze at the sudden movement.

"Let me make myself clear," she said with a low, menacing voice. "You may *never* touch me again. I will come with you willingly, but don't make the fatal mistake of assuming compliance as weakness." A firestorm raged in her eyes. "Because right this very moment, I could so easily sweep your feet out from under you, wrap my thighs around your throat"—she bent toward him with a disturbing grin—"a place we both know you love to be"—she straightened, her eyes hardening to steel points—"and with one swift twist, break the vertebrae in your neck. I taught myself how to fight with my hands tied behind my back at a very, very young age."

Alec remained silent at her waning attempt to maintain some sense of dignity, her trembling body restricted by the canvas jacket.

Alec finally nodded, decimated.

How many times had he told Ally that when people tell you who they are, believe them?

So why the holy fuck didn't he believe her?

Rubbing his thumb along his bottom lip, aware of the number of eyes tracking their every move, he caught Mercy to his right, now glaring at him with unreserved hostility and Cara standing beside her with a look of pure confusion and indecision.

"What's 'Avatar'?" he asked as they began their trek toward the fenced entrance and the medical transport vehicle.

She smiled weakly. "It means it's over and to stand down."

He nodded again.

She added, "It's our safe word."

Order Beyond Wilder Today

ACKNOWLEDGMENTS

Ah, where to begin?

First and foremost, I'd like to thank my parents, who insisted I study something practical in college as opposed to attempting a writing career straight out of high school. In their defense, they were fearful I'd end up unemployed and writing what was never going to be the next great novel and living, infinitum, in their renovated basement. And to their credit, they did manage to raise me without inflicting any bodily harm or slipping sedatives in my morning smoothies.

Benadryl doesn't count, by the way.

The least I could do was move out, go to college and give them back some peace of mind.

Turned out, Mom and Dad were right. I enjoyed a wonderful career in business where I traveled the world and humbly learned how much I didn't know. So thank you to the parental units. The life lessons learned in business and abroad garnered me tons of stories from which to feed, not to mention some hefty self-preservation skills.

I'd also like to thank my beta readers, Sharon Conway and Crystal Bobo. You gave me constructive criticism while at the same time convincing me that I had a story worth telling. You ladies are exemplary human beings, and I'm honored to have you in my life and reading my books. Over and over and over . . .

Additional thanks to beta reader Brittny Downing, also my wonderful daughter, who read all the sexy scenes written by her saintly mother, and managed not to gag . . . or managed not to tell me that she gagged. Your feedback was always clear and honest, and for that I am grateful. Feel free to forward your therapy bills to my attention. Kidding. Send them to your Dad.

Lastly, I want to thank Sherry Patterson, who has followed my writing efforts since day one and made me feel like an author before I was one. Sherry, you have no idea how your kind words and enthusiasm sparked my drive and nurtured my self confidence.

ABOUT THE AUTHOR

Lēigh lives in the suburbs of Atlanta with her husband, whom she cheekily refers to as The PoolBoy.

She recently walked away from a career in the tech industry, working a variety of positions where she sold, trained, marketed and managed... a ton of stuff. When not holed up in her office crafting stories about badass women and the men who try to tame them, she can be found walking the beach in Florida or at the gym.

    Email: leigh@leightudor.com
    Website: www.leightudor.com
    Facebook: facebook.com/Leigh.Tudor.31
    Instagram: instagram.com/leightudorauthor

ALSO BY LĒIGH TUDOR

Beyond Wilder, Book #2 Wilder Sisters Series
Loving Wilder, Book #3 Wilder Sisters Series

Made in United States
North Haven, CT
13 December 2023